Praise for *A Shrug*

"Elaine Cockrell's novel *A Shrug of* ... service by rendering in dramatic terms th...... ....se-American relocation that unfolded during World War II. I'm glad to see it in print, because it serves as a reminder of this period in our history and therefore increases the odds that we will not allow ourselves again, as a nation, to act on prejudice."

–David Guterson, PEN/Faulkner Award-winning author of *Snow Falling on Cedars*

"Elaine Cockrell has created a time, place and a people that are unforgettable. Almost cinematic in its narrative, these Japanese Americans forced into internment camps come alive. I cheered them, cried with their losses, regretted their battles and admired their resilience. Here is a new vision of Oregon showcasing a people's capacity to grow, change and treat each other with kindness despite the trauma they lived through. *A Shrug of the Shoulders* is a singular perspective of Japanese Americans making a new world out of a shattered one. I didn't want this story to end."

–Jane Kirkpatrick, award-winning author of *The Healing of Natalie Curtis*

"After exhaustive research, Elaine Cockrell takes readers into the thickets of American shame—the internment of Japanese-American citizens in World War II. Against this dark backdrop, Cockrell finds the shining stars of the human spirit that can't be dimmed by fear. The result is an uplifting story built of love and war, life and death, honor and ignorance. It is a story told through individuals and families of the Pacific Northwest who struggled while being exiles in their own country but refused to return such evil with evil."

–Bob Welch, author of *Saving My Enemy: How Two WWII Soldiers Fought Against Each Other and Later Forged a Friendship That Saved Their Lives*

"A love story, a war story set on the home front, a saga of families caught in the riptides of history, Elaine Cockrell's moving novel captures how World War II was experienced by Anglo and Japanese

Americans in the small towns and beet fields of eastern Oregon. Poignant and powerful, *A Shrug of the Shoulders* also reminds us that the war against fear, ignorance, and prejudice did not end in 1945, indeed, is never-ending."

—Alan E. Rose, author of *As If Death Summoned*

"I highly recommend *A Shrug of the Shoulders*. It belongs side by side with some of the best literature depicting the Japanese-American experience of the Second World War, including *Farewell to Manzanar* and *Snow Falling on Cedars*. You won't be able to read a reference to this era without your mind and your emotions evoking the characters in Ms. Cockrell's story."

—Rick E. George, author of *Sinister Refuge*

"*A Shrug of the Shoulders* captures bits of Japanese-American life after Pearl Harbor in an assembly center, internment camp, and Farm Security Administration labor camp near Nyssa, Oregon. It highlights the unjust internment of Japanese Americans and resident aliens, and explores not only their losses, but their resilience in the midst of such terrible discrimination and hatred. Elaine Cockrell created such a realistic story that I shed a few tears, as this tale is not unlike what my own family endured during that time."

—Mike Iseri, resident of Ontario, Oregon

"*A Shrug of the Shoulders* paints a vivid picture of WWII's internment of Japanese Americans in Eastern Oregon. Elaine Cockrell skillfully intertwines the lives of three families—two of Japanese ancestry—into a compelling story of the conflicting circumstances, emotions, viewpoints and prejudices of those touched by the internments and displacements. Cockrell's research shines through, allowing the reader to feel the devastation, persistence and rebirth of the affected Japanese Americans and the resulting effect on the non-Japanese in the community."

—Virginia Pickett, author of *A Long Road There*

A Shrug of the Shoulders

A Shrug
of the
Shoulders

A Novel

ELAINE COCKRELL

Book and cover design by Kevin Breen
Cover photograph taken by Russell Lee, from Library of
Congress, Prints & Photographs Division, Farm Security
Administration/Office of War Information Black-and-White
Negatives

ISBN: 978-1-7360127-9-6
Cataloging-in-Publication Data is available upon request

Manufactured in the United States of America

Published by
Latah Books, Spokane, Washington
www.latahbooks.com

The author may be contacted at
elaine.cockrell.author@gmail.com

To Paul Hirai,
who shared his story.

And to Dudley Kurtz,
the original gun slinger.

INDEX OF MAIN CHARACTERS

Yano (YAH-noh) Family

Chiharu (CHEE-ha-roo) — Widowed mother
George — Eldest son, vegetable and fruit farmer, and eventual recruiter for the sugar factory
Abe — Second son who struggles under George's thumb
Thomas — Third son and aspiring doctor
Pamela — Youngest and only daughter

Mita (mee-tah) Family

Kentaro (KEN-te-roh) — Father and former store owner
Tak`e (TAH-keh) — Mother and Japanese traditionalist
Molly or Momoe (MO-mo-eh) — Eldest daughter who works at both the Portland Assembly Center and then at Minidoka Internment Camp
Mary — Second daughter and Molly's confidante
Kameko (kah-MEE-koh) — Third daughter

Hertzog Family

Lee — Father and farmer
Mae — Mother
Luke — Oldest son, born on Mae's birthday
Donald — Second son, first to enlist
Sam — Third son
Ellis — Fourth son, basketball player, and musician
Emily — Youngest and only daughter

MINOR CHARACTERS

Ed and Rex Allen — Brothers and farmers from Alberta, Canada who are neighbors of the Hertzogs

Doc Yamaguchi (Yah-ma-GOO-chi) — On George's beet crew in Nyssa; later lives in Cow Hollow

Okimoto — Abe's mentor and wood carver in Minidoka Internment Camp

Shug (Shug like sugar) — Japanese Hawaiian soldier of the 442nd Regimental Combat Team

Ken Ogata — Linguist for the Army

Masayuki Higa — Linguist for the Army

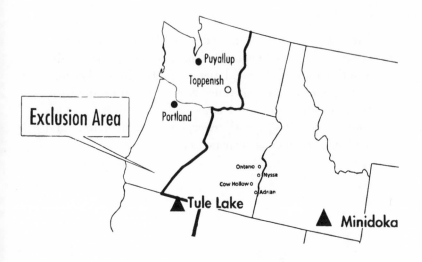

Exclusion Area

Puyallup

Toppenish

Portland

Ontario

Nyssa

Cow Hollow

Adrian

Tule Lake

Minidoka

AUTHOR'S NOTE

Ontario, Nyssa, Adrian, and Cow Hollow are all real places in Eastern Oregon that provide the setting for this historical novel. In July and August of 1942, Russell Lee took photographs of this experimental labor camp for the Farm Security Administration. I have tried to avoid real people's names, stories, and events, reimagining the home front and the Japanese American experience.

"I am for immediate removal of every Japanese on the West Coast to a point deep in the interior. I don't mean a nice part of the interior either. Herd 'em up, pack 'em off, and give 'em the inside room in the badlands. Let 'em be pinched, hungry, and dead up against it."

—Henry McLemore, *San Francisco Examiner*, January 29, 1942

CHAPTER ONE

GEORGE YANO

George's chest tightened as the sheriff pulled up at the family's farmhouse. Through the kitchen window, he watched the patrol car come to a stop in their front yard. He felt everyone else's eyes on him—his brothers, sister, and mother. In English, he asked his sister, "Do you think you can distract Mother?"

Pamela nodded, glanced at their mother, and began to clear the table. His mother also gathered a stack of dirty dishes, following Pamela into the kitchen.

George wiped his sweaty palms on his pants. "You stay here," he said to his two younger brothers. He opened the door, shut it carefully behind him, and tramped down the wooden steps.

"You George Yano?" the sheriff asked, peering over wire-rimmed glasses. The sheriff's dark hair was shot through with silver, and his beige uniform was complete with a pistol on his brown leather belt. The officer towered over George's husky five-foot-seven frame.

"Yes, sir."

George offered his hand, but when the sheriff ignored it, a chasm of tension opened.

"You the oldest male in the family?" the sheriff asked as he flipped through some documents. "Says here your father died a couple of years back."

George nodded, raking his black hair off his forehead.

"So, three males and two females?"

George nodded again, his mouth too dry to speak.

"Here's your evacuation notice."

"I've just planted our vegetable crop. The camps aren't ready yet, are they?"

1

"Every Japanese family west of Highway 97 needs to relocate. You'll go to the assembly center in Oregon first. Not the one here in Washington. That's what I came to tell you. My deputy and I'll pick you up on May seventh to take you to the train."

"The seventh? That's only five days . . ."

"Just doing what I've been told. Here's a list of what to bring." The sheriff presented a bunch of papers and said, "Fill these out and have them ready to give the soldier on the transport car."

George took the papers and watched the sheriff return to his car and drive away. May seventh, five months to the day since Japanese planes attacked Pearl Harbor. He'd have to leave the vegetables— plowing them under during wartime was considered sabotage. The fruit trees would produce whether anyone was at the farm or not.

Five days.

He'd have to tell the family. After Pearl Harbor, his mother had been so afraid he would be arrested. Now, it appeared they were all going to be locked away.

When George returned to the house, he realized the whole family had overheard the sheriff's orders. He looked to his mother, who pressed her lips together. *"Shikata ga nai,"* his mother said.

George should have known. His mother used that phrase ever since he could remember. A verbal shrug of the shoulders. An acceptance of fate. A resignation to whatever will come. *Shikata ga nai.*

George handed his mother, Chiharu, the paperwork. She turned to his brother, Abe, asking him to translate. Abe had spent five years in Japan, living with his uncle while attending school. Abe was fluent in reading and writing Japanese. The family's plan was to send him to law school, where he could help Japanese *Issei* and their *Nisei* children navigate the laws of their adopted country. Abe had broad shoulders, a heart-shaped face, and twinkling eyes. If Chiharu had a favorite child, George knew it was Abe.

And that was that. No further protest, no tears, no ranting at the gods. A simple calmness that George tried to match by stuffing his anger inside.

He needed to make a plan. After the Office of the Alien Property Custodian had frozen all Japanese assets in March, he had spent nearly all their cash to plant spring crops. He would need some money to take with them. That meant selling their few possessions.

After only a moment's reckoning, he and Abe went outside to appraise what they owned.

"What do you think?" George asked Abe as they looked over the car. "Should we sell the Ford coupe or the John Deere?"

"Father was very proud of this car. I'm sure he wouldn't want us to sell it," Abe said. The 1934 black coupe gleamed in the sunlight. The running board looked new.

"Yeah, but it's more important to keep the tractor so we can come back to farming," George said.

"If you'd already made up your mind, why'd you ask me?" Abe snapped. He often challenged George's role as head of the family since their father's death.

George's voice hardened. "You'll need to go down to the store and button it up. See if there's anything we can peddle."

George was proud of their store. He and Abe had built the small wooden structure last summer in order to sell their fruit and vegetables locally. Abe resented the decision and argued with him. Abe wanted to go to college, and George did too. He'd been a sophomore at the University of Washington, studying agriculture and business, when their father died of a brain aneurism. The best they could do was work together and send their youngest brother Thomas to school. He'd wanted to be a doctor since he was a little boy.

"Here." George threw the keys. "Park the car by the store and put a 'For sale' sign on the front window. Check each day for offers. We got four days. Let's go for two hundred bucks."

Abe grumbled under his breath as he drove away.

The next day, George went to their neighbors' house to ask if they'd take care of the farm while they were away. Mr. Franklin was in his fifties, stooped and balding, but the best farmer in the area. George had known the family for ten years. Franklin was one of the few in the Toppenish area who had been willing to sell land to a Japanese American. As an *Issei*, George's father was prohibited from owning land, but his *Nisei* son could. When George turned eighteen, Franklin sold the acreage to them.

"I'd only need thirty percent of the take," George said to Franklin, thinking his offer was a generous one. He was puzzled when Franklin didn't go for it.

"I might be able to pick some of your fruit and sell it, but it's going to be difficult to weed and irrigate your vegetables and mine. All my hired hands have enlisted."

George knew that fruit sales alone wouldn't be enough to make payments on the farm's bank loan and taxes. Why had he thought Franklin would be willing to help him in the first place? His pride made him stand up straighter, and he turned to leave.

"You selling the tractor?" Franklin asked. "I could use one."

"Not yet." His father had bought the 1938 Deere for a thousand bucks four years ago. George didn't think Franklin had the kind of money he'd want for it.

Franklin busied himself by sharpening a hoe and didn't meet George's gaze when he said, "Take care then."

***

The family worked frantically to decide what to take with them and what to store in their home. Items on the list included clothes for winter and summer, sheets, towels, and toiletries. Yet they could only take what they could carry. Thomas, sixteen, and Pamela, fourteen, tried to help their increasingly panicked mother. They packed trunks and boxes for the attic, only to paw through them to find two more towels or another set of sheets for the heavy duffle bags George and Abe would carry.

George climbed the stairs to Pamela's bedroom to check on her progress. She was standing at her window, looking at the sunset over the orchard. On her bed were all her favorite books. "You aren't thinking of putting those in your suitcase, are you?"

"Of course not." Pamela turned to him. "I'm just saying goodbye."

He stepped inside her room, something he hadn't done since she turned twelve. "I'm sorry." George swallowed hard.

"*Shikata ga nai.*" She looked around. "I'm going to miss my own room, my red ruffled curtains, my books, everything." Quiet and reserved, Pamela usually hid her feelings.

George stepped over and gave her a quick hug. He was surprised when she put her arms around his waist and laid her head on his chest. She was so small, frequently mistaken for a child instead of an adolescent. It didn't help that she wore her dark, shoulder-length hair in pigtails. George rested his chin on the top of her head.

"Are you scared?" she asked.

"A little," he said.

"Good," she said. "I didn't want to be the only one."

George gave her an extra squeeze and then left to check on Thomas. He'd packed and left the suitcase open on the bed. Inside, George noticed a carefully folded white shirt, tie, and slacks, along with jeans, Thomas's school sweater, and a couple of t-shirts. But there were no socks or underwear. Thomas's mitt and hardball were gone, so George headed outside and found him in his favorite place—seated on a tree stump and throwing the ball against the side of the shed, catching it over and over.

"Been lookin' for you," George said in greeting.

"Yeah?" Thomas combed his black hair straight back from his high forehead. He was lean, wiry, and fast. Maybe that was why he was such a good shortstop. George had difficulty treating Thomas as a young man because he hadn't had a growth spurt and his face looked so young, soft, and naïve.

"Mother filled another suitcase," George announced. "Think you could carry two?"

"Sure." Thomas sounded glad to be asked. "We leaving tomorrow?"

"That's what the sheriff said. Mother's been going through the paperwork. Looks like we're going to have another bonfire tonight."

George and Thomas looked up as they heard Abe kicking a rock up the gravel drive. "Any luck?" George asked.

Abe stopped abruptly. He jammed his hand in his pocket and drew out a handful of cash. "I sold Father's car. Only got fifty bucks." He slapped the money in George's hand.

"That's all you could get?"

"You think someone's going to pay what it's worth?" Abe glared at George, went inside, and slammed the door.

George sighed. He never seemed to get it right with his middle brother. "I'll go over to Franklin and see if he still wants the tractor. We have to have more money than this." He turned back to Thomas. "You finished packing?"

"For now."

"Throw in some socks and underwear. Then get the burn barrel started."

George crossed the road to their neighbors. Behind him, the sound of the ball hitting the shed taunted him. Not even his little brother would do as he asked.

***

George stood by the burn barrel, stirring the flames as Chiharu fed it with another letter. Shortly after that awful Sunday morning of Pearl Harbor, they burned any official documents written in Japanese. Now, they were burning everything else. Chiharu was ruthless. She wanted no ties left between the Yano family and the Empire of Japan. She read each message carefully, as if storing it in her memory, before throwing them into the fire. She burned the letters she had received in Japan from her betrothed. She had been a picture bride who first met her husband only after she'd arrived in America. George put his hand on his mother's shoulder, hoping it might comfort her.

Flames flickered in the darkness, playing light and shadow on her face. She seemed unaware of tears tracking through the ash on her cheeks. The old adage of smoke following beauty certainly applied to her. At fifty, Chiharu retained a vestige of her youthful beauty, obscured only by glasses, a few silvery strands, delicate facial lines, and a slight limp. George barely rescued the photo of his mother as a girl dressed in a flowered kimono. Later, he slit the lining of his suitcase and put it inside to take with them.

George salvaged his father's Samurai sword that hung over the mantel, Pamela's Geisha doll Abe had brought her from Japan, and his father's watch that Thomas treasured. He found a tall wooden box for the watch and doll, wrapped and tied the box in oilcloth, and put it in a hole he dug in the shed's floor. He wrapped the sword first in canvas and then in oilcloth and laid it beside the box. After he filled the hole with dirt, he ran the tractor's wheel over the space several times, leaving the front tires parked on top.

The tractor was no longer his. Franklin had offered him $100 for the John Deere, claiming it was all the cash he had on hand. George had no choice but to take it. Franklin had always been straight with him before, but this time his voice was clipped, and he avoided looking George in the eye. There was no handshake to clinch the deal.

**

On the last morning, George latched the windows and locked the doors. Abe and Thomas stood in the front yard, baggage all around them. His mother, still smelling slightly of smoke, waited on the front stoop. She wore her black winter hat and coat, holding her suitcase in front of her with both hands. She seemed numb to what was happening, lost in her mind's reveries.

"Here they come," Pamela said. "I can hear the truck."

The sheriff and a deputy drove up in a county flatbed. Three generations of another family were already in the back. George held his mother by the elbow as she stumbled down the steps.

The deputy got out and put a stool at the rear of the canvas-covered truck. "Here you are, ma'am." He helped her, then Pamela, climb into the bed.

An elderly man stood and bowed to Chiharu. She returned the bow before she took her seat. They sat stiffly on benches, heads held high, bags and trunks stacked on the sides.

The sheriff checked George's registration papers, nodding to Abe and Thomas, who stood rigid, unwilling to acknowledge the situation.

"Three males, two females," the sheriff declared. "Looks like it's all in order."

"Yes, sir." George folded the papers and put them in an inside pocket of his denim jacket.

"Here. You need to put these on." The sheriff held out stiff cards with strings attached.

"What are they?"

"ID tags. Put them on your coats."

George looked at the other Japanese passengers in the truck. All wore a white card prominently displayed. Numbers. His family was reduced to numbers. He swallowed his shame and handed out the tags. Pamela took two and helped their mother tie one around a button on her black coat. He couldn't look his brothers in the eyes when he gave them their tags; instead, he busied himself with his own. His fingers were suddenly unable to work, and he fumbled much too long on the simple task. He couldn't help comparing it to the Star of David the Jews were forced to wear in Nazi Germany.

7

Abe and Thomas threw their luggage onto the truck, then sat so their legs dangled over the end. George leaned against the inside of the truck and focused on their home. The white house was framed in black trim he had painted last summer. The apple orchard on one side was just blossoming out. The field of vegetable starts would need to be weeded in a few weeks. He was losing everything his father had expected him to protect. He had failed in his role as the eldest son. As they passed the Franklins, George spotted the John Deere parked by the haystack. One of the house curtains flicked closed, hiding the residents. No one waved goodbye.

The sky was gray and cloudy. It was sprinkling. His mother said something George didn't catch.

"What'd she say?" George asked Pamela.

"*Shikata ga nai,*" she replied. "It cannot be helped."

***

The Yanos arrived at the Portland Assembly Center after a seven-hour train ride. They joined other Japanese families in a ragged line, identification tags on their clothes. Soldiers stood on both sides of the muddy road leading to the center and watched as men, women, and children struggled off the train and walked to the gate. Two tables sat on either side of the entry gate, an official at each to process the long line of people. Over each man was a soldier holding a black umbrella. They weren't having much luck keeping the officials or their paperwork dry. After standing in the steady rain for more than an hour, the Yanos finally reached the tables. George presented their papers.

"You the man of the house?" asked the bespectacled official.

"Yes, sir." George tried to hold his end of the duffle bag out of the mud.

"Any small children?"

"No. My sister's fourteen. She's the youngest." George looked over at her and realized his baby sister was becoming a young woman. His mother, with rain beading on her black wool coat and dripping hat, clung to Pamela's arm. Pamela whispered, translating into Japanese, trying to ease her mother's fears.

"You were born here, all except your mother? Chiharu? Don't know if I'm saying it right."

The man mangled his mother's name, but George wasn't going to correct him. "Yes, we're all citizens." He felt his patience slipping.

"I'm assigning you rooms in section one. That's the farthest from the toilets, but as adults, you should be able to manage. There will be six cots in your room. Put the one you don't need in the hallway. Someone will come by and reissue it." The official stamped the papers with the entry date of May 7, 1942 and gave them back to George. "Chow is at five or so. Listen for the dinner bell. You have about an hour to get settled."

George led his family past the soldiers guarding the gates. Barbed wire surrounded them. Watchtowers loomed overhead. The Yanos were now prisoners of the United States of America, the land of the free and the home of the brave.

A stout adolescent boy led the Yanos into camp. They clung together, bumping and jostling on the way to their sleeping area in section one. Their feet clomped on the wooden floorboards, leaving behind bits of mud. Their suitcases and duffle bags banged against the plywood hallway. When they met fellow Japanese internees, they would squeeze up against the wall to allow them to pass. Chiharu bowed politely each time, especially to the elders. His mother's limp was more pronounced when she was tired. They were all cold, wet, and exhausted. Without their guide, they would have been lost.

"I've been here a couple of days now and make myself useful whenever a new trainload of folks arrives," the boy said. "We're up to a thousand now."

"Where are you from?" Thomas asked, trying to keep up with the boy.

"Portland. Arrivals east of the Willamette River will be here today as well."

"How many is the center supposed to hold?" George asked as he took his mother's suitcase and put it under his arm. He could still manage his end of the duffle.

"About three times as many as are here now. They may have to build some barracks outside the barn near the hospital."

George couldn't believe there'd be so much crowding. All these people—all of Japanese heritage—blamed for looking like the enemy. And he wasn't sure he'd ever make sense of the maze of hallways.

Eventually, they reached a burlap doorway that looked identical to all the rest.

"This is it," the boy said brightly, turning to Thomas. "When it's not raining, we meet outside and play ball. Nothing official yet. We choose up sides and play until the rain starts again. You play?"

"We both do," Abe answered. "I haven't had a chance to play since I graduated from high school last spring."

"He's a great player," Thomas said. "I play too, usually the infield."

"Check with me after supper. My name's Danny. Danny Saito." He turned and hustled back down the hall.

Abe parted the burlap door—a curtain, really—for their mother. Following her inside, he knocked on the plywood wall. "Hollow," he said. "No insulation either. The walls stop at eight feet and simply separate one room from the next. Bet it will be noisy even at night."

Chiharu sat down on the springs of the first cot, her eyes brimming with tears. Pamela sank down on the cot beside her mother and put her arm around her.

"This is where we'll live?" Chiharu said, scrunching up her nose.

The smell of dung permeated the interior. Perhaps it was because the floorboards had been placed directly over the ground, and the dirt had absorbed the urine and manure of horses, cows, and sheep for decades. A single sheet of flypaper hung from the rafters in a futile attempt to rid the stall of the flies that buzzed around them. Known previously as the Pacific International Livestock Exposition Center, Oregon officials decided the huge barn could hold the three thousand Japanese that lived in the state.

George put his mother's suitcase on one cot, and he and Abe swung the heavy duffle onto the next. Cotton mattresses sat rolled up at the head of each bed. No pillows. The only blanket was a standard Army issue, a scratchy, dull green wool.

"Do you remember where the sheets are packed?" George asked. And with that, the family began to settle in.

***

The next day, Chiharu and Pamela started to turn their small space into a makeshift home.

"We have no place to put our things, to show this is where the Yanos live," Chiharu said. She seemed to have come out of her shell as she searched the large duffle bag. "Abe, we must have some shelves. Have you seen the neighbor's room?"

Abe left and returned with some scrap lumber he found near the construction site where men were turning more stalls into rooms. He'd borrowed a hammer and began to nail the shelves together. George hurried out. He couldn't stand more noise. Besides, he was eager to figure out the rules and regulations they were to live under.

George walked from their section of the assembly center to the entry in about fifteen minutes. At first, he got turned around, but soon he learned the layout. The authorities had taken the enormous barn and divided it into seven sections. One was the chapel, while the other six contained sleeping cells. The Yano's hallway was next to the chapel near the women's shower area and the laundry. The men's showers were on the opposite end. The seventh section held bunk beds for the single men, mostly elderly. The mess hall, near the entry, was large enough for all the current residents to eat together, and it was where general meetings would be held. The men's and women's restrooms were opposite each other at the entry to the sports arena.

The barn's auction area was now set up for activities. People sat on the tiered rows surrounding the show floor and talked, wrote letters, or played the few games available. Ping pong tables were set up in the center, where a few youths hit the ball back and forth.

George asked questions, but no one knew who was in charge or how the center would be run. In frustration, he returned to the stall they'd been assigned to see what progress his mother and sister were making.

Pamela stood in the hallway, squinting at the door covering. One of her black curly pigtails traced the line of her jaw.

"What are you doing?" George asked.

"Embroidering our name on the burlap. And look." She held the door open and showed him the two shelves Abe had completed. They held a small doll, a floral vase, a framed picture of their father, and a tea set from Japan.

"Mother found the calendar from our Toppenish store. Thomas cut out a newspaper headline, 'I am an American!' And we put it together with the flag we brought. It makes a statement, don't you think?"

11

George frowned at the newsprint. Thomas might be quiet, but he showed his defiance of their internment in not-so-subtle ways.

Pamela turned back to her embroidering. "When I can't find anything else to do, I'll add spring flowers."

George forced a smile. "Good for you." He glanced at his mother, lying on her cot, her glasses on top of her head. Her eyes were shut, but he doubted she slept. "Where are Abe and Thomas now?"

"Checking out the baseball game, I think. At least Thomas took his glove and ball when they left."

George was astonished to realize the internment might turn out to be a blessing for his mother. After living in Toppenish for several years without any friends, she met the women assigned to the area around their family. By the second day, she was already helping new families settle in by showing them the dining hall and the outside laundry area. She spoke Japanese as often as she liked, no longer lost in the puzzle of English.

Abe and Thomas started making friends just as quickly. Abe was a jokester and a natural athlete. He was a couple of inches taller than George's five foot seven and just as good-looking. Thomas was slight, and he was going to be shorter than his older brothers. He was mild-mannered and eager to please. He wasn't as athletic as Abe, though he didn't seem to mind being in his brother's shadow as long as he was included in the baseball games they played nonstop.

At least Pamela stayed by their mother's side. She was short, not quite five feet. She wasn't gregarious and tended to be shy. George knew she would have the hardest time adjusting. She had brought one book of poetry by Emily Dickinson. He wondered if it afforded her any relief at all.

***

On the third night, George woke from a fitful sleep. He looked around the room and counted heads. Pamela was gone. Perhaps she'd needed to use the latrine. He sat up and put on his pants, uneasy that she was out by herself. Slipping out in his stocking feet, he tiptoed quietly on the wooden walkway. Single-lit bulbs hung intermittently from the ceiling. George walked from light bulb to light bulb all the way through the arena to the privies.

The pit toilets for the center were a matter of embarrassment for men and women alike. There were fifteen heads in a row, each with a wooden lid and a roll of toilet paper. Every evening, lye would be shoveled on top of that day's waste. At least this reduced the smell during the night. Across from the women's privies, George squatted down, resting on his heels, and waited for Pamela to emerge. When one woman came out, he asked her if anyone else was in the women's latrine. The woman shook her head in response. George slowly stood and then heard the soft sound of someone crying. He followed the sound into the mess hall and saw his sister seated at one of the benches, her head cradled on her arms on the picnic table. He sat down beside her, his back to the table, and leaned forward with his elbows on his knees. He knew she could feel him there. Her tears threatened his own emotional composure.

Pamela leaned her head on George's shoulder. She wiped her face with one hand and whispered, "I'm sorry."

George put his arm around her and pulled her closer. He laid his cheek on her forehead. "You've been a brave girl this whole time. It gets to be too much to hold in after a while."

"Are you afraid?"

"Afraid? No. I don't think anything will happen to us. I do believe we'll be jailed until the war is over."

"Jailed? But I've never done anything criminal."

"No. But we look too much like the enemy."

George and Pamela sat there. Every once in a while, she would shudder, a remnant of her weeping.

"Ready to go back?" George asked. "We should try to get some sleep."

Pamela nodded, and George put his arm around his sister and led her back through the maze to their small quarters. He lay awake, his arm resting on his forehead, and stared up at the rafters. He was the eldest son and was responsible for his family's survival. For their happiness. George turned over onto his side. Somehow, he had to find a way.

Chapter Two

Molly Mita

When Molly's family reached the Portland Assembly Center, the man processing the paperwork glanced them over, then addressed her father. "Girls, huh?" he said and snickered at Molly and her two sisters. "I'll put you near the women's shower and away from the single men's dormitory. Section two. It's a good location. Guess having three girls ought to be worth something."

Worth something, Molly thought.

She and her two sisters helped sell all the family store's merchandise, packing and consoling their parents as they frantically readied themselves to abandon their Portland home near the Willamette River.

Worth something. Her mouth felt metallic, like she'd been sucking on a tin spoon for too long.

Molly and her two younger sisters, Mary and Kameko, followed their father, Kentaro, into the big barn where all the residents from the west side of the Willamette River were told to report. Their mother Tak`e brought up the rear.

They hadn't taken more than a few steps inside when a short, bespectacled Japanese woman spoke to their father in English, "Do you have your room assignment?"

Kentaro handed her a piece of paper.

"Section two!" she yelled into the chaos of the new arrivals.

A youth of about sixteen hurried over. "I'll take that," he said. He looked at the section, row, and compartment number, then gave the paper back to Kentaro. He turned to Tak`e. "May I help you, ma'am?" She looked at him blankly. The boy repeated his question in Japanese. This time she answered and handed him her suitcase.

14

Finally, he turned to Kameko. "Do you want me to carry your suitcase too?"

"Sure," Kameko answered in English. "That's very nice of you." She smiled tentatively.

Molly shifted her heavy suitcase to her left hand. Just a little longer, she told herself.

"Come on. I'll show you where you'll be staying for the next few months." The boy took off at a rapid pace.

It was difficult to take in their new surroundings with little light and the maze of hallways. Molly tried to get her bearings. She could barely hear their guide as he pointed to his left.

"That's the mess hall. The women's latrine is on this side of the arena." He led them into the arena where animals had been auctioned off just a few weeks ago. Their footsteps echoed up to the stands all around them. "This is the activity area. We have some ping-pong tables and a sound system for dances." Kameko was translating for their mother as they hurried on.

They exited the arena, and the boy stopped at a T-intersection. "This is section two. You can go either right or left from here." He lifted the suitcase in his right hand and nodded his head down the right hall. "The men's shower is at the end." Then he pointed with Take's suitcase on the left. "The women's shower is all the way down there. So's the chapel. We'll have Catholic, Buddhist, and Protestant services there every Sunday. Otherwise, it's functioning like a small lecture hall."

Molly peered down the shadowy hallway, determined to come back and take a closer look. The group trailed after their guide. At the end of the hall, all the way to the back wall, the guide stopped. "Okay. Rooms on the left side are in Section One. Rooms on the right side are Section Two. You are in row three, unit three." He walked down the hall a short way and ducked under a heavy canvas curtain nailed above a doorway. "Here we are." He put down the two bags. Six metal cots were arranged haphazardly inside. "You can move one of the cots outside and get settled. Listen for the whistle. That's the signal for lunch." He bowed slightly to Kentaro and disappeared.

Molly put down her suitcase and stretched out her stiff fingers. Mary set her bag on one of the cots. The metal springs squeaked. Molly couldn't find her voice. This was it? There was barely enough room for five of them to stand inside. She looked above her. Two light bulbs hung down into the compartment. Molly tried the switch on the closest one. Nothing happened.

"Well," said her father, "let's unpack. Kameko, hold open the curtain. Molly, help me set this cot in the hallway."

Mary stepped over, picked up the mattress and the blanket from the extra cot, and followed her father and oldest sister. Tak`e began untying the cords to let the mattresses stretch out on the beds.

The girls shoved three of the cots to the end of the room. About six inches separated the three beds, enough room to squeeze by. Molly took the middle one, with her two younger sisters claiming those on either side. The cording used around the mattresses was tied together and strung from one side of the wall to the other, separating the room in half. Sheets could be hung with clothespins to give a modicum of privacy between the parents and their daughters. By the time the lunch whistle blew, the five beds were made.

As they retraced their steps to the mess hall, Molly was relieved to see it wasn't too crowded. Her family homed in on a spot in the far back of the room where they could sit. But it wasn't private. Three tables pushed together made up a row. An elderly man, a family with small children, and several young men joined them.

A waitress hurried over with several plates on her arms. She plopped down hash browns, dry toast, and steamed spinach flavored with vinegar. A second woman brought a large bowl of chocolate pudding for dessert and a pitcher with hot black coffee. Molly was hungry, and she looked at the offerings in dismay. She spooned a helping of spinach onto her plate and passed it to Kameko. Her sister took one whiff, grimaced, and gave it to Mary. Toast, several hash browns, and that was it. Her plate was half full. The waitress returned with more plates and bowls of the same food. She set them in front of the young men and left again. Molly cut the spinach and tasted a small bite. She would eat it as it was the only green vegetable, but she had to convince herself to swallow. *Ugh.* She was careful to put the pudding on her plate away from the vinegary remains.

***

Molly didn't react to the first typhoid vaccine, but did to the second a week later. About four hours after the injection, she developed a chill and a fever. She crawled into bed in their small compartment and pulled the wool blanket over her head. With all the noise in the center, she slept fitfully.

She woke in the afternoon to her sister nudging her shoulder.

"Here. I brought you some toast and tea," Mary said. "It's not as hot as it was. You can probably just drink it straight down. Are you feeling any better?"

Molly sat up and leaned back against the wall. Her dull, black hair was tangled from being under the covers. "Thanks," she said as she reached for her supper. "I think the fever is gone."

Mary put her hand on Molly's forehead and said, "I think so too. Do you feel well enough to go to the dance tonight?"

Mary was the caregiver of the trio of sisters. She wore her shoulder-length hair brushed back and held into place with either bobby pins or a headband. She dressed fastidiously and fussed in the same meticulous way with her needlework. Her shy, quiet manner hid an inner artist. Her sketches frequently became a pillowcase decoration or an applique on a skirt.

"You go on," Molly said. "Our section should quiet down, and I may be able to sleep some more."

Molly finished the toast and drank the tea while her family got ready for the festivities. Kameko brushed her dark hair into a tight ponytail. She was the youngest and the most adventurous of the sisters. She could curl into a corner with a book and imagine herself a character in it, certain she could be an actress on the stage or screen. If anyone rebelled against traditional values, it would be her. Molly couldn't understand why their mother wasn't worried about Kameko. Perhaps as the oldest, Molly shielded her from Tak`e's scrutiny.

She and her mother were at odds again. Tak`e was busy meeting the Japanese newly arrived in the assembly center, trying to find an appropriate match for her eldest daughter. Molly, on the other hand, was determined to find her own special young man who would share her dreams. In a way, her illness provided her a respite. When they left, Molly lay on her side and thought of her mother.

Tak`e's mild demeanor and timid smile masked a ramrod spine and a fierce loyalty to her husband first and then her daughters.

She was the shortest in the family, wore bifocals with black frames, and owned only one pair of scuffed black, low-heeled shoes. While Molly wanted to belong to the country she was born in, Tak`e found English lessons too difficult, though classes had been established in the assembly center. Molly liked to attend talks on government, history, and current events, while Tak`e wanted her to take classes in Bonsai, classical dance, or the traditional Japanese tea ceremony. It was an exhausting struggle. Only Molly's father could win an argument with Tak`e.

Even without a significant dowry, Molly was a valuable bride. She had been born in the United States and was a citizen, a *Nisei*. For an *Issei*, a *Nisei* bride was worth her weight in gold. But Molly resisted this marital path and her parents' pressure.

Just this morning, Molly had been introduced to her mother's idea of an acceptable husband. Molly had bowed to him, mentioned a headache, and fled to the compartment. She pleaded her case with her father. "He's as old as you are."

Kentaro raised his eyebrows. Molly knew she'd miscalculated. She tried again.

"If I married him and had a baby, he'd be seventy years old by the time the child graduated from high school. I could be a widow at thirty." Molly couldn't keep the panic out of her argument.

"The youngest *Issei* are just now turning thirty-five. Perhaps your mother could find a doctor or a merchant, someone you both could agree to." Kentaro's voice was placating. "I'll speak to your mother. She can do better. She just hasn't found the right man for you yet."

Molly shook away the thoughts of her mother and contemplated her father. Kentaro seemed to age by the day. Though they'd only been at the assembly center for a week or so, this relocation seemed harder on him than the previous five months. His dreams for his family shattered when the attack on Pearl Harbor made the Empire of Japan an enemy. The FBI visited them at the store and took her father in for questioning. He returned after three fretful days. Other leaders and teachers in the *Nikkei* community had also been arrested and questioned. Some had not been allowed to return, but they could at least notify their families where they were being held. They were accused of being enemy aliens if they were found with Japanese yen or a shortwave radio or owned a gun.

Then, when President Roosevelt signed an executive order in February 1942 requiring all persons of Japanese ancestry to be removed from Military Area I from Highway 97 to the West Coast, worry etched her father's forehead. Now Molly tallied the further signs of stress and worry this incarceration caused. His bowed head, slumped shoulders, slowly graying hair, and shuffling feet intimated he was not holding up well. Even his glasses reflected his depression. Black framed and a little large on his face, they were smudged and dirty most of the time. Molly began washing them every morning before the family went to breakfast.

Molly sighed and snuggled into her covers a little more. The side effects from the vaccine were gone. Now she was simply tired. Sunday would give her time to rest before her work schedule resumed. She was the only one in her family who'd managed to land a job. Molly had secured a position as intermediary between the chefs and the Army supply clerk. Being in charge of the supplies, however, didn't improve the meals much.

On Monday, when Molly and her family arrived for breakfast, the waitress placed the meal choices on a picnic table: canned plums, fried spam, mush, tea or coffee, and toast. Molly settled for toast and tea since her stomach was still a bit uneasy. Her father's plate ran with grease from the fried spam. Her mother slurped the juice from the canned plums, some of which she mashed up to put on her toast in lieu of jam. The oatmeal was the reason for the milk on their table. Usually, children under six were the only ones who were allowed to drink it. Mary and Kameko poured it on their hot cereal, tried to eat it, but gave up after a couple of bites.

"Lumpy," Mary said. She pushed her bowl away and reached for the plums.

"I'm still hungry," Kameko muttered. She took the last of the toast, a piece of spam, and folded it into a sandwich.

It wasn't that there wasn't food—it was just unpalatable. Even though the PAC hired two of the best Japanese chefs, they could only serve what they were given. Maybe lunch would be better, Molly thought as she drank the remaining tea. Molly waited until her family finished eating and then got up to leave together. The boys who were busing the tables made fast work of their bowls, cups, and saucers. Another family settled in shortly after.

Once they returned to their cubicle, Tak`e took off her shoes and laid back down on the bed. The neighboring children coughed much of the night, and the Mita family didn't get much sleep. Mary covered her mother with a black winter coat. The PAC was cold this morning, as there was no heat in the center. The girls all wore sweaters, but Kentaro put on his jacket.

They hadn't been able to pack very much of their lives to bring with them. It was drummed into everyone's head that they could take only what they could carry. Each girl managed about forty pounds, which included winter and summer clothes, bedding, and towels.

Molly had been curious to see what was so special to each family member that it couldn't be left behind. Mary gathered embroidery needles, a hoop, and several packets of thread to make things for her dowry. Her crochet hooks, knitting needles, and yarn filled every cranny in her bag. She slipped in empty notebooks for a journal. In them, she sketched people, animals, her surroundings, and wrote poetry, preferring haiku and tanka forms.

Kameko took a book of short stories, her favorite book *Little Women*, and her first pair of high heels. She slid in the newest copy of *Hollywood Times*, her guide to the latest movies. She also accommodated blank notebooks, but she used hers for scrapbooks of newspaper headlines, stories of Hollywood actresses, letters from girlfriendsand , anything else that struck her fancy. She wanted more books, so Molly and Mary each squeezed in another pair in their bags.

Her mother carefully wrapped the blue kimono and tea set she'd brought from Japan as a bride. She stuffed in two new aprons they hadn't been able to sell. Clothes were tucked in and around miso ingredients, bowls, and a saucepan. The English lessons Miss Curtis tried to teach her went in last.

Her father put in a pipe, extra tobacco, and a bottle of *sake* wrapped in a towel along with two small glasses. A small tool kit consisting of a hammer, a flat-headed screwdriver, measuring tape, a cotton rope, and nails of different sizes went in too. A hammer could be seen as a weapon, perhaps, but her father hadn't seen it explicitly forbidden.

Molly couldn't decide between the red cardigan and a blue sweater set, and she knew it was an extravagance to pack them both. In the end, she took out a second towel to make room. The cardigan would keep her warm, and the sweater set was for special times. Surely, special times were still ahead, weren't they?

The family did their best to make the compartment look like a home. Kameko and her father scrounged for scrap lumber to make a couple of shelves. Tak`e displayed her tea set from Japan while Kameko lined up the books: *Little Women* by Louisa May Alcott, poetry by Emily Dickenson, a couple of novels by Dickens, the Brontë sisters, and the current hit *The Grapes of Wrath* by John Steinbeck. Kameko read more than the other sisters, but with little to do in the center, all of them were devouring the stories. Mary hung her embroidery hoops on the wall by the side of her bed. It added color and art to the small space.

"I'll see you for lunch, if not sooner," Molly said. Mary took up the embroidery she'd started. Kameko dug out her journal and a pencil, leaned back against the wall, and started writing. Molly couldn't imagine what she'd find to write about.

Molly patted her father's shoulder as she left for the storeroom. Working gave her a purpose. She thought her father would get out of his misery if he could find something he cared about too. She sighed as she walked quickly down the hall, her heels beating out a steady rhythm on the wooden floor.

CHAPTER THREE

ELLIS HERTZOG

School was out for the summer! Ellis Hertzog walked toward one of the two school buses, thinking how different summer would be. He'd completed his sophomore year at Adrian High School, while his brother Sam had just graduated. Their older brothers, Luke and Donald, had joined the service shortly after Pearl Harbor. He hadn't seen Donald for five months now, and Luke left for the Air Corps in March. Even though the family received letters, the older brothers' absences left a huge hole. He'd never known this kind of worry or thought it could affect his parents so much. His mother rarely smiled anymore.

Ellis knew Sam planned to take advantage of an agricultural scholarship and attend two terms at Oregon State College in Corvallis. He wanted to begin basic flying school there, along with his regular classes. He'd be home this summer until college began in the middle of September, and then join the Air Corps next March when he turned nineteen.

All four sons usually helped their father, Lee, on their Eastern Oregon farm in the summers. This year's work, however, would fall on his and Sam's shoulders. Emily, the youngest and only girl, was thirteen and didn't help much in the fields. She weeded and watered in the garden with their mother and did housework.

As he considered his summer, Ellis heard angry voices behind him and was nearly knocked over by Jimmy Lewis. "Hey! Watch out!" Ellis called out.

Jimmy's feet churned in gravel as he ran past Ellis. Butch Butler followed, hooting and hollering at Jimmy as he gained ground. Jimmy almost made it around the corner when Butch pushed him down from behind. His face skidded in the rocks as he tried to break his fall with his hands. Butch picked him up by the back of his shirt and hit Jimmy with one great big blow to his eye before Ellis could get there to help his friend.

"That'll teach ya. Stay away from Jeannie! And keep your big mouth shut!"

Butch's sidekick smirked. "Way to go, Butch! Nice right cross!"

Jimmy waited until Butch moved away. He slowly and painfully sat up, his back to the building's brick wall. Ellis squatted down beside him and asked, "What happened? What'd you say to set him off?"

Jimmy had a reputation for shooting off his mouth. Sometimes his cracks were funny, but more often than not they got him into trouble.

Jimmy grimaced as he looked at his palms. He picked out a couple of small rocks and then shook his head. "I didn't say anything to him. I just told Jeannie I was going to miss her shelf this summer."

Cursed with bright red hair, Jeannie was freckled, loud, and crass. She also had the biggest breasts in Adrian High School and knew it. All the boys eyed her, but most of them were wise enough to keep their remarks to themselves.

"I didn't see Butch comin' up from behind," Jimmy said as he stood up and dusted off his shirt and pants. "Ah, gee, he tore my shirt pocket! Ma's going to kill me."

"You're lucky Butch didn't kill *you*."

Jimmy was the shortest boy in the sophomore class, though Ellis only had a couple of inches on him. Both were lean with hard muscles from all the farm work they did. They'd been best friends ever since Jimmy's family moved from Kansas.

Ellis slapped Jimmy's back companionably and said, "Maybe I'll see you around this summer. We could go swimming in the river or fishing or something."

"Yeah. I'd like that. But you know how my old man is about playing when there's work to be done." Jimmy shook his head, turned, and walked onto the bus.

Ellis worked hard too, but his folks tried to follow the scripture on Sundays. After church services, that usually meant afternoons of basketball or baseball, dips in the river, or picnics at one friend or another's. Jimmy didn't get to join in often.

Ellis stepped onto the other bus. After four miles, he and Emily got off and walked the half-mile to their house.

Emily was the youngest and every brother's favorite. Her brown hair would soon have blond streaks from the sun, and light freckles would sprinkle across her nose. Eastern Oregon sunshine claimed all of them, first with sunburns, then darker and darker tans. Ellis inherited his father's black hair and blue eyes, and his arms already showed the tan mark of short shirtsleeves. Even in May, the sun could be hot.

Ellis and Emily covered the distance to their basement home and walked through the door and down the stairs. The basement was the first step in building their house. When the farm had another good year, their parents planned to build a ground-level floor on top of it. But until then, the family made do with this subterranean space. Light came from the windows high up on the concrete walls. An adult could see outside, although Emily was still too short. The roof was flat, with black tar paper. Every winter their father worried it would leak. The chimney extended out the top, curving in a U so rain or snow wouldn't come in. Other than that, only the covered entrance stairway indicated a house existed there. To passersby, Ellis imagined theirs looked like the remains of a home, not the start of one.

It was cooler in the basement than outside this time of year. The landing at the bottom of the stairs was also the laundry room with the washtub and farm sink. A metal drainboard slanted down into the sink where their mother cleaned fruits and vegetables. She also used the sink to drain the washtub and to rinse the clothes. One door off the landing led to the bathroom with a toilet, sink, and bathtub—the first indoor facility their family ever had. The second door was to Emily's small bedroom. Ellis opened the third door leading into the kitchen. It was quiet, so he and Emily tried to step softly.

"Ellis? Emily? Is that you?" Their mother, Mae, sat at the round dining table in the family room, writing letters. Judging from the envelopes, she had finished her daily correspondence to Donald and Luke. "I'd better get these letters to the mailbox. I hope we hear from the boys today." She stood up and reached toward the bookshelf for stamps. "Ellis, your father wants you to start irrigating the top forty."

"Sure, Ma." His mother was the rock on which the family was built. She'd never seemed to age before Ellis's brothers had gone to war, yet now her dark brown hair had new strands of gray, and she needed glasses for reading. Ellis was still getting used to the changes.

Ellis headed into the boys' bedroom. With two brothers gone, he and Sam each claimed a top bunk. The two bottom beds were spotless, with the blankets and sheets tucked under, military-style. He unbuttoned his school shirt and hung it in the wardrobe. He put his jeans into his drawer, then took the work shirt and overalls off the hooks on the back of the bunk beds and put them on. As a senior, Sam finished school a week earlier and was already in the fields. Ellis hurried out of the house. Picking up a shovel in the shop, he headed out above the farmhouse to check the water.

At the top of the fields, the large, deep government ditch was like a line drawn in the desert. On one side, grayish-green sagebrush grew in large bushes. The dirt was slightly damp from the rains, but by late summer it would harden, and the sagebrush would look dead. On the near side of the ditch, though, the green fields flourished in neat rows. The water ran down the corrugations, soaking the beet shoots. Ellis whistled while he worked. Irrigating was actually pleasant in the evening, now that the ditches had all been formed. When his father first established the homestead, the soil was like fine flour. It hadn't enough tilth to hold together, but with each subsequent crop of alfalfa, the land strengthened and became productive.

This year the county agent convinced his father that beets would be in high demand, and with the war on, prices high. The only problem with beets was the labor required. Men were needed to thin them in the spring, hoe for weeds twice during the summer, and cut the tops during harvest. Ellis knew with his two older brothers in the service and Sam off to college, his father worried they wouldn't have enough hands to bring in the crop. Many of the hired hands joined up too, eager for adventure. That left many farmers in the area wondering how they were going to survive.

That evening, the Hertzog family ate dinner early. Lee was heading into Nyssa for a community meeting about the labor shortage. The sugar company was hosting it in their community room, and Welch, the president, would be the speaker.

"What will we do, Dad?" Sam asked. "Is it true that the factory's going to bring in some Japs to work? Won't that be dangerous?" Sam had been following the issue in the *Nyssa Gate City Journal* ever since the idea came up.

Many communities didn't want Japanese anywhere near them. That was especially true with the American Legion in Vale. The factory and the farmers that planted beets, however, were willing to try. Ontario and Nyssa already had some Japanese farmers who'd lived in the area for years. Ellis heard they were good neighbors. In any case, Lee would listen to both sides before he made up his mind which way to vote.

"You boys want to come?" Lee said as he knotted his tie. "You can find out firsthand what the issues are. I wonder how many men Welch thinks we need."

Sam and Ellis jumped at the chance. They rushed to their bedroom to change and joined their father in the 1939 black Ford pickup.

***

When the three Hertzogs arrived at the sugar factory's community room, Ellis realized his dad was one of the few men who dressed up— many were still in their overalls. Most had washed up, but it was hard to clean all the grime worn into their hands and the dirt lodged under their nails. His father noticed their neighbor, Ed Allen, sitting near the front and took a chair beside him.

"Full house tonight," Ed said. "You boys come to see the action?"

"Yessir. Pa didn't have to ask us twice," Sam said.

Ellis looked around. The farmers were talking quietly among themselves. Men sat with their arms crossed over their chests. Several had their hats on their knees. He saw their neighbor, Mr. Inghels, sitting across the way. The Dutchman had immigrated to the area only a couple of years earlier, joining several families who had come to Adrian from Holland. He'd established a dairy not far from the Hertzog's farm. A large man, he sired two equally tall twin girls. Where he tended to be dour and morose, his girls were always giggling together behind their hands. Ellis had the unfortunate luck to be seated in front of them in nearly every class.

Ernie Butler, Butch's father, stood against the back wall. He was a slight, short man, about five foot six, with a dark mustache and closely set brown eyes. He was known for wearing cowboy boots with two-inch heels and a shiny belt buckle he'd won as a young bull rider. Instead of being a farmer, he raised cattle and ran them on federal land in Jordan Valley. He had no need of Japanese workers. Butch slouched beside him, hands in his jean's pockets. He was already as tall as his father and just as muscular. Ernie was talking with another man, arguing loudly that Japanese shouldn't be allowed to work in the fields.

"I don't want any more of 'em leasing or buying land. I don't."

"The Japanese are good farmers," said Ernie's companion. "Just look at Tanaka. His fields are some of the finest around. We need that help until the war is over."

"And how long is that goin' to be? The Brits have been fighting the Nazis since '38. That's four years already. If we have Japanese here for four years, you can bet they'll get a toehold in our area. They're tenacious!"

Ellis caught Butch's eye and looked away quickly, but not before Butch scowled at him. Ellis turned around in his chair and faced forward, sinking a little. No way did he want to encourage Butch's attention. He could hear the men's heated conversation continuing.

"Didn't the FBI arrest any Japs they felt were dangerous when they raided those homes over in Ontario?"

"They only arrested two. How do you know they got 'em all?"

Ellis remembered the FBI raids. One of the Japanese who'd been arrested was rumored to have a stash of yen, while the other man possessed a shortwave radio and a couple of cameras. They'd been sent to FBI headquarters in Portland. The feds also arrested two Germans and one Italian for having hunting rifles and shotguns, but they'd been released.

Welch walked into the community room. He towered over the Nyssa mayor who was with him. Welch was red-headed, with long, freckled arms. He normally wore his shirtsleeves rolled up, leaving the blond hair on his arms visible. Tonight, however, he wore a jacket, shirt and tie, and black slacks. His presence commanded attention. When the room quieted, Welch called the meeting to order.

"Good evening, men. It's great to get such a good turnout. As you know, I've been to the Portland Assembly Center where the Japanese are being held. Although the governor has signed documentation permitting the Japanese to come here and work, and the federal government has agreed, the Japanese themselves still have to want to come. At the meeting we held there, one of the men referred to the negative comments recently made by Idaho's governor. They're worried about their safety. We need to assure them we'll treat them well, that housing will be adequate, and wages will be competitive."

Ed raised his hand and stood up to speak. "What about *our* safety, our women and children? Who's going to guard the Japs at night?"

Ellis had never thought of being in danger. He listened carefully as Welch explained.

"These men are not considered threats. They didn't break any laws or cause any problems in their previous communities. They won't be inside a fence or have guards, but a curfew of eight p.m. will be established in the camp. Any violators of the curfew will be sent back to Portland. A Farm Security Administration director and assistant director will be in charge. These Japanese want to show their patriotism by helping save your crops. They want to earn more than the wages they get paid in the center in order to help their own families survive. We've screened them. These are good men."

The farmers murmured among themselves. Inghels asked the next question. "Will the Japs be able to buy or lease land for themselves?" This question was at the root of the problem with the American Legion and the Grange.

Welch looked at the mayor, who stood up. "Governor Sprague answered that last month. The law says Japanese who are American citizens can buy and lease land. We know some community groups have asked their members not to sell or lease to the Japanese, but we also know the government can't prevent it."

Ellis heard Ernie swear behind him.

Welch went on. "We have Japanese farmers in the Treasure Valley who have been tending to their land for twenty years or more. They've been here longer than you have, Mr. Inghels."

Ellis didn't know how well Inghels took that comment. Then he heard a man loudly exclaim to his neighbor, "See? I told you! Them Japs gonna take over!"

Lots of men commented to their neighbors, and the swell of voices stopped Welch from continuing. The government's ads touting the Owyhee Irrigation Project and the promise of water brought many of the farmers to the area in the last five to seven years after their own farms were blown away in the dust bowl of Oklahoma and Kansas.

"We have a right to this land," someone said.

"We got here before these Japs!" called out another.

"My family's been here since the Civil War!" Ernie exclaimed.

The mayor stepped up to the podium. "Quiet down, men! If we can't have an orderly meeting, we'll put an end to it now, and you'll all have to plow your fields under!"

An uneasy quiet resumed.

"Now, about numbers," Welch continued. "Very few Japanese have signed up so far. I have the names of fifteen men, mostly young men over eighteen, who are willing to come. If they discover their fears are not founded, working conditions are good, and we treat them fairly, they'll write back to Portland and tell the others. This is our only chance to recruit the labor force we need. It'll take about four hundred to work the beets this spring. That doesn't include potatoes, onions, and the other crops. The first group will be here tomorrow. We need them to convince others that this is a good deal."

The room vibrated with tension.

"Fifteen men? What good will that do?"

Welch tamped down the panic in the men's voices and moved to the crux of the issue. "So, we're going to vote. All those in favor of working with Japanese labor, raise your hands."

Ellis looked around. Slowly, farmers were lifting their hands. No one could afford to plow their beets under. His father and Ed joined with the others.

"Any opposed?"

The question hung in the air like a rattlesnake waiting to strike.

"Seeing none, the vote has passed unanimously."

Ellis let out the breath he hadn't realized he was holding. He wondered how this experiment would work out.

CHAPTER FOUR

ABE YANO

The Portland Assembly Center, or the PAC, wasn't as bad as Abe thought it would be. He loved baseball, and, at first, games were organized haphazardly. A bunch of guys would show up on the baseball diamond, choose sides, and play. Even if there were only six boys per team, that was enough for a game. As more and more people arrived, there were enough for nine or even ten on a team. A second diamond was fashioned, and four teams played at a time. Abe could pitch and play infield and soon became captain of a team. He made sure Danny Saito and his brother Thomas were on the team. Thomas played second or third base, while Danny was terrific as shortstop or catcher. Being outside was a relief from their Expo center confinement. And when he and George had another dust-up, Abe could bash a baseball instead of his brother.

Their disagreements had increased here in the PAC. Now, however, they were conducted in fierce whispers, hissing words back and forth. George was self-righteous in his role as eldest brother. Abe taunted him, mocking his tone. Pamela and Thomas ducked their heads and escaped whenever they could. Their mother followed the emotion from one son's face to another, not understanding a word they spit but dismayed at them for fighting. Abe found refuge on the baseball field.

At nineteen, Abe was one of the older boys playing. He enjoyed joshing the other boys and eating together for lunch and dinner. After a few days, though, he became restless. Thomas had found a job in the mess hall with Danny. He was setting up and clearing off after meals. Pay was only twelve dollars a month, but it was more than anyone else in their family earned. Abe decided a job would give him more purpose than playing baseball.

"Mr. Johnson?" Abe asked. He read the man's name from a plaque sitting on the battered wooden desk in the administration office.

"Yes, son? What can I do for you?" Mr. Johnson's desk was covered with stacks of papers. Abe recognized the registration forms George had handed in; they looked like requisitions for food and building supplies.

"I'd like to find some work if you have it. I'm good with my hands. I can build whatever you need." Abe stood tall, hoping his youth wouldn't prevent Mr. Johnson from taking him seriously.

"I need a furniture builder. You have any experience with that?"

"Yes, sir. I worked in our shop class at Toppenish High School, constructing shelves, side tables, and dressers. Last year my brother and I built a small store to sell fruit and vegetables." Abe couldn't believe he was using the family store as part of his resume. He hated that store. It seemed a taunt to him about not going on to college.

Mr. Johnson nodded his head. "We just got permission to construct a library for the center. We need shelves, desks, and a few chairs. Then we'll need a table and chairs for the newspaper room. I just hired one man, but we need another. We pay sixteen dollars a month. That sound okay to you?"

The wage was very low, but he'd be contributing to the family's well-being. "Sure. That sounds good. What about tools?"

"Come with me. I'll introduce you to Robert and show you the plans for the library."

***

On his second day working on the library, Abe attached a third bookshelf to the wall. The room was small, and the shelves wouldn't hold much, but with folks checking out the books, they could accommodate more than just this small space would handle. He knew a library would be a lifeline for Pamela.

He looked up and saw his brother stomping down the long hallway. George wanted Abe to attend a meeting in the mess hall, and Abe hadn't mentioned the job he needed to get to. He took the nails out of his mouth.

"Is the meeting over?"

"I didn't realize you were helping with the library construction. I tracked down Thomas at a baseball game, and he told me where to find you."

Abe knew he'd hurt his older brother's feelings again. If he felt ambushed, even good news like getting a job made George touchy.

"These are great shelves." George glanced around the small room and saw Abe's co-worker. "Can you talk?"

Abe spoke to the other man. "Hey, Robert, I'm going to take a short break, get some water."

Robert nodded, and Abe led George to a quiet spot.

"What's up?" Abe asked.

"I signed up to go to Eastern Oregon tomorrow."

"Tomorrow? That's sudden." Abe could tell George was excited.

"I'll be checking out the working conditions as one of a crew of fifteen laborers."

Abe looked at him. It would be just like his brother to sign him up, too, without asking. "Am I going?"

George shook his head. "You need to stay here and be in charge of the family. I'll be counting on you. Thought we'd talk about it tonight."

Abe looked at his older brother for several seconds. Then he grinned and took a small jab at his brother's plan. "Let's make it short. There's a dance tonight, and I want to meet some new girls."

Abe watched as George's face hardened.

"Don't worry!" Abe laughed. "I only have a few hours to kick up my heels before you leave. I want to make the most of it." He slapped George on the back as they returned to the library. "It wouldn't hurt you to look at the beauties in camp either!"

George walked away, shaking his head.

***

Abe loved to dance. He could feel the rhythm in his feet. The physical education teachers at Toppenish High School had taught the students how to dance the waltz, polka, foxtrot, and jitterbug. Abe had also learned to square dance. He'd learned the steps quickly and was a favorite partner. The only problem was the girls. Somehow, they got the idea that if he danced with them, they had a claim to him. That was why Abe danced with as many girls as he could. He didn't want to show any favorites. And some of them giggled. What was that all about?

With so little to do, most of the families had come to the arena to see what was going on. Some just talked in the stands while chaperoning younger family members. A ping-pong tournament took the attention of the younger boys. Off to one side, a few girls were practicing dance moves. Of his family, only Thomas had come to dance. He had the same PE teachers as Abe and was at least comfortable with the dance steps. Pamela sat in the stands, ever the observer. The girls were outnumbered by the males, which made it a bit harder to have a partner for every dance, but Abe was determined to try. He'd never seen so many Japanese women in one place at the same time.

As the music played, Abe began asking girls to dance. If a gal was tapping her feet to the music, that was a good sign. He learned where the girls were from, where they'd gone to school, first names, and maybe what they liked to do before the internment. The songs blasted out from a radio, made louder by a microphone. Each song was three or four minutes long. Then Abe walked each girl back to where she'd been before and thanked her, often turning to another girl standing close by. "Care to dance?"

Abe knew that George and their mother were in their room, packing a small suitcase. In the back of Abe's mind, behind his ready smile, he felt guilty. His brother was going to earn more in a week than Abe would in a month. As the eldest son, George was trying to save the farm.

Abe spun a girl out and then in, and gathered her in his arms before another swing. What was this one's name? He couldn't remember.

His thoughts turned to Thomas. George still planned on sending Thomas to medical school with the money they made on the farm. Their mother, Chiharu, put every spare dime into a decorative cookie tin earmarked for Thomas's education. Abe tried not to begrudge Thomas the dream of being a doctor. He knew his brother would make an excellent physician. It was just that his own dream of being a lawyer and the preparation of his Japanese schooling had been set aside, no longer important. Thomas even called him "Number Two" as a joke.

The dance was nearly over when Abe approached his sister. "Come on, Pamela. They're going to play a foxtrot as the last song. Let's show off the Yano sister."

Pamela set down the notebook she had been writing in, smiled, and took Abe's hand to climb down the benches. Abe was so much taller than his sister. The top of her head barely reached his shoulders. He put his hand in the middle of her back and placed her right hand in his left, and away they went. He was pleased Pamela hadn't refused his invitation. Sometimes his baby sister surprised him.

***

The next morning at breakfast, George was giving Abe instructions. "Don't put my bed out into the hall until I'm sure this labor camp is going to work. The administration might put the family into a smaller stall if they figure out we have just four people left."

Abe clenched his teeth. It made his jaw flex and drew attention to his high cheekbones. Even when irritated, he looked handsome. Some girls walked by the picnic table where he, George, and Thomas were sitting. One girl covered her mouth as she giggled with her friends. Abe lifted his hand in greeting, which made all the girls whisper together more.

"What if there are vigilantes?" Thomas worried. "What if the camp is attacked? Are you sure this is a good idea?"

"That's why the fifteen of us are going. We'll check it out and send word back to you. I don't think women will be welcome in camp, so you both need to stay here with Mother and Pamela," George said.

George picked up his suitcase and walked outside, Abe and Thomas following. A small crowd gathered to see the men off. A couple of armed soldiers escorted the men as they walked to the train. George looked back and waved. Abe couldn't help it. He had to rib his brother one more time.

"Bye, George! Get a blister for me!"

Chapter Five

George

Always the funny one, George thought as he and the others walked to the train. He wondered how Abe would do in his new role as head of the family. Maybe the responsibility would make him grow up.

George had been at the PAC for fifteen days. He'd nearly gone crazy with the confinement, the guard towers, the small stall serving as their home. Of the three men in his family, only he had not been able to get a job to bring more than a pittance of money. When Welch, the man from the sugar factory, offered the men a chance to work in the fields south of Nyssa, Oregon, he'd jumped at it. He still couldn't get the money he'd make in the fields to add up to the bank mortgage and taxes, but he was better off trying than pacing the hallways of the Expo Center.

He'd first told his mother of his decision. When he returned from the meeting, she was lying down on a cot, not an unusual sight. She had removed the sturdy black heels and had tucked her anklet-clad feet under her faded print dress. Her hair had a few gray strands running through it, pulled back in a bun. She opened her eyes when George cleared his throat. Sitting up, she reached for her glasses and smiled tentatively at him. He knelt in front of her.

"How was the meeting? What did you find out?" she asked in Japanese.

"Mother, I think I can get us out of here," George said softly. It was so easy for sound to carry to the cubicles next to them. "I've volunteered to go to Eastern Oregon to thin beets. I have to leave tomorrow."

"So soon?" She looked at George steadily. He knew she would

not question his decision as the eldest son and head of the family. As a mother, however, she could not keep the concerns for him to herself. She put her hand on the side of his face. "My son, is it safe for you to go?"

"That is why I must go. A number of us volunteered to be scouts for the rest of the camp. I can earn some money and perhaps find us a better place to live that's out of the military zone."

"We've only been here two weeks. Surely our situation is not that urgent."

"We don't know how long we have to stay here, Mother. You've seen the doctor twice already."

His mother frowned. "I would not want you hurt because of my discomfort."

At George's reminder of their poor living situation, his mother nodded her head in agreement.

"Then this is a good plan," she said. "Just be careful, be safe. You will write to us?"

And that was it. Perhaps he should feel guilty that his decision was so easy to make. He was concerned Abe wouldn't be able to handle everything. Really, the only problem in the family was between the two of them. Surely if other issues arose, the mail would be fast enough to relay them.

The men reached the train station in a few minutes. They were led past the passenger cars to the last ones on the track. The guards opened the door to a cattle car and told the men to get in.

"We're riding in an open car?" one of the men asked. "You didn't tell us that! It'll be cold and stink to high heaven."

Johnson conferred with a guard, who jogged back in the direction of the camp. "Sorry, men. We couldn't get permission for you to ride in the passenger section. You can sweep it out before the train gets started. I've sent a man back for some blankets and a bucket you can use as a privy."

George saw a shovel leaning against the door. He was darned if he'd let some dirty straw stand in his way. "I'll do it." He hoisted himself up, took the shovel, and began in the back, clearing out the dirty mixture of hay and manure. His eyes stung from the urine.

Another man got up and handed George a bandana. "Here. Cover your mouth and nose with this." He put on his own bandana and grabbed a second shovel. With both men working, the car was soon emptied. A couple of bales of clean straw were stacked to one side. They broke one open and strewed the new layer on the hard floor. The stench was less but still lingered in the air.

By this time, the soldier was back with scratchy, greenish-brown wool blankets and a large, galvanized five-gallon bucket. As each man climbed into the car, he was handed a blanket, sack lunch, and a jar of water. They settled around the car as best they could.

An armed guard boosted himself up into the front. The War Relocation Administration officials required that he accompany the men to Huntington, where Welch would pick them up in a truck for their last leg to their new camp in Nyssa. He moved the pail to the front of the car, in the corner opposite the door. Another soldier handed up a sturdy wooden armchair and his World War I-era rifle. The man stationed himself right by the door.

"Speak English!" he barked. "I don't want anyone whispering. Ask my permission to use the bucket. Everyone else, stay seated. Better not plan to escape. No Nip will slip away under my watch!"

George looked him over. He was at least twenty years older, had dark, beady eyes, and wore his belt taut under a rounded belly. Physically, he wasn't very intimidating. But that didn't mean he wasn't dangerous. The man patted his gun and stroked the butt of it, as if to reassure himself that if a problem arose, his gun would provide the solution. He sat down with his back against the wall and remained aloof, his rifle resting on the chair arms.

George sat down across from the guard, his blanket spread on the straw. He laid his suitcase flat and put the sack of food on top. The smell—and the guard—killed any appetite he might have had. In a couple of hours, he might feel differently.

The train whistled twice and then slowly began to move. With the spaced slats on the sides, George could see the shadowy images of Portland as the train gathered speed. Blackout curtains hid the city along the railway. The train chugged along as the sun outlined Mt. Hood in the distance. He opened his suitcase and pulled out his denim jacket. He had his old baseball cap too, but no gloves. The guard watched every movement he made. Leaning back against the swaying car and closing his eyes, George hoped he'd made the right decision.

***

The tracks followed the Columbia River for miles, slowly leaving the lush greenness of the Willamette Valley behind. In forty short miles, the train passed the magnificent Multnomah Falls, Hood River, The Dalles, and then Celilo Falls. Soon waterfalls gave way to craggy rock faces, which slid almost to the river. The towering firs were gone, replaced by lichens growing on dark rock. Tugboats pushed the occasional barge upriver through the columnar basalt. Stubby, water-starved trees fought the stony landscape for survival.

George felt like those trees: water-starved and fighting against great odds. It wasn't just the prejudice and distrust the guard emanated. The hard work to survive also meant saving for the family farm. He had signed up to be a hired laborer. He knew wages would be low.

As they headed southeast, George knew this was the closest he'd be to his home in Toppenish until the war was over. He had to admit he was homesick, but the home he missed no longer existed. It hadn't since his father died. His parents had raised his brothers and sister between the old world of Japan and the new one of the United States. His father insisted that each boy be named after a famous president: George Washington, Thomas Jefferson, and Abraham Lincoln. His sister's original name was Junko, meaning "pure and genuine child." Her first-grade teacher, however, couldn't imagine anyone called "junk" and insisted she change her name to Pamela. From that time forward, Pamela refused to answer to anything else.

He wondered how Franklin was doing—if he was farming both places. The garden would be coming to life now, the plants growing in the rows. Bees would be pollinating the trees and setting the fruit. He'd fertilized them two days before they left. The abundance of the life he'd left contrasted with the barrenness he expected in Eastern Oregon.

At Highway 97, they finally reached the border of the military zone. The tracks turned away from the Columbia River, heading overland toward Pendleton. The land flattened out. Farmers here produced wheat and other dryland crops. Grain elevators stood beside the rails, waiting for the harvest. Here, deciduous trees existed only around the canals or homes where well water kept them alive. In this third week of May, though, the land was greener due to early spring. The light greenish-blue of sagebrush sprinkled color on the barren landscape.

As the train began its slow ascent up the Blue Mountains, the men began eating some of the food in their sacks. They had spam sandwiches, celery slices, carrot sticks, and some cheese. Other than pouring their drinking water on their hands, there was no way to wash.

The group grew less wary and began to share their names and backgrounds. There were two shopkeepers and one doctor in the group. Twelve of the fifteen were farmers. They came from Hillsboro, Gresham, and Hood River. George was the only one from Washington. Most were like George and had raised vegetables and picked fruit from orchards. Some had grown onions and potatoes, but none of them knew about sugar beets. A few were married, had small children, and were more anxious about leaving the center. Dr. Yamaguchi had practiced in Portland and had his medical bag with him.

"I've never done field work before," Yamaguchi said. "Instead of asking you men to turn your head and cough, I'll be asking you to massage my back!"

The men laughed.

"I'm sure you'll be treating our blisters," said a young man who had worked in the Hood River orchards. "We'll get used to it, though. We should harden up in a week or so. I'm sure we can gain the respect of any man who works with us. We'll show the farmers we're true patriots and think first of our country."

"You may show some of those folks, but there's no way a regular American will be fooled!" The guard had followed the conversation, looking intently at each man as he spoke. He stood up, his face flushed with anger. Both hands gripped his gun. "You Japs are the enemy, and I'll never forget that!"

The tension that had subsided rose again. George was on high alert until the guard slowly sat down. The men quit talking and hunched down into their blankets. They watched the guard as carefully as he watched them. The men rode the last two hours in total silence.

Toward midafternoon, the train came to a stop at the Huntington station. The guard slid the cattle car's door back, and Welch was there to greet them. George was relieved to see a friendly face after the hostile soldier.

"I've got a truck over there," Welch said to the men. "Carry your gear and find a seat. Nyssa is another two hours away."

The men helped each other down as they disembarked. They carried the blankets and suitcases and, in twos and threes, walked over to the vehicle. The soldier started toward the truck, but Welch stopped him. "I've got it from here."

"You got a gun with you?"

Welch narrowed his eyes. "I told you I'll handle it from here. Your orders are to return on the next train." He gave the soldier a couple of bucks and watched as he retreated into the hotel. Welch opened the passenger door after the last man had settled in the back, got in, and told the driver to pull out.

The ride from Huntington seemed interminable. The men were free to talk now, but with no shade from the sun, several of them nodded off. The truck descended into the valley, entering Ontario. They passed by a Catholic hospital located on a hill overlooking the town. Another twelve miles of farmland passed by before they entered Nyssa.

As the truck drove through town, George craned his neck, looking at the stores and schools on the highway. On one, he saw a sign reading: "No Japs served here."

Doc read the sign out loud and said, "Good to know they aren't cannibals."

It took a moment for the men to get Doc's joke. The laughter eased the tension and the worry of what they would find in their new surroundings. The vigilante fears seemed more credible now.

The truck turned south and traveled through farming country once again. The ditches flowed with water, and irrigation pipes lined the banks, drawing the brown liquid to rows upon rows of crops. Occasionally, land was not irrigated, and the dry, parched soil yielded nothing but sagebrush. The farmhouses were modest, certainly nothing to indicate wealth. George saw his first basement house, and another dwelling nearby seemed like nothing more than a lean-to. But everywhere there were sugar beets. There would be no shortage of work.

The truck crossed railroad tracks, turned left off the road, and rolled down a knoll into the camp. The driver shut off the motor. The engine ticked in the cooler air as the men sat quietly, none of them quite ready to step out. George silently compared the new camp with the assembly center in Portland: no gate to block the entrance, no barbed wire fence surrounding it, no guard tower with a soldier pointing a gun at them. Instead, under a tarp lit with a lantern, two men stirred a couple of pots. The area was stark, with no trees and little grass. Welch had said they'd be living in tents, and a few were set up nearby. Newly built outhouses perched on the hard dirt several yards away. Picnic tables were arranged outside the cook tent under a shelter. Down a few hundred feet from camp, the Snake River flowed, swift and menacing in the near dark. Two men with clipboards in their hands emerged from a small wooden structure to greet them. George was relieved to see they didn't carry guns. It seemed that the Amalgamated Sugar Company had gone to some effort to make sure the camp was ready for the first volunteers.

Welch got out. "We're here, men. Let's get you settled before dinner."

They got off the truck and stood in a ragged line to be assigned their tents. The director and assistant director were polite, efficient, and business-like. George found the tent he would be sharing with Dr. Yamaguchi. Doc glanced up from the cot he had already chosen. He was an older, slender man, about the same height as George. His dark-rimmed glasses frequently slid down his nose. He wore a sleeveless white undershirt beneath a white dress shirt. His black cotton pants grazed his black dress shoes. He didn't look like any farmer George had ever seen. At least he could tell a good joke.

The tent's bottom two feet were comprised of a wooden, square foundation with a doorway cut into it. Strong canvas material provided the top and sides. Ropes pulled up the side of the canvas and allowed a breeze to blow through, chasing heat from the enclosure. They could only stand up in the center of the tent, as it peaked at about six feet. George put his gear on the other cot. This would be home for as long as the work lasted.

Talking quietly among themselves, they began to line up for chow. Stew bubbled in two large pots, and the smell of freshly baked bread made George's stomach growl. Cherry pies for dessert sat by pots of fresh coffee. Red and white checkered tablecloths covered five wooden tables with benches. The director and assistant director sat with Welch, separating themselves from the rest of the men. George overheard them talking about how to divide them into work crews.

Welch lit another hanging lantern. The evening was cool, with a slight breeze. Moths batted at the lantern's light, and crickets chirped their evening song. Men filled their plates. Quiet laughter broke the night's stillness.

George was finishing his stew when a farmer walked across the road and hailed the men. Welch walked toward the man and shook his hand. George watched the exchange for any signs of trouble. The farmer reached up and tilted back his short-brimmed hat. He was Japanese! George didn't know that other *Nikkei* lived in the area.

Welch walked toward the laborers with the farmer. "Men, this is Mr. Tanaka. He lives across the road in the two-story house and farms the eighty acres he owns there. He's raising celery, onions, potatoes, and about forty acres of beets this year."

The men murmured their hellos as Tanaka bowed to them. He was an older man with white-streaked hair and dark eyebrows. He wore clean, patched bib overalls atop a short-sleeved t-shirt and scuffed leather boots. George shook his hand and felt the calluses on his palm. His handshake was firm, and his eyes held George's as they were introduced.

"Welcome to Malheur County!" Mr. Tanaka said. "My family is most eager to make you comfortable here. The community is anxious to have your help in the beet fields. I will be here tomorrow morning to help Mr. Welch when the farmers come to pick you up. I wanted to meet you this evening to answer any questions you may have, and to let you know my home is just across the road. You would be most welcome guests at any time."

George nodded his head along with the other men. Tanaka's invitation seemed genuine and sincere.

"Thank you, Henry." Welch turned and spoke to the men one last time. "I'm going to head home and let the driver return the truck to the sugar factory. Breakfast is at five thirty. Farmers will be here at six. Get a good night's rest; you'll need it." Welch shook hands with the director and assistant director and with that, he was gone.

Tanaka spent a half hour more with the work crew. He was a jovial man, happy to greet the new arrivals. According to him, there were several Japanese families living in Nyssa and Adrian and more in and around Ontario. He had settled in the area nearly twenty years ago. As the man talked, the cooks washed up, left another pot of coffee for the men, turned off the lanterns in the eating area, and left. The directors went into their quarters and retired for the night as well. Tanaka also said good night and walked back to his house. The men were alone and without a sentry for the first time since they entered the assembly center. George poured the last of the coffee for anyone who wanted it, and the men spoke quietly around a table. With the directors gone, the remaining tension dissipated. No one said anything of consequence, but the freedom to speak Japanese or English as they chose felt like a quiet rebellion. The stars overhead, accompanied by a quarter moon, added to George's sense of peace. His soul stretched like a cat. After a time, the men withdrew to their tents.

George looked up at the stars before he entered. The Big Dipper and the North Star shimmered overhead. It was quiet here. No guards, no watchtowers, no fences. His sigh of relief was audible. Doc, sitting across from him, smiled. "How does it feel to be out of jail?"

"Good." George grinned. "Damn good."

Chapter Six

Molly

Molly thought of herself as a juggler with at least four balls she needed to keep in the air. Every once in a while, one would drop, and she'd have to catch the other three before she could pick up the one lying dusty and dirty on the ground. Then she'd begin juggling again, never knowing which one would drop next. The one she was worried about the most was her father.

Kentaro had always been ethical, sharp, and resilient. Molly believed his financial burden would have been much lighter if he'd had even one son. She'd never heard him complain, though. He radiated strength and warmth instead. He wasn't affectionate, but his concern for his family let Molly know of his deep, abiding love. He wasn't just strong for his family; he had been a leader in *Nihonmachi*, or Japan Town in Portland. But now he was remote, distant, always focused on some middle distance Molly couldn't see.

She didn't have to worry about her mother. The compartment became the center of Tak`e's social life. Women were always visiting and checking in with each other. That didn't bother Molly, as she worked several hours a day. Mary smiled at the women and continued her needlework, knitting, or crocheting. Her work drew admiring comments and sometimes a companion who needed advice on her own project. Kameko found friends and left the compartment to search them out if it became too noisy with gossip. Kentaro couldn't abide all the women and began wandering through the complex, pacing and pacing and pacing.

Usually, Molly would spy her father going back and forth. She waited by an intersection, and when she saw him, she hurried to catch up to keep him company as he walked the many halls of the center. She tried many topics of conversation, but Kentaro's contributions were few and usually mumbled.

"How about walking outside?" she asked. "It's a nice day, and we could watch one of the baseball games."

They walked by the canteen and post office. Someone was hammering in the storeroom next to that. The pounding outside her head added to the headache she felt beginning.

The baseball field was near the Military Police barracks. They watched an inning while Molly explained the game as best she could. Even a home run didn't pique her father's interest. Without saying anything, he turned and wended his way back into the big barn. Molly gave a shrug. She'd try again the next day.

One afternoon, Molly stood between Section One and Section Two. She hadn't seen her father for quite some time. Many people were in the hallways, but not Kentaro. She'd already checked the chapel/lecture hall. She'd walked through the arena twice. The men's dorm was off-limits for her, but if her father was there, he'd have mentioned a friend or a conversation he'd had. There were no clues he'd ventured to that section. She tried to puzzle out where he might be.

She entered the arena for the third time and looked around carefully. He was sitting in the shadows at the top of the stands right above the exit, once again staring off at nothing. Molly waved at him, but it didn't bring him out of his reverie. Holding onto the splintering railing on one side of the stairs, she began climbing and got close enough to him that she could make out his features. Tears dripped from under his smudged glasses. He wasn't making a sound, no sobbing, no heavy breathing. Molly was so shocked, she retraced her steps, slowly, quietly. She had never seen a man cry before. Especially her father. She didn't know how to help him.

The next morning after breakfast, Tak`e reached into her purse for a pen and paper to write to Miss Curtis, her English tutor from church. Not finding either, she dumped the contents out on the bed. "*Aihee!* My wallet is gone. It had ten dollars in it. Someone has taken it. Who would do such a thing?"

Molly looked at her father. Kentaro had buried money from the store under a floorboard in a hole he dug in the dirt. His bed sat on top of it. He shook his head slightly at the family. There was no sign it had been disturbed.

Molly pulled out the suitcase from under her bed. Nearly empty, it bounced on the cot. She owned two purses, one black and one white, but kept her money pinned into the inside of one of the suitcase pockets. It was still there. "I have mine," she said.

Mary checked on her savings. It was wrapped in one of the white pillowcases she'd brought to embroider. Kameko didn't have a purse or money but looked through her belongings. "It doesn't look like anyone searched my suitcase."

"Someone must have seen your purse under the bed and taken your wallet on a whim. I'll go tell the administrator what was stolen," Kentaro said. "Tak`e, come with me. Molly, would you let the families in our section know? They will want to check their possessions too."

It was the first time since they'd arrived that Molly's father had taken charge of anything. She was delighted to obey. Stopping outside the canvas curtains of each family, the noise level rose as people expressed their dismay. One other person had something stolen too— an alarm clock. Such an odd thing to steal, Molly thought.

The theft of Tak`e's purse put a damper on them all. However, it prompted the appointment of an acting Japanese governing group inside the PAC. The military declared the *Issei* ineligible to be elected leaders, as they couldn't be U.S. citizens. That meant the second generation, the *Nisei*, were promoted to leadership roles over their elders. That didn't sit well with Molly's father. "They're just a bunch of kids," he complained.

The current president of the Japanese American Citizens League, Kane Kasai, was appointed as the temporary leader of the assembly center until all the Japanese in the Military War Zone arrived and could vote. All meetings were conducted in English.

Over the next week, more thefts in the center continued. Mr. Kasai called a meeting of all the victims to make a list of stolen items. Molly's parents attended. When Kentaro and Tak`e returned, Molly was surprised to see her father looking brighter, as though he'd been taken off a shelf, dusted, and wound up. He was standing more erect and had a determined look on his face.

"I have been appointed one of four watchmen for the center," he announced. "I'll be working a six-hour shift from noon to six p.m. Of course, it's a volunteer position, but it is much needed if we have a thief living among us."

"I hope it's not too dangerous, my husband," said Tak`e.

"It will only be dangerous for the thief," Kentaro said. "I want to catch him in the act. Mr. Kasai also informed us that a hospital is being set up near the barracks. We will have one ward for women and one for men. We may also have an isolation unit in case we need to quarantine people who become sick with typhoid fever or whooping cough or even polio. We are fortunate enough to have two Japanese doctors and four nurses."

"And a dentist," Tak`e added.

"What about a library?" Kameko asked. "Did anyone say there would be a library?"

"Not yet, but give us time. I'm sure Mr. Kasai has a list of items to accomplish. Perhaps a library is on it. Now I must go talk to the other men," Kentaro said. "Mr. Kasai needs names of other volunteers."

For the first time since they'd arrived, Kentaro strode out purposefully. As he walked, he removed his glasses and, holding them up to the light, polished them with a handkerchief. Molly followed her father until he turned into the single men's dorm room, and she went the opposite way to the storeroom. She was surprised by how light her own steps felt.

***

When Molly received her first check, she bought a radio for her father. The electricity was turned on at seven o'clock, and he would be able to listen to the news and track the Pacific battles on a map he'd tucked away in his duffle bag. Her second purchase was a hot plate so her mother could make tea and soup. Miss Curtis agreed to bring the items on Saturday to a specially fenced area where visitors could see the internees. Molly stood on one side and Miss Curtis on the other. Before she could give Molly the items she'd bought, they were inspected by a guard outside the fence, passed to a guard inside the fence, and then to Molly.

Molly thought of Miss Curtis as a fussy woman, a bit overweight, with a tendency to wear hats with fake flowers. She had a weak chin and small, watery blue eyes. She seemed puffy and out of breath much of the time. Today, Molly waited at the gate as patiently as she could, until her mother's English tutor appeared, panting hard.

"Here I am, dear," Miss Curtis said. "Sorry I'm late. I had to search for a grocery that still carried dried fish and greens for miso. Those are a bit difficult to come by nowadays. One merchant actually ran me out of his store for asking for 'foreign food'."

"I am so sorry!" Molly searched Miss Curtis's face. She hadn't thought of Miss Curtis as a brave woman before. "Where did you have to go to find it?"

"In Gresham. That was the closest store."

"Gresham!" Molly exclaimed. "I didn't mean for you to drive fifteen miles out of your way."

"That's alright. I was asked by several families to buy similar ingredients, so I stocked up. I won't have to make the trip again for about a month." Miss Curtis removed her hat and wiped at the sweat trickling down her temples.

"What are you doing now that your English classes have ended?" Molly wondered how Miss Curtis was getting by without the small stipend from the church.

"I've taken in a boarder, one of the women missionaries who had to leave Japan last fall. With her rent subsidy, we're getting along. We haven't found another church that wants our help, though. We may follow you to the internment camps and see if we can help there. At least I found a kindred spirit."

"We are most appreciative of your help here. How much do I owe you?" Molly asked, mentally adding fifty cents for the gas to Gresham and back. She put the money in an envelope, then gave it to the guard to pass through to Miss Curtis.

Miss Curtis noted the additional funds. "Thank you. I'll be able to assist others with your generosity."

As Molly left with the treasures, another Japanese woman waited to speak with Miss Curtis. Molly's family wasn't the only one to ask her for favors.

***

Molly's job swirled around how many residents there were, how many people ate at the first seating and how many at the second. She tried to eat during the second shift and then restock the kitchen. The cooks took their own meals after everyone else had eaten, and Molly frequently joined them to make any last-minute adjustments. Then she went to speak to the soldiers who brought over the supplies from the warehouse, requesting exact numbers of canned meat, canned fruits and vegetables, coffee, tea, and milk. If she was lucky, she could procure fresh fruit and vegetables. Occasionally, canned tuna, halibut, or salmon would arrive from the canneries in Astoria. Despite how much she tried, starches slowly replaced fresh produce.

Pancakes, toast, sandwiches, rolls, waffles, and cereals were easier to make than individual helpings of fried fish. The cooks tried to replicate *miso*, a Japanese soup consisting of tofu, dried fish, and seaweed or kelp. They substituted chard or kale for the kelp and added green onions. The canned fish replaced the dried. Sometimes the soup was tasty, but no one called it *miso*. Rice was also more difficult to obtain than potatoes. No one had time to make pasta. People complained about the food more than anything.

Molly's only free time came in the afternoon. If it was good weather, she'd go outside to watch a baseball game or just walk in the sunshine. She couldn't go far, and the guards around the fence's perimeter bothered her. Watchtowers stood at intervals around the fence, with two soldiers in each, watching from above like hawks. It made her rethink the desire for fresh air.

One day as she walked outside, she spied a group of girls practicing jitterbug moves as two guards watched. The men encouraged the girls to twirl under each other's arms and to flip over each other's backs. As she walked closer, she recognized Kameko among them.

"Kameko!" Molly called.

When her sister looked up, Molly beckoned her over. "What do you think you're doing?"

Kameko was flushed, and her hair had come loose from her ponytail. "We're just practicing. It's almost Saturday night."

"Take your girlfriends and practice in the arena. It's not fitting for you to be showing off for the soldiers." Molly couldn't believe what she was saying. She sounded stiff and old and stodgy.

"They're just like the boys at school. Only eighteen!" Kameko whined.

"Come on. Call your friends. I'll show you the moves I know," Molly said, sweetening the offer. She was one of the most skilled dancers in the center.

"Really? My friends would love that," Kameko said. She rushed back over to tell her friends the good news.

Molly smiled at the girls and nodded coldly to the soldiers as they headed back inside the big barn. She was going to have to watch Kameko more carefully.

***

The next afternoon, Molly headed for their cubicle. Kentaro was on duty, and their mother and Kameko were doing the laundry. She removed her shoes for the last few feet so as not to disturb Mary's nap. Ducking under the canvas hanging in the doorway, she surprised her sister. Mary was curled up on a narrow cot, a tatted kerchief catching tears.

"What is it? What's wrong?" Molly stepped quickly to the middle bed, sat down, and began to stroke her sister's forehead.

Mary sniffed and wiped her eyes. "I'm sorry. I thought I could have a good cry while everyone's gone."

"You can cry in front of me," Molly said. "I think everyone needs a good cry every now and then."

"You seem so strong. I just can't take this crowding, the noise, no privacy. The only place I can call my own is this stupid cot." Mary sat up and leaned back against the wall. "Even now, the neighbors can hear us," she whispered.

"Trade me places," Molly said. "I'll brush your hair. Close your eyes and breathe deeply. It will help, I promise."

They switched places, and Molly took her sister's blue hairband out and removed the bobby pins on each side. As she stroked the shiny black hair, Mary closed her eyes. Every once in a while, a tear escaped. "Breathe," Molly said. She poured her love into the smooth caresses, changing the angle of the strokes. After a good long while, she put down the brush and massaged her sister's back.

"Feel better?"

Mary opened her eyes, the tears gone. She nodded.

"I'll go to the mess hall and get us some tea."

When Molly returned, the girls curled their legs underneath them on their cots, white bobby socks keeping their feet warm. For the moment, their cares slipped away, the tears forgotten.

Tea. Sisterhood.

A respite.

CHAPTER SEVEN

ELLIS

S am and Ellis were at breakfast when their father walked into the house. Ellis helped himself to some scrambled eggs his mother had put on the table and then passed them to his older brother. Toast and ham were already on his plate.

As his father washed up, he turned to them and said, "You boys are going to help the Allens thin beets for a week or so. Then they'll help with ours. Ed only got four Japs as a crew in the lottery."

"You've seen 'em? Boy, Ed is up early!" Ellis was having a hard time keeping his eyes open.

"Are you sure they should mix with Japanese?" Ellis's mother Mae frowned, drying her hands on her apron.

"I'm sure the boys can handle themselves." Lee sat down and reached for the eggs.

Ellis's ears perked up. His father believed he made men by challenging his sons in practical ways. He seldom taught the boys how to do something, but let them figure it out for themselves. Only when they got into serious trouble would he bail them out. It made Ellis very observant. He watched carefully whenever he took something apart, knowing he'd have to get it back together too. Somehow, hoeing the beets was going to make Sam and him better men.

Sam looked at Ellis across the table and raised his eyebrows. Ellis shrugged. Neither added to the conversation as they ate.

The Hertzog boys walked up to the field where Ed and Rex Allen and the Japanese had already started work. They'd brought their own short-handled hoes. The others were halfway down the first row, not too far ahead of them. Ed and Rex were demonstrating how to thin, leaving about a foot between each beet. Occasionally, when two beets grew on top of each other, one had to be pulled up by hand. The men stepped one foot in front of the other, walking in the narrow corrugations, careful not to step on the plants.

The boys dropped their water bags and started in. Ellis tried not to stare, but he couldn't identify any difference between them and those that lived in their community. Three of them looked to be the same height as Ellis, but the one called George was at least five foot eight. He weighed as much as Sam, maybe more. Ellis guessed George was big enough to have played football in high school. He didn't expect any of them to be that tall. The other three looked to be older than George. A couple wore glasses. All had dark hair, eyes, and eyebrows, but their faces were distinct. They looked like ordinary men. What had he expected?

Ellis continued to listen to the men as they hoed. They called one man who was in his mid-thirties "Doc." Why would a doctor be working in the fields? It didn't make any sense. And Doc didn't wear jeans. He was in black cotton slacks and a white shirt. The shirt was open at the neck, and the sleeves were rolled up, but it was definitely a shirt for Sundays. Ellis peeked again when Doc stopped to empty dirt from his black leather shoes.

At the end of the first row, Rex turned the corner first, Ed following closely behind. Rex stopped and inspected each of the Japanese workers' rows. "There's not quite enough space here between these two beets, Doc," Rex said. "Otherwise, you men are doin' fine. Get a drink, stretch a bit, and then let's pick up the pace."

As the Japanese took a stretch break, Sam caught up with them. Ellis was right behind. Sam didn't stop, but turned the corner and kept going. Ellis took a quick stretch and started down his next row. The Japanese looked at the two boys and started back to work, faster this time. Ellis got the feeling George was trying to keep up with him.

After a bit, George asked Ellis, "Do you have any extra short-handled hoes?"

"They're in the box behind the tractor," Ellis said. "You'll need to stretch more if you use the short ones. I've seen men develop bad backs. You want to be careful."

George stood up and jogged to the tractor. Despite Ellis's warning, he exchanged the long-handled hoe the sugar factory had provided for a sturdy short one.

"This looks like it was recently sharpened," Ellis said. "That'll help too."

By the beginning of the third row, Ellis and George settled into a quiet rhythm, each silently challenging the other to stay caught up.

After the men worked for two hours, Rex stopped. He took a long drink of water, letting some of it wash down his face and chest. As each man came to the end of the row, he also stopped. Soon, all eight men and boys were stretching, getting a drink, and exchanging a few words. Files were placed at the end of the rows, and Sam used the break to sharpen his hoe. Rex asked each worker to show him his hands. A couple of the crew and Ellis were getting blisters.

"Didn't bring any gloves with you?" Rex asked.

"We won't be able to buy any until our first payday. We'll have to buy our own hoes and files then too," George said a little defensively. He took off his shirt, leaving his undershirt. The sun beat down on them. It was going to be a hot one.

Rex grunted, then walked over to the tractor box and pulled out some gloves. He hit them on his trouser leg, knocking off some dried mud. The men put them on and flexed their fingers, making them more pliable. The gloves were too big for Ellis though. He wrapped his bandana around his hand, covering the tender spot between his thumb and his first finger. Sam tied it in place.

"Why didn't you bring gloves?" Sam sounded impatient.

Ellis just shrugged. "I thought my hands were tough enough, but apparently not."

By now, all the men were equipped with short hoes. The long-handled ones were new, but the blades hadn't been sharpened at the camp.

The men began again. Three of the Japanese stayed close to each other, talking. Doc seemed to have a sense of humor the others enjoyed. George stayed even with Ellis. Rex and Sam were competing with each other and gradually got a couple of rows ahead. Ed worked somewhere in between.

After two hours of working side by side, George broke the silence. "So, Ellis, how old are you?"

"Sixteen. I'll be a junior this fall." Ellis was glad George wanted to converse. It would take his mind off his aching back.

"I thought you were about my brother's age."

"Yeah? Where's he?"

"He's at the Portland Assembly Center with my mother, brother and sister."

"Locked up?" Ellis was shocked.

George looked over at Ellis and frowned. "They're at the livestock expo, surrounded by barbed wire. Yes."

An uncomfortable silence followed the reply. Ellis finally blurted out the question he'd been holding in all morning. "What'd you do?"

"What do you mean?" George asked.

"Didn't you have to do something wrong? I mean, tell some secrets or sabotage something or shoot at someone?"

"Nope. Just livin' my life. I'd finished planting the crops at my own farm over in Toppenish when we were forced into the center in Portland."

Ellis was impressed that a man as young as George owned his own place. "Then why'd they lock you up?"

"The official reason is we're of Japanese ancestry and lived in the military zone. The unofficial reason?" George shook his head. "I'm still tryin' to figure it out."

Ellis was puzzled. It seemed to him that the government had some explaining to do. Something wasn't right.

***

As the day wore on, Ellis's back ached more and more. Instead of leaning over from his waist, he started thinning on his knees. It was slower, but his back and buttocks appreciated the change. George followed suit.

At the end of one row, Ellis said, "You can use your hoe to massage your back, like this." He put the hoe's handle across the small of his back and ran it up and down his spine. Then he put it across his shoulder muscles and did the same.

George tried it. "That is better."

They both bent backwards and leaned from side to side.

"How long've you been thinning beets?" George asked.

Ellis thought a bit. "I started when I was nine, following my father. As he hoed, I'd pull weeds and take out the double-growing beets. Pa could go faster that way. When I was thirteen, I could thin for about a half day before my back gave out. Last year was the first year I could thin all day. And then I'd only get a half an acre done."

"That's ten rows?"

"Yep. I'm hoping I can average more like sixteen this year. Rex can do twenty. That's what most experienced men can do."

At noon, the men reported to Ed how many rows each had accomplished. George and Ellis reported their eight. Doc, the slowest thinner, completed five rows; others six. Rex and Sam finished eleven and Ed ten.

Ed turned to George, "If you're going to be the crew boss, you're going to need a notebook too. Not everybody is as honest as me."

Crew boss, huh? Ellis was surprised that the youngest man of the four was going to be the crew boss. Maybe George had more experience with agriculture than the others.

Ellis and Sam headed to the Hertzog farm where their mother cooked their dinner. In a farming community, the noon meal was the biggest of the day. The men had worked six hours and needed more sustenance to finish their physical labors. What was left of the noon hour the Hertzog men used for a catnap. Supper was in the evening, with irrigating or homework following that. It wasn't unusual to work sunrise to sunset.

***

At the end of the day, Ellis listened as the crew reported in. Ed recorded twenty rows each for himself, Sam, and Rex. George and he both finished sixteen. The other three thinned ten rows, equivalent to a half-acre each. Doc wouldn't have finished his tenth row had George not helped him. Forty-six rows for the Japanese crew's first day. That was only three dollars.

"At this rate, it will take us eight days for forty acres," Rex said. "We've got to speed it up. You'll do better with more experience." Rex took the men's gloves and short hoes and returned them to the tractor's box.

George picked up the long-handled hoes from the sugar factory. "Is it okay to take a couple of files to make our hoes sharp for tomorrow?" he asked.

Rex handed him a couple. "You'll have to share."

"We can do that," George said.

Ellis and Sam found their water canteens and short hoes and followed Ed as he lumbered back to the truck.

George boosted Doc into the bed of the truck while the rest of the crew wearily climbed up. Ellis was worried about Doc. He wasn't in good shape. He'd had to stop several times to rest and lie on his back over the ditch bank. He couldn't walk straight, but hunched over. The other two members of the crew were mum with fatigue.

"You might have to give Doc a massage when you get back to camp so he doesn't get cramps tonight," Ellis suggested.

George nodded. Ellis was surprised when George opened the cab's door to sit up front with Ed. Maybe he still had a few questions. Sam and Ellis stood up on either side of the pickup on the running boards, holding onto the open windows for a quick ride back to their farm. Ed slowed down when he got to their place, and they jumped off.

"See ya tomorrow!" Ed called. "Stretch out those sore muscles!"

The crew and Ed waved to the boys as the truck picked up speed.

Ellis was so tired he was limping. They stopped at the water pump outside the fenced yard to wash off some of the day's grime.

"You go first," Sam said. He worked the pump's arm a couple of times, and the water gushed out.

Ellis pulled off his undershirt. He scrubbed his dirty hands first and then put his head directly into the flowing water to let it soak his hair, face, and neck. He then stood to the side so Sam could do the same. The water didn't ease his exhaustion, but washing sticky sweat off his skin and out of his hair made him feel better.

Ellis flopped down in the yard, under the shade tree. Sam soon joined him. "How'd you do today? That blister get any worse?"

Ellis inspected his hands. "A little. I may have to pop it before tomorrow. How'd you do?"

"I stayed up with Rex. Hope he's as tired as I am. He's fast for an old geezer."

Sam opened one eye and looked over. "What'd you think of the Japs?"

"It was weird. I felt sorry for Doc. And talking to George was like talking with you. If I didn't look at 'em, they didn't seem to be any different than we are."

"A Jap lover, huh?"

Ellis felt like Sam had slapped him. "You mean we gotta hate 'em?"

"No-o-o. But there's gotta be some reason they're the enemy."

Later during mealtime, Ellis continued to turn Sam's reply over in his mind. Meals with the Hertzog family were usually quiet, so his reservedness went unnoticed. The men were hungry after the day's toil.

"Another slice of bread?" Mae asked her husband. The females waited on their men until they'd eaten their fill and then filled their own plates with what was left over.

As they finished, Emily removed the plates. Mae took the freshly brewed coffee and poured Lee a cup. She cut everyone a piece of angel food cake left over from Sunday's dinner.

Lee poured the hot coffee into his saucer. When he was in the Great War, he had burned his lips drinking from a tin cup, and his mouth was still tender. He blew across the surface gently, careful not to spill. Then he quietly slurped it into his mouth. "Ahh. Wonderful, Mae."

She smiled.

"How'd it go today?" Lee asked.

"Fine with me." Sam stretched his arms over his head. "Japs sure were slow, though. Except for the one that kept up with Ellis here. He looked like he was catchin' on."

Ellis felt redness creep up his neck. He hated being the central character in Sam's dramas.

"Did you speak to him?" Mae asked her youngest son. "Did he know English?"

"He didn't talk much," Ellis said. "He just kept watching me. He threw out his long-handled hoe after his second row. George didn't speak any Japanese that I heard. He talked English like we do."

"George?" Mae said. "I don't think it's good to get too friendly."

"Ellis is a Jap lover," Emily said, sniggering behind her hand.

"Am not!" It was one thing to have Sam caution him about his conflicted feelings and another altogether to have Emily call him a name at the dinner table. "But I don't get it. I asked George what he and his family had done to get into trouble. He said they were locked up just because he has Japanese ancestry. Isn't it illegal to lock someone up if he hasn't done anything wrong?"

Mae took in a sharp breath. "If President Roosevelt thinks the Japs are a danger, that's enough for me. Don't you go feeling sorry for that man. If we get invaded by the Jap Empire, you'd soon see who's loyal and who's not."

Lee cleared his throat. "I hope you boys are working hard and pleasing Rex and Ed. Best leave the politics out of the beet field." He got up. "Sam, time to milk the cows. Emily, let your mother have a break tonight. You can do the dishes." Lee left unsaid what the family knew. Ellis would practice the piano.

Mae had inherited her folks' piano. She would get out the hymnal and practice the old tunes. Church meetings were held in the high school gym, and no one else could accompany the congregation's singing, so Mae always had. She tried to get Emily to learn to play, but she found all kinds of reasons not to practice. Ellis, however, couldn't stay away from the keys. He'd watched Mae's hands and soon could pick out a tune himself. She taught him to read the notes, and Ellis started playing at nine years old. Soon he was playing for church and the school choir, for weddings and funerals. He could sightread anything put in front of him.

Mae thought the whole family recognized his musical gift and supported it. Most of the time, that was true, but Sam kidded him about all the milking he had to do so Ellis could practice. And Ellis couldn't count the number of times he'd been called a sissy by the boys his age.

As he started to play, Mae sat down in the rocking chair. She picked up a sock and began to darn. Knowing his mother was listening, Ellis played some of the older songs his aunts had sung in his grandmother's home. They'd been able to sing in harmony, and their workdays were lighter for it. Mae had been more of a singer before the hard work of living faded the tunes. Ellis tried to give her back some of the pleasure she once knew. He was always pleased when he heard her humming along.

Sam came into the kitchen, sloshing milk pails as he went. "Here's the milk, Ma! I'm going back out to help Pa finish the irrigating." He left as loudly as he'd come in.

Mae put down the darning and got up. Ellis rose from the piano and went into the kitchen to help his mother with the pails.

"Is that a blister?" she asked him.

Ellis looked at the slightly raised red skin. "It's a bit sore, Ma, but it hasn't turned into a blister yet. It'll be all right." He paused, trying to phrase his request in the right tone. "I wanted to ask if I could borrow the car on Saturday night. I haven't had a chance to see my friends since school got out. It's not for a date or anything. Maybe you could ask Pa?"

"We'll discuss it. But the gas is rationed, you know. We don't often make frivolous trips to town. This doesn't mean you'll miss out on church on Sunday, though."

Ellis couldn't remember the last time he'd missed a sermon. Attendance was simply a foregone conclusion. His mother picked up the darning and Emily joined them with a book. He sat back down at the piano and lost himself in the music.

CHAPTER EIGHT

ABE

Abe struggled to attach the last leg to a table for the camp office. He heard Pamela coming before he saw her. He guessed from the insistent heels beating on the wooden floorboards that she needed his help with something.

"Finally!" she said in greeting. "I've been looking all over for you. We need privacy. I need to talk to you about Mother."

"Close the door. There's no one else here. What's up?"

Pamela struggled to find the right words. "You know how the toilets are open? No partitions between?"

Abe nodded but didn't know if he wanted to hear this. He'd only been the head of the family for a little more than a week, and already he wanted George to return. He picked up another table leg and averted his eyes from his sister's troubled face.

Pamela swallowed and then hurried to finish. "Mother can't sit there long enough. She can't . . . can't . . ." She blew out her breath.

"You mean she's constipated."

"Yes! She hurts! She's curled up on the bed right now, holding her stomach. You've got to do something!"

Abe fiddled with the table leg, thinking. "Tell you what. You go to the doctor. Tell him what's wrong and get some medicine for her. I'll go talk to Mr. Kasai about the problem. Maybe we can find a solution."

Pamela nodded. She opened the door and headed outside to the makeshift hospital.

Abe set out to find Kasai. As he passed the general manager's office, he saw Johnson, Kasai, and two other Japanese men in conversation. He tapped on the door. Johnson crooked his index finger and motioned him in. Kasai looked surprised at this young man disrupting the meeting.

"What can I do for you, son?" asked Johnson.

Abe colored up slightly. It was an awkward subject, but he couldn't think of any way but straight to the point. "Would it be possible to do something about the women's toilet facilities, sir?"

Kasai shook his head. "You need to bring this to the Japanese council. If you have a specific concern, we can address it there."

"Yes, sir, I know that's the normal procedure. I just happened to see you here," Abe said. He wondered if by cutting corners, he had insulted Kasai.

"What is it we need to fix?" Johnson asked.

"There isn't any privacy, sir. My mother finds it extremely embarrassing to use the facilities, and now she needs to go see a doctor for some relief. And this isn't the first time. Could we put up some stalls?"

"There isn't any budget for that. We're still constructing barracks outside the main building, getting ready for the people coming from Wapato and Yakima. Can you come up with anything using the wood from the scrap pile? I don't know of anything else."

"Thank you, sir. I'll see what I can do." Abe left frustrated.

Johnson's office was next door to the kitchen and storage room. As he passed by, Abe saw the Army delivering B-rations for the cooks. There were canned goods, smoked meats, beans, rice, flour, and sugar, all delivered in boxes and some wooden crates. When the soldiers finished unloading, the cooks opened them and began sorting the contents.

"What are you going to do with those boxes?" Abe asked.

One of the men looked up. "We'll flatten and burn them."

"Would you mind if I take them? And the crates?" An idea had formed in his mind.

"Not at all. You want to flatten them for us?"

"Sure!" Abe got to work.

The next morning, Abe put up a sign in front of the women's lavatory: "Closed for repair. Please use the men's restroom." He'd warned the men at breakfast that the facilities would be closed for an hour. Abe and some of the boys from the baseball team fashioned cardboard walls about five feet tall. They laid scrap board on either side of each toilet to hold the partitions in place. With only cardboard to use, they couldn't make a door, but at least the partitions would separate each stall. Pamela assured Abe that the blanket she carried back and forth would work as a door. In an hour, they were finished. They took down the sign in front of a line of women that stretched all the way down the hall. Several of the women bowed, and others applauded their efforts. The women wasted no time admiring the new partitions.

Abe nodded as Pamela and his mother entered the restroom. He hoped the rest of his responsibilities were solved as easily.

***

On the evening of May 26th, Thomas and Abe helped Danny's family carry their luggage to the gate. This was the first large group to leave Portland for the Tule Lake Relocation Camp—seventy families in all. The FBI had arrested Danny's father right after Pearl Harbor. He hadn't been charged with anything, but the family didn't know where he was for nearly six months. Now he'd been transferred to the relocation center at Tule Lake in northern California. The family would join him there.

Armed men stood guard, making sure no one slipped out the barbed wire fence in the confusion. The train taking them to northern California stood nearby, and many families were already being loaded. Danny's mother and younger sister said goodbye to their friends. Thomas handed Danny the duffel bag he'd carried to the gate.

"Any news when you'll get the approval to leave for Nyssa?" Danny asked.

Thomas shook his head. "Johnson has a call in to Welch to see if the company will sponsor families. We don't know what Mother would do to help. Abe doesn't want her working in the fields. Pamela will probably stay in camp. She might help watch the children if other families start to go. At least Abe and I'll be able to thin beets."

"Write to me!" said Danny. "I'll let you know how it is at Tule Lake."

"I will," said Thomas. "Hope you see your father soon. Take care of the womenfolk."

Danny slowly walked between the armed guards, through the gate, and disappeared.

A little girl carried a doll and a toy parasol beside her mother who held an infant. One of the soldiers reached out to steady an old man who stumbled and nearly fell. Many folks were gathered outside to wave goodbye.

"What have we done to deserve this?" Thomas asked Abe as they watched the last of the group load onto the train.

Abe had no idea how to answer that question. It haunted all of them. Instead, he opted for a more optimistic observation. "Tule Lake should be better than the assembly center. How could it be worse?"

Danny poked his head out a train window and waved goodbye. Then the windows closed, and black curtains slid down to hide the Japanese from public view.

***

The next morning, Abe was working on his second cup of coffee in the mess hall when he heard a gunshot. Everyone froze. A second shot rang through the stillness. Abe left his coffee on the table and ran outside.

A man laid face first on the ground clutching his stomach. His legs dug into the ground. Abe knelt beside him, turned him over, and pried his fingers away. A dime-sized hole showed between his fingers. Blood trickled out.

"I've been shot! Someone shot me!" His cook's hat fell off, revealing blond hair.

A guard ran up, holding an Enfield rifle in his hands. "Get away! Get away from him!" He pointed the gun at Abe, motioning threateningly.

Abe stood up beside the cook with both hands in the air. "Don't shoot, mister! I didn't do anything."

The guard crouched beside the cook, alternately looking down at him and then up at the crowd beginning to form. "My god, I didn't know he was one of us! I thought he was a Jap stealing supplies from the storage room."

Abe noticed Thomas running past and reached out to restrain him. "What are you doing out here?" Abe asked. "Get back! Do you want to get shot too?"

Thomas couldn't look away. A mother rushed by, carrying her little boy in her arms, one hand covering the boy's eyes.

"Help me," the cook whispered. His skin was turning gray, and he sweated profusely.

One of the Japanese doctors pushed through the growing crowd. He knelt beside the cook and began to take his pulse. "It's rapid and weak. We need a blanket. This man is in shock." One of the men ran inside.

Three soldiers ran through the gate, surrounding the victim, their rifles pointed at the crowd. "Move back! Who shot this man? What happened here?"

The doctor continued to minister to the bleeding man. One of the soldiers walked over and pointed his gun at the physician.

A sergeant rushed up to take charge of the chaos. "What are you doing?" he said to the soldier. "Can't you see the man's helping?"

The sergeant listened as the guard babbled out his story. He ordered another soldier to take the guard's rifle and escort him away.

"I thought he was a Jap!" the guard protested faintly as he was taken to the military barracks.

"Am I going to die?" the injured man panted. "I am, aren't I? I'm going to bleed to death!"

A woman put her hands over her ears and rushed back into the center as two men came running from the center's infirmary with a stretcher and blankets.

Another doctor arrived with his medical bag. "Quickly! We have to get this man to a hospital. We can't handle it here. He needs surgery now!"

Thomas stood on his toes, looking over Abe's shoulder. Abe could feel Thomas's body trembling as he held him.

The men picked up the cook and moved him onto a stretcher. He lay quietly, unnaturally still. More guards came running up and encircled the crowd. For a moment, it looked as though they weren't going to allow the Japanese doctor outside the fence.

The sergeant shouted, "Are you crazy? Who cares if he's a Jap! He's a doc, ain't he?"

The doctor climbed into the car alongside the stretcher, monitoring the cook's vital signs. A soldier climbed in the other side, and the driver took off, horn blaring. Other soldiers moved the crowd back into the compound.

Abe gently moved Thomas inside. They sat together at one of the picnic tables. He put his arm around Thomas's shoulders, as though to shield him from what he had witnessed. The crowd milled around the mess hall, talking excitedly.

"I heard the first shot," one man said. "That's when the cook turned around. The second shot hit him."

"He was shot *inside* the fence," said another.

"I didn't hear the guard shout a warning before he pulled the trigger."

"A gut shot is the worst. It doesn't kill right away. A deer can walk for miles, bleeding internally until it collapses."

"The guard repeatedly defended himself, saying he thought the victim was a Jap. And that he'd been stealing."

"The cook was unarmed. How can it be right to shoot a defenseless man?"

As the morning wore on, the story flew around the assembly center. Lunchtime arrived, and still there was no news. By mid-afternoon, Abe saw the doctor get out of a car and walk into the gate. Members of the camp's council gathered in their meeting room. Hours later, Abe learned the cook had died of his wounds. He hadn't been a thief. He'd requisitioned some coffee for the soldiers' mess.

Most people stayed inside the rest of the day. Baseball games were canceled. Women who needed to do laundry put it off. Many went to their rooms and tried to understand what had happened. Their situation had changed. The guard truly believed they were the enemy. He had shot to kill. Everyone was jumpy. Even though it had been a white guard killing a white cook, the Japanese didn't want to give any more guards an excuse to get trigger-happy.

***

That afternoon, Abe walked by Johnson's office and saw him slouched at his desk, his graying head in both hands. When Abe walked in, Johnson looked up.

"What can I do for you?" Johnson asked.

"I need to get my family out of here. That guard pointed his gun at me too. It was a miracle I wasn't shot. Can you expedite the paperwork?"

"I haven't received final word. Welch is still working on it. No one wants women at the camp."

Johnson seemed unsteady, and Abe knew he'd have to push him to get the answer he wanted. "Ma can cook rice. She'll be a cook."

"And your sister? She's too young to be employed."

"Employed? You think the farmers are going to care she's fourteen? The farm kids are out there thinning beets right now. At least she's old enough not to have to be cared for. And maybe she could care for younger children once families realize they can go too." Abe paced in front of the only man who could get his family on the train to Eastern Oregon.

Johnson held Abe's gaze. Abe swallowed hard and continued.

"You can't stand in the way of us getting out of here. If Thomas or I had been shot instead of a soldier, the news would alarm the Japanese community. The orderly internment would end, and more violence could occur. Let Welch know the situation. He'll understand." Abe stopped and looked at Johnson. "I hate this war, sir. We Japanese are the victims now, but we won't be the only ones."

"I'm afraid you're right, son." He stared off into the distance. "I'm afraid you're right." He nodded his head. "My decision is made. Get your family ready. You can leave tonight on the train."

"Will we be able to get word to my brother that we're coming?"

"No, it's too late for that. You'll have to surprise him. I'll get the paperwork started. The train leaves at seven."

"We'll be ready," Abe said. He worried about George, though. His older brother didn't like surprises.

Chapter Nine

George

George rode back to the labor camp, tired after another long day. He and his crew had finished Allen's farm in six days and started working for a second farmer. George could now finish twenty rows a day, while the rest of the men managed between fifteen and seventeen. He felt the satisfaction of a job well done.

As the truck pulled into the camp, George saw newly erected tents. Instead of six, there were now sixteen. Were more workers joining them? George jumped off the truck bed and headed into his tent to get his shower gear. It looked like they were the first crew back. He wouldn't have to wait in line.

As he walked to the shower, he looked over to the new tents. Men were inside one of them, arranging cots and settling in. He heard someone hit a ball. Was there a baseball game starting? It must be the new recruits. After a day in the fields, the other men wouldn't have the energy.

"Way to go, Thomas! Nice hit!"

Was that Abe's voice? It couldn't be. The paperwork wasn't finished. He didn't have anything ready yet for his mother or Pamela. George detoured around the showers. Could Abe and Thomas have left the women alone in the assembly center? Surely not!

Yet there they were! Abe pitched batting practice to Thomas while a young man crouched down, catching any ball Thomas missed. George stood there, both hands on his hips. What the hell was going on?

Thomas hit a foul ball toward George who reached out with his free hand and snagged it on the fly.

Abe recognized his brother and broke into a grin. "Hey! Looks like you've had a hard day. How's work going?"

Thomas and Abe jogged toward him. They slowed down as George glowered at them.

"What are you doing here?" George snapped. "I told you to get the paperwork ready, not leave Mother and Pamela! Is this the way you handle family responsibility?"

Thomas glared right back. "We didn't leave Mother and Pamela. They came too."

George looked at Thomas incredulously. "They're here? In a camp of men?"

Abe's face darkened, his voice rising with each word. "That's the way you are! You jump to conclusions without knowing the facts. You have no faith in us!"

"Facts? What facts could cause you to bring the family here without preparation? What was so bad at the assembly center that you had to come without discussing it with me?"

Abe lowered his voice and told George what had happened. George was stunned. He looked at Thomas and back to Abe. "Someone was killed? A soldier held you two off with a gun? You might have been shot?"

Abe went on, emphasizing each point. "No one would leave the expo barn after that. If a guard could shoot a white cook thinking he was Japanese, we were in trouble. The guns are pointed in, not out. I shouldn't have to explain all this to you. You should trust me. It's obvious you don't."

Abe turned abruptly and started walking to the new tents. Thomas shook his head at George and ran to catch up with Abe. The family hadn't been reunited for ten minutes, and already George was at war with Abe. And now Thomas.

George tried to take it in. He looked past Thomas and Abe and saw his mother and Pamela walking across the road, coming from Tanaka's farm. Their heads were together, and they were talking and laughing. George jogged over to meet them.

"Mother! Pamela! You're here!" George noticed their wet hair and towels.

"Yes, we are, my son." His mother hugged him and held him a fraction longer. It had only been ten days since they'd seen each other, but so much had happened in that time. "We met the Tanaka family. You're right! They are so nice. They invited us to take our baths at their home until Abe gets the bath built here at camp. Mr. Welch has been busy with plans for us all day."

Pamela beamed. "The tent is nicer than our cubicle was. We've got it all set up. Aren't you going to take a shower? You'll be late for supper!"

George was speechless. He watched his mother and sister continue on to their tent. Several of the men bowed to them and gave them a happy greeting. Chiharu responded in Japanese, bowing and smiling in return. His family was here. George couldn't get used to the idea. He turned around to go shower. Several men backed up the line. Yep, it looked like he was going to be late for chow.

***

The last Sunday of May was a welcome day of rest. The family couldn't wait for afternoon to come. Camp regulations allowed one three-hour trip to town each Sunday afternoon. For the first time, the factory was sending trucks for them to see a specially arranged movie and to do some shopping. Most hadn't been into Nyssa yet, and the theatre was showing *Tortilla Flat* with Spencer Tracy and Hedy Lemarr. The drugstore would be open afterwards. It had a soda fountain where folks could buy an ice cream cone or a milkshake or necessities they might need.

George gave each family member a quarter to spend. With the movie only a dime, Thomas and Pamela were anxious to see what else they might buy.

Thomas said, "I deserve to spend some money on myself. See these?" He showed Pamela his blisters on the palms of his hands. "These are worth at least a chocolate malt."

At 1:30, two trucks pulled up. The men put a stool at the back of each truck as a step, then helped the women and children up and onto the truck bed. Chiharu and Pamela climbed in, both in their nicest dresses. Abe, George and Thomas stood on the sides, allowing older men, women and children to take a wooden middle bench. George understood Thomas's excitement, but he was apprehensive. He'd been in town a couple of times and was always leery about what their reception might be.

As the truck lumbered into Nyssa, a 1940 Ford came up alongside them. A young man in the passenger seat rolled down the window and yelled, "Someone let you Japs out of jail? You better not let us catch you alone!" The car swerved around them and sped away.

Japs. Would they ever outlive that derogatory term?

The caravan entered Nyssa and slowed down. It looked about the same size as Toppenish. Rounding a curve, George pointed out the schools. The high school was fairly new, but the elementary school looked at least twenty years old. The trees on the grounds were mature and provided shaded grass. After the dusty, dry labor camp, the shaded lawn looked like a park.

Thomas pointed out a baseball field in the back of the park that stood out in the hot sunshine, dusty and well used. A tall fence provided the backstop. The infield grass was healthy and recently mowed.

"I miss playing ball with Danny," Thomas said. "That was one good thing about Portland."

The trucks turned right onto Main Street. Most of the stores were closed on Sundays, but they could see colorful displays in the windows. A sign pointed to the public library and a city park. The street was nearly deserted when the trucks pulled in at the lone theater.

Thomas jumped down first and set the step down. George landed beside him, putting his hands up to steady the women. Abe lifted two children to the street while the rest of the men climbed down. The movie started at 2:00 and would last at least two hours, with the cartoons and newsreel added. Just enough time to buy some popcorn.

Their mother said, "I won't go in. I'll look in the windows and rest here on the curb."

"I'll translate for you," Abe said. "You can't spend two hours window-shopping. It will be good for you to hear it so you can work on your English. Besides, I don't want to give those boys in the car any opportunity to make our lives worse."

Their mother looked around. "If it will make you feel better, I guess I will. It is my first movie. It feels so extravagant."

The ticket seller worked the booth quickly, and the Yanos slowly entered the theatre. Pamela couldn't resist a bag of popcorn, while Thomas settled for a Coca-Cola. George realized the movie was only for the Japanese. No Caucasians were in the audience. Most of the Japanese were speaking English if they could. The whole thing made George uneasy.

Chiharu and Abe made their way into a small back room designed for families. It was soundproof so the audience wouldn't be disturbed by crying babies. The room would be perfect for Abe's translating.

George settled down in a plush seat between Thomas and Pamela just as the picture show opened with a newsreel. The announcer's booming voice first reported on the Kaiser Shipyards being built in Portland and Vancouver. "Workers are needed from all over the United States. Men and women are being hired as fast as they can get off the train. A housing boom has begun to provide homes, apartments, and rooms for folks arriving eager to work."

The next story showed the naval battle of the Coral Sea. "Nippon forces try to invade Port Moresby, New Guinea in early May." The screen showed a fierce battle scene. An American bomb hit a Japanese ship, and Thomas stood up and cheered. He raised his fist in the air, his shadow on the screen.

At his side, George pulled at his arm. "Sit down. Sit down, Thomas." George tried to shush him, but his little brother didn't listen.

"Yah! Take that. And that!" He was yelling at the top of his lungs.

The usher stepped into the theatre through the curtain and watched from the back, his arms folded in front of him. George was embarrassed.

Soon, more people in the audience were on their feet. Some were yelling, some crying, some stood in stunned silence. The announcer's voice boomed throughout the theatre. "The battle ends in a draw with Commander Inoue recalling his fleet. The battle is a strategic victory for the Allies as the Japanese forces are turned back for the first time."

Thomas was breathing heavily and clenched and released his fists several times.

"I hate the damned Japs!" He looked around at the others. "Look what they've done to us!" Trembling, he slowly sank into his seat.

Someone behind them said, "*Shikata ga nai.*"

George reflected on that phrase: It cannot be helped. Was that the answer his little brother needed to hear? George put his arm around Thomas, but he shook it off. He'd never seen Thomas this angry before. He remembered the principle of *gaman* his father had tried to teach him before his death. It was the determined silence a man used to endure the unbearable with grace. Perhaps the Japan his father had known had something to teach him and his brothers. At least he could try. The news ended, and a cartoon began. George was startled to hear Pamela laugh. He settled back. He'd talk to Thomas and maybe even Abe when they got back to camp.

***

George finally got out of the theatre and onto the street. After Thomas's outburst, he hadn't been able to concentrate on the movie at all. He thought of his father's teachings. How could he steer his youngest brother into being a good man with all the anger, conflict, and distrust around them? He couldn't deny that having his family reunited gave him additional burdens. He felt the responsibility of being first-born settle heavily on his shoulders like a yoke on an ox.

Most of the Japanese were still inside the drugstore when the trucks from the sugar factory pulled up.

Welch got out and approached George. "How was the movie?"

"Good," George said. He tried to remember something about the movie he could share. "I've always liked Spencer Tracy."

The small talk distracted him from his somber thoughts. He watched as the cashier and soda jerk in the drugstore filled the orders. Neither man made any conversation. He could tell they were ill at ease. At least there was no overt prejudice showing.

"How is the labor camp working out?" George asked. He couldn't think of anything else to talk to Welch about. "Do you think it's a success?"

"We need about a hundred more workers. The farmers are panicking. It doesn't look good for the beets."

"I could go back to Portland and recruit some more," George offered. "It would have to be a paid position, though, since I would lose at least two days of work traveling back and forth on the train."

"That's a great idea!" Welch replied. "You could reassure new workers about the safety and conditions here better than I could." Welch considered it more and then said, "Each trip you take, we'll pay for the train ticket and expenses along the way. I'll give you a fifty-cent bounty for every worker you recruit, plus the six dollars a day you've been earning in the field. What do you think?"

George didn't know how the other Japanese would feel about a bounty. It felt like the wanted posters in the Old West. But this was an answer to one of his problems. He would be doing something to save the family farm.

"It's a deal, sir."

"How about taking the train tonight?"

He'd have to leave Abe in charge again. Maybe he could handle Thomas better. George tried not to acknowledge the relief he felt.

"I'll get my things together right away."

Chapter Ten

Molly

Molly had been in the supply room when the military cook came in, frantic about the lack of coffee for the soldier's mess.

"The officers get real sulky if they don't have coffee all the time," the soldier said. "They can't wait until we get our supplies in. Do you have any I can borrow? I'll bring some back tonight."

"Sure." Molly looked around for something to put it in. She found a small tin with a lid and filled it to the top. "Need anything else? Sugar? Cream?"

"Nah. This'll do," the soldier said. "Thanks."

She'd given it to him, knowing that a new shipment of goods was being unloaded. She went back to taking inventory until she noticed a mother run inside the center, covering her son's eyes with her hand.

Molly stepped into the hall. "What is it? What's happening?"

"A soldier just shot a white cook, mistaking him for a Japanese thief! The guards are yelling at everyone and have their guns out. Be careful!"

Molly made her way to the entrance to see if it was the same man she had just helped. It was. He was lying on the ground, surrounded by soldiers and a doctor who knelt beside him. Coffee spilled out onto the ground to one side, the tin squashed. Molly was stunned. He was just a kid. She watched from the doorway as the victim was loaded into a car and taken to the hospital.

For days after, she couldn't help thinking about that poor blond kid. It colored her pleasure in her job, creating a shadow even on the sunniest days.

A week later, a group of Japanese arrived from Yakima, Kennewick, and Wapato. Today, more were expected. The young men sporting cowboy hats made quite a splash among the younger girls. Molly thought the fashion a bit silly, but her youngest sister Kameko was enthralled. Too bad her mother wasn't trying to find a match for Kameko in the high school set. She would have been fine with any number of the older boys. In two days, the center swelled by fifteen hundred more people. That gave both Tak`e and Molly more options for a match. Molly was on a hunt.

The assembly center had a routine. Saturday was dance night. At least it would give Molly a chance to observe the men. She was a popular dance partner and tried not to judge each man by how many times he stepped on her toes. She put on her light blue sweater set that went with her pleated blue plaid skirt. Her hair was clean and bounced on her shoulders. She hoped she looked her best. It was almost time for lunch.

As she walked through the arena, Molly noticed a young man talking in the middle of a group. She overheard enough of the conversation to realize he was talking about conditions in the Eastern Oregon camp. There was a train leaving Sunday evening which would be taking interested workers to a little town called Nyssa. Now that families could go, more of the young married men were interested. She wondered who this young man was.

He was a bit taller than average, a wrinkle-free complexion, with dark hair brushed back from his face. He was intent on the conversation. He talked enthusiastically and developed a rapport with the men. Clearly, he was a leader and had ambition. He had a soft mouth and a slight awkwardness that Molly found endearing. With his white shirt sleeves rolled up to his elbows, he talked with his hands and then rested them on his hips as he listened. Yes, he would do, Molly thought. If only she could talk with him, see if she could set sparks flying between them.

She sat down on a bench where she could see people coming in for lunch, hoping to spot the young man she'd seen earlier. When he didn't arrive—he must be assigned to the second shift—she tried not to be disappointed.

After lunch, Molly wanted to see if she could spot the fellow again. "Kameko, do you want to take your book and journal to the arena?

I'll go with you." Molly turned to Mary. "Do you want to come too?"

As they walked to the arena, Molly glanced down each hallway to see if her mystery man was there. She wondered when he'd arrived in Portland and how often he visited the center. Sure enough, when the Mita girls settled down on the bleachers together, Molly spotted him. This time, he was talking to some of the older boys, those eighteen and nineteen. She heard him say, "Aren't you tired of playing baseball yet? You could use your own money and buy something for yourself. Or give it to your folks to save for after the war."

After the war. Molly couldn't imagine how far in the future that would be.

"Do you know his name yet?" Mary asked.

Molly swung her head around. She forgot how perceptive Mary was. "No. This is the first time I've seen him. Do you know anything about him?"

"Only that his family is also in Eastern Oregon. They left the same day the military cook was shot. I think the family name is Yano."

Yano. Molly watched him for a bit longer. He threw his head back and laughed, then slapped a couple of the men on the back. He walked out and turned left toward the men's dorm. Most single men in the dorm were elderly *Issei.* Those men hadn't been as lucky as some. Whereas Molly's father was able to send for a bride, these men never found a wife. They had no families. A few younger single men lived in the barracks too. Molly's generation respected the *Issei.* They were the first to settle up and down the coast in Washington, Oregon, and California. Many had been fishermen or farmers. Some lucky few catered to their own by running stores, laundries, or hotels. Her father visited the *Issei* men often, sometimes taking the *sake* he'd brought.

That night at the dance, Molly searched for the Yano man. Even when she danced with her favorite partners, she remained distracted. When she missed an underarm swing, her partner complained. "Where are you tonight? Aren't you feeling well? I can't tell if you're going to follow my lead or not."

Molly paid closer attention but left the dance soon after. How could she be lovesick already? She didn't even know this Yano character. And yet, she went to bed miserable.

The next morning, Molly saw Mr. Yano several times, always surrounded by other males. It was completely against her character to be forward, but she didn't know how else to meet him. At the second lunch period, Molly spotted him sitting alone at a table. Screwing up her courage, she walked over and sat down. He didn't even notice.

"Why so glum, chum?" Molly blurted.

The man looked up into her dancing, black eyes. He was about her age, maybe a bit older. Molly grinned and shook her shiny black hair so it bounced on her shoulders. He seemed irritated with her glib question. He frowned and concentrated on his plate.

Molly tried again. "Aren't you the guy who's trying to get folks signed up to go to Eastern Oregon?" She looked him up and down, taking in his white cotton shirt with rolled-up sleeves. He looked good in field clothes. "You sure are tan. I've been watching you ever since you landed in town." Molly babbled away. She was so embarrassed at his silence and how idiotic her chatter seemed to be.

"Yes, I'm the recruiter. I'm George Yano."

"*George* Yano. I've been asking all over the expo center about you. I'm Molly Mita."

"Pleased to meet you," George replied. He cut his pork chop and put a forkful into his mouth. Molly and George sat in awkward silence. People beside them finished their meals and cleared off their dishes. Perhaps George wasn't interested.

"Sorry. I didn't mean to be rude. I thought maybe you were lonely and could use some company. I'll leave you to finish in peace." Molly stood up.

"Don't go," George said. "Sit down. Keep me company." He smiled wobblily, and her heart melted. "I'm terrible around girls."

"Ah! But I'm not 'girls.'" She smiled as she slowly sank back down. Her voice softened. "I'm just Molly. And you can just be George." She dared to touch his hand with her index finger. There it was, the spark she wondered about. "You must think I'm terribly forward, but we don't have much time to get to know each other. Don't you leave tonight on the train?"

***

The rest of the day went smoother. George seemed to be more at ease if they walked while they talked. After the rain the day before, the sky was clear, and the rhododendrons planted around the center's grass were vibrant in their reds, pinks, and yellows. Molly ambled alongside George, her hands clasped behind her. It was too soon to hold hands. But she looked into his eyes and watched them become warmer, his glances longer, and his laughter more frequent. They talked about their families, what had happened to Mita's Merchandise, and how George was trying to retain the family farm. Every once in a while, another man interrupted to confirm he would be on the evening train.

As they watched a baseball game, George told her how his brother Abe had surprised him when he brought the family to Eastern Oregon. He also mentioned a letter he'd recently received from their old neighbor, who told George he wouldn't be harvesting the Yanos' crops after all.

"No wonder you were a glum chum." She squeezed his arm in sympathy.

"I'd been counting on money from the harvest to pay the property taxes, reduce the bank loan, and save for a new start when the war is over. That's why being a recruiter for the sugar company is a real blessing." George paused. "What about you? How's your father reacting to the loss of his store?"

Molly shared her worries about her father's inactivity, the black glasses that were always dirty, and his introspective silences. When it was time for Molly to join her family for supper, she asked, "Will you write to me?" She held her breath.

"Sure. It will help us get to know each other. I've never written to any girl before."

"I'm just Molly, remember? I'm not just any girl." She smiled up at him.

George nodded his head. "See you on my next trip."

"All right." She walked him to the men's dorm. It was hard to let him go. She wondered if he would write or if they'd see each other again. What if he knew of her plan to marry? She was going to have to toy with this big fish if she wanted to land him.

CHAPTER ELEVEN

ELLIS

Ellis eased the family's '39 Ford sedan out of the driveway and onto the gravel road. He didn't want to stir up too much dust because he'd just washed the car. He picked up Jimmy, and soon they were on their way to Nyssa.

"This is great!" Jimmy said. He blew cigarette smoke out of the side of his mouth. The pack barely made a dent in his front pocket. Ellis could see a couple more but knew Jimmy was going to have to ration them out to last the night.

Jimmy turned down the radio and put out the butt. His face lit up, and he reached over to pound Ellis on the back. "Our first Saturday night on the town!" Jimmy turned up the radio again to hear Glen Miller's band and lit another cigarette. "You wanna share a smoke?"

Ellis didn't smoke—his mother didn't like it when his father had an occasional one. He didn't think she'd be able to tell, though. It was hours before they'd get home. "Sure. I'll take a puff."

Jimmy held the red glow of the lighter next to the tip of the cigarette and inhaled. He coughed as he put the lighter back. "Boy, that burned all the way down."

Ellis took a drag and began to cough. "I've never smoked before," he said, spitting tiny fragments of tobacco from his mouth.

"No kidding. It is kind of messy, but I'm not wasting it. Don't know when I'll be able to lift the next ones." Jimmy winked at Ellis.

"You mean, you stole 'em? From your dad?" Ellis knew Jimmy never had any money.

"My mom took 'em from my dad. She sneaks a puff every now and then. I found where she stashes hers." Jimmy looked smug. "She might miss 'em, but she's not gonna ask any questions."

Ellis avoided looking at Jimmy. He didn't want to be square, but he'd never steal from his own folks. He didn't understand his friend sometimes. He reached the highway, looked both ways, and carefully pulled out.

He was almost to Nyssa when he reached Garrison Corner. It was well known that this intersection was a dangerous one. It crossed the railroad tracks twice. Ahead of them, the road continued to the new Japanese labor camp. The boys could see the administration building's flagpole in the distance. The sagebrush and the land's descent to the river hid the tents from view.

"Go straight," Jimmy said. "I want to see how many Japs are here now."

Ellis licked his lips. "What do we say if one of them comes out and asks us what we're doing?"

"We can tell 'em we're going down to the river."

Ellis hesitated and pulled over to the side of the road.

"Must be supper time," Jimmy said. "I can see the smoke from the campfire."

Just then, a pickup rolled past them. In the back was a Japanese thinning crew returning from the day's labor.

Jimmy rolled down his window and stuck out his head. "Welcome to farming, slant eyes! Bet your backs hurt. You can name your blisters after me."

Ellis snickered and looked out to see the men's reactions. He recognized Doc and George and ducked his head. He hoped they hadn't seen him. He waited until they were gone and then pulled out, bumped over the tracks, and spun gravel behind his wheels as he took off.

"Whew! Never thought I'd see you speeding," Jimmy said.

Ellis's neck was a blotchy red.

As they continued driving, Jimmy came clean about not having money for the movie. "I'll just sit on the bumper and watch the action until you get out."

"Nah. I don't want to go without you."

"How about driving to Ontario?" Jimmy suggested. "We could cruise the main drag, see what's happening."

"Don't have a ration card. Just one trip to Nyssa a week." Ellis could feel Jimmy's excitement ebb.

"So, let's get a malt and park at the high school lot," Jimmy said. "I hear the kids go there and listen to the radio and talk. We might even meet some girls."

Ellis faked an enthusiasm he didn't feel. He hoped the night wasn't going to be a total bust.

The Boise radio station played big band music exclusively at night. "In the Mood" was one of Ellis's favorites, and he tapped his foot to the beat as he sat on the hood of the car. Jimmy was talking to some kids from Nyssa. An old pickup turned into the parking lot, and Ellis sat up straight. It was Jeannie, and it looked like Butch was with her.

"Jimmy, it's Butch!" Ellis scrambled off the bumper and hustled over to his friend.

Jeannie drove into the center of the parking lot, beeping the horn. The group of teens parted and gawked at the new arrivals. Jimmy ducked behind Ellis. He still had a yellow bruise around his eye from the last time Butch objected to Jimmy admiring Jeannie's boobs.

Jeannie, however, had seen Jimmy. When she bounded out of the truck, she headed straight for him. She wore a new-to-her dress, perhaps one she had bought at the church rummage sale, and the buttons strained at the bodice.

"Jimmy!" she cried, hugging him to her. "My biggest fan!"

Jimmy broke free and smiled a loopy grin. "Hi, Jeannie. How's your summer?"

Ellis couldn't understand Jimmy's attraction. Jeannie was loud, crass, and red: red hair, red freckles, red arm hair. She had a tendency to wear red too. Although her dress was a faded, non-descript white cotton, Jeannie had tried to fancy it up with a red ribbon around her waist and red rickrack on the sleeves and hem. A blaring brass band all by herself.

Butch scowled as he caught up. "I thought I told you to stay away from my girl."

"You don't need to worry about Jimmy," Jeannie smiled. She mussed up Jimmy's hair with her hands. "He wouldn't know what to do with me if he had a chance." She turned to Butch, put her arms through his, and stood on her tiptoes to give him a quick kiss. "Come on, handsome. Let's see what's doin'."

The boys watched as Jeannie swished away. She was jabbering at Butch even as she put on a show for them. "Jeannie's almost too much for Butch to handle," Ellis said. "I'm surprised she hasn't gone for an older guy."

"I sure would like that chance." Jimmy sighed.

"You couldn't handle her, and besides, Butch would kill you." Ellis couldn't believe Jimmy hadn't learned his lesson.

"It would be worth it," Jimmy said. "She's a dream."

Later that evening, as Ellis and Jimmy were getting in the car to go home, Butch banged the roof loudly with his flat hand. "Hey, Hertzog, I need a ride home. Jeannie's short on gas. You go right by my road. Drop me off, huh?"

Ellis's mind raced. He needed to come up with an excuse quick. "Sorry, Butch. We're runnin' late, and I'm going to miss my curfew."

"Move over, ya pansy. I'll drive. You poke along like an old woman." Butch opened the driver's door and pushed Ellis over.

Ellis crowded Jimmy, who said, "Hey, watch it."

Butch settled in and revved up the motor. "This is great. I'm surprised your folks let you have the car tonight."

"It's the first time. Don't drive too fast." Ellis knew he'd lost control of the situation. He moved his legs away from the gears.

As Butch peeled out, he waved goodbye to Jeannie, who blew him a last kiss. Ellis exchanged a frantic look with Jimmy.

On the way home that night, the sky was pitch black. Most of the farmhouses were too, although every once in a while, a light would peek through the edge of a blackout curtain. The stars shone above, sprinkled like sugar on piecrust. The moon wasn't out yet. Butch raced the car around the curves. The caboose lights of a train became visible as Butch caught up to it. The train only had a few cars and was lumbering toward Adrian.

"What do you think, boys? If I don't stop at Garrison Corner, I'll bet I can beat it."

"No!" Ellis cried. "Stop! Stop the car. I'm going to drive." Ellis reached for the steering wheel and tried to elbow Butch out of the way. The car lurched from side to side.

"You're the one who's going to make us wreck." Butch punched Ellis on the side of his head. "Get back."

Butch put his foot down hard on the gas pedal, and the car pulled ahead of the train. In the dim light of the locomotive, the boys could see the engineer shake his fist at them. Butch ran through the stop sign and made a sharp right. The car fishtailed. He punched the gas again, trying to get over the second set of tracks.

"It's gonna hit us!" Ellis yelled as he heard the squeal of the train's brakes. Jimmy threw his arms up in front of him and screamed.

The car shot over the rails as the train blasted its whistle. Suddenly, Ellis heard the sound of metal shrieking on metal, and the car flipped violently around. It came to a rest, its headlights glaring against the moving iron wheels of the train.

The brakeman shouted at the boys from the caboose as it rolled past. "You're lucky you didn't get yourselves killed! Stupid kids!"

Butch opened the driver's door and vomited onto the roadbed. Jimmy had been thrown across Ellis and landed on the gearshift. He groaned in pain.

Ellis gingerly touched his forehead. "Ouch. Musta hit the window."

"Are you all right, Jimmy?" Butch asked, wiping his mouth with his shirtsleeve. He shook Jimmy by his shoulder, but all he got was another moan. "You were driving," Butch insisted. He looked at Ellis. "You got that? No way I'm takin' the blame for this."

The two boys got out of the car and started around to the back. The rear bumper had torn loose from one side, but it was still attached in the center and on the driver's side.

"Wow. That was close." Ellis looked Butch full in the face. "You coulda killed us."

"It was your fault. You shouldn't a grabbed the steering wheel."

Someone ran up the road from the labor camp holding a lantern. "Are you all right? Anyone get hurt?" It was Doc, with George trailing behind him.

"Something's wrong with Jimmy."

Ellis tugged the car door open, and Doc asked, "Where does it hurt, son? Lie back on the seat. Don't try to get up." Doc pulled up Jimmy's shirt. Red marks on his side showed clearly where he'd landed on the gearshift.

Butch looked at Ellis. "You know that Jap?"

Ellis nodded his head. "He's part of a crew hoeing at Rex and Ed Allen's place. I worked with 'em."

"Then you better back me up on who was drivin'. Even with

them." Butch pointed at Doc and George with his chin. His voice was low, almost a hiss.

"You may have broken a rib," Doc said to Jimmy. He opened his medical bag and began rooting around.

George came around the back of the car. "This your folks's car?"

"Yeah." Ellis licked his lips. "I was tryin' to beat the train." His voice sounded hesitant. He cleared his throat and said it again, this time with more certainty.

Butch looked down at the ground and shook his head. George looked at the boy and back at Ellis.

"My folks are gonna kill me," Ellis said.

Others from the camp were arriving at the accident scene. A couple more brought lanterns and began to direct oncoming cars around the area. Butch saw another friend driving back from Nyssa. He waved his arm to stop the car and then got in. "See ya, Ellis."

Ellis watched silently as Butch left the scene.

"He a friend of yours?" George asked.

"Not any longer."

Ellis could hear the men talking quietly, some in Japanese. He went back to check out the damage done to the car.

George squatted and examined the bumper. "With a little luck, you could pound it back into position and put a new bolt into the car to hold it in place." He pointed to the body. "Your father could weld it together here where the original bolt tore it in two. It looks drivable, though. You'll be able to make it home okay."

Jimmy sat up as Doc wrapped a dressing around his torso.

After seeing to him, the doctor checked Ellis. "You're going to have a knot on your head."

"I can't stop shaking," Ellis said. "Even my stomach is quivering."

"That's the adrenaline. It'll pass." Doc put his stethoscope back into his bag. "Guess I don't need to tell you how lucky you are. Cars don't fare too well against trains."

"How's Jimmy?"

"He'll be fine in a couple of weeks. He probably has a cracked rib or two."

A couple of weeks. Jimmy's father wasn't going to like that much.

Ellis got into the car and backed it onto the road. He turned it around and braked beside George, who stood just outside the driver's side window.

Ellis looked at George and swallowed hard. "You know it was us that yelled at you when you came home tonight."

"I saw you duck."

"It wasn't me who called the names."

"No?"

Ellis couldn't hold George's gaze.

"Take it easy the rest of the way home," George advised. "You've got some explaining to do."

Ellis slowly drove off. Jimmy laid his head on the back of the seat and closed his eyes. He wrapped his arms around his ribs and held himself.

"Sorry," Ellis said.

Jimmy grunted in reply.

Ellis would have to face Jimmy's father first and then his own. He gripped the wheel tightly and began rehearsing in his mind the lies he was going to tell. Nothing he could think of was good enough to excuse what had happened. Some Saturday night this turned out to be.

CHAPTER TWELVE

ABE

Abe sat still as Pamela carefully cut his hair outside the tent at the labor camp. The barber shears were a new family purchase and Abe her third customer, as George and Thomas had gone first. After six haircuts, the shears would pay for themselves. Abe held up a mirror so he could see Pamela's progress. So far, her hand held steady, but she'd slipped once with Thomas, making a gouge in his hair right above his ear.

"Just a bit more in the back and I'll be done," said Pamela. After a few moments, she came around and stood in front of him, chewing the inside of her bottom lip. "It's even on the sides. What do you think?"

Abe held the mirror to each side and then up above his head. "Looks good to me. Pretty soon you'll get a reputation as a barber, and the men will all line up."

Pamela blushed. "Doc has already asked me if he can be next. At least he's a friend of the family."

"See there? A new way to make a living. Better than hoeing beets!" Abe teased.

He hurried back inside the tent he and Thomas shared to finish his hair. He rubbed some Brilliantine into his hair, parted it on the side, and then tried to make a couple of waves in the top part. He let a styled strand fall onto his forehead—a single, subtle, jet-black curl. He put on a white dress shirt, tucked it into his black dress pants, and rolled up the shirtsleeves a couple of times. Black dress shoes shone from the polishing he'd given them the night before. He was ready.

Abe walked by his mother sitting on a wooden step outside her tent with her face upturned.

"The heavens are at peace tonight," Chiharu murmured to him.

Abe stopped, gazed at the stars, and said, "You seem philosophic tonight."

"I am. Sometimes when I look up, I feel as if I bear a sky's worth of sorrows."

Abe looked into his mother's eyes and replied softly, "We all need joy in our lives too. Even if we have to pretend a bit. Dancing will ease our burdens for tonight. Put aside your cares and enjoy the company of new friends and our new community."

Chiharu nodded her head and let out a deep sigh. "Let's try your way. Let me freshen up a bit." She disappeared into the tent and returned with modest heels on, her hair combed out of its knot at the base of her neck, and no apron. The last time she had removed her apron was on the train trip to Eastern Oregon. It was her uniform. She hooked her arm inside Abe's, and they set out across the highway to the Tanaka house.

***

The entire camp was excited about the first Saturday night dance on Tanaka's lawn. The newly formed Girls Club sponsored it. Mr. Welch had a jukebox delivered from the factory's cafeteria, the men carried over a couple of benches from the mess hall, and sodas were available for purchase. The dance itself was free, but the jukebox cost a nickel per song. On each poster announcing the dance, the plea "Bring nickels!" stood out. The Tanakas did their part too. They'd hung lanterns on a couple of the trees, put out the chairs they had, and invited the local Japanese community to meet those living in the labor camp.

Moths flitted around the lights, and crickets chirped in the background. A half-moon waxing in the sky added to the shimmering stars. An owl hooted from Tanaka's barn, and a distant murmur of conversation drifted over the assemblage.

Abe escorted his mother to a chair in the middle of some older women. Blankets were laid on the grass for the younger children and babies. One mother sat with her young son, allowing him to crawl from one side of her to the other. Even young parents wanted to enjoy the evening's entertainment.

Jiggling the nickels in his pocket, Abe walked over to Thomas who was looking at the music listings in the jukebox. "You want to keep this machine going?" Abe asked. He handed Thomas a handful of coins. "It'd give you a way to be here without having to dance."

Thomas took the money gratefully. "I've already got requests. You want any particular tune?"

"Try three fast ones and then a slow one. I don't care which. As we get closer to the end, make it one fast one and end it with three slow ones. I'll let you know if the mix isn't right." Thomas nodded. Abe knew he'd take his jukebox responsibilities seriously.

He wandered over to the galvanized tub filled with ice and sodas. Pamela waited there for the first customer. She had swooped her hair up into a tight ponytail and wore a pink sweater set to match her black, gray, and pink A-line skirt.

"You're lookin' good tonight, sis," Abe said. He bought a Coke with another nickel and waited while a younger girl opened it for him. He was early. He tried not to show that his nerves were tingling. It wouldn't do his suave reputation any good.

The door of the house banged open, and a man in uniform came down the stairs. Abe had heard Tanaka's daughter's beau was home on leave. He'd been in the Army before the war broke out.

Lucky guy, Abe thought. He envied the man in uniform. He'd trade in his hoe for a rifle any day.

Abe joined George standing with a group of men milling around on the lawn. He nodded to the Army man and decided to talk to him later. Right now, the men were talking about invasion fever running high on the West Coast. Even at the labor camp, the news troubled the men.

"How do you think the Imperial Japanese would treat us if they did invade?" one man asked.

"I don't think we'd fare too well," the Army man replied. "We'd be treated as traitors, probably, and executed."

Abe grew more pensive than he'd been before. What a night for a dance, he thought. He tried to shake off the dark mood. First his mother and then this.

Fortunately, Thomas started the first song. It was an upbeat tune from the Les Brown Orchestra called "Let's Dance." The clarinet wailed a fast, jazzy intro, the perfect way to begin the party.

All the girls were in their own group. It took a lot of courage for Abe to cross the lawn and ask one of them to dance. Thank goodness she didn't refuse. Away they went. Abe started off with the basic steps of the swing to see how well the girl could dance. Not bad! He pushed her out, then in, then under his arms. Around them, a few others also began moving to the beat, some obviously just learning.

"Whew!" Abe said. "What's your name?"

"Janice."

He nodded his head when she answered, promptly forgot it, and swung her away from him again. The short song ended, and Abe asked his partner if she'd like to dance to another song.

"Sure," she said.

"I'm sorry. What did you say your name was again?" Abe looked at the girl this time, tried to hear the person and not the echo of war.

"Janice," the girl said. "I live in Nyssa and go to high school there. I'm a junior."

The second song began, and Abe and Janice began to move to the music.

"Where'd you learn to dance so well?" Abe asked.

"At school. We have an eight-week unit in all kinds of dancing."

Abe felt a tap on his shoulder and gave away his partner to a young man. He waved his farewell and looked around to see who else was available.

Across the lawn, Pamela was trying to learn the swing with one of the girls. Abe walked over and began to teach her: *Slow, slow, quick, quick. Slow, slow, quick, quick*. When she got the hang of it, Abe took her out on the lawn to show her more. He was awarded for all his coaching when Pamela giggled. Her face lit up, and her ponytail swung around as she twirled. Someone tapped on his shoulder, and he handed off his sister to a younger boy.

"Be nice," Abe warned. "She's my sister."

When it was time for a slow song, Abe deliberately chose a girl who'd not yet been asked. The music was in four/four time and easy to move to. The girl's name was Betty. Abe showed her the steps— right, left, right, together; right, left, right, together—and by the end of the song, Betty was looking over his shoulder instead of at her feet. Abe twirled her under his arm in a final, grand move. Again, he was rewarded with a shy smile. Abe grinned and walked her back to her seat. The night was getting better.

Abe noticed the Army fellow sitting by himself. The Tanaka girl was nowhere around, so Abe walked over and introduced himself.

"I'm Roger," the young man replied.

"I haven't seen many *Nisei* in uniform," Abe said as he sat down.

"No. And the Army isn't taking any more Japanese for a while either," Roger said. "They don't know what to do with us. I'm on leave now, but when I get back, I'll be on KP duty or guard duty or something equally mundane. They won't even let me train with a real gun. The guys who were in the Air Corps all got grounded, although I heard of one tail gunner whose crew rebelled and took him up anyway."

"I tried to enlist right after Pearl Harbor but was turned away," Abe admitted.

"Yeah?" Roger looked at him closely. "You might as well wait until the Army decides what they want to do. Unless you like peeling potatoes."

Abe didn't. He looked out as more and more couples began to dance. He just felt stuck—first in Toppenish, then in Portland, and now here. Roger's girl approached the two men. Abe nodded as Roger led his fiancé to the lawn. At least there were girls to distract him.

Chapter Thirteen

George

The new recruits George brought from Portland gave the farmers a fighting chance to save the beet crop as the second round of weeding and thinning began. George was gratified when Ed Allen asked for his group specifically. His new crew consisted of Doc and his two brothers.

"Are we thinning with the Hertzog boys again?" George asked Ed as he climbed from the cab of the pickup.

"Yep."

"Should be able to finish in five days easy, then," George said, giving Ed a friendly handshake. "Even Doc can hoe sixteen rows a day now."

"You haven't heard, huh? Ellis lost two of his friends in a drowning accident. He's been out of sorts since then." Ed frowned. "But he's still working. His father insists it'll do him good, but he's slow. I understand his oldest brother Luke is coming home on leave. Ellis always did look up to him. Maybe that'll help."

"Tough break. Thanks for letting me know." George thought of the grief he and his brothers suffered when their father died unexpectedly. In his experience, only time cured grief. No pill or shot made time move any faster. "We worked together before. Even if Ellis won't talk, maybe he'll take some comfort in my presence."

George didn't notice Ed's sharp glance.

When Ed, the Yanos and Doc got to the fields, Rex and the Hertzog boys had just arrived. It was a pleasant early morning as doves cooed on the electrical wires. Sharpened short hoes lay out in rows, waiting for the men. Ed introduced Thomas and Abe while Rex made sure everyone had gloves. George studied Ellis and noted his distraction. When they spread out, Abe took the row next to Ellis's older brother Sam. Rex settled in right beside them.

"You boys want a little competition?" Rex asked. "Experience versus youth?" He smiled like a wily coyote looking at a couple of rabbits. "Let's go."

Doc and Ed laughed and started in together. That left George, Thomas, and Ellis.

"Ready?" George asked.

Ellis said nothing but started in. He looked like he was hoeing in his sleep. George did two rows to Ellis's one so he could stay beside the heartsick boy. Thomas worked ahead and soon was matching Doc and Ed. They gradually left Ellis and George behind.

About halfway through the morning, just when the sweat began to trickle down George's back, Ellis interrupted their steady pace and said, "I keep having the same nightmare."

"Yeah?" George didn't pry for more details. If Ellis wanted to talk, George wanted to listen.

"I keep trying to save Ma and my sister from drowning, but I can't. In the dream, I jump into the water, but it doesn't make any difference. Just when they're about to drown, I scream my whole family awake. Every night." For the first time, Ellis's eyes were clear and alert. Tears wet his cheeks, and as he wiped them with a gloved hand, dirt smeared his freckles. "You know about my friends drowning?"

George nodded.

"Ever since Jimmy and Jeannie drowned, I can't sleep. I'm exhausted but I still can't sleep."

George knew Ellis's dreams were pockmarked with guilt. "So, what happened? Feel like telling me?"

And so, as George worked beside Ellis, the details of the drownings bubbled up one by one.

"It's just a recurring dream. I see Jeannie—lifeless, bloodless, blue lips—staring at me with her green eyes. I wake up frightened, heart pounding so hard I think I'm having a heart attack. At first, Sam would wake me gently. Now he throws a pillow at me. If I don't wake up, he's shaking me or slapping me. Anything to stop me whimpering."

Ellis hoed a bit more and then looked up at George. "See, I could never swim well. Dog paddle, always with my head above water. Made me tired." Ellis pulled up a weed too close to a beet to get it with his hoe. "We'd been swimming for a couple of hours at Flat Rock in the Malheur River when I decided to get out, dry off, and change into my clothes. Butch got out right after me. I guess I thought Jimmy and Jeannie would be right behind us."

He paused for so long George thought the confession was over.

Then Ellis continued. "Jimmy always had a crush on Jeannie. Maybe with Butch outta sight, he thought he'd try his luck with her." He looked back down. "I dunno." Ellis stopped in his row and stood up. He stared across the field, but George could tell Ellis wasn't seeing the beets and the men hoeing them. He was in his memories, reliving the horror of the tragedy.

"Jeannie was sunning herself on a smooth, black lava rock on the far side. All the kids would dive from that rock into the deep pool. I thought Jimmy knew it would be over his head to get over there . . . I heard Jimmy cry out, Jeannie yelling at him to kick his feet and try to make it to the bank. I could hear panic in her voice. That's when I turned around and started running back . . ." Ellis focused his eyes on George. "Jeannie surfaced once and yelled to get a branch for Jimmy and her to hold on to. I found one, pushed it into the water where I'd seen Jeannie before. I could feel her grab it, but then she let go."

Again, Ellis stopped the telling. He shuddered as if he'd been holding back tears. "I don't know where Butch had been, but he came running up and dove in. He surfaced, hanging onto Jeannie's arm, but couldn't get the rest of her and Jimmy up. Somehow they were entangled. I waded in to help as best I could, and when Butch came up next, he had Jimmy's leg. We pulled and pulled and finally got the two bodies back on the shore."

George studied Ellis's face, his eyes reflecting the agony of the memory.

"It was too late, of course," Ellis said quietly. "Jimmy had his arm inside Jeannie's back strap, twisted around. Butch and I got them apart and laid them side by side . . . Even dead, Jeannie was beautiful. Her skin was so white, her lips so blue, her hair so red . . . Butch and me, we couldn't even cry. I was shocked to see her eyes open, just staring at me. Those green eyes." Ellis shivered, goosebumps raising on his arms in the hot sun.

Ellis smiled a crooked grimace and mused, "I always wondered if

Jimmy was trying to cross the river to flirt with Jeannie . . . Guess I'll never know."

He bent over, slowly beginning to hoe the never-ending row. George reached over and grabbed a couple of beets ahead of Ellis. No wonder the kid was still so shaken up.

At noon, Ellis fell asleep in the shade of the poplar trees while the men finished their lunches.

"It's gonna be a scorcher today," Doc said. "Don't know whether I want to take my shirt off so I'm cooler or whether I want to keep my shirt on so I don't get sunburned."

"I'm keeping my hat on," said Ed as he adjusted his wide-brimmed hat. "Last time I burned my bald head, it hurt to lie down on a pillow." Ed tied a bandana above his eyes to catch the sweat and settled the hat around his graying rim of hair. "How're you doing, Thomas? You gonna keep up with me this afternoon?"

"Hope so. I thought I'd pester Doc with questions about the medical profession," Thomas answered.

"Oh?" Doc turned Thomas's hands over and looked for blisters. "What kind of medicine are you thinking about?"

"Surgery. I've always wanted to operate on patients. Just don't know what parts I want to concentrate on."

Sam pushed himself up and walked over to Ellis.

"You might just let him sleep," George said. "He told me he's exhausted."

"I know." Sam's voice had an edge to it. "I'm the one that wakes him out of that nightmare he keeps having." He shook his brother on the shoulder. "Pa thinks he needs to get on with life. No excuses."

Ellis opened his eyes, yawned, and stretched both arms over his head. "Okay. I'm up."

Sam offered him a hand, and Ellis rose to his feet. He swayed to one side, but Sam steadied him.

"You okay?" Sam asked him.

"Sure. Ready to go."

Doc exchanged a worried look with George as they fell in behind the Hertzog brothers.

The men stopped at the outside pump to fill up their canteens and then trudged back to the field.

The afternoon's work continued unabated. Sam, Abe, and Rex slogged through more rows. Their catcalls and hoots from the morning's contest were replaced by grunts and moans in the afternoon's toil as the sun beat down on them and heat waves shimmered over the field.

At the midafternoon break near the irrigation ditch, Ed made Rex, Abe, and Sam stop for water. "Listen, fellas," Ed began, "You workin' yourselves to death on this one day won't help me get this whole field hoed. If you don't drink and take a breather, you'll get heatstroke, and then where will I be?"

George unscrewed the lid on his canteen and washed some of the dirt out of his mouth. The warm water left a metallic aftertaste. Beside him, Ellis swayed and then slowly slid down to the ground before George could catch him.

"Doc," George stammered, "something's wrong with Ellis. His face is beet red."

Doc hurried over and put his hand on the side of Ellis's neck. "His pulse is light and thready."

"What can I do?" Sam bent over his brother. He patted Ellis's face, trying to bring him to.

"Put something under his head. Get his feet raised." Doc looked over at the rest of the men standing around. "Somebody bring me a wet bandana."

The men leaped to follow Doc's barked-out instructions. Still, Ellis did not revive.

"What's wrong with him?" Sam sounded panicked.

"Dehydrated, I imagine. We need to get his body temperature down," Doc said tightly. He turned to Ed. "You got a bathtub?"

Ed shook his head. "Only thing we got is a horse trough, and it's empty."

"Then let's put him in the ditch," Doc said. "That'll cool him down."

George started to take off his shoes, but Sam shoved him aside and climbed into the water, boots and all. "I'm his brother. I'll hold him."

George took Ellis's head and shoulders, and Abe lifted him by his knees. They carried him over to Sam.

"Put Ellis's head in your arms with his feet downstream," Doc instructed.

As Doc splashed Ellis's face, he slowly came to. When Ellis felt the water around him, he screamed. "Ma! Em! Where are you?" He thrashed around even as Sam tried to calm him.

Then Sam shook Ellis hard. "Stop it! Quit screaming. You're having that nightmare again."

Ellis turned halfway and sobbed in Sam's arms. The brown ditch water swirled around the brothers.

"We need to take him home," Doc advised. "He should be in bed."

Rex ran to the pickup, drove it on the adjacent road, and idled it beside the ditch.

George planted his feet in the mud and helped Ellis stand. He put Ellis's arm around his shoulder, and between Sam and him, Ellis managed to shuffle toward the vehicle. Doc slid in the cab beside him, Sam hopped into the bed, and Rex put the pickup in gear. He drove slowly down the road and into the Hertzog's driveway.

Ed gathered the canteens and took them to the house to refill. He insisted the men rest in what shade there was. After a quarter hour, the men began again. By the time Rex, Doc and Sam returned to the field, Abe had completed so many rows, they agreed to defer the competition to the next day.

"How's Ellis?" George asked Doc, once they were alone.

"In bed where he belongs. His mama has seen heatstroke before. She wasn't too happy to take my advice about it. She kept telling me they have their own family doctor. I got the distinct feeling I wasn't too welcome."

When the men quit that evening, Doc went to check on Ellis as he'd promised. George wasn't surprised when Mrs. Hertzog took a step back and shut the door in Doc's face.

CHAPTER FOURTEEN

MOLLY

Molly's father frowned as he sorted through the mail and found the first letter. When he found the second one, his eyebrows raised, and he locked eyes with Molly. "And who is this George Yano? He is at the Eastern Oregon camp, yes?"

"*Hai*," Molly answered. She raised her chin and answered a bit defensively. "He is the new recruiter for the sugar beet company there."

Her sisters both knew about George, of course. He wasn't exactly a secret. Tak`e frowned at the two girls and said to Molly, "Let me see that."

Molly handed the unopened letter to her mother, knowing she couldn't read English.

Tak`e sniffed it, squinted at the handwriting, and turned it upside down and around. "Smell like *inu*."

Molly knew her mother was insulting George before she'd even met him. An *inu* in Japanese meant *dog*. Molly put her hand out for the letter. Tak`e reluctantly gave it back.

"When will we meet this young man?" her father asked.

Kameko peeked over the book she was reading. Mary stopped mid-stitch. Tak`e folded her arms and looked between her husband and her eldest daughter.

Molly stood tall and took a deep breath. "He'll be here Saturday morning. I'm sure you'll make him feel like a welcome visitor."

"A most welcome visitor," Kentaro repeated. "Of course."

"Harrumph," her mother said.

***

The train pulled in at about ten on a sunny, warm morning. Molly waited impatiently for George to be cleared at the entry gate. She had washed and curled her hair the night before to create the black, silky pageboy which bounced on her shoulders. The new red dress buttoned up the front with a Peter Pan white collar. The black patent-leather belt encircled her narrow waist. She showed off her slender legs and wore white anklets inside newly shined black flats.

George smiled as he approached her.

"Hey, big guy! Got a date for the hop tonight?" Molly teased. She didn't know if they could pick up the easy banter they'd had in the past.

He grinned down at her, his brown eyes turning warm. "Did you get my letters?" He shifted the suitcase to the other side so they could walk closer to each other, and Molly slipped her hand into the bend of his elbow.

Molly nodded. She slowed down and looked up at him. "My father wants to meet you." She paused. "He's a bit old-fashioned. I hope you don't mind."

George put his suitcase down on the ground. He held Molly by both arms, his eyes searching her face. "I want to do this right. If your father wants to meet me, I'll try to make a good impression. But he might be disappointed," George warned. "I'm not a lawyer or a doctor."

"Not many of those around here," Molly said, trying to reassure him. "I told him you are the recruiter though."

"So, he knows about me?"

"And he knows about the letters."

They sauntered into the expo barn, heads together while Molly prepared George for the man he was about to meet.

Much too soon, they reached the Mitas' compartment. George set his small suitcase down in the hallway, brushed his jacket, and stood tall.

"Here we go." Molly gave him a smile, pulled aside the canvas curtain, and bowed to her father and mother.

Her father was a bit taller than George and more slender. As he stood up, he straightened his stooped shoulders, shook hands with George, and nodded as Molly introduced him in English.

George turned to Molly's mother and bowed respectfully to her. Mrs. Mita returned the bow, both hands flat on her thighs. Molly didn't know how George knew to be more traditional with her mother, but a handshake with her father and a bow to her mother was exactly right.

Molly then introduced her younger sisters, Mary and Kameko, who were sitting on the cots. Kameko's black bangs skimmed her eyebrows; her long straight hair, parted in the middle, hung down to her shoulders. She looked around her parents and waved to George, covering a giggle with her hand. Whereas Molly had been nervous before, now she was simply irritated with her little sister.

Mary looked more seriously than Molly and, if possible, seemed more nervous than George. She stood to be introduced, but instead of bowing, she held out a limp hand. George shook it awkwardly. Mrs. Mita bustled about in the small space, setting out some dried mangoes. Mary and Kameko left to get some tea from the mess hall.

"I don't believe I know your father," Mr. Mita said, gesturing for George to sit on a stool he'd borrowed from the neighbors. Molly sat at the end of her cot, silently apologizing to George as Kentaro slowly peeled away information about the Yano family, question by question.

"No, sir. My father died two years ago from a brain aneurism. I am the eldest son. We have forty acres in Toppenish and grow vegetables and pick fruit to sell in our family store." George paused. His face reddened, and he shrugged. "At least, that's what we did before the internment."

"I understand you are recruiting workers for the Nyssa sugar factory?"

"Yes. I'm trying to find a way to support my family and still save for our farm expenses. I wish to return to it when the war is over."

"And you've been writing letters to my eldest daughter?"

Molly's gaze lifted from the floor to focus on George. At least she had told George her father knew about them.

"I—I have. I wish to further our acquaintance—with your permission."

Mr. Mita cocked his head and studied George. "These are unsettled times. Normally, we would employ a matchmaker to make arrangements for our daughter. We are not in Japan, of course. If your intentions are honorable—"

"They are," George interrupted. "Begging your pardon, sir." He ducked his head in apology.

"Molly may be seen with you, but only with the escort of one of her sisters. Please be careful of my daughter's reputation."

George looked quickly at Molly. He turned back to Mr. Mita. "I will treat her as honorably as I would my own sister."

"Ah. You have a sister? Tell me more about your family." Mr. Mita enfolded his hands around one knee and leaned back.

George took the tea Mrs. Mita offered. When he lifted the cup to his lips, his hands trembled, and he spilled some on the floor. He moved his foot over the spot and answered more questions, this time from Mrs. Mita in Japanese.

Molly had never heard George speak Japanese. She could tell he was more comfortable in English. Molly helped lighten the mood when she could, and even Kameko pitched in.

After a half hour, Mr. Mita stood up and offered his hand to George once more. "It was good to meet you. We must let you get on with your business in the center."

George handed his cup to Molly and smiled at her. He bowed once again to Mrs. Mita. Then in front of her parents, he asked, "May I escort you to the dance this evening?"

"Yes, please. I would enjoy that."

"Please ask one of your sisters to accompany us."

"I'll go," Kameko said.

Molly couldn't imagine she would be able to keep Kameko's curiosity at bay.

George bowed to her, his eyes twinkling. He opened the canvas flap, picked up his suitcase, and was gone.

Molly turned with a questioning look for her father. He gave a short nod. George had passed inspection.

***

Molly didn't know who was more excited, her or her little sister. In a way, it was Molly's first date. She'd gone to activities at school, but there was never anyone special. Kameko asked to style Molly's hair. Whereas Mary and Kameko cut their bangs just above the eyebrow, Molly grew her hair out and generally parted it in the middle. Kameko drew the tresses back from Molly's face, accentuating her high cheekbones and small ears. The pageboy from earlier in the day cascaded from each side into a smooth roll that rested just above Molly's shoulder. Kameko used bobby pins to keep the hair back and wove a red satin ribbon under the pageboy. She tied a neat bow and stood back to survey her work.

Turning her head this way and that, Kameko said, "You are the prettiest one of us."

"I hope I am tonight anyway," Molly sighed.

Kameko put her hair in a ponytail, then in pigtails, and now had brushed it out. "I don't know what to do with my hair."

"Aren't you going to be dancing too?" asked Mary. "At least with your girlfriends. Why don't you wear it in pigtails and keep it out of your face? I've a blue ribbon we could cut in two."

By the time George arrived to escort Molly to the arena, Kameko was so excited she couldn't just walk. She skipped ahead, then turned around and walked backwards. Molly tried to keep pace beside George in the narrow halls but had to step in front of him if anyone passed heading in the other direction. Her parents and Mary followed at a distance. Molly tried not to mind, knowing her father had given George the benefit of the doubt.

Molly had not thought to ask George if he could dance. She soon learned he could manage a foxtrot in four/four time, but anything else was beyond his abilities. She had not thought about the young men who asked her to dance multiple times, nor the occasions they tapped George on the shoulder to take Molly away. She tried to return to where George was waiting between each dance, but it was never for very long. It was the first time she'd wished she wasn't such a good dancer.

About a third of the way through the two-hour dance, Molly caught a glimpse of George on the outskirts of the arena. Kameko and her friends were practicing the swing, and they were showing George the steps. She couldn't hear them, but George was smiling, and Kameko looked animated. He was learning the basic steps and swung Kameko under his arm, only to lose his grip. Kameko nearly fell. Molly briefly lost sight of them, but when she caught a glimpse again, they were both laughing. As soon as the song ended, Molly wended her way back through the crowd toward George. Kameko saw her first.

"Molly! We're teaching George to dance. He's never had lessons before." Kameko's eyes sparkled, and her cheeks were red from exertion.

Another song came on the loudspeaker.

"May I have this dance?" George asked. He held out his hand to Molly.

She put her hand in his, and they started out with the basic swing steps. "You're good!" she exclaimed, not meaning to sound so surprised.

"I'm learning," George corrected. "I've never had such an enthusiastic teacher. She said she learned all her steps from you."

Molly thought of the day she'd enticed Kameko and her friends away from showing their dance moves to the soldiers leering from the other side of the fence. She never dreamed Kameko would return the favor in such a considerate way. Molly shook her head at one of the many partners coming her way. At the end of the song, Kameko clapped her hands, and Molly beamed at George. She hardly recognized her glum chum.

CHAPTER FIFTEEN

ELLIS

The passenger train hissed its arrival at the Nyssa Depot. A porter jumped out of the car and set down a step for the passengers.

Luke waved his arm high overhead, calling, "Ma! Pa! I'm here!" He stepped down off the train steps in full Army Air Force uniform, his tie neatly knotted and tucked into his olive-green, belted jacket.

The family hurried toward him, Mae in the lead. Luke put down his duffle bag and threw both arms around her. She kissed him tearfully on the cheek and held him tightly. Luke gripped his father's hand as Sam slapped him on his back.

Luke's second hug was for his sister Emily. "You've grown! You must be all of five feet now!" He lifted her off the ground and shook her like a rag doll. Emily laughed in delight.

Sam punched Luke's arm and said, "You've got another stripe! Not just a private anymore, huh?" The two brothers tussled briefly until Luke's hat fell on the ground.

Luke picked it up, dusted it off, and then turned to Ellis. "I understand you've had a tough summer, little brother." Luke studied him for another moment. "What's with the dark circles and worry lines, huh?"

Ellis turned his head aside, his dark, straight hair falling over his eyes. He squirmed under Luke's scrutiny. He didn't want to break down and spoil Luke's homecoming, but his emotions were a jumbled mess. Just having Luke home was reason enough for tears of joy. But his tears were a conglomerate of misery, grief, and exhaustion. If he wasn't careful, he'd be blubbering like a baby.

The train blew three short blasts and slowly began to roll forward. The moment passed. Ellis took a deep breath.

Then the family all began talking at once, vying for Luke's attention and bringing him up to date on local news. Ellis hefted the duffle bag and stumbled after the family to the car. Luke was home.

***

Luke's Army leave followed a pattern that combined farm labor and pleasure. The four males worked every day until about four o'clock. Mae would either have a picnic supper ready for them to take to the river, or they'd change clothes to visit family and friends. Each night, they got home with enough light left to finish the evening's irrigation.

The only wrinkle came on Saturday night when Luke wanted to borrow the family car to take a girl to the picture show. Their mother said nothing, but the smile disappeared from her face. Meanwhile, Luke wasn't subtle about forging ahead with his plans.

Sam and Ellis stood around as Luke shaved and whistled while he dressed.

"Do you think we'll ever be so confident with girls?" Ellis asked Sam. Neither of them had asked a girl out.

"Not me," Sam said. "So far, they're just shorter pals—except they make me nervous!"

Luke overheard them. "You're going to have to decide whether to choose the ones Ma wants you to date or pick for yourself. I'm not letting Ma's disapproval get in the way of me having a good time. It's not like I'm getting married or anything." Luke patted some Old Spice on his clean-shaven face. "You can bet that if I were going out with one of the girls in the youth group, Ma'd be all smiles. I like to date ones she doesn't know, just to keep my options open. Who knows what could happen to me when I finally ship out?"

Sam and Ellis exchanged grimaces. Theys knew firsthand their mother worried about Luke more than any other son. He had a wild streak and got himself into trouble more often than not. However, Luke and Mae shared an October birthday, and she considered him a gift from God forever after—no matter what he did or didn't do. The rest of the family supported him in his quiet rebellion. His father filled

105

the car with rationed gas, and Emily ironed his uniform. Sam and Ellis did extra chores to fill in the work gap, yet the house held its breath while he was gone.

***

The next morning, Ellis shook Luke awake. "Come on, it's time for flapjacks!"

Luke moaned and put an arm over his eyes.

"You know what Ma says about Saturday nights getting in the way of church the next morning." Ellis handed Luke a cup of coffee. "Hop to!"

"You're worse than my drill sergeant in basic," Luke said. "I'll be there in two shakes."

The second week of Luke's leave, the family revived their basketball games after supper and before the evening's irrigating. Ellis and Luke scrambled against Sam and their father Lee. If Luke talked sweetly enough, their mother joined. She'd been a roving forward as a girl on her high school team. Then Emily had to play to keep the teams even.

Ellis's advantage in basketball was that he was left-handed. He was fast, hard to guard, and even harder to block. He had a really tricky shot Luke called his "gunslinger." Ellis brought the basketball up his left side and fired from chest high—almost like a shotput. It wasn't a jump shot, wasn't a lay-in—it was his own brand. Ellis learned to shoot that way when he was little and the basketball was so heavy he had to heave it. Luke hooted with laughter every time Ellis faked out Sam and made a basket.

After the last game of the night, Ellis bent over, sucked in air, and wiped away the sweat running into his eyes. Luke pounded his back in congratulations. Ellis straightened up and beamed at Luke. It was his first normal smile the family had seen in nearly two months. Sam groused about the loss, but all the while, he grinned too.

***

The last night Luke was home, the family ate around their round, wooden table. There were no guests, no extended family, no friends. Mae asked if Luke wanted a going-away party, but he said no. He just wanted to be home. The conversation was subdued—the topic, war. Lee's *National Geographic* world map hung on the wall, with pins representing the various battles. On the US continent, pins were stuck where Luke and the second oldest brother Donald were stationed. Luke's new training would take place in Blythe, California. He was leaving on the morning train for Portland and would continue south from there.

"Now that you know how to march and shoot, what else is there to learn?" Emily asked. "You already know how to fly."

Luke smiled. "I'm going to learn to fly all kinds of planes, including single and multi-engine airplanes. I'll be learning about navigation, formation flying and night flying. Don't worry, little sister, the Army Air Force will find something for me to do!"

"How much more training will you have before they ship you overseas?" Mae asked.

"That's the million-dollar question. The Army doesn't tell lowly soldiers like me." Luke smiled at her gently. "I'll write to you and let you know what I can."

"Yeah, Ma. Loose lips sink ships!" Emily teased.

"I bought something while I was in Nyssa yesterday," Luke said. He got up, went into the boys' bedroom, and came back with a flat paper sack. He handed it to Ellis.

Ellis's hands shook slightly as he took out the gift of sheet music. "Don't Sit Under the Apple Tree." It was a hit song from The Andrews Sisters who were the current rage, blasting out on every radio. Ellis struggled to find the right words.

"You know I'm pretty rusty. I haven't touched the keys for a while." He walked to the piano and pulled out the bench. He began sight-reading a difficult phrase here and there. Finally, after plinking out the harder sections, he started at the beginning.

Luke patted his leg in time to the rhythm. Ellis missed fewer and fewer notes as he grew more confident. The second time through, the rhythm was up to speed, and Emily hummed along.

When Ellis finished, he turned to Luke and said, "Thanks, big brother. It's swell."

Luke nodded his head. "Glad you like it."

Mae picked up the hymnal from the top of the piano and handed it to Ellis. "Would you play some of our favorite hymns? A few for Luke's journey. We've missed your music."

Without opening the book, he began to play hymns he knew by heart. Luke put his arm around his mother and began singing in his tenor voice, "The Lord watch between me and thee." Mae joined in, singing alto in harmony with her son. "The Lord watch between me and thee, when we are absent one from another."

Ellis's joy and sorrow mingled with the melody, and the swelling music enveloped the family.

CHAPTER SIXTEEN

ABE

The sun was low in the evening sky when Abe and Thomas got in from the fields. To their surprise, the size of the camp had more than doubled. Tents had sprung up everywhere. One director shouted orders to the men erecting a women's shower area and an outhouse. Multiple hammers competed with the supper bell for the attention of new residents. The cooks now numbered four, and the serving line for supper ballooned.

"Look! There, standing in line." Abe nudged his brother in the ribs. "We've got new girls in the camp. There must be a half dozen more. Boy, the dance at Tanaka's on Saturday night is gonna be great!"

"Yeah," Thomas said. "If all these people are George's doing, he must be back. You can be second fiddle again."

His younger brother's comment set Abe's teeth on edge. His relationship with his older brother was always prickly. After each absence, when George reasserted his authority as head of the family, Abe didn't like the person he became, reverting to snide comments and slight rebellions. Abe felt himself go back and forth between being a man and a boy.

When they entered the tent, George greeted his brothers and handed Thomas a letter from Danny that he'd brought back from the assembly center. Thomas perched on a stool and scanned it hungrily. Every now and then, he looked up to share what was happening at Tule Lake.

"It snowed there in May!" Thomas cried. "There wasn't enough heat; Danny says they were all cold . . . Danny's family has part of a barracks, big enough for six people. The walls are thicker and go all the

109

way up to the roof, but Danny says they can still hear their neighbors . . . The camp isn't finished. The fence around it isn't complete yet, and the guard towers are only at the entrance gate so far . . . Lots of people are coming from California. The city kids think they're hot stuff. Danny doesn't like 'em. He wishes he was still playing baseball with me." Thomas read the end of the letter, folded it, and put it under his pillow.

"You still miss him, don't you?" Abe asked. He got out his shower gear and a clean t-shirt.

"He's my best friend," Thomas said as he joined Abe on the walk to the showers. "I haven't found anyone else who could be serious one minute and joking the next. He's the only one outside of our family I've ever really talked to about becoming a doctor."

Thomas was quiet throughout dinner. Later, he flopped down on his cot and started to write a reply. "Danny's going to be surprised we're here in Nyssa. I wonder if he's seen his dad yet. He didn't mention it."

"Isn't that the reason they went to Tule Lake?" Abe asked. "To be reunited with Danny's father? Mr. Saito was under suspicion of being an enemy alien. Maybe Danny's mortified and doesn't want to write about it."

"Maybe." Thomas bit his bottom lip. "I hoped he'd set more store by me as his friend. He should know I'd never think less of him."

"Tough letter to write," Abe observed. "He'll know you value him if you keep being his pen pal."

George also took out some stationery and began to toil over a letter. Abe watched his older brother write a sentence, cross it out, think awhile, and then begin again. Every once in a while, he chuckled to himself.

"Who ya writing to?"

"Never you mind. Keep your nose out of my business." George got out a clean sheet of paper and began copying the letter again.

"Sure, big brother."

Abe whistled a low tune, lay back on his cot, and tossed a baseball into the air. "Maybe some mysterious lady will keep you off my back."

George didn't answer, and Abe smiled to himself. He had never known George to be romantic. It made him seem a bit vulnerable instead of so authoritative. A new woman in George's life would give Abe new material to tease his brother about too.

***

As the labor camp expanded, the Farm Security Administration asked the people there to form a council to help write the rules and regulations so there wouldn't be any disagreements among the county sheriff, the two camp administrators, the sugar factory, and the workers. George was elected to the council, and Abe appointed as one of two security guards. It gave Abe an insight into how the camp worked as he observed the meetings.

Invasion fever on the West Coast was running high in June 1942, and Abe worried about the rising hysteria. He was concerned about vigilante action against the local Japanese by young hotheads. The news close to home wasn't reassuring. A small Japanese force had invaded part of the Aleutian Islands off mainland Alaska, and a few days later, on June 7th, an American freighter was torpedoed and sunk off the Washington coast. The Navy blamed a Japanese submarine called I-26. Later, news arrived that momentum on the Pacific front had turned around, with the U. S. Navy decisively winning the Battle of Midway in early June. Four Japanese aircraft carriers and a heavy cruiser had been sunk.

Abe and George handed the newspapers back and forth in the late evening, trying to establish a timeline for what was happening in the wider world.

"My girl Molly wrote that Johnson imposed a curfew in the assembly center," said George. "Everyone has to be inside by nine o'clock for quiet hour and then lights off at ten. The sun hasn't even set by nine."

"Molly, huh?" Abe commented. "Never known you to have a girl before. Isn't this a first?"

Abe was genuinely curious. He hoped George would open up so they could talk about this new development in his brother's life. Instead, George reddened. He raised the newspaper high enough that it blocked Abe's view.

Must be serious, Abe thought. He rolled up an outdated copy of the newspaper and bopped George over the head as he left the tent to visit his mother and sister.

***

Even as alarmist headlines stoked invasion fears, farmers' demands for labor grew. George left again for Portland and returned with fifty more workers. The Nyssa camp bulged. New workers expanded to other crops when the beet thinning was done. Men were haying, driving tractors, and irrigating. Women worked with celery and lettuce, transplanting the starts into the cultivated fields. They hoed weeds, taking older children with the, and leaving their youngest in camp.

Pamela and other older girls took care of the young children, creating games and reading stories. The Nyssa library ran a bookmobile out to the camp every week. Abe was amazed at all the books Pamela checked out for herself and for her charges. Pamela's position was a volunteer, one that she shared with the other members of the FSA Girls Club.

The camp wasn't large enough to house all the workers. Welch sent out a plea to local farmers, asking them to consider taking the workers in as tenants. The Farm Security Administration had to approve each site, asking the farmers to meet the minimum requirements of running water, electricity, fair compensation, and shade.

On the night of June 21st and early morning of June 22nd, a Japanese submarine fired shells at Fort Stevens near Astoria. Soldiers on guard were ordered not to fire back because commanders didn't want the sub to home in on the fort and possibly damage the barracks or the battery emplacements. Luckily, the only damage done by the sub's guns was to the baseball field's backstop. Still, the news frightened Oregonians even more.

That afternoon, Sheriff Hamilton came out to the camp to meet with the directors and the camp council. Abe listened as the sheriff told them of the local reaction to the shelling. A drunken farmer had beaten up his Japanese worker for no apparent reason. The sheriff ended up arresting the farmer for disturbing the peace.

Disturbing the peace? Abe thought the man should have clearly been arrested for assault. Abe's face hardened as the sheriff tried to explain his way through the decision.

"I've brought the injured man here to the camp," the sheriff said. "It's the safest place for him to recover. Doc, can you give me a hand?"

Dr. Yamaguchi walked to the sheriff's car and helped the injured man out. "I'm going to need help to get this fella to the infirmary."

Abe ran over and took him by an elbow while Doc supported him on the other side. As he stood, the man groaned in pain. His face was cut, swollen, and bloody. His nose looked broken, and with the way the man was favoring his left side, perhaps some ribs were too. They escorted him the short distance to the clinic's door as he stepped gingerly on the powdery dust.

Abe was incensed. He returned to overhear the sheriff continue with his explanation.

"I don't understand why he didn't fight back," the sheriff said. "The man was drunk, and it would have been easy to get away. Instead, he curled into a ball on the ground and let himself get beaten. I don't get it."

Abe understood. A Japanese alone in such a situation would likely be arrested if he fought his white boss. Abe fumed.

A modest crowd had gathered, and the sheriff told them, "I wish I could tell you there won't be any more situations like this, but I can't. We're running a fine line, invitin' the Japanese to work here while farmers are scared to death you'll become the fifth column for invading forces. I'm tryin' to keep a lid on the situation. That farmer won't get any more help, so I'm hopin' it'll be a warning to the community. We've gotta keep everyone in line."

Tensions were running high with those in the camp, and Abe and his security partner traded watch all night. Although they each carried a club and a whistle to warn others, their only useful weapon was the administration building's telephone and the sheriff on the other end. Thankfully, the only noises Abe reported were an owl hooting and crickets chirping.

On Monday, the newspaper reported the assault, and Welch was quoted. He warned farmers that the federal government would stop the labor program if another incident like that occurred, and an editorial backed up Welch's threat. But it didn't stop one hundred and thirty Japanese from returning to Portland that evening. That was nearly the size of the entire workforce George had recently recruited. Yet Abe could understand the reasoning.

One of those who returned was Abe's fellow watchman. That left only Abe to listen for night sounds and subtle warnings. George checked on the remaining workers, those who stayed at the labor camp and those who were living on outlying farms. About sixty men, some with family members, counted as the remaining work force. At least Doc had stayed, he and his family. That left their work crew intact. Around the camp, George barked out orders and grew more rigid in his demands. After another dust-up between Abe and George, Abe left their tent to get away from the simmering tension.

He walked down to the Snake River and plopped down on the grassy bank. The deep, flowing water enabled him to ponder the bigger picture of his role as second fiddle. How was he going to become his own man? To discover who he really was? Every once in a while, a fish splashed to the surface and nipped at a bug, leaving a small ring of ripples that disappeared in the current. An owl hooted from a distant tree, and frogs croaked from the river's edge.

Abe got up and searched for a flat, oval rock and tossed one sideways, making it skip three times before it sank. He felt an affinity with that rock. Each time it skimmed the surface, Abe urged it on to find the strength for another airborne leap. And yet the rock could not stop its fate of being swallowed by the river. Surely, if he threw hard enough, another flat rock could skip its way to the opposite shore and escape drowning. Abe chucked rock after rock after rock, venting his anger and frustration.

Only when the moon took its place among the constellations did Abe retrace his steps to the tent he shared with his two brothers. In the morning, he vowed to move into one of the vacant shelters. Perhaps physical distance would help achieve an emotional separation and room to grow into the man he wanted to become.

CHAPTER SEVENTEEN

GEORGE

George arrived in Portland on the evening train. He hadn't come as the recruiter this time. Welch told him that until the Japanese got settled in their internment camps, the Farm Security Administration wouldn't approve more workers. Hence, the sugar factory was not paying for this trip, though Welch did give George the travel documents he needed to return to the military zone. With no wages and the expense of the train ticket, George was spending the equivalent of a week's salary on this visit. But he'd promised Molly he would return for the PAC's final dance in the middle of August.

Molly and her sister Kameko were waiting for him. They held hands, and Kameko waved excitedly at him with her free one. He opened his bag to have it searched and then walked through the gate. As soon as he entered, Molly rushed forward into his arms.

"I'm so glad you came. I was afraid something had happened."

"The passenger train was sidelined several times for the freight trains. Sorry I'm late."

"I thought you were going to be here when the transfer lists were posted. That was this morning."

George paused. His frustrations of no pay for four days plus the cost of the train ticket were his to bear. He came to see Molly, and that was what she needed to hear.

"I'm here now. I wanted to be here earlier, but I wasn't the train engineer." He smiled gently at her. "We have four days to be together. Let's enjoy them."

Stricken, she looked into his face. "I didn't think. I'm sorry. I didn't realize . . . this must be a lot to ask of you."

George offered Molly his arm. "This trip is just for us. No matter the sacrifice, I wanted to be here now. Especially with everyone getting split up and transported to different internment camps. I wouldn't miss the opportunity to hold you in my arms again at the All Center Farewell Dance."

Molly smiled up at him uncertainly but took his arm. Subdued, they joined Kameko, who had waited at the big doors, and walked into the center.

"I don't know where your family is going," George said. "Which camp will it be?"

"We're going to Minidoka in Hunt, Idaho," Molly replied. "I understand it's near Twin Falls. I'd never heard of it before."

He released a breath in relief. "That's great! I'll be recruiting there and at Tule Lake for the harvest. We'll still be able to see each other."

"Then let's enjoy the days we have now. Everyone here has mixed emotions about who is going where. There are a couple of baseball games going on. The recreation center is full of people visiting and sharing the news. What would you like to do?"

"There's a movie tonight I'd like to see," Kameko chimed in.

George smiled at her. She was as peppy as her oldest sister. He wondered how much privacy he'd get with Molly with Kameko as their chaperone.

The girls waited outside the single men's dorm while George dropped off his bag. Arm in arm, they caught up with each other's lives. As they passed by the administrative offices, Johnson saw them.

"George!" Johnson called out. "Are you here to pick up the lists? I should have known Welch would send you."

"What do you mean, sir? I don't understand."

"All the people you've recruited to work at Nyssa have been assigned to camps. Until the government gives each family member permission for an indefinite leave, the government has oversight. Anyway, your family has been assigned to a camp too."

George jerked back. He assumed they'd be assigned to Nyssa and not an overarching camp. A thousand thoughts raced through his mind. Would he and his family be behind a fence too? They would, unless he could find a way out.

To Johnson, he said, "Yes, I should have realized that. Ordinarily, I'd consider it my duty to take the lists to Welch. However, I'm staying for several days to attend the farewell celebrations and the last dance."

"Then I'll go ahead and send them with the mailbag on tonight's train. You might want to see where your family will be going." Mr. Johnson looked over his glasses at him.

"I'll go do that now, sir. I saw where the lists are posted."

Molly and Kameko had to run a bit to keep up with George as they retraced their steps to the bulletin board. He began with Tule Lake, running his finger down the eighty or so names. Not there. Next was Heart Mountain, Wyoming, a list of nearly a thousand. George's heart pounded, his blood surging in his ears.

Molly's voice broke in. "Your family is listed here at Minidoka. We'll be together!"

George looked up, at first not comprehending. They would be going to Minidoka along with the Mitas? Then he would be with Molly. He could see her every day. And Kameko. Instead of letters carrying their relationship forward, it would be the two of them doing it together. The prospect of this increased intimacy dulled the pain of relocation. Perhaps Molly's father would accept him as a future son-in-law if Mr. Mita knew him better.

Despite these advantages, George's thoughts turned to the downsides. He didn't want to live with twenty-three hundred people from the PAC. Behind a fence. With watchtowers filled with armed men. Acid gathered in his mouth at the thought. The close proximity of so many people shattered the internal peace he felt working outside in the sun. Even sharing a tent with his two brothers was better than living in the crowded compartments here. And in the labor camp, there was no smell of manure. George blanched at the idea of their life in Minidoka.

This wasn't his plan for the family. He wanted to find a place in Nyssa to spend the winter and spring, finding what work he and Abe could do. The farmers paid more in Nyssa, which meant saving the family farm in Toppenish was still possible.

He could pursue that indefinite leave. But then he wouldn't be with Molly. George realized his face had given away this internal struggle when Molly touched his arm.

"Folks are already getting mail from Minidoka," she said. "Camp Harmony, those folks gathered at the Tacoma fairgrounds, were assigned there too. That's about six thousand people settling in. We'll be joining them in two or three weeks."

So not just the folks from Portland. Eighty-five hundred people. George added another fifteen hundred staff to guard and administer Minidoka.

"Do you know anyone there?" George asked, trying not to show his panic as they walked outside into the sunshine. A faint cheer went up at the crack of a baseball bat.

"Not yet," Molly replied. "But they're in the same situation we're in. I try to look at it as friends I haven't met. I've never lived in such a large city of *Nikkei*."

"An internment camp, Molly. Not a city."

"I know." Molly looked up at George. "I wonder how long we'll be there."

"A single day is one too many."

The crowd noise from the baseball game seemed incongruous with the discussion of confinement. A game of teamwork juxtaposed with isolation and tedium.

George shook his head. "Sorry."

"It's okay." Molly's smile was small. "Let's change the subject, shall we? *Shikata ga nai*."

***

The All Center Farewell Dance was at once a celebration of friendship and a marker of looming separation. The cooks used much of the sugar rations to scrape together cookies and punch. The recreation department hired a local dance band called the Woody Hite Orchestra. The former Thiel Restaurant was the only place in the center that had a hardwood floor suitable for dancing.

George approached the Mitas' canvas doorway to walk Molly to the dance, Kameko in tow. He knocked on the plywood wall and stood back a bit. It was his last night in town. He and Molly had spent every minute of the past three days together. It was going to be harder to leave her this time, especially because they didn't know when they'd see each other again.

George cleared his throat. At least he was prepared to dance this time.

Molly pulled aside the canvas doorway and motioned George in. "You look very nice tonight," she murmured.

He stepped inside and shook Mr. Mita's hand and bowed to Mrs. Mita. George recognized Molly's red dress with black buttons down the front and a thin black belt to accentuate her small waist. The whole family, including Mary and Kameko, was ready to go.

The dance was a bit subdued at first. Only a few couples stepped out for the first foxtrot. "Let's boogie a bit, shall we?" the lead singer asked. As the big band heated up and the dancers matched the tempo, the night took on a life of its own. The dance floor filled up as the woes of the assembly center came second to the music.

George tried to spend as much time with Molly as he could, but every time he started to dance with her, someone tapped his shoulder and cut in. He asked both Mary and Kameko to dance a couple of times, but he had no desire to ask anyone else. He was surprised to see Mr. and Mrs. Mita glide around the floor whenever the band played a foxtrot or waltz. He could barely manage the swing, even though he remembered some of the steps Kameko had taught him before. He didn't get much practice in Eastern Oregon.

One of Molly's partners was especially talented. He could throw her over his back and up in the air. Molly matched him step by step. Her peppy dancing made George smile. He wasn't jealous; he enjoyed watching her. She danced around him, waving both hands over her head in time to the music, teasing him. What a great gal she was!

At the end of the evening, he took Molly into his arms for the last waltz and refused to give her up no matter how many times his shoulder was tapped. She looked at the various men and shrugged her shoulders. After the third one was rebuffed, no one else tried. He tucked Molly's head under his chin, closed his eyes, and swayed to the music. She just fit. At the end of the dance, it was all George could do not to kiss her. Looking up, however, he saw Molly's father watching them. He released Molly and stood beside her as the band played the last song. Most of the internees sang the words. "God bless America, land that I love..."

When the song ended, the lights came on full force. Curfew began in fifteen minutes.

Molly turned around, reached out for both of his hands, and

squeezed them. "Good night, George. I'll see you at breakfast before your train leaves."

Over her head, George saw Mrs. Mita frown. He walked Molly over to her parents, respectfully bid them a good night, and the family left the area. The band members were striking the bandstand, and the cleanup crew took down the decorations.

The young man who had danced the swing several times with Molly walked up to him. "So, you're the recruiter for the farmers in Nyssa?"

George nodded and put out his hand. The young man ignored it and continued, "Molly's the best of the bunch. You treat her nice, 'cause if you don't, I'll be here to pick up the pieces. You're the reason she won't look at me twice." He turned around and walked away into one of the many corridors of the center.

George returned to his cot in the men's dormitory. That talented dancer was right to challenge George. What had he done to truly commit to Molly?

George tossed and turned all night.

The next morning at breakfast, Molly sat across from George. With Kameko as their constant companion, they made small talk, saying nothing of importance. The biggest problem of the center was no privacy, especially for what George wanted to say. It was only when Molly walked him out of the center toward the gate that he finally got it out.

"Molly, will you be my girl? I know it might not be fair. I know we don't see each other very much. I—"

Molly put her index finger against his mouth. "I am your girl. I have been since that first day when you were my glum chum."

"I don't have a class ring or a pin or anything. I wish you could wear something of mine to show the world you're taken."

She laughed lightly. "Let's not give my father a heart attack. He cautioned me last night not to set my hopes on you. But it's too late. I already have." She looked back at the entrance to the center. Kameko had her back to them. Molly kissed him goodbye once on the cheek, then once on his lips. "Write to me. We have three weeks before we leave for Idaho. You still don't know what you'll be doing after the harvest. We may have the winter together at Minidoka."

George walked away, thrilled about Molly. As he boarded the train, though, his mind returned to his family obligations. Molly seemed to put him in a trance. Minidoka? Did it make sense to go there for the winter? He hated the feeling of being enclosed behind barbed wire. What about Nyssa? Wouldn't his family be better off in a rental home, or as a tenant? Thomas and Pamela still needed to finish school. How would he take care of one more person? And if they married and had kids? He'd never thought of himself as a husband, a father.

While the train built up speed, George tried to think through the dilemma, stymied by the war between his head and his heart.

CHAPTER EIGHTEEN

MOLLY

Molly leaned her head against her wadded-up knit sweater, cushioning the vibrating wall. This was the second day of their journey by train to Minidoka Relocation Camp near Hunt, Idaho, and she had a headache. Their departure had been delayed due to her father's pneumonia, and he barely had enough strength to travel. She glanced over at him, sitting upright, his eyes closed behind his glasses and head bobbing as he dozed. Mary and Kameko had joined a couple of friends and quietly conversed up front. Her mother sat beside her, embroidering a handkerchief. Their luggage occupied the racks above them while a canvas duffle bag had been stuffed beneath their seats.

She never realized how exhausting a trip could be. Their train must have had the lowest priority. She'd lost count of how many times they'd been sidetracked. The Japanese were told to keep the blackout curtains pulled down, and with no windows open, the heat was stifling. Armed soldiers walked up and down the aisles intimidating everyone and barking out orders for the slightest offense. Children were fussy, and babies cried. The only relief was when it was their turn to go to the dining car.

Molly thought she'd be pleased to get out of the center. That was all she and her family talked about. Surely conditions in Minidoka would be better. However, as the center had gradually emptied of familiar friends and acquaintances, doubts began to grow. When her father became ill, he had been hospitalized in the camp's infirmary and, because her mother spoke so little English, Molly took his place as head of the family. She collected their identification tags and found a cane to aid him. She helped her mother pack the family's belongings, labeled each bag and suitcase, and stripped the apartment of any personality. Even though the stall was horribly small, they'd tried to make a home of it. Now, it was as if they'd been erased once again.

Aboard the train, her sunny disposition gradually faded to reluctant dismay. Her headache dogged every thought she had. Her hair was mussed, her clothes wrinkled, and she was thirsty. The trip seemed interminable. Worry about her father made it that much worse.

It was late afternoon when the train stopped at the tiny town of Eden, Idaho. Everyone began to stir. The Mita girls stood and brushed their clothes down and, even though it was mid-September, put on the winter coats they'd worn to save space in their suitcases.

"We're here, folks!" shouted a soldier. "Gather up your luggage and make sure the ID tags are on them. Trucks will take them to the camp. There are buses outside to take you the rest of the way."

Molly hefted a large canvas bag onto the seat and reached over her head for the family's suitcases. Then she steadied her father as he teetered on his feet. Looking at his gray face, she saw beads of sweat on his brow. She realized she would have to manage his valise too. He would have a rough time walking, even using his cane.

Mary and Kameko stepped up to carry one suitcase each and also managed the canvas bag.

"Can you handle that?" Molly asked. What would she do without her sisters? She followed, carrying her own suitcase and her father's.

Her mother wrapped one arm around her husband to bear some of his weight. When Molly reached the platform, she put her bags aside and turned to help her mother. Together, they eased her father down the dangerous steps.

"Thank you," her father said, swaying slightly.

Trucks were at the siding, and soldiers loaded the luggage into the beds. School buses from Jerome, Rupert, and Eden were loading men, women, and children. Molly was grateful these windows didn't have blackout curtains. As people claimed their seats, they slid open the panes to capture what breeze there was.

"Excuse me, sir," Molly spoke to a tall, bald, uniformed man who acted like he was in charge. "How far is it to Minidoka? My father is ill. He was in the infirmary with pneumonia before we left. His fever has returned, and I don't think he can hold up much longer."

The uniformed man looked over her head to Kentaro who was leaning against Tak`e with his eyes closed. "It's a couple of miles," he said, "but I have a car. If I take your father and mother to the camp's hospital, can you manage?"

"Yes. But they don't speak much English."

"We have interpreters at the hospital. They'll be well taken care of. Can you give them their registration papers?"

Molly walked over to her mother and explained what was going to happen. The man hustled to his sedan and opened the back door. Molly and Tak`e supported Kentaro as they walked him over and helped him into the back seat. Tak`e climbed in on the other side.

Molly handed her mother the registration papers and tried to reassure her. "I'll see you there," she said.

As the trucks, cars, and buses left the train, Molly, Mary, and Kameko followed the rest of the crowd and loaded onto the remaining bus. The train blew its whistle, and the porters stepped back on the railway cars. As Molly looked out the window, the contrast between Western Oregon and Idaho's Snake River Plain couldn't have been greater. Instead of the lush greens of Portland, the Snake River Plain was a desert with only sagebrush and small greasewood trees. The dry flat land was known for its extreme temperatures and dust storms. While the assembly center had been uncomfortable with the smells and flies, it was pleasant to go outside and sit under the shade to read a book or talk to friends. Looking around, Molly felt as lifeless as the land around her.

The bus turned onto Hunt Road, and they could see the camp in the distance. There was no fence around it yet, but several watchtowers and a couple of water towers could be seen dotting the desert. The bus crossed over a deep canal and pulled into a parking area beside the other buses.

A uniformed officer barked out orders. "Stay with your families, please. Join the registration line with the others, and be sure to have your paperwork ready."

Molly led the way as Kameko and Mary followed closely behind.

"What's that smell?" Kameko wrinkled her nose. "It can't be cow manure!"

Molly shushed her sister as they exited the bus. At the bottom of the steps, Molly asked the guard, "Do you know where the hospital is?"

"It's inside the entrance to the left, by Area One. Ask anyone. They'll show you."

Molly hadn't realized the consequences of being among the last residents to arrive at the camp. As she checked in for her family, the administrator told her there were no barracks ready for them; they were still being built. "You'll have to bed down in the recreation center for Block 23. It's public space, so each morning, you'll have to get up, fold the bedding, and stack the cots on one side to make room for the activities offered during the day. Others will be sleeping there also. You'll have to change clothes and wash in the laundry rooms."

Molly blinked back tears as she signed the papers to acknowledge the requisitioned cots, blankets, pillows, and mattresses.

"My father, Mr. Mita, was brought in earlier by car," Molly said. "He's still recovering from pneumonia. My mother is with him at the hospital. When can we go see them?"

"You and your sisters need to see the physician first and then go on over to Block 23. After you've received your bedding and baggage, you can check. If your mother comes, I'll send her over to your block as well."

"She doesn't speak much English. Is there someone who can escort her? And can you tell me where we pick up our mail?" Molly hadn't heard from George in a week.

"Listen, lady, we deal with folks who speak only Japanese all the time." The administrator's voice cracked with annoyance. "We'll take care of any complications. Your block manager will have all mail delivery in building twelve, but it will take a while to sort all of the mail that's come in for the Portland group."

Molly bit back any more questions. She picked up the suitcases and trudged over to the next line.

"Why do we need to see a doctor?" Mary whispered. She hated needles and the requirement of up-to-date immunizations.

"I have our shot records right here. I can't imagine we'll need any more." Molly was so tired of standing in line after line and waiting and waiting and waiting.

"Do you think Papa will have to stay in the hospital?" Kameko asked. She was Father's favorite. During his last stay in the infirmary, she was the only one who could get him to eat and drink enough to recover his strength.

"I hope so, since we don't have our own room yet. This trip wasn't good for him. But don't worry. The hospital here should be better than the infirmary we had in Portland. By the time he recovers, we might have our own place. I hope it's soon." Molly closed her eyes and put a hand to her head. "I have such a headache."

Mary held her hand up to her sister's forehead. "No fever. You never complain. It must be a doozy."

The line moved faster than Molly thought. Before she knew it, a youth had been assigned to take them to Block 23.

Compared to the assembly center, Minidoka was huge. As Molly, Mary, and Kameko struggled to stay up with their guide, they looked around in bewilderment. The camp followed the shape of a swift, flowing river that curled around like a boomerang, with the administration building, staff housing area and motor pool in the center. Blocks one through nineteen were on one wing, while blocks twenty-one through forty-four were on the other.

"Where's the hospital?" Molly asked the teen.

"It's near blocks four and six, all the way across camp from where you'll be. You gonna try to work? If you are, don't forget to sign up. That's in block two, building fifteen."

The young man began to give the sisters the lowdown on how the blocks were arranged, and how they functioned.

"What's the smell?" asked Kameko, tucking her nose into her coat collar.

"That's the pit toilets. Overnight, lime is added, and it cuts the smell, but with the usage during the day—well, let's just say you want to do your duty early in the morning."

"How awful!" Kameko exclaimed.

"As the old folks say, *Shikata ga nai*. Here we are." Their guide carried Tak`e's suitcase to a corner of the large recreation room and put it near stacked cots with blankets and pillows mounded around them. "Better claim your beds. Hope you girls get your own room soon." With that, the youth left.

Molly sank to the floor, exhausted. She was so tired, she felt physically ill. She leaned her head back against the wall and closed her eyes. She still had to find her mother and father.

"Here. I thought you could use this." Mary held out a cup of hot tea. "I asked around to see if we could get anything before supper."

Molly gratefully took the cup from her sister.

"I got some aspirin out of my bag. These might make you feel better." Kameko dropped two pills into Molly's hand.

Mary and Kameko sat down on each side of Molly with their own cups of tea. After taking the aspirin, Molly slipped her free hand into Mary's. Kameko leaned her head on Molly's shoulder. The three sisters sat beside each other, getting what comfort they could.

CHAPTER NINETEEN

ELLIS

Ellis lay on his stomach, a pillow over his head. Last night, by moonlight, they'd loaded the beet truck for the final time. After such a long day, he desperately needed more sleep. Exhausted, he pulled the pillow off his head and saw it was still dark out.

"Ellis!" his mother shouted. "I've called you twice now. Next time it's a bucket of water. You'll end up with no time to eat breakfast and late to the fields."

Ellis could tell his mother was losing patience. He pushed up on his elbows, swung both legs around, and then dropped off the top bunk. His mother was a woman of her word. If he didn't hustle now, he'd not only face her wrath but teasing from the other workers along with his father's silent disapproval.

"I'm coming, Ma!"

He'd shaken out his denims the night before, but it hadn't done much good. They were stiff from the dirt and sweat of the previous four days. Finger-combing his dark, straight hair, he hustled to the kitchen and quickly sat down to breakfast.

"Looks like you need some coffee to get you going," Emily said, setting a brimming, steaming cup in front of him.

Ellis added some cream and a teaspoon of sugar. Coffee smelled better than it tasted. Somehow, he'd graduated to drinking coffee this fall. With Sam off to college, and Ellis now the only son at home, maybe he'd become a man in his family's eyes. Emily put a plate of bacon and eggs in front of him and went back for the mush that would stick with him until the noon meal.

"Pop has been out for at least a half hour," Emily said. "I heard the truck heading down the road for the beet dump. He's going to try to be first in line. Ed's pickup already went by to get the Jap workers. If you don't hurry up—"

"Okay, okay, Sis, I'm eating as fast as I can. Ma's nagging is enough. I don't need yours too."

Ellis gulped down the coffee, finished the oatmeal, and headed up the stairs with two slices of bacon in his hand.

His mother greeted him by the hand pump. "Here's your water bag. See you out there."

"What do you mean?"

"I'm going to top beets today too."

"You? But it's man's work! You've never worked in the fields before. Besides, who's going to cook for the crew?"

"Emily's going to do the prep work," his mother said. "I'll come in a bit early to help for the last hour. It'll work. With Sam gone, we're extra short on labor. I've found an old pair of overalls of Sam's that fit well enough."

Ellis's ears turned red. His mother in pants? Ladies her age didn't do that. Even when she worked in the garden, she wore dresses and an apron. She usually knelt on an old piece of flour sacking as she weeded row upon row.

"Does Pa know you're coming?"

"Never you mind about your pa. It'll be a done thing before he's back from the beet dump."

"But the Allens will see you and . . . and the Yanos. I'll work extra hard, Ma. Really, you don't need to come."

Ma looked at Ellis with that steely stare he knew so well. It was useless to argue with her when she had that attitude. Sighing in resignation, he picked up his water bag and beet knife and hustled down the road.

Rex was already in the field, hooking up his team of horses to the beet puller. The implement was large enough to handle two rows at a time. It cut the roots under the large beets and popped them to the surface. They weighed between eight and twelve pounds. Ellis and the crew would hook the beet with the rounded top of the knife, cut the green foliage off the tops, and leave them in the furrows. When they topped enough for a load, they'd stop and throw them in. Usually, Ellis could fit a beet in one hand, but sometimes he needed two. Yesterday, the crew had enough moonlight to fill the truck a fourth time.

"Hiya, Ellis. You ready to go today?" said Rex. "We might as well get started. The others will catch up soon enough."

Ellis followed the puller down on its first pass. The beets were muddy but still white enough to stand out in the early morning light. He hooked the beet and brought it up to his knee with his right hand. He usually needed only one strike with the knife to cut the top off. The beets didn't seem heavy at first, and his wrists were getting stronger, but they were still sore by the end of the day.

The goal was to top and load a truck per person. If they had Rex, Ed, Pa, and him, they might manage an acre a day. With forty acres in beets on each farm, the men knew they had to go faster than that. If the beets froze, they would turn to mush. Ed and Pa had decided to get a Japanese crew beginning today, although they could only get three men. Maybe that was why Ma was determined to help. They should be able to double the number of beets harvested yesterday.

Ed pulled into the field with George Yano and his two brothers in the truck bed. Ellis hadn't seen them since he'd fainted from heatstroke. He shook each brother's hand and made sure he looked them in the eye. Thomas was so slender he didn't look fit enough to work the field. Maybe wiry was the better term. Ellis was trying to make up his mind when Abe put words to what he was thinking.

"We'll all be learning how to top beets today, but I'm willing to wager a nickel that Thomas here will be able to keep up with Ellis in about three days." Abe took a nickel out of his jeans pocket.

Rex reached into his pocket and brought out a second nickel. "I'll take that bet. Ellis has been working the fields for several years now. No way Thomas will pick it up that fast!"

"Give the nickels to me then," Ed said. "I'll hold them until we find out who wins."

In all the joshing around, Ellis hadn't seen his mother arrive.

"Morning," she said. At the sound of a woman's voice, the men turned around. Mae smiled. "It's easy to see why you men have to load your beets in the moonlight, with you wasting time getting started."

"What are you doing out here, Mae? Does Lee know you're . . . ah . . . ." For once, Rex seemed tongue-tied.

Ellis ducked his head. Now she'd done it! They'd all seen her in overalls. She'd tied her hair in a bandana and had her water jug and knife in her hands.

"You'll have to show me what to do as well," she said. "Thought I'd get my training at the same time as these Japs. Well?" Mae arched an eyebrow. "Let's get started."

Rex jogged over to the team, picked up the traces, and put the beet puller in motion. Ellis went back to where he'd been, leaving Ed to talk to his new crew about the fine art of topping beets. It made him uneasy when his mother called George and his brothers "Japs" right to their faces. It sounded disrespectful. But he knew better than to say anything.

By the time his father returned with the truck, Mae had her rhythm down. He didn't see his father say anything to her. Lee picked up a knife and went to work in the rows beside her. Every once in a while, Ellis saw his dad grab a beet from his mom's row, helping her keep up. Ellis started doing the same. It still shocked him, the fact that she was working beside them. He never would have guessed his mother would be willing to be a part of the crew. And he never would have thought his father would let her.

***

On the third day of the harvest, Ellis felt like he'd been put on the spot. A nickel wasn't much to wager, but it wasn't all that was at stake if he failed to keep up with Thomas. Rex always bantered with George and Abe better than he did. He'd rather stay out of the limelight, but now everyone was ribbing him. If he stood up to stretch his back, Abe would tell Rex he knew his nickel was safe. If he happened to top two or three beets in a row with one whack of the knife, Rex would brag. As far as he could tell, he and Thomas were the only two not wanting to involve themselves in this "friendly" harvest competition.

When his mother arrived at the field, the teasing and banter always stopped. The wager was still on, though, so he and Thomas worked steadily, not saying a word.

With three Yanos, the two Allen brothers, and Ellis's family working, it didn't take long to top enough beets for a truckload. His father let down the sides of the bed, and they began pitching in the beets. Soon, the stack rose high enough that the beets were rolling down the pile and back onto the ground. Ellis helped his father put up the side rack, and the men threw the beets higher. The Ford truck could carry about four tons, and in the plowed ground, the engine strained under that much weight.

Rex got inside to drive it to the train siding, known as the Overstreet Beet Dump. "Mae, you want a ride back to the house? Isn't it about time for you to be back in your kitchen?"

"I can manage an hour more," she replied. "Emily's doing fine. Don't be so concerned about filling that stomach of yours!"

Ellis felt a twinge of shame. No Japanese he knew had been invited to eat inside a farmer's house. It didn't help that the radio reported that Prime Minister Tojo had flown incendiary devices over the forests in southwest Oregon. Japanese forces had tried to set fires twice in September, the last time a few days ago. It kept folks jumpy and concerned about an invasion, although the balloon bombs hadn't done any damage.

Drinking from his water bag and stretching back and forth, Ellis was aware that his hands were rough and callused from all the work he'd done throughout the summer. Getting a jump on Thomas, he picked up his knife and headed back down the row he'd been working. To his surprise, Thomas fell in beside him, matching him beet for beet.

His mother left the field about an hour before noon, walking down to the farmhouse. The basement was a symbol of the poverty his family lived in. His father had constructed it in 1935, shortly after proving up on the homestead. They hadn't had a good enough year yet to build the main floor on the foundation. That was one reason to plant beets. The sugar factory paid them weekly based on the tonnage they delivered to the Overstreet dump. It was known as a cash crop.

"Do you miss school?"

Ellis glanced up in surprise when Thomas's question brought him out of his somber thoughts. "Sure. I actually like school. What about you?" Ellis asked.

"I liked it when we lived in Toppenish. I'm kind of nervous about going here." Thomas bent down to pick up another beet.

"It's the first time all the high schools have closed for the harvest. Did you hear about Nyssa?" Ellis asked. "The shops aren't opening until late to give the employees time to help out in the mornings. Even the teachers are out in the fields."

"How long do you think we'll be working? Until the end of October?" Thomas asked.

"Yeah. I can't see us getting started in school until at least the end of the month. Where will you be going?"

"I don't think my brother has decided where we're going to live yet. We're supposed to report to the Minidoka Internment Camp in Idaho, but we're on temporary leave. Sleeping in a tent at the labor camp is getting pretty cold for my mother and sister. I hear they're talking about putting some of us at the old Civilian Conservation Corps camp at Cow Hollow. Then I'd go to school in Nyssa."

"You two are sure yakkin'. Getting slower by the syllable." George's wry observation stopped them short. Ellis risked a glance at Thomas, who'd set his jaw at George's criticism. Ellis shut up and picked up the pace.

By noon, the crew had filled two truckloads and started topping beets for the third. Rex had already returned from the dump. They were managing much better than they had two days before. Even Ellis's father was happy with their progress.

"Dinnertime. Let's head for the house," said his father.

The men put their knives by the beet puller and drank the last of the water in their bags. Ed unhooked the team, took them over to the horse trough to drink their fill, and put grain in their feedbags. He slipped them around the horses' noses and over their ears.

"Your Emily is sure a good cook." Rex patted his stomach.

"She's doing just fine," Lee said. "Normally, she plays second fiddle to her ma." He turned to the Yano brothers. "Why don't you boys come down to the house and sit under the shade of our trees? The grass has grown in pretty well this year, and you can eat your lunch there."

"That would be nice, Mr. Hertzog. Thanks," George said.

The Yanos picked up their lunch pails and walked behind the others until they reached the Hertzog's place.

As they went in the gate to the yard, Ellis turned to Thomas. "Sorry you can't come in. My ma's still touchy about . . ." His voice trailed off.

"See you when you get done," Thomas said simply. He and his brothers collapsed under the red and yellow leaves of the oak tree.

Ellis felt like Thomas had let him off the hook. He bowed his head and slipped down the steps into the cool of the house.

CHAPTER TWENTY

ABE

The early fall evening was a pleasant time, even in the labor camp. Doves perched on the camp's wires, cooing soft songs. The cooks banged pots and pans as they cleaned up from supper. An occasional car drove by on the highway, a few hundred feet away. Abe was constructing an *ofuro*, a soaking tub, as his contribution for the camp's upgrade. The camp required four hours of work a week from each adult resident. Some people buried the garbage, some gardened, some cleaned the shower stalls or spread lime into the pit toilets. Abe used his carpentry skills.

Abe was nostalgic for the hot baths of Japan he experienced as a boy in his uncle's home. He wanted to figure out a way for a man to both soak his sore muscles and cleanse his mind. The ancient Shinto tenets believed in expelling evil, both in the body and mind, using the purifying attributes of water. He was working on some steps that led to a raised platform when he saw George walking over to him. He clutched a letter in his hand. Molly must have written again.

"How's this gonna work?" George studied the wooden box with a tin bottom. It was sitting on a foundation of brick about two feet above the ground. Abe had managed to construct a tightly sealed tub with rudimentary tools.

"Well, I have to build a firebox underneath the tub to heat the water, so that means putting the bathhouse up a couple of steps. I put it in an enclosure for privacy and need a lid to go over the tub to keep the water hot. Usually, a wooden frame rests on the tin so it won't burn the soaker. To tell you the truth, I haven't figured it all out." Abe picked up his hammer. "What about you? You got that problem solved yet?"

"What problem is that?" George asked.

"The one that's making you grind your teeth at night and keeps your brow all wrinkled up." Abe nailed down the boards for the first step.

"Here I think I can hide troubles from you, and I'm broadcasting them like the daily news." George shook his head. "I've been trying to puzzle out whether we can stay here for the winter."

Abe quit hammering and sat back. "I thought we had to report to Minidoka after the harvest."

"Welch thinks he can get deferments for us to stay in the Nyssa area. The internment camps are crowded, and many folks here are settled in with farmers. We'd have to find housing for our family as they'll close down the labor camp after the harvest."

"I'd rather go to Idaho. I feel like we've abandoned the others that were in the assembly center with us."

"You can't go, Abe. I need the money you're making to save the farm."

"What'd you say?" Abe's voice was quiet but intense, and he focused on his older brother. It was one thing for George to be the eldest son but another for him to determine Abe's future.

"You can't go. I need you here." George looked down and kicked the toe of his boot into the ground. "Thing is, the bank took over our store when we had no money from the harvest in Toppenish. I used it as collateral."

"After all the fighting we've done about that store, you just let it go? Why didn't you talk to me sooner?"

"I'm the one in charge of the legal and financial dealings. You know that." George never failed to remind Abe that he was in charge.

"What about the money from the tractor? Did you spend it too? And Father's car?" Abe's voice grew in volume.

"I sent that first. The bank said it wasn't enough. I have to send most of the cash we've saved this summer for the rest of the payment."

"Why talk to me about it now?" Abe had no idea the money was so tight. "Seems you've already made the decisions."

"Thomas may have to work until the harvest is in. That would help."

"Thomas needs to be in school." Abe emphasized each word. "Remember? He's gonna be a doctor."

"If we lose the farm, he won't be able to go to college," George snapped.

"You haven't spent Thomas's college savings, right?" Abe glared at George.

George shook his head. "Mother keeps the money in a tin that never leaves her sight."

"I didn't realize we were in such financial straits." Abe partially pounded a nail, stopped and thought a bit, and then said, "I always hated that store." He punctuated his feelings with a final blow.

"What do you think about going to Minidoka after the harvest?" George asked.

Abe plunked down the hammer and sat on the platform, his legs dangling over the side. "It wouldn't cost us anything. No need to buy furnishings of our own, which we'd have to do if we rent here. I still want to go to Idaho when we get to the point I can. What do you know of the conditions there?"

"It's pretty bad. My girl just got there. Here." George handed him Molly's letter. "Read it yourself."

Abe studied the letter and then glanced up at his older brother. "Molly, huh? She nice?"

"A gem."

Abe couldn't believe George was finally letting him into his romantic life. He opened the letter tentatively, not wanting to tear the fragile paper. A faint whiff of perfume tickled his nose.

September 14, 1942

Dearest Chum,

So sorry I haven't written. Father has been ill, first with pneumonia and now with food poisoning. The hospital isn't ready, and with the latrines unsanitary, a dozen more have become sick. We are surrounded by desolate country, with only gray-blue sagebrush and tumbleweeds. At least there are no fences and no gates yet. Only the manned watchtowers loom over us.

When are you and your family coming? There are opportunities to work in the fields around Twin Falls as you are doing there in Nyssa. Some stay in FSA camps, but I would miss you too much for you to do that. Many Minidokans are helping with construction of the barracks, although at times the dust storms are so bad all work stops as no one can breathe or see beyond a foot or two. When they finish, we'll be able to move out of the crowded recreation hall into a one-room family area. It should be quieter and certainly more private.

I think I have found a job as a teacher's aide. I've never worked with children before, but that was the only position available. I won't bring in much money to help the family, but my sister Mary is looking for work too. Father is too ill to help.

I miss you. I keep thinking about the last time we danced and I was in your arms. When I ache for you, I close my eyes and remember your touch, your smell, and your soft lips.

I'm still your girl,
Molly

Abe read Molly's last loving sentences and scrutinized his brother. No wonder Abe had to wake him from his daydreams sometimes.

"Doesn't sound like a picnic," Abe acknowledged. "But how can we afford to stay here? We're getting squeezed. Sorry, big brother. I don't see a good option."

"Neither do I." George tapped the letter against the palm of his hand. "Thanks for listening. Let me know if you think of something." George walked away, one hand shoved deep into his pocket.

Abe hopped down from the platform. He should be trying to help George instead of grousing all the time. The farm meant a lot to their father, and George had taken on the burden of trying to save it. Abe couldn't see how it was possible. He shook his head, put some nails into his mouth, and began to pound in the boards for the last step. He wondered if a good, hot soak would clear the thoughts in George's head. It would be a gift—his big brother would be the first to try it out.

When he was finished, Abe wandered over to the mess area of the labor camp where his mother and Pamela were fixing all the lunches that would fill the metal pails for the harvest crews. The talk with George had unsettled him, and he needed to confer with his mother. Even with Pamela there, Abe knew he could speak openly.

When he arrived, Chiharu was working with several loaves she'd baked that day. She sliced each loaf and prepared thirty sandwiches at a time, about half of what was needed. She would insert a slice of spam in the morning. Sometimes carrots or a cold baked potato or a boiled egg would be substituted for cookies. Chiharu varied the lunches, working with the ingredients she had on hand.

Abe was relieved to see that no one else was there besides his mother and Pamela. He washed his hands at the metal basin, dried them, and then stepped over to greet his mother. He folded the waxed paper on three sides, tucking the bread in each envelope, making sure the spam could be added easily. Chiharu looked up at him and smiled her thanks. Pamela added the bread to the lunch pails and then buckled the lid closed.

Abe tried to think of a subtle way to begin the conversation, but nothing came to mind except a straight-out plunge. "Has George talked to you about his plan for us after the harvest is over?"

Chiharu looked up at Abe. "He tells me only when he is sure of his path. He has not spoken to me. He has shared something with you?"

"If he could find a way, he would like to stay in Nyssa for the winter and enroll Thomas and Pamela in school."

"And you are uneasy with this idea?"

"We are assigned to Minidoka. The barracks are not complete, and the need for carpentry skills is acute."

"For which you would earn a pittance."

Abe winced. His mother could read him like a book. "I wish to be of use rather than consider what I would earn."

"What about us?" Pamela asked. "Are the schools in Minidoka finished? Would Thomas and I find classes started?"

"I don't know about the high school. The elementary school is beginning soon."

Pamela worked behind Abe, taking sandwiches several at a time to put in the pails. She said, "I know George hates the noise and watchtowers and large numbers of people. He would rather us be in a safer place."

"How do you know that?"

Pamela shrugged. "He's like me. He'd do anything not to have soldiers surround us with their guns."

"Could we remain in Nyssa?" Chiharu asked.

"If we get permission, but we'd need to rent a place. The FSA and the sugar factory will close the labor camp after the harvest. We'd have to make our own way."

"Can we not do this? Has George not saved the money we have put aside from our labors?"

"The taxes and the mortgage on the farm used most of it."

Chiharu nodded. "Good. George has preserved his father's dream. We must not question this decision."

"But where will we live, Mother?" Abe didn't mean to speak so loudly or to be so exasperated.

"Be patient, Abe. Anxiety for tomorrow does not make today any more peaceful." Chiharu patted Abe's shoulder. "George will find a way."

That was not the answer Abe was searching for.

CHAPTER TWENTY-ONE

GEORGE

George and his brothers climbed down from the dusty farm truck. He winced as he rubbed his lower back. Even the ablest of bodies were sore after twelve hours in the field. It was the beginning of October, and the harvest was well underway. The nights were getting colder and the sunsets earlier and earlier. The deciduous trees were losing their yellow and red leaves. All of nature's clues were telling George he was almost out of time to decide where the family would spend the winter. The labor camp would close at the end of the beet harvest. He picked up the mail from the administration building and saw a letter from Molly. She wrote to him nearly every day. Instead of heading for the shower, he read it on his way to the tent.

October 3, 1942

Dearest Chum,

I'm blue today. I miss you so much. There are times I can't keep my chin up, when I wonder how we'll make it through. I cry at night, using my pillow to muffle the sounds, and know others do the same. Last night Kameko crawled onto my cot, interrupting my tears, and we held each other. She has a sixth sense, that one. She is the youngest yet, in some ways, the most attuned to my emotions. I am blessed to have her.

I am worried about us. This is the most important time of our lives to be together, to build on the relationship we have, yet we're apart. I need your strength, your steadfastness, your courage. I ache for you to hold me. I know you need me too. I can look into your eyes and read your soul. I will always be your Molly, your helpmate. I need you beside me. When will you come to Minidoka? That question is my constant companion.

141

I too can be a glum chum.

Much love,
Molly

George read Molly's brief letter over and over. How could he not go to Minidoka? That question was *his* constant companion. He still didn't have a place for the family this winter, but he hadn't given up hope either. When he finally emerged from his emotional fog, Pamela was sitting beside him on the cot. She quietly watched him.

"Sorry. Didn't know you were here," George croaked. He cleared his throat, trying to rid himself of the lump.

"She must mean a lot to you, this girl." Pamela nodded toward the letter, now clutched so tightly in his hand it was nearly crumpled into a ball.

George let out a sigh and smoothed it out on his leg. Wordlessly, he handed it to her.

After she'd read it, Pamela looked at her brother intently. "She loves you very much." She glanced over the letter again and then added, "And you love her."

George didn't know how to react to Pamela's observation. Instead, he reached under the bed and pulled out the old shoebox where he kept Molly's letters. He added the newest one to the stack and slid it back.

"How long has it been since you've seen her?"

"Last time I went to Portland—August. Now she's at Minidoka."

"And that's where we may end up."

"Yeah. That's the problem."

"Because you don't want to go?"

"No, I don't." George's face flushed. He turned to look at his fifteen-year-old sister. She had her foot up on his bed, her chin resting on her knee. Her black bangs rested on her eyebrows as she regarded him.

"I don't want to go either. Guards, so many people, no privacy." Pamela sat forward. "Couldn't you bring her here?"

"Here? Her father doesn't want to work in the fields, and he has suffered some physical setbacks. I asked him before, and he said no."

"No. Molly. Not her whole family. Just her."

"You mean—marry her?" Stunned, his black eyes searched his

sister's face. "Bring her here as . . . as . . . my wife?" He wiped both hands on his jeans.

"Seems like the sensible thing to do." Nodding, Pamela stood up. "Course, you'd have to find a way to ask her." She cocked her head. "Can you write a love letter?"

George watched his sister walk away, pigtails swinging side to side, dusting off the back of her dress.

Write a love letter. Marry Molly.

It seemed so simple when Pamela said it. But he hadn't planned to marry. Not yet. His thoughts began to whirl as he considered this new possibility.

***

A couple days later, George attended a camp council meeting. Welch was there, as were Abe, the sheriff, Doc, and the two administrators.

"What's the situation in Nyssa for the new labor camp there, the one between the railroad tracks and the Snake River?" one of the administrators asked.

"The cabins are still under construction," Welch answered. "They're in the middle of putting in the plumbing and electricity. They'll be ready for occupancy in a couple of weeks."

"How many will be able to live there?"

"There's room for about two hundred workers," Welch said. "The temporary labor camp in Vale has been finished for about a hundred. The CCC camp at Cow Hollow can hold another two hundred, but they have to figure out what's wrong with the water first. It shouldn't take too long to turn it over to FSA supervision after that. We have another hundred and fifty workers living on individual farms scattered throughout Malheur County. We're still short a hundred and fifty workers to finish the harvest. We have tents here for temporary workers with so many folks going to alternative spots."

Welch paused in his narrative and turned to look at George. "I know with only you and Abe as laborers, your family is quite far down on the list for housing. Sorry I haven't come up with anything yet."

George hid his disappointment and said, trying to sound casual,

"Would it help if I went on a recruiting trip to Minidoka? There may be some who would come here to work and live in the labor camp. We may have exhausted the Portland folk, but those who were at Camp Harmony near Tacoma haven't been asked yet."

"That might be worthwhile." Welch paused. "It would be your last trip, though. After that, it will be too close to the first freeze."

"I understand." George tried not to sound too excited. "If you'll draw up the paperwork, I'll get my bag packed and be on tonight's train."

Welch nodded, the meeting ended, and George hurried over to his tent. How was he going to ask Molly to marry him when he didn't know where they'd be living for the winter? He had this one chance to convince her. Already, he was rehearsing what he would say.

***

When George arrived at the Minidoka office, Mr. Stafford hesitated, not certain he would let him into the camp. "You aren't a permanent resident, and you aren't staying. It's highly unusual for you to be a visitor here when technically you are on work leave and reside at the labor camp in Nyssa."

Stafford was at least fifty, with thinning brown hair and a bald spot in the back. He was heavyset, as round above his belt as below. "Excuse me while I look over your paperwork."

George waited impatiently. Had he traveled all this way for nothing? Was it possible he wouldn't even see Molly?

After a while, Stafford reappeared. "Welch from the Amalgamated Sugar Factory vouched for you. He said you'd likely be back in the spring to recruit for planting and thinning season, but this would be your only visit this fall. We'll have a meeting of the Block Representatives tomorrow after lunch. You can talk to them then and sign up as many workers as you can get for Nyssa and Ontario. The train going back leaves the next day early in the morning. Be sure you're ready." Stafford reached over the counter and shook George's hand. Then he turned to a young man with thick reading glasses who sat in front of a typewriter. "Harold? Would you walk this young man to Block 39? Get him settled in."

"Of course, sir."

George walked with Harold to Block 39. He knew Molly's family had been moved to Block 23. Perhaps they wouldn't be so far apart. He wanted to see her first, before he lost his nerve. He only had two nights and would be leaving on the third day. He hadn't managed to buy an engagement ring yet and knew he had to ask Mr. Mita for Molly's hand. He wished he weren't so nervous, but then again, he'd never asked anyone to marry him before.

CHAPTER TWENTY-TWO

MOLLY

Molly hurried across the large expanse between Huntsville Elementary School in Area One to residential Block 23 in Area Two. She was still confused occasionally by the size of the internment camp. Row upon row of tar-papered barracks looked like a rat's maze. The only thing that distinguished one barrack from another were the flowers and herb gardens planted outside the apartments of those who had first arrived from Camp Harmony.

Molly followed the main pathway in her rubber boots, holding an ugly brown coat close to her. It had been raining so much the raised footpath was the only way to avoid standing puddles. Many people were out in a lull between showers, and occasionally, Molly had to step off the pathway to allow others to pass. It was only when she crossed into Area Two that she began to recognize folks.

Molly and her family had moved out of the recreation hall and were living in the high school section in a room that would become a classroom. The barracks in Blocks 41, 42, and 44 were still being finished. The Mitas would be settled in one of those by the end of October.

The high school couldn't open yet, as there were no textbooks, no desks, and few teachers. However, the two elementary schools would begin tomorrow for grades one through six. Molly was going to work with a fifth-grade teacher, Miss Shepherd, in Stafford Elementary School, named after the camp's director.

Molly jumped over puddle after puddle as she got closer to her barracks. As she walked, she thought about George. He wrote to her faithfully, though she never found out enough about his life to imagine him in it. She was familiar with the names of his brothers and sister and knew about his hopes and dreams. She smiled to herself at his awkward declarations of love. He always closed his letters in that way, and sometimes she started at the end and then went back to the beginning. She picked up her pace, hoping a letter waited for her.

It took Molly almost fifteen minutes to get to Block 23. Her father had been dismissed from the hospital a week ago. As she neared her family's room, she saw him sitting outside on the steps enjoying the weak sunshine. His hands were clasped around one knee, and he was leaning backwards. His eyes were closed behind his thick glasses, and his thin face tilted up to get the most out of the rays. Molly could see his wrist bones extending out his shirtsleeves. She hated to disturb him.

"*Konnichiwa, Otoosan*," she said in greeting.

"*Konnichiwa, Musumesan*. How has your day been?"

"Good. I came to get Kameko to help me get the classroom ready for tomorrow."

"Thank you for that. She has too much idle time. We are fortunate you and Mary have found employment here."

Until her father regained his strength, he could not work. Mary's and Molly's jobs would bring in thirty-two dollars a month. Her mother was sewing in the recreation building, and although that enterprise was worthwhile, it only qualified them for a monthly clothing stipend. Thankfully, their patchwork of jobs was enough to survive on.

"Please excuse me, *Otoosan*." Molly bowed briefly to her father as he stood to let her pass.

The outside door opened to a landing. On the left was the Ashida family's apartment, and on the right was the Mita family's room. It contained five metal cots and a cast iron stove to burn wood or coal. They had no tables, no shelves, and no chairs. Others who had been there longer had scrounged lumber scraps to make furniture, but Molly's father had no experience with building things. Molly hoped their wages would be enough to pay for a few simple pieces.

She knocked on the door twice to give warning to anyone inside, bent down to remove her muddy boots, and waited a moment before entering in her stocking feet. Kameko sat up, blinking her eyes and brushing her hair back from her face.

"Were you sleeping?" Molly walked over and put her hand on Kameko's forehead. "You don't have a fever."

"I'm not sick. I was reading and fell asleep. I'm so bored!"

"I'm going over to Stafford Elementary to see what I can do to get the classroom ready. Why don't you come with me?"

"All right. When do you think the high school will open?" Kameko was anxious to start her freshman year. "I mean, it's crummy waiting around all the time. At least in Portland, we had things we could do."

"Patience, Kameko. Things are getting better, slowly but surely. Your oxfords are going to get dirty. Why don't you wear the boots?"

Someone else knocked on the door. Molly waited for her father to enter. The second time, the rapping was louder. Kameko opened the door a few inches.

A male voice asked, "Is Molly here?"

Molly sat still on Kameko's bed.

It couldn't be.

Kameko turned and grinned at her sister, nodding.

George stuck his head around the corner. "Molly?"

"George!" Molly ran to him, and he enfolded her in his arms.

Kameko turned quickly and looked out the window, her back to her sister. Then the Ashidas' door opened as well, the mother-in-law poking her head out. When she saw Molly in George's arms, she sniffed and shut it quietly.

Molly's joy dimmed a little as George released her. She tugged at her dress, glanced quickly at her sister, and said quietly, "Father?"

"He knows I'm here," George said smiling. "I caught him before he headed over to the recreation building."

George stood outside the doorway in his muddy shoes, and Molly couldn't invite him into the family's area without parents present.

"Is there somewhere we can go?" George preempted. "Kameko too, of course."

Molly smiled quickly at her sister. "Shall we take him to the classroom? Maybe he can help us put up some shelves and the maps. Let me get a knife to clean our shoes, and then we'll go."

"Classroom? You got that assistant position?"

"Yes, for fifth grade. The children are so excited! We begin tomorrow."

As they got ready, George waited outside on the steps. She had so much to tell him. She wondered how long he would be at Minidoka. He and his family should be able to move here as soon as the harvest ended. She waited impatiently while Kameko pulled on boots, found a coat in the suitcase, and tied a scarf around her head. Soon they stepped out to join George, Molly leading the way, chatting and beaming up at him.

***

That night, George ate with the Mita family in the mess hall. Mr. Mita dominated the conversation as he explained the organization of Minidoka.

"As a block, we all share the dining hall, laundry and showers, and recreation hall. There are nearly ten thousand people here at camp, four times as large as the assembly center in Portland. The Caucasian staff live near the entrance in units holding two families or two single teachers. The military police have their barracks outside the camp perimeter, also near the entrance."

To anyone curious enough to visit their table, Molly's father introduced George as a friend of the family and as the recruiter for the sugar factory in Nyssa. After dinner, Molly, her sisters, and George walked to the recreation building. There were two ping-pong tables and several places where people played games. A local radio station featured a Benny Goodman song.

Kameko went to find a board game to entertain them. "How's Monopoly? There are enough pieces for six."

"I'll go ask a couple more if they want to join us," Mary said. "There are so few games, we shouldn't hog it."

Molly took the brief opportunity to reach across the table and squeeze George's hand. "I'm sorry there's no privacy. Quiet hours begin at ten, so we have a little time. How are you?"

"I work and keep busy and then I get a letter from you. The whole world seems flat without you." George smiled at her tenderly. "Tell me about your teaching assistant job."

"It's a good position. I'll be working under Miss Shepherd. She's been teaching for almost twenty years here in Idaho. She told me she always wanted to be a missionary but was afraid to go abroad. She feels a foreign country came to her." Molly looked down and then back up into George's eyes. "I keep telling her I'm an American citizen. It just doesn't seem to register."

"I need to talk to you. Do you think we can slip away somehow?"

Molly had thought about this earlier and already had a plan. "Meet me in the laundry building an hour after curfew begins. I'll have to wait for Father and Mother to go to sleep. I can't be gone long." Molly knew she shouldn't sneak behind her parents' backs or violate curfew, but somehow being with George trumped everything else.

George nodded as Mary and two more girls came up to their table. They played Monopoly for the next two hours and teased each other as they traded properties back and forth. Molly didn't mind being in jail for three turns because then she could watch George. She studied the expressions on his face, trying to fix them in her mind. She wondered where the rendezvous in the laundry room would take them. She'd stolen only two kisses before he left Portland in August.

"George, it's your turn. You didn't even notice that Mary landed on your property. You're going to become the banker if you lose!" Kameko reminded him.

Molly laughed. She wasn't the only one who'd lost track of the game.

***

That evening, Molly rose from the bed quietly. She could hear her father snoring softly and her mother breathing gently. She put a coat over her pajamas and picked up her shoes. As she glanced down at her sisters, Mary stared back. Molly put a finger to her lips, Mary nodded, and Molly tiptoed out the door. She shut it behind her and slipped on her shoes.

The night was quiet. Smoke from the potbelly stoves rose from several compartments' chimneys. The stars twinkled in the black sky. With no cloud cover, it was colder than usual. Molly quickly walked to the sanitation building in the middle of their block. The laundry, latrines, and showers were all in one place; they just weren't working yet.

As she opened the main sanitation building's door, she caught a glimpse of George ducking into the entrance of the laundry. She rounded the corner and ran right into him. George's lips smothered her nervous giggle. Although they had exchanged quick, surreptitious kisses before, this was their first impassioned one. George broke it off and began to whisper to her, but Molly hushed him, took his hand, and led him to the corner farthest from the opening.

She could barely see George in the darkened room. She pulled away from him for a moment and felt his face with her fingertips. He had a high forehead with a long, handsome nose. His cheekbones were well-defined. As she explored his face, she could tell he was smiling. He had dimples in his cheeks and a strong jaw. Her fingers traced a muscular neck and an Adam's apple. A hint of aftershave lotion nearly made her swoon.

She kissed him softly and said, "I love you."

"I love you too, Molly." George kissed her lips again. "It's so hard being away from each other."

Molly was so nervous that she couldn't quit talking. "I don't understand how I can feel this deeply about you when we've known each other for only four months," she whispered.

He kissed her neck.

"I live for your letters."

He kissed her eyelids. She left her eyes closed and enjoyed the new sensations George created in her.

They heard someone whistling outside the building. She slid behind him and held her breath. It had to be one of the camp's policemen. A beam of light shot across the laundry area before sweeping the rest of the building. The guard walked on, resuming his tune.

"That was close." George turned to face Molly. "What would he do if he caught us?"

"I don't know. Perhaps escort me back to my unit—and my parents. I would be so ashamed. I have to get back. I'm sure I've been gone too long already." She put her arms around his neck. "Goodnight, George. Give me something to dream about?"

George drew her into him and kissed her softly. "I haven't told you anything about my plans. About us being together."

"I know." Molly paused a moment. "But I really must go."

"I'll see you tomorrow then. Do you want me to walk back with you at least part of the way?"

"No. I don't want anyone to see us together until . . ." Molly's voice trailed off.

"Until I've spoken to your father?"

"We have so much to talk about." She stepped closer to him and whispered into his ear. "I love you." She rained a series of soft kisses along his cheekbones, over his nose, and across the other side of his face. "Sweet dreams."

***

Molly's first day as a teacher's aide flew by. She stood at the doorway and greeted the thirty-three fifth graders as they filed into Miss Shepherd's classroom. Miss Shepherd was an experienced teacher. Her short, reddish-blonde hair was parted in the middle and curled tightly. She wore brown glasses shaped like cat's eyes, and her green eyes were flecked with gold. She was a stoic woman until she laughed, and then Molly wanted to laugh with her.

Students used picnic tables for desks, which was the best the camp could do for now. Six to eight students would sit at each, facing each other. When the students came into the classroom, the boys clumped together, and the girls sat on the opposite side. Two Caucasian boys, sons of teachers, isolated themselves in the back. Molly could tell from Miss Shepherd's frown that this wouldn't do.

Molly would oversee homeroom in the morning and study hall in the afternoon by herself. This was the only day Miss Shepherd would be with her during that time. She prepared Molly to take roll and give each child an American name if they didn't have one.

"Your parents were sensible, giving you your name," Miss Shepherd said. "I'll never be able to remember all these foreign ones."

Molly didn't tell Miss Shepherd that a first-grade teacher had been the first to call her Molly, the closest she could come to "Momoe," her real name. "I'll call you Molly so you can practice your 'L' sounds," her former teacher had said. "Most Japanese have such a hard time with it." Mary had the same teacher the following year that renamed her too, but she was gone by the time Kameko started school. That was why Kameko still had her Japanese name.

As long as she was renaming some of the children, Molly decided to integrate the classroom too.

"Stand up, children, and go to the back of the room. When I call your name, please sit at the next place at the table. You'll be seated alphabetically until we get to know you."

Two little girls held hands, clinging to each other. They waited silently.

Molly called each student's name, wrote their English names by their Japanese ones, and filled out a seating chart as she went. She asked each child without an English name to pick one as their first assignment. If Miss Shepherd required renaming, Molly at least wanted to give the students and their families some control over what their American names would be.

Many of the children didn't know each other, but most had at least a friend or two. There were groans and cheers as the children filled the tables, greeting each other with nods and small bows. The white boys were split up too, one a Barnes and the other a Wilson. The two little girls holding hands turned out to be cousins, both Sakamotos, and they climbed onto the bench together. Molly's underlying motivation for putting the children in a seating chart was to give the subtle message she was in charge. When she was done, however, half the children had their backs to the front of the room. That wouldn't do.

"Children, please stand up and turn your tables sideways so that I can see your faces and you can see me too."

All the control Molly had achieved was lost in the ensuing chaos. Benches hit the floor as the students climbed off them. The tables were so heavy, it took four or five children to turn each one. Molly intervened a couple of times to get the angles right. The clamoring voices made a mockery of the uneasy silence that began the day.

Miss Shepherd got up from her desk, crossed over to the doorway, and turned off the light. All the children stopped talking and looked over at her. "Thank you," she said in a mild voice. "Please be seated again, and listen for further instructions from Miss Mita." The class settled down immediately.

Molly made a mental note of the simple way to gain the children's attention. She handed out card stock and asked each student to write his or her name on it and to locate it above their spot at the table. "Use your best penmanship. Make it legible and neat. You may decorate it if you wish. For those of you who will choose your English name as homework, you will need to take these home to fill in this evening."

Molly helped hand out papers, collected them, supervised the children at their morning and afternoon recesses, ate lunch in the same mess hall, and assisted Miss Shepherd in any way she could. The students had a page each of addition, subtraction, multiplication, and division to complete during study hall at the end of the day. They were asked to write a letter to Miss Shepherd, introducing themselves to her. Molly allowed them to talk quietly and help each other. When they got too noisy, she remembered the teacher's trick and turned the light off and on. When it was time for the students to leave, she reminded them of their homework—to bring back an American name written on their name tag. At 3:25, the students put on their coats and lined up at the door. Molly let them leave one by one, trying to call them by name. She remembered about twenty of them. She'd do better tomorrow.

Molly had barely sat down when Miss Shepherd bustled into the room. "How do you think it went today?"

"The children were respectful and attentive. They seem eager to learn and happy to be back in school. That trick with the light really works, Miss Shepherd."

"I was pleased with how well you did, too. If we're going to work together as a team, you need to call me Alice. When the children are here, we'll have to be more formal, but not now. So . . . tomorrow. Let me show you how we'll structure the day . . ."

***

An hour later, Molly arrived home. She had a few minutes to lie down before supper began. At her doorway, she heard a hammer pounding inside. When she opened her door, she saw George and her father putting up nails in one corner of the room. Mary was hanging up the family's coats by the door. Molly slid her wrap off and added it to the others. Her mother was threading a rope through the hem of a sheet.

Kameko put a doily on top of her suitcase and slid it between two cots. She put her geisha doll on top of the doily and said, "There. That adds some decoration."

"George is helping us get the room settled," Molly's mother said in greeting. "He has an idea for separating the room so we will have a bit more privacy." She gave the rope to George, who stood on a rustic wooden chair, tied one end of the rope to the nail on the side of the stud, and brought the other end to the nail on the crossbeam at the ceiling.

Molly sank down on her cot, sliding her shoes underneath. Her eyes sought George's, and she smiled up at him, content to watch the bustle of action. To be honest, she was too tired to match the energy in the room.

Her father brought a new bench over for her inspection. "George showed me how to make it. I have enough wood for another one and plans for a table."

"I'll be able to hang our laundry inside to dry too." Her mother seemed happy with all the new uses for the ropes. "I have another sheet I can hem after dinner."

"Can you hang our flag and this pretty table runner? It would give us some decoration for the wall." Mary was showing the two items to George.

"Where do you want to put the table, Father?" Kameko asked, intent on arranging the small room to its best advantage. "Here under the window so you'll have some light? Or right in the center under the hanging bulb?"

Molly put her feet up and lay her head on her pillow. Amid the noise and confusion, she shut her eyes and rested.

***

That evening in the recreation hall, Molly led George to a pair of chairs in the corner. Although everyone in the room could see them, the noise from the radio and the chatter of friends and neighbors made the corner an oasis of privacy.

"You're leaving in the morning?" Molly asked.

"Yes. I've recruited another fifty workers, mostly from Seattle and Tacoma." George paused and licked his lips. "You know, I won't be back until spring."

"Spring?" Molly leaned forward and gripped George's hand. "I thought your family was assigned to Minidoka and would be here after the harvest!"

"I . . . I want to come be with you, but I hope to find lodging in the CCC camp. Thomas and—"

Molly interrupted him. "You *want* to be away from me? Why not come here?"

"I can't make enough money."

"Money? That's more important than we are?"

"No, Molly. I don't mean it that way. I want you to marry me."

Molly let go of George's hand. "Marry you?" Her hands tightened into fists. "This is the way you propose?"

"This is coming out all wrong." George reached over to her. "I want you to marry me and live in Nyssa with my family."

"I can't." She sat back abruptly. "You're not the only one with family to care for. I have a job for the winter too, you know." She answered in a flat voice, her face struggling to hide her emotions.

"I know that." George swiped his face with his hand. Small beads of perspiration appeared on his forehead. "I didn't mean for the conversation to go this way. I love you! I want us to be together too. It's just that Eastern Oregon . . . I mean . . ."

"I don't think you know what you mean," Molly spat, leaning away from him and folding her arms across her chest.

"I can't be cooped up," George said. "I'd die here behind a fence with guards and watchtowers! I'm trying to make enough money to save our farm. I have to pay off the bank loan, and more taxes are due next spring. I don't want to lose everything my father and I have worked for." George's voice was pleading, his hands reaching out to her in frustration.

"My father lost everything," Molly said. "Perhaps it would be better if you had, too. Then you'd know what really matters in life." She stood, her expression unreadable. "Goodbye, George. I'll see you in the spring."

Molly fled the recreation area and barely made it outside before bursting into tears. She ran back to the apartment. The lights were off inside, and she was glad her parents had gone to bed early. She stood outside for a moment, getting herself under control. Slipping off her shoes, she tiptoed to her bed, found her pajamas under her pillow, and undressed.

"Momoe?" Her father spoke to her from his side of the curtain.

"*Hai, Otoosan.*"

"Your young man leaves tomorrow?"

"*Hai.*" Her voice quavered.

"He is a good man. He has not yet matured into the man he will be, but he has promise. Be patient with him. He will learn."

"*Hai*, Papa. I am afraid for us. He says he'll stay near Nyssa this winter."

"Momoe, if your mother and I could find each other across the ocean, you and George can manage the distance across Idaho!" Her father laughed wryly.

Molly climbed into bed. *If* George wanted to meet her halfway. Maybe he didn't love her as much as she loved him.

CHAPTER TWENTY-THREE

ELLIS

Ellis's favorite time of the year was when the fields went dormant. He didn't have to hoe, irrigate, or top beets. Instead, as daylight faded earlier, he spent hours practicing the piano and trombone. He lived in a world of flats, sharps, and rhythm. Yet even his music wasn't the same as before the war. New hits filled the airwaves, and he practiced "The Boogie Woogie Bugle Boy of Company B." Those Andrew Sisters recorded one smash after another.

The war invaded the kitchen, too, in the form of food ration cards. The maps of the war theater dominated the wall catty-corner to the dining room table. With two brothers in the service and Sam at Oregon State College, the contrast between war and peace was even more stark. Mae immersed herself in writing daily letters to Ellis's three brothers, and the postman's delivery was a cause for celebration or gloom. Even his mild-mannered father was dour, surly, and morose. A dark cloud of disquiet hung over Ellis.

***

One afternoon, Ellis opened the postbox and brought in a letter from Luke. His mother saved it until after the family had eaten and then read it out loud for all to enjoy.

November 5, 1942

Dear Family,
I've received new orders. I'm shipping out, although I can't tell you where.

"Oh, no! He's going to the front." Mae crushed the letter to her chest.

"Probably Africa," Lee guessed. "The British are fighting Rommel in El Alamein for the second time."

Mae smoothed out the note and continued.

I won't be able to come home first, as I've had leave within the last six months. I'll be working in logistics, although why the Army wants a flier to work on the ground, I don't know. As the comics say, 'When you gotta go, you gotta go.' I'll try to write frequently, but sometimes events get in the way.
Know that I love you and I'll come home to you.
Luke

Mae sniffed a bit and wiped her eyes. "I always feel our boys are safe as long as they are billeted in the States."

"One thing to be thankful for is that he'll be working in logistics," Lee reminded her. "All the boys want to see action, and he'll be disappointed not to be flying. But he'll be safer this way."

"What's logistics?" asked Emily.

"He'll be dispensing tents, cots, food, fuel, parts, and repairs—all that kind of thing. He'll be in the rear lines."

"Then that's good, right, Ma?" Ellis wanted his mother to see the silver lining of Luke's letter.

"I hope so." She dropped her eyes to the letter to read it through one more time. "I wonder when Donald will go. He enlisted before Luke."

Lee got up and went to the world map hanging on the wall. Emily and Ellis joined their father, trying to digest what was happening in the battles that could soon involve their brother.

Mae sat alone, staring off into a middle ground of gloom.

***

After Luke's letter, something began to gnaw at Ellis's father. Usually, Lee enjoyed the slower pace of his winter chores. He'd putter in his shop, mending harnesses and repairing equipment to use in the spring. He'd whistle or listen to the radio's programs. This year, however, Ellis thought he seemed restless, taciturn, and lost in his thoughts. He wished his father were more verbal, but Lee tended to stew over issues until he either figured out what he was going to do or the worry subsided. Until then, Ellis fretted too.

Each night, the family listened to the evening radio broadcasts. On November the 8th, II Corps attacked the Vichy French Atlantic naval base in Casablanca. It was the first land and sea operations the United States had fought in. By November 10th, Americans surrounded the port, and the city surrendered. In a newspaper photo, British warplanes called Supermarine Spitfires were shipped by sea and assembled at RAF North Front, Gibraltar by American and British soldiers. They put together 116 aircraft in eleven days.

"Do you think that's where Luke is going, Pa?" Emily asked.

"Could be. The censors will keep him quiet about location and mission. Who knows who's listening in?"

Ellis watched his father's concentration. On the family map, Lee color-coded the pins: red for Nazis, yellow for Japanese, green for Italians, white for English, and blue for the Americans. Every time he stuck in a pin, it seemed as though his mouth clamped tighter. Three days later, the British recaptured Tobruk, Libya. On November 22nd, Lee moved the second Nazi front to Stalingrad in Russia. In the Pacific, the Marines were fighting the Japanese over a tiny speck of an island few had ever heard of—Guadalcanal.

After three weeks of nightly winter routine, Lee finally opened his mouth. "I can't just sit here while the war is being fought all around the world. I know I'm too old to fight, but I can still be of use. I know how to weld and how to fix and build things. I'm going to Portland to apply for a job at the Kaiser Shipyard for the winter."

"But you've done your part!" Mae protested. "You served in the Great War. And we have two sons in this one."

"Please understand. I have to help with the war effort." Lee covered Mae's hand with his own.

"But we'll be alone!" Mae snatched back her hand. "How will we manage without you?"

Emily and Ellis exchanged glances. Their parents had never fought in front of them before.

"I'll send home most of the money I make. We'll get ahead some. We need extra in case we hire any Japanese next spring. I doubt we'll be able to farm as many acres as last year with labor scarce as it is."

"And the chores? How will we manage them?"

"Ellis can milk the cows. I've finished what few repairs there were. I need to go."

"No. You don't *need* to go. You *want* to go!" Mae's voice broke with the accusation.

His father took a deep, audible breath. When he spoke again, his tone was flat. Detached. "I'll be leaving Friday after we've celebrated Thanksgiving. That will give you some time to pack for me. I won't need much."

"And what about Christmas? Can the war effort spare you for a day then?" Mae asked hotly.

"I might get the day off, but I doubt I'll have more time than that. War doesn't stop for holidays." His father reached across the table and held his mother's hand. "War means sacrifice. Even for us at home. I won't be risking my life, but perhaps making ships for the Navy will get our boys into the fight sooner and get Hitler, Mussolini, and Tojo out of the war business."

He stood up, signaling the end of their conversation.

***

After Thanksgiving, Ellis, Emily and Mae saw Lee off at the train station. On the drive home, Mae vented her frustrations.

"I know your father feels this effort is necessary and that as a man, he needs to go work on the ships. But our family is important too. We used to have a happy family of seven, and now it's only us."

Ellis listened silently. He knew there was no point in arguing with his mother. Perhaps she felt she needed her children to agree with her.

"Before Pearl Harbor," she continued, "I had a plan for all of you kids. Each son would help the next go to college. I knew all the girls you could pick for brides."

Ellis remembered Luke's warning about dating the girls from the youth group and hid a grin.

"Your father would make a success of the homestead with all of his sons helping. We would have something to leave you and the grandchildren." Her eyes gleamed with her vision of their future.

Then she looked at Ellis and said bitterly, "Now it's chaos! The Jap attack on Pearl Harbor ruined everything. If it hadn't been for Tojo and Hirohito, we'd have stayed out of this fight."

Ellis watched the speedometer as his mother approached a sharp turn. "Careful, Ma. You're going too fast."

Mae slowed the car, but her rant continued. "Your father is going to live somewhere in Portland, Sam is in Corvallis, Luke shipped out to who-knows-where, and Donald will be the next one to leave the States." She hit the steering wheel with the palm of her hand. "I hate this war! What it's doing to all of us." The car swerved as Mae pulled out to pass the car ahead of her. "I can't control what's happening. I feel like a marionette, being yanked this way and that by all those strings."

Emily gripped Ellis's hand as their mother pulled back into her own lane.

"It's all right, Ma," Ellis said. "Calm down. We'll be fine."

His mother bit her lower lip. She slowed down and drove more carefully. She didn't speak again until she turned off the highway. "And your father left us!" His mother sounded so bewildered. "I didn't think he'd ever do that."

She drove into the driveway, turned off the engine, and covered her face with her hands. "You kids go on. I have to pull myself together."

Ellis held his sister's hand for the first time in years as they made their way into the yard and down the stairs into the house.

When they reached the kitchen, Emily turned into him and put her head on his chest. In a small voice, she asked, "What are we going to do? I'm so scared. And we're all alone."

"No, we're not. We just need to give Ma some time." They stood together for a few minutes, then Ellis took her arms and held her out so he could see her face. "Let's fix the fire and get something ready for supper. Ma will be in soon."

"Do you think it'd be all right if I moved into the bedroom with her?" Emily asked. "I'd feel safer if we were closer together at night."

"I don't think she'd mind. Why don't you go on and move some of your stuff into Pa's drawer? I'll see what there is to eat."

By the time Mae came inside, Ellis and Emily had set the table, fixed a hash that made the room fragrant with cooked onions, and warmed the house with a hearty fire. As the only male left in the household, Ellis said the traditional blessing before they ate. Afterward, he reached over and squeezed his mother's hand.

"We'll be fine, Ma. We just have to have courage, that's all."

Emily smiled at him from across the table, and they began their first meal with just the three of them.

After supper, Ellis turned on the radio to listen to the news. Further gasoline rationing would begin on December first. As the broadcaster relayed new war events, Ellis picked up a blue pin and stuck it into the map of Italy. The United States had bombed the Naples harbor.

CHAPTER TWENTY-FOUR

ABE

Abe stepped into one of the five barracks that had sheltered the Civilian Conservation Corps boys. They were responsible for the government pipes and ditches bringing water to the sagebrush desert from the Owyhee Dam. Once war was declared, the young men between the ages of eighteen and twenty-three joined the service, abandoning the CCC. Known as BR 43—Bureau of Reclamation, camp number 43—the Farm Security Administration had turned it over to the War Relocation Authority as a Japanese relocation facility beginning in November 1942. The locals called it "Cow Hollow."

Abe examined the simple construction, knowing the barracks were considered portable. Each CCC camp was made with the same materials, same floorplans, and same construction. Forty men stayed in each barrack, with forty cots and forty footlockers. The barracks were twenty by one hundred and thirty feet. Three dusty, black, cast-iron stoves located in the middle and at each end provided heat. There was no insulation in the walls nor in the open-beamed ceiling.

The Yano family would occupy the middle section of the building. It was certainly larger than the compartments at the Portland Assembly Center or the tents at the labor camp. Unfortunately, materials for solid walls to separate the living units were scarce. Perhaps the FSA would be able to spare some canvas from the tents they'd just taken down. Or they could tear down one of the barracks and reuse the wood to create internal walls. Abe was sure there was plenty of work to do.

First, though, each compartment needed to be cleaned. Cobwebs covered the windows and rafters. He hadn't seen any bat droppings but was on the lookout. Feral cats roamed the grounds, so perhaps the mice and rats were under control.

It was better than the tents at the labor camp, Abe thought, but nowhere as nice as their home in Toppenish. He recalled his conversation with his mother—that they would live where they were destined to be. Somehow, George finagled the housing. His mother Chiharu would serve as one of the cooks, and Thomas would set up for meals and wash dishes. Neither George nor Abe had formal positions—hence, no pay. That gave the family twenty-four dollars a month. Not even a dollar a day. Instead, Abe would volunteer as a carpenter and general repairman, and George would continue as a camp board member.

Abe set down his toolbox beside a stack of Pamela's books. A string of light bulbs ran down the middle of the exposed rafters, and small windows were spaced every four feet or so on both sides. A two-hole latrine sat behind the unit for the barrack's use. The board planned to convert the water system so each unit would have running water and an inside toilet, but that would take some time. There were no tables or chairs. That was a project Abe could start on right away if he could find some scrap lumber.

So, this is what George had chosen over spending the winter with Molly at Minidoka. Abe was sure he wouldn't have made the same decision. Molly sounded too sweet. At least the Yanos didn't have to buy furniture, an expense they could ill afford. Abe looked at the forty cots. He remembered that the fifth barracks was going to be used as storage. They could move most cots out of the middle section, leaving only the five his family needed.

His musings were interrupted when Thomas and George entered with the duffle bag and two suitcases. Pamela followed, struggling with two suitcases, her own and their mother's. Chiharu toted a bushel basket full of dishes, pictures, and the embossed tin she used as a bank. Doctor Yamaguchi set aside two suitcases and his medical bag.

"If you see a brown leather one, I'm still missing it," Doc said.

Abe hurried out to the heap of luggage the sugar factory trucks had dumped to the side of the circular drive and found Doc's suitcase underneath the stack. The leather bag had survived another move, but one side of the handle had broken. Abe sighed. It seemed as though he was fixing, mending, or patching something every day.

Abe returned, passed Doc his suitcase, and asked him how things were going.

"About as good as can be expected," Doc replied. "The missus is anxious to make up the beds and have me build a fire. Just not enough time in the day to make everyone happy."

"The CCC boys left us kindling and some wood," Abe said. "Do you want me to bring some over? I can start a fire for you."

"I wouldn't want to leave you short."

"It's okay. I'll chop some more. I saw branches in a heap out by a shed when we drove in. The cooks will have supper ready by six."

Abe headed out to the woodpile.

That afternoon was busy for all the new residents. Men and older boys came to get the wood Abe chopped, and soon smoke billowed out of the various chimneys. When Abe finally had split enough wood for everyone, he stacked the extra under a lean-to. He wiped the sweat from his brow and swung his arms back and forth. He knew whenever he couldn't find something else to do, he could always add to the woodpile.

When he came inside, Abe realized his mother was still in the mess hall, preparing the evening's meal. George had gone to town for additional groceries. And Pamela and Thomas had rearranged the remaining beds in their portion of the barracks. Already, Cow Hollow was starting to feel more permanent, more like a home. Just in time too. Temperatures were dropping fast.

***

After a week in the CCC camp, Abe and George were at odds again. Abe had gritted his teeth for so long, his jaw ached. George snapped at him for anything and nothing, and then quickly apologized. That rankled Abe as much as anything. If George knew he was in the wrong, why snap at Abe in the first place? In desperation—and also because Abe was sure he was going to haul off and hit his brother before too long—he turned to his mother.

"What is wrong with George?" he asked her. "He's up, down, and sideways. I'm losing my patience with him!"

"It has to be about Molly. He cannot decide what to do."

"You mean the girl who was writing him all those letters?"

"Yes. But the letters have stopped coming. You didn't notice?"

Abe turned his head sideways, thinking through recent events. "Something must have happened when George went to Minidoka. He hasn't been the same since. Now that I think about it, he's also stopped writing. I used to enjoy how much each composition tortured him as he wrote it."

"And you, my son? What have you been contemplating?"

Abe looked at his mother in surprise. She had an uncanny way of reading his mind. "I've been thinking of leaving Cow Hollow and going to Minidoka to rejoin the group from Portland. I enjoyed helping with the construction projects there and know Minidoka needs skilled carpenters. I feel I would be more useful there."

"Then what is stopping you?"

"I should be here to help George."

"No one can help him with his heart except himself. Still, be gentle when you tell him. He won't have you around to spar with and he will miss you."

Abe nodded and excused himself. He walked one orbit around the camp, just to let the idea settle in, then went to find his older brother.

He found George whacking at sagebrush outside the camp area. His coat lay on the ground, and perspiration glistened on his forehead. His arms and shoulder muscles flexed as he hefted the ax above his head. Then, he brought it down hard on the hapless roots. C-r-r-a-c-k! On the ground were branches and twigs ready to haul to the covered woodpile. George separated kindling from the rest.

"You tryin' to kill that sagebrush?" Abe asked, announcing himself. "It needs to be in large enough pieces to burn for a while, you know."

George hit the root one last time, severing it. "'Bout time you showed yourself! You can haul this wood back to the pile and bring out another axe. Even if you aren't getting paid, you can make yourself useful."

Abe took a calming breath. "That's what I came to talk to you about. I don't feel like I'm pulling my weight here. I can't find any paid work. I've been thinking about heading to Minidoka. I hear they pay their skilled workers sixteen dollars a month. That would be enough for me, and I could help the folks there. The camp is still under construction."

George stopped his swing and lowered the ax. "The watchtowers don't bother you? The soldiers? The mess halls? The latrines? You know the dust blows continually, and it's been in the low twenties there."

"I can put up with it—as long as I keep busy. I'll get caught up in projects and ignore the rest."

"Then you're a better man than I am. I get the willies inside that camp." George looked away for a bit, contemplating something. Then he asked, "Would you do me a favor? Would you look up my girl, see how she and her folks are getting on? You don't have to tell her I asked you to. Just write to me and let me know how it's going."

"Anything in particular you want me to find out? Any message to take to her?"

"I . . . I . . . can't think of anything."

Abe had never seen George so unsure of himself. "What's stopping you from communicating with Molly?"

"Money. Survival. Obligation. We got so serious so fast." George shook his head. "How can I write to her if I can't include her in any future I can envision? I've written to Franklin asking about farming our place this coming year. Renting it to him. That would bring in some money to replace what I took out from Thomas's college fund for this month's mortgage. Then there are taxes this spring and—"

"What? You took money put aside for Thomas? Out of Mother's tin. Did you ask her?"

George looked guilty. "She doesn't know yet. I hope to replace it before she notices."

"I can't believe you stole the money." Abe looked for some sign of contrition. Instead, George's face hardened.

"The farm comes first, not some vague plan to send Thomas to medical school. The family must understand that."

Abe shoved George so hard, he stumbled backward and fell.

"Don't get up," Abe said. He stood over him, breathing hard. "I don't want to hit you."

George narrowed his eyes at his younger brother. They'd been in disagreements before, but Abe had never been physical.

George yelled up at Abe. "Maybe you'd just better go!"

"I will." Abe bit off his words. "Every cent I send goes back into the tin for Thomas. Do you understand? Your priorities are all fouled up." He kicked the stack of kindling, scattering it far and wide. "Family comes first, not the damn farm."

"Don't ask for my blessing," George warned. He sat up slowly.

"I don't need yours." Abe's fists rested on his hips. "I already have Mother's."

There was nothing left for the brothers to say.

CHAPTER TWENTY-FIVE

GEORGE

George found his mother moaning and lying on the floor, clutching her belly in the CCC camp kitchen. It was mid-morning in December, and no one else was around. He rushed over to her and knelt down. "What's wrong? Are you hurt?"

"It's nothing. A small pain. It will go away." Panting, she tried to sit up. Tiny sweat beads dotted her forehead. She laid back down and drew her knees up to her chest.

"How long have you felt this way?" George touched her forehead. She was burning up.

"My stomach was hurting when I got up this morning, but now I have pain farther down in my abdomen."

George took off his jacket and put it under her head. "I'm going to get Doc. I'll be right back."

Her weak protests followed him out the kitchen door. He ran to the small dispensary where the physician's family lived and pounded on the door. Doc's youngest son opened it as Doc came out of the back room. He already had his black medical bag in hand.

"What's happened? Who's hurt?" Doc asked.

"It's my mother. She's got a fever and is clutching her stomach. It's something wrong with her gut. She's in the mess hall."

"Could be several causes. We may need to take her to the hospital in Ontario. Can you get a car or a truck ready just in case?"

By the time George got the camp's truck and drove it to the kitchen, Doc had his stethoscope on Chiharu's belly, asking questions.

"I do not wish to be trouble. Surely I will recover . . ." Chiharu trailed off.

When he saw George, Doc barked, "Call the hospital and tell them we are bringing in a patient who might have an inflamed appendix. I hope we're in time, and it hasn't ruptured yet. If you see anyone on your way to the office, send 'em to me. I'll need help getting her into the truck."

Five minutes later, George was racing to the highway, with Doc in the seat talking reassuringly to his mother. When he pulled into the emergency entrance forty-five minutes later, Chiharu was biting on Doc's handkerchief to keep from crying out in pain.

When emergency attendants came out to the pickup and opened the door, Doc told them his fears: namely, that Chiharu had a ruptured appendix.

The attendants ushered them inside, where a physician took the lead. He noted Doc's stethoscope. "You a doctor?"

"Yes, sir. I serve the Japanese laborers and their families," Doc said.

"She doesn't speak English?" the physician asked, motioning toward Chiharu.

"Not much. If you would permit me to observe, I could also translate for Mrs. Yano and you."

It seemed clear to George that Doc didn't want to let his patient out of sight.

"It's a bit unusual, but we seem to live in unusual times," the physician said.

George walked beside his mother, holding her hand until he reached the operating room door.

"You can't go any farther, young man," the physician said. "We'll find you in the waiting room once we're finished."

George kissed his mother's hand, and the physician wheeled Chiharu into an examination room. The doors swooshed shut behind them.

George tried to contain his nerves, first by pacing the floor and then by napping in short stints, his head resting against the wall. His eyes were closed, and he was snoring softly when someone patted him on the knee.

"George?" he heard. "Wake up."

"Huh? Yeah, I'm awake." He sat up and rubbed his hands over his face. Doc was bent over, looking at him. "How's Mom? How'd it go?"

"The appendix has been removed, but it was perforated.

Fortunately, the doctors had sulfa drugs available, and they have packed the abdominal cavity and the layers of the wound. I don't think the infection spread too far. Your mother will be in the hospital at least two weeks. She'll need you with her when she wakes up."

"She's going to be all right?"

"There's a risk of infection. It's possible something could go wrong. But these doctors used the most modern surgical techniques, and sulfa is almost a miracle drug. Your mother is a strong woman. She'll fight for her life."

"You couldn't have done the operation?"

"No. I'm not a member of the staff, but I observed it. I believe the doctors here have done the best they can."

George turned away as he struggled to keep his emotions in check. His father had taught him the virtue of *gaman*, a Buddhist belief of stoic endurance, of self-control, discipline, and strength in distressing times. He focused his mind away from the swirl of emotions and on the practical problems that could be solved. "So, if I stay with Mom, how are you going to get back to the camp?"

"I thought I would drive back, get Thomas and Pamela, and return. It will take a couple of hours. You can think of what arrangements to make while I'm gone."

George reached into his pocket. "Here's the key. Have Pamela pack a small bag so she can stay overnight if needed. Which way is the recovery room?"

***

After a two-week stay, Chiharu still was not well enough to come home. The abdominal infection complicated her recovery, but at least she hadn't required a second surgery. Pamela stayed at the hospital for the first week, until the doctors said Chiharu was out of danger. George saw her every morning, so he could catch the doctors as they made their rounds.

The hospital bills grew until they reached the point George knew was coming: It would take the rest of their savings to pay them. For the second time, George found his mother's colorful, embossed tin and took out the rest of the money they had saved for Thomas's college fund. His hand trembled as he held it. He knew it was not enough to foot the tax bill owed on their Toppenish farm nor the spring mortgage payments. He had held onto the farm less than a year. He recalled the threat in his brother's voice, that this money was for Thomas and he wasn't to touch it. He folded it and put it in his pocket. *Shikata ga nai.* Surely Abe would understand.

In the weeks of uncertainty about whether their mother would live, George had done a lot of thinking. Not only was the farm lost, but the family was fractured. He wished he could talk to Abe. He missed his brother. No point in worrying his mother about her condition, and Thomas and Pamela were too young—no use bothering them either. He sure made a mess of things. Maybe this was what Molly meant when she told him he didn't understand what was important in life.

He needed to be upfront with Abe about the hospital bills and ask for his forgiveness for using the money earmarked for Thomas. But more than anything, now that he had nothing to offer Molly, he needed to tell her how much he loved her. He was no longer that dashing recruiter with a shining future. He may have waited too long. Molly may have given up on him.

With a heavy heart, George sat down to write three letters: one to the bank, one to ask Franklin if he wanted to buy the farm, and one to Abe. Then he needed to find a way to go to Minidoka and see Molly. He didn't trust his letter-writing skills enough to write that fine of a love letter.

Chapter Twenty-Six

Molly

Molly had never felt heartbreak before. And now, it had been a month and a half since George had visited Minidoka. He hadn't written since she'd turned down his proposal. She felt as though she could cry at any moment. If Miss Curtis didn't depend on her to be at school every day, she would have stayed in bed with the covers over her head. At least at school, the children distracted her with their demands for her full attention.

Molly trudged through the snow to the apartment. When she arrived, no one was there. She shrugged out of her coat and hung it on a nail by her bed. Rubbing her arms, she opened the potbelly stove and stirred the coals. She propped sagebrush branches on top. That would warm the room nicely.

Mary came in then, removing the scarf from her head. "A young man came into the educational building today asking about you."

"Really? Anyone you recognize?"

"I think he was in the PAC with us but left with his family for the sugar beet fields in Nyssa. I can't remember his name, though." Mary frowned.

"He's not another suitor Mother might have sent?" With George out of the picture, her mother had once again stepped up her matchmaking ways.

"No. He's your age or perhaps mine. Cute, though." Mary arched her eyebrows mischievously.

"What did you tell him?"

"That you were a teacher's aide at one of the elementary school buildings. I just confirmed that you were an employee. If you want to find him, he works in the carpentry shop."

"How do you know that? Did he tell you?"

"He had his toolbox with him and some sawdust on his pants. I thought it best to let you decide if you wanted to talk with him or not."

"Thanks, Mary. Curious, huh?"

***

Molly heard a hammer pounding in the maintenance building. She followed the sound into a shop and saw a handsome young man building a crude teacher's desk. A hand drill and a rip saw lay nearby. He was concentrating so hard on his task that she observed him for a minute. When he paused, she said, "I hear you're looking for me."

He looked up at her over the desk's flat surface, then brushed sawdust from his hands and asked, "Are you Molly?"

"Molly Mita, yes. Who are you?" She gazed at him curiously.

"Abe Yano."

"George's brother?" Her eyes widened. "Is he here too?"

"No. I came alone."

Molly's hopeful face fell back into a neutral countenance. "Where's the rest of your family?"

"They're staying at an old CCC camp near Nyssa." Abe tilted his head to one side as he looked her up and down. "You're as pretty as George described. No wonder he's a mess."

"A mess?" Molly asked, stricken. "What is the matter with him? Is he ill?"

"He's sick, all right," Abe said. "His heart is broken."

"Please. Don't toy with me. I haven't heard from him in six or seven weeks. We used to write letters every day. How is he?"

"Miserable, frightened, angry, short-tempered, abrupt. His emotions are all over the place. None of them good."

"Did George send you?" Molly asked.

"In a way." Abe paused. He didn't think Molly needed to know about his and George's estrangement. "I wanted to come help out, but he has our family settled now and our two younger siblings in school. He asked me to check on you and let him know how you're doing. Will you write to him?"

"No, Abe. He must take the first step."

"What do I tell him then?"

Molly shrugged. "He needs to ask me himself. How hard can it be to pick up a pen and write?"

Abe laughed. "I sure hope love is easier than this for me."

Molly smiled a bit crookedly. "I didn't expect it to be this hard either."

An uncomfortable silence added to the difficult situation.

"Listen," Abe began, "I sorta told George I'd check to see how your family was doing. Would it be okay if I meet the rest of the Mitas?"

Molly thought about it for a bit. "Just don't give my mother any ideas. She's looking high and low for a husband for me."

Abe laughed. "George doesn't fit the bill?"

"He might for me," Molly said, "but I think she's getting desperate. Anyway, we'll be at the recreation center tonight. Stop by, and I'll introduce you."

***

Molly kept a lookout for Abe as she and her sisters and friends played their usual game of Monopoly. Her parents sat together in the corner in the same spot she and George had quarreled. They were reading a couple of newspapers from other internment camps. It was one way to follow the lawsuits filed against the United States government for their imprisonment. It also let them keep track of friends who'd gone to other sites: Wyoming or Tule Lake in California.

When Abe finally came in the door, he had a letter in his hand and he looked upset. Molly waved to get his attention. Abe held the letter behind his back as he was introduced to Mary, Kameko, and their friends.

Abe did a double take when he met Mary. "Aren't you the one I asked about Molly?"

Mary nodded her head and smiled at her wiles.

"I'll have to keep my wits about me when you're around," Abe teased.

When Molly led him to her parents, Abe greeted them in Japanese and bowed formally. "Father, this is Abe Yano, brother to George. Mother, this is Abe."

Her parents bowed back, and Mr. Mita said, "Your Japanese is fluent. Where did you go to school?"

"In Japan. My uncle and his family allowed me to stay with them for five years while I learned to read and write in Japanese. I hoped to be a bilingual lawyer and represent Japanese-American clients. I still have that dream, but it has been deferred for now." Abe hoped he didn't sound too proud of his interrupted plans. "George asked me to check in with the Mita family to be sure you are well and finally settled here. I understand it was a few weeks before you were able to have your own apartment."

"It is kind of your brother to be concerned. Please assure him of our welfare," Mr. Mita replied.

Abe glanced over at Mrs. Mita. She was listening intently.

"And your family? I hope they are well," Mr. Mita said.

Abe brought out a letter from his back pocket. "Actually, I just learned that my mother has undergone surgery for a ruptured appendix. Dr. Yamaguchi assures me she will be well, but it will take time to recover."

"Oh, no, Abe!" Molly exclaimed. "You just found out?"

Abe nodded his head.

"I'm so sorry to hear your news," Molly said, switching back to English as her parents excused themselves from the table. "Why don't you sit here? I'll leave you alone so you can reply."

Molly returned to her sisters and friends, but the game had grown old, and they were putting the pieces and the money back into the cardboard box. Molly quietly told her sisters what she'd learned about Mrs. Yano.

Mary looked over at Abe as he wrote his letter and said, "He looks so forlorn. I wonder if he needs company."

Molly peered closer at her sister. She'd never known Mary to express interest in any man before. "I think it's too soon. Maybe when he finishes writing."

Mary reached into her bag for her crocheting. Molly hid her smile. Abe had already made a big impression on Mary. Molly couldn't imagine her shy sister grabbing *his* attention.

George. Poor man. Her heart ached for him and his mother. It would be all too easy to write to him first. But then he wouldn't learn the lesson she knew he needed. He wasn't yet a man who knew how to care for others on their terms. And really, what could she say to a man she wasn't sure loved her?

CHAPTER TWENTY-SEVEN

ELLIS

Ellis came home from school with his pocket torn and his band music muddied. Mae found him in the kitchen, trying to clean the music with a damp rag.

"What happened?"

"Nothin'. Just dropped my music, is all." Ellis kept working patiently, cleaning off the mud but not rubbing so hard as to eliminate the print.

Mae moved around Ellis to inspect his efforts more closely. "Your pocket is torn!" She looked up into Ellis's eyes. "Tell me the truth, son. What happened?"

Ellis bent down and blew on the spot he'd been working on. "Nothin'. Let it go, Ma."

"If you're not goin' to tell her, I will." Emily came into the kitchen, bright spots on her cheeks.

"Tell me what?"

Ellis turned around, facing his younger sister. "Em! Let it go. You know Pa's rule. If I need help, I'll ask for it."

If he was supposed to be the man of the house with his father working at the shipping yards in Portland, he needed to be strong. That didn't mean just physically strong. He needed to be mentally and emotionally strong too. Butch might beat him up, but he'd never outsmart him.

"Someday, Butch is going to really hurt you, and then it'll be too late," Emily said. "Ma needs to know what's goin' on!"

"Butch Butler? He's still after you for Jeannie and Jimmy's drownings?" Mae asked. "He was there too, wasn't he?"

"He's never stopped blaming Ellis," Emily said. "Except now, he does small things, like knock Ellis's books out of his arms or push him into the lockers. Today, when he hit the books out of Ellis's arms and his music went flying, Butch walked right over top of them in his muddy boots. Didn't say a word." Emily's whole face flushed a bright red.

"And your pocket? How did that happen?" Mae persisted.

"Butch tried to slam my locker shut," Ellis confessed, "but it caught on my pocket. I think you can fix it. It doesn't look too bad."

"He does things like this every day?"

"It's really not that bad, Ma. The principal told him if he hit me, he'd be out of school for good."

Emily's voice raised a couple octaves. "The only reason he hasn't beat you up is that your friends try to be around all the time. He's going to catch you alone one of these days. I just know it!"

"I'll go talk to the Butlers," Mae said. "We don't need to involve the school. Surely, they'll talk to Butch."

"No, Ma!" Ellis lowered the volume. "It'll just make it worse. Then I'll be a momma's boy. Leave it alone. I'll ask for help if I need it."

***

"Mornin', Ellis," Stan called. Stan was the center for the boys' varsity basketball team and towered above Ellis. At five and a half feet, Ellis would have given the world just to gain two inches of Stan's height. "I need some help with a couple of math problems, if you don't mind, before we head off to class."

"Sure thing," Ellis said.

What Ellis lacked in height, he had in brains. Learning didn't come easy, but he was a hard worker, diligent, and did his homework every night. He was first in his class but had to work hard to keep it that way.

"I see your pocket got fixed," Stan said gently. "Wish I'd seen Butch do that. I would'a slowed him down a tad."

"Butch is my problem," Ellis said. "I don't want him to think I'm hiding behind anyone."

"Butch has been calling you a 'runt.' I've heard him. He's trying to find a way to get you to fight him."

"Calling me names won't do it," Ellis said stiffly.

"He's finding that out. He's still looking for the trigger to set you off. I wouldn't be surprised if it's something under the belt, something that truly makes you angry. Can you think when you get mad?"

"I don't know." Ellis knew he'd have to be really ticked off to fight. Butch was mean, nasty, and underhanded. Ellis doubted he'd come out the winner in any physical confrontation with him. "I can't imagine what he'd come up with that would make me want to fight. I wish he'd just leave me alone."

"I don't think he's gonna grant that wish."

Most of the boys at Adrian High School tried to steer clear of Butch and his friends. They cut against the current of what most kids deemed friendly. If they found someone they could get a rise out of, the whole gang turned on the victim. Ellis ran interference for many kids, especially the loners. Besides, he had an ace in his pocket—Stan. He hated to see kids resort to violence. Stan usually hugged his opponent into submission. He'd come upon two kids fighting, put his big arms around the back of the angriest one, and pin their elbows to their side. It worked almost every time. Ellis never saw Stan angry. He just acted disappointed with the kids who couldn't find a peaceful way to settle their disagreements.

Besides, it was basketball season, Ellis's favorite sport. He loved hearing the hoots from his teammates and fans when he danced around an opponent and made a shot. As a junior guard, he was at the peak of his high school career. The only part of the season that dampened Ellis's enthusiasm was his father's absence that winter. He'd never missed a home game before.

Stan was over six feet and weighed a healthy one-sixty. With his long arms, he was the obvious center for the team. It was the best when he blocked an opponent, which led to a quick outlet pass and Ellis's gunslinger shot. The coach depended on the duo to score a majority of the team's points. Ellis frequently stole the ball and raced down the court for an easy two. Stan didn't run so much as lumber. He was typically the last teammate to get in position so the team could run their half-court plays.

The second guard was Andrew, one of Butch's group. If Stan heard Andrew say something nasty to Ellis, Stan wouldn't pass the ball to him. If Andrew yelled an atta-boy to Ellis, he could count on the ball. As basketball season progressed, Andrew backed off heckling Ellis.

"It's like training a dog," Stan explained to Ellis one day. "I reinforce the behavior I want to see."

The basketball team practiced the last period of the school day so they could still ride the buses home. It just made more sense with gasoline rations and the fact that some of the guys had to walk home as far as twenty miles. The junior varsity used half the gym, and the varsity the other half. Scrimmages took place Tuesdays and Thursdays. Ellis loved those the best. Half the time, the principal came in to watch practices and help the coach. Games were always on Friday nights.

The team began their season with two wins against Weiser and Payette, two schools across the Snake River in Idaho, and then played Vale, Nyssa, and Ontario twice each. At the end of the season, Adrian was in first place with seven wins and one loss. The varsity team headed to LaGrande for their conference playoffs.

LaGrande was home to the Eastern Oregon Normal School. It was where Luke had gone to school for his freshman and sophomore years. It had the largest gymnasium in Eastern Oregon, so the teams gathered there. Eight teams were in the playoffs, with a double-elimination setup. Adrian played Cove first on Friday afternoon and won handily, 46-33. That night they played Union High and again won 35-29. The two wins placed Adrian in the top four teams for Saturday's games. On Saturday morning, Adrian played North Powder, a team that was also undefeated. The coach gathered the team into a huddle before the game.

"Stan, I want you passing to Andrew and our frontcourt as often as you can, so long as we're winning. We want to shield Ellis from the spotlight so we can use him tonight. Ya got that? He's our secret weapon, and we don't want to use him until we have to. If Powder gets within four points, go ahead and get Ellis involved. But Ellis, none of your gunslinger shots until tonight. We need to play smart, not just hard!" The coach looked around at the boys. "This is your game to shine, Andrew. Stan, be disciplined. Play a good defense. Hustle. Everyone ready?"

The team put their right hands inside the circle and yelled, "Let's go, Antelopes!" and the game was on.

Try as hard as North Powder could, they never pulled within four.

Andrew made six baskets, and Stan made five. The other members of the team scored when they could. Ellis accounted for eight points. They walked off the floor with their third win of the tournament, all set for the game that night. Vale and North Powder were vying for third and fourth place at six. Adrian was to play Burns for the first-place trophy at eight.

This would be their big night.

***

Ellis had held back for so long that he could feel adrenaline running up and down his arms like ants at a picnic. He'd been using his right arm a heck of a lot, never showing his left-handedness. When he focused, when he was single-minded, he bit his tongue on the left side. Stan told him once that if he played poker, that would be his "tell." The opponent would know he had a great hand.

After warming up on the floor, Stan and Ellis went out to meet the co-captains of the Burns Bulldogs.

"Keep it clean, boys," the referee said. "We gotta call a championship game tight or the fans will have our heads. May the best team win."

The players shook hands, the ref blew the whistle, and Stan and the Burns' center crouched down for the tip-off. Stan's long arm reached the ball, and he tapped it over to Ellis, and the game began. From the very first, the game was fast. The Adrian Antelopes lived up to their name. The Bulldogs tried to keep up, but the first quarter ended 17-13 in Adrian's favor.

In the second quarter, Ellis lurked behind a player or two, waiting for a bit of inattention. He'd steal the ball and head downcourt. His focus was always on that orange basketball. He made his first gunslinger shot using his left hand. Stan, however, kept feeding the ball to Andrew. The two guards passed the ball in turn to the two forwards, and the lead seesawed back and forth. By the half, the score was 31-29, Burns leading.

In the locker room, the coach urged the boys to let loose. "The Bulldogs think we've been playing our hearts out when we've been using our heads. Now let's show them what we're made of. Pick up the pace. Stan, let's show them what Ellis can do. Andrew, hit the shots that you can. Pass off to the forwards if it makes sense. But Ellis, now's your time. No more holding back."

From the very start of the second half, Ellis stole the ball and raced down the court, shoes squeaking, side-stepping his opponent with ease. He used his gunslinger shot, confusing those looking to block it. Ellis's tongue protruded from his mouth, making Stan smile. The Antelope fans cheered wildly.

It was all background noise to Ellis. He was singled-minded. At the end of the third quarter, the Antelopes led 40-35. Ellis had scored eight of the Antelopes' eleven points in the quarter. During the fourth quarter, the Bulldogs tried setting up a few plays, but they lost their momentum. The Antelopes pulled away to win the game 48-39. Ellis broke the school record for the most points in a single game at twenty-one. The only person Ellis knew who had scored more was his mother, a guard like him, who held the family record at twenty-three from her College of Idaho days.

When his focus cleared and Ellis became aware of the crowd around him, he was surprised to find his father and Sam there.

"Way to go! Great game," Sam said. He pounded Ellis on his back.

Ellis's father gave him a hug and said, "Sam and I couldn't stay away. We timed our train trip so we'd see you play. I thought Adrian would make the playoffs. Nice to see you take the conference title."

Ellis grinned. He and Stan accepted the trophy for the team along with the first-place ribbon. The reporter for the LaGrande *Observer* lined up the team with Stan in the center, down to the shortest two players, Ellis and Tommy.

"No way!" Stan said. He reached over and pulled Ellis in front of him. "The guy with the most points belongs in front."

Ellis held the trophy self-consciously as the flashbulb went off. He thought nothing could dampen the thrill of that tournament.

Chapter Twenty-Eight

Abe

Hurrying through the cold January day, Abe entered the barracks. The room he shared with five others was warm, but the coal bucket sat empty. Before he got too comfortable, he grabbed it and headed back outside to the coal pile in the middle of their block. He shivered as he filled it and handed the shovel to another young man waiting his turn. The low-grade coal barely heated the tar papered rooms, but it was easier to gather than sagebrush.

When Abe returned, Okimoto spoke to him, thanking him for the coal. "*Arigato, Yano-san.*" He bowed to Abe, who returned the gesture.

Abe was the youngest man in these quarters; Okimoto, the eldest in his eighties. Abe knew he had lived in Gresham, worked as a laborer for other Japanese, and never married, but that was about all. Okimoto seldom ventured out except to eat and take a shower. Occasionally, he shuffled outside camp in his old navy coat, looking for greasewood found in the dry, alkaline land. He carved small, richly detailed figurines only four to five inches high, some of men, some of women, and some of nature. Right now, he was working on a child, its face suddenly revealed in the light brown grain of the branch.

How he found beauty inside a piece of wood, Abe couldn't figure out. "The child is beautiful, Okimoto-san. I work with wood too, but only in practical ways. It doesn't speak to me the way it must to you."

"But with your creations, we can sit, eat, and study! These figurines aren't as useful."

"The wood is alive!" Abe described the figures sitting in the windows around the room. "The child cries, the old woman's back aches, the young man throws a perfect pitch! Your creations have soul, music, laughter. They inspire!"

185

Okimoto-san smiled and bowed his head. "I am honored. Perhaps you would walk with me to our fine dinner in the mess hall. We shall see if the cooks are similarly inspired."

***

Abe went to the dance at the recreation center on Friday night. He wasn't really all that keen on going but he craved anything that broke the monotony of camp. The younger girls hid their giggles behind their hands as he walked by, searching for a partner. He danced with them all, so no one girl could lay claim to him. He understood why Molly had captured George, but he'd not seen anyone who thrilled him in that special way.

About halfway through the evening, Abe went across the room to speak to Mr. and Mrs. Mita.

Mr. Mita had recovered from pneumonia and dysentery, and regained most of his strength. "In fact," he said, "I am now the fireman for our sanitation building. I shovel the coal into the furnace to provide hot water for showers and the laundry."

Given Mr. Mita's age, Abe was surprised that he had such a physical job. It would only pay $12 a month as it wasn't a skilled position. Still, the hours were short—six each day—with three shifts. The fire was banked at midnight so the water wouldn't freeze and started up to full capacity at six the next morning.

"I am fortunate to be a morning person. I finish work in time for lunch and a nap!" Mr. Mita smiled and chuckled softly, then turned serious. "But indeed, I am pleased to be able to contribute to our family's well-being."

"How do you like the table and chairs?" Abe asked. He'd been able to hoard enough scraps and a few larger pieces to build the Mitas some basic furniture. Mrs. Mita had requested a table where Kameko could study and they could sit to enjoy a cup of tea. She had used flour sacks to make a tablecloth and asked Abe to string the central hanging light over the table, much like George had done in Portland. His next project for them was a bookcase.

"You take good care of our family," Mr. Mita said. "We do not wish to be a burden to you."

"My brother cannot be in two places. I am fulfilling his wishes."

The band began a slow foxtrot. Abe noticed Mary sitting next to her mother and asked Mr. Mita, "May I have the honor of dancing with your second daughter, sir?"

Mary looked up, startled. Abe held out his hand and bowed to her. "If you would give me the pleasure?"

Her mother encouraged her. "Go, go, go! You should be with young people."

Mary, flustered, began with an apology. "I'm not very good. I'll step on your toes."

Abe tucked her into his arms, his dark eyes looking into hers. "I've never met a girl yet who couldn't follow me. Do you feel my hand in the middle of your back? The pressure there tells you which way to move. Let me worry about the dance steps."

"I don't make conversation easily. I . . . I don't know what to say . . ."

"Then don't say anything. Let's enjoy the music."

***

Abe found all kinds of ways to keep busy by helping his fellow internees. Instead of complaining about the cold, he found a way to divert water from the canal and created a shallow pond southwest of Block 44 for ice skating. After that, families ordered skates from Sears, Roebuck & Co. or bought skates while on leave to Twin Falls, Jerome, or Rupert. Abe then managed to snare a few oil barrels from the maintenance department to burn wood as warming stations for cold hands. Instead of huddling inside their small rooms, people learned how to skate. Girls shared skates with each other, and the boys were soon showing off, learning to navigate backwards. Abe chuckled as one boy literally skated circles around two girls holding on to each other as they wobbled across the ice.

He worried, though, as he watched Okimoto slipping further and further away from reality. The old man had to be cajoled into eating, and Abe began carrying food from the mess hall at breakfast so he would be spared the harsh cold. After his shift, Abe would often find the food untouched and Okimoto curled up on his bed in his coat.

"You must eat, *Okimoto-san*." Abe sat on the edge of the elder man's cot.

"Why, my son? I am a burden to you and to these people."

"Nonsense. I am learning to be a better man because of you. My own father died when I was eighteen. I have no elder to teach me the ways of the world. I would be honored if you would let me care for you as a true son would."

Okimoto lifted his shaky hand off his bed and put it on the side of Abe's face. "If for a time I can help mold you into the fine man you will become, I would consider that an honor such as I have not had in this life."

"Then come with me to the evening meal. We will both build our strength through the efforts of the mess cooks." Abe helped Okimoto stand. He buttoned the old, blue wool coat and pulled down a wool scarf from a nail. He covered Okimoto's bald head and tucked the ends into the coat. After he bundled the old man up, he supported him with one arm, and they stepped out into the icy night.

***

Abe was surprised to learn the old man began his life in the new world in Alaska in the fish canneries.

"It is a world of light and darkness," Okimoto explained to Abe one evening. "When the sun rules, the land is bathed in light for twenty hours. That is when we worked double or even triple shifts, cutting off salmon heads and tails, gutting them, throwing them into large bins. The owners liked us because we worked fast, hard, and for less money. Then in the winter, the sun wanes, and it stays dark for much of the day. If we saved enough, we would catch a ride on one of the last ships and go to Seattle or Portland for the winter. Once there, I was lucky if I could find a job in a laundry where it was warm. Otherwise, I worked on the docks, unloading cargo, or in a hotel, washing dishes. I did whatever I could find.

"At first, I sent money to my parents. Times were hard for them, and they would use it to feed the family or pay for schooling for my eldest brother. But then I, too, had difficulty finding work. One winter, when I was in my early thirties, I had to live on what I saved. My parents' letters were angry, demanding. I hadn't seen them for almost fifteen years. I didn't reply to them."

Okimoto retreated into himself, lost in the past. Frequently, his stories would trail off before he finished them. Abe knew to leave him alone then.

Slowly, however, the old man's previous life took shape. Abe loved to watch the gnarled, arthritic hands carve the greasewood and reveal birds, animals of the desert, salmon, or an elaborate handle for a cane.

"Would you allow me to make the base for the cane?" Abe asked. "With your gift and my practicality, we could make a beautiful, useful tool to help with your balance."

It was Okimoto's turn to watch as Abe fashioned the sturdy staff and fit together their gifts of passion and practicality to form a handsome walking stick.

"It turns my slow shuffling into a fashionable, sauntering pace," Okimoto said in appreciation. "Very nice, Abe. *Arigato*, my son."

A few days into February, Okimoto retreated into his stories of Alaska, but this time he told Abe of the Inuit he met. He talked about how if the tribe suffered, an elder Inuit might sacrifice himself by walking into the wilderness. Better to die of exposure than to burden their community.

"I believe I am a burden here in this life," the old man continued. "I struggle to overcome the shame brought on our heads by the Japanese bombs at Pearl Harbor. That shame hangs over me always, and the weight of it gets heavier."

Abe was shaken. He still struggled to understand Okimoto's point of view about death. It was so different from his own.

***

When Abe came in from work a few days later, he noticed that Okimoto had spread out his statues, one lying on each bed for each member of their room. Abe's small wooden face stared up at him. It was carved out of black greasewood and finished with a clear varnish. It was beautiful. Okimoto's cane was gone, and worry began niggling at Abe. He left for dinner, intent on finding the old man in the dining room.

When he got back around six thirty, Okimoto had still not returned. Abe asked the others if they had seen him. One of them said Okimoto had left earlier in the day to gather more greasewood for carving, but he hadn't seen him since.

His concern growing, Abe went to the common area, asking folks if they had seen the old man. An elderly woman said she had eaten breakfast across from him that morning but hadn't seen him at lunch.

At eight forty-five, fifteen minutes before lights out, Abe hurried to the administration headquarters, telling the man on duty, "An old man from Block 44 is missing. People who saw him last say he went out into the desert to look for greasewood. I can find no one who saw him at lunch or later. I need to go search for him!"

"You have no idea which way he went?" the man on duty asked. "We'll need to form a search party, and it's too late tonight. I'll let the director know about it in the morning. He can call for an aerial search. In the meantime, I'll have the men in the watchtowers light lanterns. Maybe the old man will see them and come in on his own."

"But it's so cold! I don't mind going out there," Abe pleaded.

"Then we'd have two missing men. I can't let you go."

Abe jogged back across camp to his room. It was freezing outside. The night had no cloud cover, which meant the temperature would drop even more. A halfmoon shone brightly overhead, and stars filled the sky. Okimoto might find his way back, or perhaps the old man found shelter and could start a fire. He did have his old wool coat. If he'd gotten lost, surely, he could be found tomorrow. In the back of Abe's mind, however, he remembered Okimoto's story of the Inuit. Abe sat on his cot, struggling to understand how an old man freezing to death brought dignity and honor to his memory.

The next day, the director ordered an aerial search. A biplane flew back and forth across the frozen flatlands. The co-pilot used binoculars, trying to spot an old man waving a cane at them or at least an old blue wool coat. They had no luck.

On the third day, Abe joined a couple hundred others as they scoured the desert. About two miles from camp, a call rang out. Okimoto's body had been found.

How the old man died was anybody's guess. The doctors could find no sign of a heart attack or stroke. There were no marks on the body. The official cause of death was exposure.

Abe knew the old man best. He identified the body and was given his effects. He set the cane by his cot. The gnarled handle would always remind him of Okimoto. The old blue wool coat was still serviceable. He searched through the pockets. Nothing. Then he reached for the sculpture Okimoto had given him, looking for any kind of insight at all. He looked into the emerging young man's face and then felt something carved into its base. He turned it upside down. "For my son, Abe. Live your life with honor."

Live your life with honor.

CHAPTER TWENTY-NINE

GEORGE

George entered the gate of the Nyssa Amalgamated Sugar Factory. He had an appointment to see Welch this morning. He blew out the breath he unconsciously held and tried to calm his nerves. Spring was here. Wildflowers bloomed among the sagebrush, but it was way too early to need a recruiter. Farmers were starting to get their fields ready, but the beets hadn't been planted yet. He was two months early. Yet here he stood. George had to convince Welch to sponsor a trip to Minidoka.

Welch's secretary asked George to wait for a few minutes. "He's finishing up with Mr. Allen."

"Allen? Ed or Rex Allen?"

"Oh, you know them? It's Ed. He's looking for some field hands for this spring. He and his brother built two bunkhouses over the winter, and they're hoping to find at least eight men to live there."

At that moment, the two men came out. "I'll let you know if I find anyone needing a place to stay and who would be willing to live out at your farm full-time. You're a bit isolated, you know, with Adrian being the nearest town. Most people find Nyssa and Ontario more desirable."

Ed shook Welch's hand and turned around. "George! It's good to see you." He shook George's hand. "You recruiting for the factory again this year?"

"I hope so, sir. That's what I've come to talk to Mr. Welch about."

"Where are you living now? In case I need to contact you."

"We're at the CCC camp in Cow Hollow."

"Oh? Any single men at Cow Hollow?"

"No, sir. Only families. But everyone is willing to work. My brother and sister are looking for jobs after school gets out in the afternoons and on Saturdays. This summer, they'll be working wherever I am."

"Well, keep me in mind. Thanks for your help, Mr. Welch." Ed tipped his hat in the secretary's direction. "Ma'am."

George followed Welch into his office and closed the door. He didn't know how this meeting would go, and he didn't want the secretary listening in. Welch offered him a chair in front of his desk. Even though the seat was comfortable and warm, George found himself squirming. He forced himself to calm down.

Welch took the lead. "I'm glad you called to meet me today. I probably should've come out to see you." Welch's skin flushed a mild red. "I need to come out with it. You were so successful in your recruitment efforts, you've worked your way out of a job. There are twelve hundred Japanese living in Malheur County now. We don't need any more laborers for the crops, so we don't need a recruiter anymore."

George was stunned. He had a little money left to get to Minidoka, but how was he going to get in? Welch was the only one who could provide papers, sugar factory identification, permission. He got up from his chair and walked toward the window, trying to formulate an argument. He turned toward Welch. "You were honest with me. I need to come out with my situation too. I need you to sponsor me for one more trip. Just one." As Welch started to shake his head, George pressed his point. "It won't cost the factory anything. I need you to give me the paperwork to get me inside Minidoka one more time. There's a girl I want to marry . . ."

A half hour later, George emerged from the factory's main door with the needed forms in hand. Welch had called the director of Minidoka with some story about George contacting the workers who volunteered during the harvest. It was the last time Welch could help. If Molly didn't agree to marry him . . . if she was so upset at not hearing from him all winter . . . George couldn't allow himself to think those thoughts. He stopped at the telegraph office to send a wire to Molly, then bought his train ticket for the next week. All the while, his hands trembled.

"There's a girl I want to marry."

The words dogged his every step.

***

The next day, George was surprised to see Ed Allen pull up in front of his Cow Hollow cabin. As George came around the front of Ed's gray Ford truck, Ed met him with a handshake.

"Seeing you at the sugar factory yesterday got me and Rex thinking," Ed said. "With no single men around, we'd like to take you on as our hired man and move you and your family into one of the two new bunkhouses we built. You're the best worker we've seen. And with your connections, you'll be able to recruit some workers for us when things get busy around the farm. You could probably find some work with the Hertzogs too. What do you think?"

George removed his hat and swept his hair off his forehead. He knew a steady job with a secure monthly income would be better for the family, even though it meant moving again. Thomas and Pamela would have to change schools. It might make Molly's father more assured of George's ability to take care of a wife. After a bit of negotiation, George shook Ed's hand on the deal.

Neither Pamela nor Thomas said much about the move to the Allen's farm. Although they had both made friends at Nyssa High School, they accepted George's latest decision. Both were aware their farm in Toppenish had been lost and that the family was financially fragile.

"Will I ever have my own room again?" Pamela asked. "Will I ever see my books?"

"Maybe after the war." George tried to comfort her as best he could.

She and her mother had shared a tent, then cots in the main living area at the CCC cabin. When Chiharu heard Pamela yearning for a room of her own, she chided her. "Close your eyes, and then you are alone."

***

Two days later, the Allens arrived at the CCC camp with their pickup to collect the Yanos' belongings which easily fit in the bed of the truck. Rex and Ed introduced themselves to George's mother, towering over her by at least a foot. She could manage their names and seemed to understand what they were telling her. The two brothers called her Mrs. Yano, not attempting 'Chiharu.' As the men got into the cab, their bulk pillowed Chiharo's slight frame in the middle. George thought the brothers might be uncomfortable on the way back, but he didn't want his mother riding in the truck bed. The gravel road would be dusty, and he didn't want her breathing it in. Even though her condition had improved, he was still concerned for her health.

When they arrived at the farm, Ed backed up the pickup to the door of the first bunkhouse. The Yanos unloaded their scant possessions and took stock of their rooms. The kitchen had an electric range, used but in working order. There was a countertop next to it with open shelves above and below. A cast-iron skillet and a stew pot were sitting on the back burners. The room had two windows that opened, allowing for a cross breeze. They placed their old wooden table and three chairs and an apple crate under one of them. The water pump was outside between the two bunkhouses, and two outhouses were located several yards behind them. It wasn't much different from the cabins at the CCC camp.

An open doorway led into the bedroom, which also contained two windows on either side of the room. It had two bunk beds with a stuffed mattress on each bed and hooks on the ends of the upper bunks. Nails were pounded into the walls between the bunks so clothes could be hung. There were no dressers, no closets, no rugs, and no curtains on any window. The men had put a single light bulb in the center of each room, each with its own switch.

After Chiharu looked around, she went up to Ed and said, "Okay. Home. Good." She bowed to him and Rex.

Turning to George, Rex said, "Tell your mama we're real glad to have her here. We've ordered a potbelly stove for this corner of the room. It'll be here in a couple of weeks. It should keep the bunkhouse toasty during the cool nights and in the winter. We'll see what else we can do to make it less sparse."

"Don't worry about that," George said. "We'll make our own way now that I'm working. After I make my trip to Minidoka in a couple of days, I'll be ready to start."

The Allens tipped their hats to Chiharu and Pamela and took their leave. As the Yanos were unpacking and getting settled, someone knocked on the door. Rex had a small rocker in his hands. It was made of dark walnut with a cushioned, embroidered seat.

"Would you see to it that your mother gets this?" Rex said. "It was our mama's. We've carted it all the way from the bald prairie in Alberta, and neither of us can sit on it. We'd just bust it up. We'd feel real special if your mama would use it for herself."

"Are you sure?" George looked from the chair to Rex and back again.

"Your mama's been through a lot. She deserves some comfort at the end of the day."

After George thanked Rex, he brought the chair in and turned to his mother to explain. She patted it, felt the curves of the wood, and sat down. It was so petite that her feet reached the floor. She rocked back and forth, petting the smoothness of the wood.

CHAPTER THIRTY

MOLLY

At noon, Molly was eating her lunch while watching the elementary children on the playground. It was the middle of March, still chilly, but the sun shone from a clear sky, promising an early spring. Molly munched on a couple of raw carrots, saving her apple for last.

Kameko ran up to her, panting and out of breath. "You have a telegram from George! I knew you'd want to read it right away."

Molly took it from her sister and turned it over in her hands. "What if it's bad news?" She squeezed Kameko's hand and looked into her eyes. "I can't read it now." She looked out at the children jumping rope and playing softball. "Thank you, Kameko. I know you're disappointed, but I'll wait until school is finished for the day."

Kameko turned to go home. Molly knew her younger sister wanted to read the telegram too, but this was the first time in nearly five months she'd heard from George. She wanted some privacy to read whatever was so important that he'd send a telegram. She put the thin, yellow message in her skirt pocket. When the bell rang to call the children in, Molly followed the last ones into the classroom.

All afternoon, she was distracted. Even the fifth graders noticed. Every once in a while, she'd pat her skirt pocket to make sure the missive was still there. Instead of seeing the raised hands asking for help, she gazed out over the children's heads. They began to call to her to get her attention, and then she'd startle and rush from one child to the next. Their normal afternoon routine bumped along like a car with a flat tire.

Finally, when school was out for the day, Miss Shepherd sent her home. "You must not be feeling well, dear. I've never seen you so absentminded. Perhaps you're coming down with something . . ."

When Molly returned home, she was relieved no one else was there. Her hands were so cold, they trembled as she carefully opened the telegram.

`Farm lost. Mother recovered from surgery.`
`Arriving Minidoka March 31.`

She read it again, trying to tease meaning from the few words George had sent.

At twenty, her life felt stalled. All winter she had waited for some news, some indication of what George felt for her. Now he was coming—he would be here the first days of spring—but the few words said little else. Was he angry with her? Did he still love her? Why was he coming? The questions swirled around in her mind. She closed her eyes and tried to think.

Just then, Mary quietly entered their compartment. Molly was so happy to see her, she thrust the telegram toward her.

"Here. What do you make of it? George is coming, but I don't know if he still loves me." Molly let out the tension she was feeling through her tears.

After a few moments, Mary sat beside her. "Is that what you get out of his telegram?" Molly turned over to face her sister. "You need to read it through his eyes. He may feel he has nothing to offer you. He couldn't come before, but now he can."

Molly sat up. "Doesn't he know possessions aren't as important as he is to me?"

"The farm meant much more than a possession, hmm? Abe tells me George fought to keep it because it was his father's legacy." Mary smiled sympathetically at her older sister. "What are you going to tell Father and Mother?"

"I don't know yet. I need to think about this." Molly scowled. She had waited so long for George to write. Now he was coming to see her—even better than a letter—but the news had knocked her off-kilter. She didn't know what to think.

When Kameko asked Molly about the telegram she had delivered, Molly quoted the words verbatim. "That was it?" Kameko asked. "Wow. He sure doesn't know how to be romantic."

Molly raised one eyebrow.

Hastily, Kameko added, "At least he's coming to see you. You must have a ton of questions to ask him."

***

For three days, Molly stewed over the communication. She spent long hours in contemplation, staring off into a vague middle distance. Then Molly received another letter from George explaining in depth the loss of the farm and of his mother's slow recovery. But still he did not write of his feelings. She wrote in her diary several times a day, and she and Mary braved the rainy spring weather to walk together and talk. The gray skies mirrored her dark moodiness. Occasionally, she would notice her father looking at her with concern. She managed a small smile but said nothing. Finally, she made up her mind.

"Otoosan," she said to him, "I wish to speak to you and Okaasan about my happiness, my future. Privately."

The family had returned from supper in the mess hall, and Kameko was beginning her lessons. Mary looked up from her embroidery.

"Momoe, we are past the time for secrets in our family," Kentaro said as he leaned forward, concern on his face. "Please, tell us what has been bothering you."

"I am in love with George Yano, and I wish your permission to marry him."

Kameko ducked her head into her textbook, and Mary lowered her needlework to her lap. Molly held her breath as she waited for her parents' reactions. As the eldest sister, she had always been the bold one.

Her mother looked askance at Molly. "Marrying for love is a Western idea. We are better suited to choose your husband. Your father and I have been married many years, and we did not know each other before we became man and wife." She shook her head at Molly. "You need to beg your father's forgiveness for being so impertinent. Choosing your own husband? This is not permissible."

Holding her breath, Molly turned to her father. "Otoosan? Will you give us your blessing?"

Her father put his hand on her mother's arm, restraining her from any further protest. "George has not asked you to marry him, is that not so? He has not spoken to me to ask for you as his wife. This is highly unusual." He ran his hand through his hair and shook his head. "Tell me what you are thinking. How can you ask this of us?"

"George wrote me recently. He has lost his farm, his store, and the family's home. He has lost his pride." Molly looked down at her hands clasped tightly in her lap. "He is coming to see me in a few days."

"This loss means he will not yet ask for your hand in marriage," her mother said. "He will not approach your father with this shame on his head."

Molly looked up and said sharply, "Forgive me, Mother, for speaking so. Father also lost everything he worked for in Portland. That was not his fault. He was forced by the government to sell everything in such a short time. George held onto his farm for nearly a year. Surely there is no more shame in his loss than in Father's."

"Hsst! No more!" Her mother drew back.

No one spoke for several moments. Molly turned toward her father, who looked thoughtfully at his wife and then at each daughter. Kameko looked at him over the top of her book while Mary offered a small smile.

"I do not blame George for losing his family's fortune. What I am concerned with is how he will support a wife and children. I must ask, Momoe. I have to ask." He tilted his head to the side and looked at Molly intently. "How do you know he wants you as his wife?"

Molly faltered. She squared her chin and told her father the hard truth she knew to be true. "I don't know. He hasn't said anything to me about marriage in the letter. But he loves me, Father, and I love him. Why else would he be coming?"

CHAPTER THIRTY-ONE

ELLIS

Ellis plowed under the last of the winter alfalfa in the east field near their house. Alfalfa was known locally as green manure. His father was going to rotate half of the beet crop this year to wheat. Ellis didn't understand all the scientific reasoning yet, but the soil sure was better than when his father homesteaded the acreage in 1934.

This was the first spring he hadn't been able to play baseball. He could manage practices and home games, but away games meant he wouldn't be able to work those evenings on the farm. His father and sister would have the cows to milk and the fields to ready, adding significantly to their own work. He just couldn't ask that of them—he was still trying to be a man, not a boy. Adrian's baseball team would have to carry on without him. Like most teams from small towns, they'd have to fill in with sophomores and even freshmen.

After he plowed, he attached the harrow and used it to break up the big dirt clods. Ellis was known throughout the small community as being the fastest harrower. He went from farmer to farmer, earning enough wages to pay for gasoline and wear on the tractor to his father, and still came out with a profit. As he worked up and down the field, he thought of his brothers.

Luke was in Africa with the II Corps. When German General Field Marshall Rommel went right through the American forces at Kasserine Pass toward Algeria, the family worried for three weeks. They'd finally received a letter from Luke, and, although it didn't say too much, they knew he'd survived. He was allowed to tell them he was behind the front lines, flying newly repaired aircraft.

Ellis pulled up the harrow, turned around the tractor, and set the harrow back down where he'd left off. Driving up and down the field was mindless work. His thoughts settled on Donald, the only infantry recruit in his family. He was still stateside. His letters were all about the training he was getting in communications. He was funny, upbeat, and still a private. Eventually, he hoped he'd be transferred to England for the big invasion. In the meantime, he wrote about going on a weekend pass, enjoying the USO clubs, "training" new officers, and marching, marching, marching.

Ellis continued harrowing until dusk, then rode the tractor to the house, thinking about his third brother. Sam had been called up within two weeks after his second term ended and reported to Fort Lewis near Tacoma, Washington on March 20th. Ellis wondered which branch of the service he'd choose when his time came as he drove into the equipment yard and lowered the harrow to the ground.

After washing up for supper, he still had a few minutes before the meal was ready, so he walked over to the maps on the wall. His dad had replaced the world map with ones of the United States, the Mediterranean, Africa, and Europe and western Russia in order to see more detail. The most recent National Geographic magazine included a map of the Pacific, including the Philippines, Australia, and all the way over to Japan. Ellis was fascinated with all the exotic names of the islands where naval battles were being fought.

Emily came up with the idea of using a different colored yarn for each brother. Whenever one moved to a different training base, she would run the yarn from one pin to the next. It made the map all the more interesting as each brother began crisscrossing first the United States, and now Africa.

Ellis still hadn't figured out what he wanted to do in the war. He wasn't enamored with flying the way Luke and Sam were. Donald seemed to be marching in circles. Ellis wanted to do something different and only had a year to decide before he'd be joining too.

"Ellis! Supper's on!" his mother called.

Ellis left the maps and his ruminations and went to the table.

***

Saturday morning, Ellis drove the tractor with the plow attachment to the Allens' eighty acres. As he drove into their equipment yard, he saw Thomas Yano spading up the new garden plot next to the bunkhouses. He hadn't seen Thomas since last fall. He'd heard the Yanos were living in the Allens' bunkhouse, but he hadn't seen anyone yet. He hopped off the tractor to say hi.

"Boy, am I glad to see you." Thomas stood the shovel up in the dirt and walked over to Ellis. "Anything to get a break. Ma wants everything done yesterday!"

"How are the new bunkhouses?"

"Good. We're really glad to be here. I haven't seen Ma this happy for a long time."

At that moment, the door opened and a girl about Emily's age stepped out. She began walking toward Thomas, spied Ellis, and stopped. She would have gone back inside, but her brother stopped her.

"Pamela! Come meet Ellis," Thomas said.

She turned around and walked shyly up to her brother. Standing behind him, she raised her eyes high enough to glimpse Ellis. Her greeting was so soft Ellis could barely make it out.

"Ellis is the same age as me," Thomas informed Pamela. "How old is your sister?" he asked Ellis.

"Emily is fifteen now. She's just finishing her freshman year."

"Pamela is sixteen, so a year older."

"It's great to meet you," Ellis said. "Haven't had neighbors near our age live so close."

An older woman looked outside at the three teenagers and said something in Japanese. Pamela replied and turned to go back inside. "Hope to meet your sister soon."

"Bye." Ellis turned back. "That your mom?"

"Yeah. She doesn't speak much English, though living here, I think she'll learn. It's funny watching Rex and Ed communicate with her. Ma tries out the few words she knows. She likes them, and the old guys seem fond of her already."

"Do you know where Ed is?" Ellis asked. "I'm supposed to start on their fields today."

"I saw him walk into the barn just a few minutes ago."

"You going to finish out the school year in Nyssa?" Ellis was curious as to why Thomas and Pamela hadn't already enrolled at Adrian High School.

"No, it's too hard with gas rationing. We got our assignments and will turn them in before the end of the school year. Any Japanese in Adrian High?"

"Just one. His family has lived here for a long time. You and your sister will make quite a stir next fall."

"At least we won't be the first."

The two boys parted, each preparing the ground for new growth.

CHAPTER THIRTY-TWO

ABE

Abe couldn't believe that President Roosevelt had changed his mind on February 1, 1943. He probably had no idea how much his waffling over creating an all-Japanese-American combat team would upset so many lives in the internment camps. The company would be made up of volunteers from both the mainland and the territory of Hawaii and be called the 442nd Regimental Combat Team. A year after the attack on Pearl Harbor, the government finally wanted Japanese Americans to volunteer.

Abe fumed at the news that the team would be segregated from Caucasians. The Negroes were also in segregated units. He wondered when the Army, Navy, and Air Corps would discover that all American blood was red. He thought back to Okimoto-san and his message, "Live with honor." What exactly did that mean in this situation? He'd tried once before to enlist but was qualified as IV-C, a category described as "an alien not acceptable to armed forces." As a United States citizen, he and many others felt insulted by being classified as aliens. Would he ever obtain the rights of true citizenship? Did he even want to serve his country under this cloud of internment and racial prejudice? Yet showing his patriotism meant a great deal to Abe.

Then, an even worse insult arrived in the form of the War Relocation Authority's loyalty questionnaire. Most of the questions were innocuous, but all the camps over the inland west were upset, unsure, and divided over two of them. Question twenty-seven asked if the respondent would be willing to serve in the armed forces of the United States on combat duty wherever he was ordered. The *Issei* were mostly in their fifties and older. Would they have to enlist? What about the women? If they said yes and had children, would they be required to leave them? Would they have to fight?

Question twenty-eight asked the respondent if he would swear unqualified allegiance to the United States, faithfully defend it, and foreswear any allegiance to the Japanese emperor. American-born children could answer yes, but what about the *Issei*? They were not allowed by law to be American citizens. If they swore allegiance to the United States, did that mean they became stateless persons, with no country wanting them? The *Issei* whispered in camp that the questionnaire was one more trick by the government to deprive them of their remaining property, savings, and anything they had left in storage. Their worst fear was that they would be separated from their *Nisei* children and grandchildren and sent back to Japan after the war. Editorials soon appeared in the ten camps' newspapers, which were mailed back and forth. Some *Nisei* answered no to protect their parents.

Fortunately, Minidoka's director, Stafford, understood how the questions could be misunderstood. Abe went with the Mitas to their block meeting as Stafford and the *Nisei* councilmen explained the government's intentions. Although some directors of other camps refused to revise the original questions, Stafford rewrote question twenty-seven, asking eligible, single women if they were willing to volunteer for the Army Nurse Corps or Women's Auxiliary Army Corps. For question twenty-eight, the revised question read, "Will you swear to abide by the laws of the United States and take no action which would in any way interfere with the war effort of the United States?" Answering "yes/yes" would enable internees to resettle farther inland, obtain indefinite leave clearances, and, for Abe, serve in the military. Ninety-seven percent of Minidokans answered in the affirmative twice, and the turmoil settled down. Other camps weren't so lucky, and the issue continued to fill the editorial pages of their newspapers.

Mr. Mita was clear in his stance. "I don't think we will leave the camp before the war is over, but I do want to portray our loyalty to the United States. If any of my daughters want to join the Women's Auxiliary Army Corps, go to a university, or obtain employment in Chicago or Michigan or Ohio, I don't want to stand in their way."

"What if your daughter wanted to get married and join her husband?" Abe asked.

"Ah! You're trying to trick me." He wagged his finger in Abe's face. "Your brother needs to ask me that question, not his proxy."

Abe still couldn't decide whether to volunteer or wait to be drafted. Recently, whenever he had an issue to wrestle with, he talked it through best with Mary. Without specifically arranging to meet, he usually found her in the recreation hall in the evening doing some kind of needlework.

Mary was there and smiled up at Abe when he approached. She removed her multicolored embroidery thread from the chair next to her, making room for Abe to sit. When he settled down, Mary quietly began to arrange the thread into separate colors on Abe's knees.

"I talked to the Army recruiters today," Abe said.

"What did you find out?"

"I registered for the draft but would rather pick how I serve, if I can. I've always been good with my hands, but the recruiter surprised me by his interest in the time I spent in Japan learning to read and write the language."

"I'm surprised you told them. Did your education make them doubt your patriotism?" Mary rearranged the pink and added orange thread.

"Apparently, the intelligence branch of the service needs literate men who might be able to crack the Imperial Japanese code, or interpret in the battlefield, or interrogate captured prisoners." Abe watched absently as Mary separated the light blues from the darker ones. "I could wind up fighting my cousins," he continued. "Who knows?" He imagined the emperor drawing a line between his uncle's family and his own.

"My father and mother also have family living in Japan," Mary said. "We haven't heard from them since Pearl Harbor. We find it difficult to imagine our relatives as the enemy."

"George carries a map wherever he goes and marks the battles against Japan. Each tiny X symbolizes ships blowing up, men bombing targets, the generals plotting their strategy. Hundreds — thousands — dying each day." He was quiet for several minutes. "An old man once told me to live my life with honor . . ."

He watched Mary thread her needle with royal blue, the same

color as the blue background on the U.S. flag. Abe knew it symbolized justice, vigilance, and perseverance. If he showed those same traits, would he prove to his country that he belonged?

"I think I'm going to volunteer, Mary."

She dropped her embroidery hoop, and it clattered on the floor. Abe bent to retrieve it. When he returned it to her, her eyes were brimmed with tears.

"You're going to volunteer?" Mary blinked her eyes rapidly, and her expression sobered.

"I have to do my part. I want to make sure the American government knows that we are fighting as U.S. citizens and that we believe in the ideals of this country."

"You know people in other camps don't feel this way. Some even want to go back to Japan after the war."

"I know. People are saying the folks here in Minidoka are the most loyal of all ten camps." Abe looked tenderly at Mary and rubbed his hand against her cheek. "Sorry to go so soon when we've just begun to get to know each other. See you tomorrow night?" Suddenly, seeing Mary every night until he was gone was important to him.

"Of course. I'll be here." She squeezed his hand.

Abe gathered the threads off his knees and handed them to her. As he left, she was once again arranging thread on the empty chair beside her.

***

Abe wrote to his family about his decision. He realized he probably wouldn't be able to see them before he shipped out. He ended his letter with an aside to George:

I've looked out for the Mitas as you asked. The father recovered his health and is able to hold down a job. Molly and Mary are both working in the same jobs as when you saw them last. Their plans are to stay in Minidoka until the war is over. I couldn't make any headway on your behalf. But if it makes you feel any better, Molly seems to be as miserable as you are. Abe

***

The first volunteers from Minidoka were scheduled to leave in March. The night before, Abe dressed carefully in his suit and walked to the rec center where his block section was honoring the men leaving for duty. He carried with him a wooden box he made and Okimoto's cane and placed them carefully underneath his folding chair. He and the other young men sat behind the podium and listened to speech after speech. Looking out into the crowd, Abe could see the Mitas. Kameko had informally adopted him into the Mita clan, she informed him. She and her friends would write to Abe and the soldiers in his unit.

"We'll make cookies and send you warm socks," Kameko said. "Whatever you need."

But it wasn't Kameko's eyes he looked into.

The last speaker ended his address, saying, "We have been asked to sacrifice our sons to the land of their birth. May you bring honor and glory to you, to your parents, and to your country, the United States of America."

The audience stood, clapping politely. The Mitas, in the third row, beamed proudly. Abe shook hand after hand, quickly losing track of how many *Nisei* patted him on the back. Finally, the crowd began to thin. Abe picked up the box and the cane and made his way over to the Mita family.

Abe turned to Mr. Mita. "Sir, Okimoto-san and I made this cane together. I hope you will accept this as a token of my esteem for you and your family."

Mita bowed to Abe as he took the cane. "It is both beautiful and practical. I will keep it and use it when I need the support a cane can provide."

"Would you hold this for me?" He handed Mary his small box and walked over to the refreshment table to pick up two cups of punch.

As he made his way back, Mary settled in a corner a bit away from all the excitement. She put the box under her seat and accepted the cup from him. They sat next to each other, observing the couples starting to dance.

Abe reached for Mary's hand. "Would you write to me while I'm gone? I'd like to know what's going on here, how everybody's doing." His voice became a whisper. "I'd like to know someone thinks of me in a special way, someone who would miss me."

"Don't you have a lot of girls here who would write to you? A couple of them are eyeing you now, hoping you'll ask them to dance." Mary tugged her hand away, knowing someone would see them.

When he realized he was embarrassing her, he sat up straighter. "Here. There's something else I want to show you."

He reached under her chair and lifted the box to his knees. Opening it, he drew out Okimoto's statue of Abe's face emerging from the wood. "I want you to keep this for me. I see myself in this face, coming into my own as a man. I'm not there yet, but I'm trying to find my way. I'll return from the war to get it, wherever you are."

"It's beautiful! Your eyes are the same." Mary turned the head over and read the words carved on the base. "Live with honor." She looked at him squarely. "All right. I'll write to you. You'll be my only soldier boy."

"I'll write back as often as I can. Do you have a picture I can take with me?"

"I have a high school picture from a year ago. What about you? I'd like one of you too." She gently rewrapped the figurine and put it in its small chest. Picking up her punch, she leaned back in her chair and smiled gently at Abe.

Abe finished his drink. "Will you dance with me? This may be our last night together for a long, long time."

As they glided together across the floor, Mary followed Abe flawlessly. Her awkward bumbling had disappeared. She was graceful, beautiful in his arms.

Chapter Thirty-Three

George

George arrived in Minidoka on the last Friday in March on the afternoon train. He walked briskly to Block 44 in the single men's area, entered the room, and stashed his bag under an empty cot. In it was a navy-blue suit he'd worn to his high school graduation. He hoped it still fit—and that he'd have a reason to wear it again.

He'd never been so nervous. He wiped his sweaty palms on his pants. The first step would be knocking on the Mitas' door. He'd just have to fake the courage he didn't feel. He didn't know if Molly would agree to see him, let alone marry him. George hoped to come into camp quietly, apologize for the winter's angst, get married in a small, intimate service, and leave as quietly as he'd come. With Molly, of course. If she'd have him. He patted his jeans pocket where he kept a wedding band for Molly. Surely, they'd have some privacy. He had so much to talk to her about. And her father—George still had to face her father. George swallowed hard and tried to think what he would say to Mr. Mita.

He found the Mitas' barracks, stepped into the common doorway, and knocked on the door. Mr. Mita opened it and bowed to him with a stiff formality. George returned the bow and noticed no one else was in the room.

"Good evening, sir. I was hoping Molly would be here."

"She, her sisters, and her mother are at the recreation center. I wanted a few moments for us to talk. Please. Come in."

George stepped inside and took a look around. He could see some of the changes Abe had made. Where the sixth cot could have been, a small table and two chairs sat. Another chair was between two cots.

Framed pictures of George and Abe were on it, each picture turned toward a different bed.

Mita noticed the direction of his gaze. "You can see the Yano family has made an impression on our own. Mary writes to Abe every day, and he corresponds with her. You and Molly, however, have not written much at all this winter. She has been upset for many months, and now, suddenly, you are here. I want to know what she means to you."

Shame coursed through George's body. He walked over to the coat rack and hung his hat. He took off his coat slowly, trying to buy a few more seconds. Then he turned and stood up straighter. "I haven't known what to say to her. Every time I picked up a pen, I could see her face when she learned my family wouldn't be coming to Minidoka. I was afraid of more responsibility, of having a wife and children before I could get my feet on the ground. I wasn't man enough yet."

"And now? Would you call yourself a man now?" Mr. Mita cocked his head at George. His eyes reminded George of obsidian rocks, dark, shiny yet opaque. He didn't offer George a seat.

"Yes, sir. I believe I am." George paused and took in Mr. Mita's stern countenance. "I've come to ask your permission to marry Molly and take her home with me. She is the most important person in my world, and I love her very much."

Mr. Mita frowned. "How will you support her?"

"I have a place to live and a job year-round. We'll live with my family. My mother can teach her how to garden. She'll have the company of my younger sister. You know what a fine man Abe is. He sends money each month for Thomas's college fund, and Thomas works after school and on weekends. Our goal is to get back on our feet and send Thomas to college. He aspires to be a doctor. We have to start over again, but with Molly by my side, we will find a way."

"I notice you say 'we'."

"That is what I have learned over the winter. Family works better together as a unit. Sometimes it is necessary to grow through self-reflection, and I have done much of that throughout the winter. I've also learned that sometimes growth comes only through pain. I learned to listen to others and work hard. I'm ready to accept the responsibilities of being a husband."

"I hope you are. Please, sit down." Mr. Mita settled himself in one chair and indicated the chair on the other side of the table. "Do you know why Molly is so set on you?"

George looked at Mr. Mita in bewilderment. "How can I explain to you what I don't understand myself? She loves me—and I love her too—but to explain why? I feel like it's a miracle."

"Will you be as loyal to her as she has been to you? Will you stay by her side when life is cruel? She has changed this winter. Your silence hurt her."

"I'm sorry to hear that, sir. I need to make it up to her. And I swear I will be loyal to her throughout our lives together and shield her as much as I can from the misfortunes we may share."

"You will be gentle with her? Give her the children she wants? Let her see us?"

"Yes, sir."

"Then I will send her to meet with you. You have my permission to marry—if this is what Molly wants too." When George's face lit up, Mr. Mita noticed and cautioned him. "I don't know whether Molly will agree. She requested some privacy for your reunion." Mr. Mita stood up, picked a jacket off one of the nails, and left the room without glancing back.

George sat quietly for a few minutes. He couldn't believe Mr. Mita was willing to let Molly wed. The life they would have together seemed so basic, so rudimentary as itinerant farmers. And so glorious. He thought of holding Molly in his arms every day. He was going to see her in a few minutes. What would he say to her? Would she want to get married? She had refused him before. He stood up and walked over to look at the pictures of himself and Abe.

So, Abe and Mary were writing to each other. He picked up the picture of his brother in his Army uniform. Must have been taken right when he got to basic training. His own picture with Molly was from the night of the All Center Farewell Dance. He could see the decorations behind them. Molly had brought the photographer over—it was the man who had warned George to take good care of her. His rival. He wondered if Molly ever knew how the guy felt about her. He had just picked up a carving of a face emerging from a piece of wood—Abe's?—when Molly opened the door.

"Molly." He put down the carving and walked over to meet

her. He reached out his hands and held hers. "I have treated you so shabbily. Can you ever forgive me?"

Molly studied George for what seemed like hours.

Finally, she said, "You hurt me by not writing. I'm worried that your silence is a substitute for difficult conversations we must be able to have. I thought you didn't want me anymore, that perhaps you didn't love me."

George understood this wasn't going to be easy. "I've never stopped loving you. In fact, I believe I love you more now than I did when we parted last fall." He dropped Molly's hands and began pacing back and forth across the floor. "I've learned a lot over the winter." He stopped and put his hands on her shoulders. "The most important realization is that I cherish you more than anyone. Why I had to lose everything to understand that, I don't know. I'm sorry you had to endure my silence for me to learn about myself. Can you forgive me?"

Molly turned away from George's pleading face. She sat down at the table in the chair her father had just vacated, hiding her trembling hands in her lap. "I was very angry at first. I knew about your mother's illness and the hospital bills because of Abe. I spent many weeks wondering if you'd learn the lessons I thought you needed. I didn't understand that I had some growing up to do myself." She raised her eyes and scrutinized George. "I'm sorry too that I sent you away. I didn't listen to what you needed, but put myself and my family first."

"But Molly—"

"Let me finish." She took a deep, cleansing breath. "I didn't write to you either, you know." She paused. "If our relationship is to work for the rest of our lives, we have to listen to each other, to weigh each other's needs, to say hard truths gently. Our love for each other may help us, but it isn't enough. I learned that over the winter. There must be commitment, not only to each other, but to *us*. We must honor our union. It must come first, before all else. Can you do that?"

He enveloped her in his arms. "Yes, Molly." He knelt down in front of her and asked, "Will you marry me? Will you be my wife?"

Molly hesitated a moment and then said, "Yes. Oh, yes. I don't want to be apart ever again."

George drew the tiny box from his pocket, opened it, and turned it to her. A gold wedding band gleamed. "Take it out, Molly. Read what it says on the inside."

Molly removed the ring and turning it, read, "'For all eternity.' It's beautiful." She looked at him and laughed softly.

"I wanted to make sure I did this right. My sister is a fierce critic of romance." They both laughed as George sat beside Molly. "She's anxious to meet you."

"You haven't kissed me yet."

George leaned over and softly met her lips with his own. "I've imagined your soft kisses every night."

"Close your eyes." Molly moved toward him and softly, ever so slowly kissed him on his cheek, his forehead, his temple, his other cheek, his chin. They felt like butterfly kisses. The last one was on his lips.

CHAPTER THIRTY-FOUR

MOLLY

The first decision Molly had to make was whether she was going to be a Japanese bride or a modern bride. Was she going to be married in a Buddhist ceremony or a Christian one? Such a conundrum surrounded a simple desire to marry George. Fortunately, George understood.

"It's a question all *Nikkei* are answering in a variety of ways," George said. "Abe decided to volunteer in the U.S. military, whereas many refuse to fight. Do we honor the place we come from or strive to fit into our new nation? Do we continue to teach our children Japanese or English or both? Do we live in Japan Town or as farmers in Eastern Oregon? These are not small questions. What do you *want* to do?"

"First, I must talk to Mother," Molly said. "I don't want to hurt her feelings, but I can't imagine a traditional Japanese wedding."

George agreed. "Let's try our best to straddle the two worlds."

***

Molly found her mother in the recreation building, sorting through the latest clothing donations from churches in Oregon and Washington. She mended some, fixed torn hemlines, added buttons, and, if nothing else, saved good material for another garment. For this work, the Mitas received a clothing allowance each month. Fortunately, her mother was working by herself, and Molly felt free to talk.

"Mother, I know you kept your traditional blue kimono and obi you wore for your wedding with Father—"

"And the white split-toed socks and shoes," her mother added.

"But I can't imagine myself with the stark black makeup over a white facial powder. I don't think George would recognize me!"

"What are you trying to say, Momoe?" Her mother pressed her lips together.

"I don't mean to hurt you. I don't feel comfortable wearing a white bridal gown either—that is just as foreign to me. I want to be a modern bride and wear something more like a suit. It's practical, and I can wear it on many occasions instead of just one."

"It will be all right with you if I wear it? Many Japanese will want to dress in kimono."

"Of course, Mother." Molly was pleased with the compromise.

"Perhaps my *other* daughters will feel more traditional." She sniffed in displeasure, and her face resumed its frown.

When Molly shared the bargain with Mary, her sister suggested they look at the donated clothing their mother had been going through. "Not to find something to wear, but to find good cloth we could use to make you a suit or a dress with a jacket. We could cut it down."

"In a week?" Molly was doubtful.

But they were in luck. A plum-colored, light-weight wool suit was in one of the latest boxes. A rather large lady must have donated it.

"Perfect!" Mary turned it over and looked for runs, stains, or moth holes. There was only one run.

"But what will I wear on my head? A hat? Flowers?" Molly's shoulder-length hair gave her lots of possibilities.

"That's Kameko's specialty. Let's give her that project," Mary suggested. Molly readily agreed. Kameko was always fiddling with their hairstyles.

Molly's mother spoke to one of her friends about Mary's plan. In no time, someone loaned them a sewing machine. A sewing circle soon formed, and the women buzzed with activity. Without a dress form to use, Molly was poked and prodded, measured and fitted. The jacket was single-breasted with navy buttons down the front. Mary managed to salvage enough of the material to make a peplum hem on the jacket. The suit's straight skirt had a small pleat. Kameko demanded Molly's time, too, as she styled Molly's hair this way and that, showing her all the possibilities for the big day.

***

The day of their nuptials was Saturday, the same day as their train trip back to Eastern Oregon. The interdenominational minister for the internment camp gathered the community together for the joyful occasion. George asked a man in his bachelor's bunk to stand up with him. He seemed like the proper choice since the man had been a friend of Abe's. Mary acted as Molly's maid of honor. As Molly walked down the aisle with her father, her hand gently hooked in his elbow, George beamed at her. A lavender grosgrain silk ribbon was pinned on the top of her head, and a small lavender veil covered her face. She carried a single white iris accented with yellow and purple. Mr. Mita gave his daughter in marriage to George and moved to his seat by Mrs. Mita. Molly moved to take George's arm. When the minister ended the ceremony with the traditional invitation for George to kiss his bride, he lifted the veil from Molly's face. She smiled and blinked back happy tears. He kissed her tenderly. Never had a decision felt so right.

It was nighttime when the newlyweds finally made it to the Allens' farm. The train trip added to the exhaustion of the wedding and the ache of saying goodbye to her parents and sisters. Molly could tell George was tired too. Ed Allen, George's boss, met them at the Nyssa depot and then drove an additional half hour to the farm. But when they pulled up to the bunkhouse, the lights were still on. George's family came out to greet them.

"Molly, this is my mother, Chiharu," George said.

Molly bowed to a tiny woman with glasses and salt-and-pepper hair.

"*Konnichiwa*," Chiharu said.

"*Konnichiwa*," Molly repeated.

"This is my brother, Thomas," George said, reaching over and mussing his brother's hair. "The smartest Yano."

Thomas stepped forward and shook Molly's hand. She was surprised Thomas was the same height as she was. He was lean and seemed serious.

Then George's sister approached. "I'm Pamela," the girl said, introducing herself. Her dark hair rested on her shoulders. "You're just as beautiful as George said." She kissed Molly on the side of her face and squeezed her hand.

Molly smiled at Pamela. "What a lovely sister you are."

"Come in," George said. "You can see where we live. It isn't a whole lot better than the barracks at Minidoka, but we have two rooms: one for cooking and one for sleeping."

Molly briefly inspected the bunkhouse and wondered about the sleeping arrangements for the night. Maybe George could bring the mattress from his bunk bed into the kitchen, and they could sleep on the floor. She certainly didn't want to sleep in the same room as the rest of the family on her wedding night.

Then her mother-in-law smiled and said to George, "Bring Momoe. We have a surprise for you."

Thomas picked up their luggage, and Pamela followed. They crossed the open space between the two bunkhouses and opened the door to the nearest section. George and Molly stepped inside.

The room glimmered in soft candlelight. Curtains hung on the two windows, and two small, woven, reed rugs covered the floor on each side of the bed. A quilt covered the double mattress, with embroidered sheets and matching pillowcases. Simple tables sat on each side.

"How did you manage this?" George asked.

Pamela said, "I did the embroidery, and Mother made the rugs from reeds we gathered at the river. The Allens put together the bedframe, and Thomas built the two tables. We were glad you stayed in Minidoka an extra week. Don't know if we'd have finished without that additional time."

"It's beautiful!" Molly turned to her new mother-in-law and bowed. "*Arigato gozaimashita*. Thank you."

Chiharu beamed and bowed back. Then she turned and motioned Pamela and Thomas from the room. As she closed the door, she whispered to George, "*Oyasumi-nasai*. Good night."

CHAPTER THIRTY-FIVE

ELLIS

Ellis listened to his father and Ed Allen discuss how they'd share workers this year. Now that the Yanos were living and working on the Allens' place, the labor shortage didn't seem to be so dire. However, there were only four adult men, Thomas and himself. That made six. They needed the equivalent of two more men to make up a crew that could thin both places. Because the Allens had their place thinned first last year, the crew would start on the Hertzog farm this time.

"George insists his sister, mother, and wife can work beside us. Your wife and daughter willing to do the same?" Ed asked.

"They'll be able to give us some help. Mae still has her garden, and Emily will be doing more of the cooking. They can probably thin for three or four hours in the morning. I'd rather not have them out in the heat of the day."

"Sounds good."

Ellis found the hoes and separated the handles from the blades. Sitting at the grinding wheel, he started its rotation by pushing on the pedals, alternating his feet. When he finished sharpening them, he put short handles in most of them but outfitted a couple with long ones. Sharpening the hoes had always been his father's job, but Ellis was picking it up this summer. He threw in a couple of files in case they needed them during the day. He'd find the water bags, too, and make sure there were no holes. He was no longer a kid who needed to be told what to do.

It didn't surprise him that the first morning of beet thinning was tense, confusing, and demanding. The women and girls had thinned their gardens, but nothing as difficult as beet fields. At first, Ed demonstrated how to hoe, with Pamela translating for her mother. Ellis's mother could hardly be polite to the Japanese women. She abruptly started off on her own but didn't leave enough room between each beet.

"Whoa, Mae," Lee called out. "These are sugar beets, not turnips. A mature beet needs a foot of room. Slow down and leave more space." He hoed beside her for the first row or two.

Emily and her long-handled hoe were pulling up beets as well as weeds. On his way back up on his second row, Ellis stopped and took it away from her. "Here, sis. Try the short-handled one. It might be easier." He slowed down and worked beside her until she got the hang of it.

He watched Thomas's sister from afar. Pamela was so careful that it took her an hour to finish her first row. Whenever Rex or Ed said anything critical to her, she cried.

"Hey, Thomas, try helping your sister," Ellis said discreetly. "She's scared to death she's going to do something wrong. You might coach her some."

Thomas glanced at his sister and headed over.

Ellis really got a kick out of watching George. He had prided himself last year on thinning as fast as Ellis did. Now, he was so distracted by Molly working beside him, he couldn't tend to his own row. With the men tripping over all the women, Rex grew disgusted and moved down the field to thin by himself. That left Ed with Chiharu. He was the only one with patience remaining.

At eleven, when the women left the field, the men stopped for water at one end. No one said the obvious until Rex finally exploded. "This won't work! The five women got eleven rows done. I only did eight instead of my usual ten. How many did you do, George?"

"Six."

"Ed?" Rex asked.

"Seven."

"At this rate, it'll take us all the way through June," Rex groaned. "What're we going to do?"

"Let's think on it," Lee said. "We've got work to catch up on." His father picked up his hoe and began again. "We've got an hour before dinner."

Ellis got back to thinning. Every now and then, he'd recall George hovering over Molly or Ed trying to communicate with Mrs. Yano and grin.

"What're you laughin' at?" George was trying to keep up with him again.

"Nothin', George. Not a thing."

***

The next morning, Ellis watched Ed diplomatically change the order of who hoed where. He placed Chiharu at the first row. Without making it obvious, Ed placed George as far away from his new bride as he could.

With this placement change, the second day was much less entertaining and much more productive. Ellis hoed side by side with Thomas, falling into a comfortable pace. George took fewer breaks, but when he did, he'd find Molly and rub her back. Chiharu worked faster than Molly, frequently finishing her row and helping her daughter-in-law complete hers. Ellis could tell the fieldwork was difficult for Molly. She was slowing down instead of getting faster.

When Mae finished her six rows, she left the field early, telling Emily to stay until she was done. Ellis was ashamed of her. She should have helped the other women finish, but she didn't. At least with her gone, Ellis felt free to hoe beside the two girls for their last rows.

Ellis tried a neutral topic to see if he could get to know Pamela some. "I know Thomas likes school. How 'bout you?"

"Yes. I miss it," Pamela said. "I also miss the bookmobile that came to camp. Do you ever have it come out here?"

"It stops in Adrian at the elementary building every third week. We have to go there. But we have quite a few books at our house too. Maybe I could bring you some."

"That would be wonderful." Pamela pulled a weed out by hand. "What do you like about school? What's your favorite subject?"

"Music, I guess. I play the piano for choir concerts and the trombone for the high school band. What about you?"

"I love to sing. I've just never really had the chance. There's a choir class then in Adrian?"

Emily entered into the conversation now that their mother had left the field. "Yes. I'm in it. Mr. Russell does all the music, and he's a good director. Sometimes we get to sing modern songs, not only the highbrow stuff."

Thomas, Ellis, Emily, and Pamela chatted comfortably for the last half hour before the girls were done. At eleven, Ellis waved goodbye reluctantly.

The women finished their thirty rows but were visibly tired and sore. Emily limped up the road to their basement house. Pamela slowly followed her mother and sister-in-law, wiping away the trickles of sweat from her forehead. Bits of Molly's hair came out of her ponytail and stuck to her red face.

Chiharu put an arm around Molly and supported her back to the bunkhouse. "*Shikata ga nai.*"

"What does that mean? *Shikata ga nai.*" Ellis butchered the words. "I hear your mom say it all the time."

Thomas looked a bit embarrassed. "It's kind of like telling Molly not to worry about hoeing well in the fields. Her family was from Portland. They didn't even have a garden."

"She doesn't have to work, does she?"

"You don't know Molly. She'll never quit. She's like George in that way."

With experience, Ellis thought, the women's stamina would improve. He sure hoped his mother's attitude did. She still wouldn't talk to the Japanese family.

At the break, Rex checked the men's progress, noting it was much better. Their ragtag thinning crew was settling into a productive routine.

CHAPTER THIRTY-SIX

ABE

Abe arrived in Hattiesburg, Mississippi after five days and nights on a passenger train.

"Camp Shelby!" the porter announced.

The men groaned, stretched, and gathered their things. As Abe stepped down, the humidity hit him in the face. After the dry desert heat in both Eastern Oregon and Minidoka, this would take some getting used to. He removed the suit coat and threw it over his shoulder. A fedora shaded his eyes.

He'd received a ticket with his orders to report to base by April 1, 1943. He and several others traveled together from Minidoka. As they got closer to Camp Shelby, men of all races piled in. At first, they sang, told jokes, and played poker. For the last fifty miles, however, the men sat two to a seat, staring out the windows, unsure of what would happen to them when they got to basic training. Abe was nervous about the Jim Crow south. He didn't know how he'd be treated as a Japanese. Would he be shunned? Heck, it was alright with him if no one ever spoke to him. But threatened? Even killed?

An officer yelled at the men swarming in front of the station. They were instructed to separate into three groups: whites, Negroes, and Japanese. *Here we go*, thought Abe. All over, he noticed other signs of discrimination: white toilets, colored toilets, whites in the front of the bus, colored in the back. Abe didn't know where he fit in with his brown skin. He was told to sit in the front with the whites, yet he felt an affinity with the Negroes. He knew what it felt like to be called a *Jap*, as if he were the enemy.

The men from Minidoka joined others from various internment camps. They picked up their suitcases, duffle bags, or backpacks and shuffled off to their induction station. Abe assembled outside and listened to a sergeant tell them where they were going and what they were going to do. He cocked his head at the sarge's southern twang. Instead of being lulled by the softness of the dialect, Abe heard a hint of shrewdness.

"All right, men. Listen up!" shouted the Caucasian officer. "This is the reception area. Say farewell to the civilian life you once enjoyed."

Abe learned he'd be in basic training for seventeen weeks in small unit training and physical conditioning. After that, he'd have forty-four weeks of unit training, combined-arms training, and maneuvers to be ready for combat. Other men would soon arrive from Hawaii to join the combat team. By the time Abe collected his pack, cartridge belt, canteen, tent-half, mess kit, and gas mask, it was time for supper. Abe moved to one of the lines. He was hungry. Chow couldn't come fast enough.

***

The next day, the men were divided into companies. Those that arrived from the internment camps took their exams for the next three days. They took the Army General Classification Test (AGCT) and trade tests (clerical, mechanical, etc.) and had a fifteen-minute interview on work experience, education, training, sports, and hobbies. Each company had room for non-commissioned officers of sergeants and corporals. With the results, the non-com officers were chosen before the Hawaiians arrived. Few officer positions remained unfilled.

Not only did they take exams, but they were also inoculated against several diseases, including malaria since mosquitos carried malaria in Mississippi. Abe's dark curl of hair, the one that endeared him to Mary, landed on the barber's floor. With Abe's experience in construction both at Portland Assembly Center and at Minidoka Internment Center, they offered him a non-combat position among other carpenters and engineers. But Abe refused. He had his heart set on fighting with the 442nd.

***

In mid-April, the Hawaiians joined the internees. Abe met his first one when he was shoved out of line for dinner. "Get in the back of the line. Me and my buddies go first."

"Sorry," Abe mumbled.

The man laughed, and his pals joined in. Abe could tell he was going to have some adjusting to do. It might even involve fists.

The big man's name was Shug. He was *Hapa*, mixed-race, and bigger than most Japanese, at five foot ten, two hundred pounds.

Shug and his buddies all spoke pidgin rather than standard English. If Abe shut his eyes and just let the sounds wash over him, he could make out the general meaning of what they were saying. Maybe not word for word, but the essence. Shug, on the other hand, could mimic Abe to perfection, with a slight haughtiness, nose-in-the-air English. The act got another laugh from his admiring buddies.

Abe and the mainland Japanese soon learned the Hawaiians loved to play craps, poker, and pick a fight. The fights were never fair, with all the Hawaiian buddies jumping in to beat up one or two mainlanders. Name-calling soon followed. Hawaiians called the stateside Japanese "Kotonks," the sound of heads banging together like coconuts. Abe and his friends began calling the Hawaiians "Buddhaheads," an obvious reference to Buddhism but also a play on the Japanese *buta*, or "pig." And the fights were on. Nothing resembled a combat team, but rather a rollicking mud bath, the two sides never agreeing on anything. Their commanders despaired and lectured the men frequently during the morning rollcall.

After the fourth fight between Shug and Abe, Sarge tied the men's legs together at the ankle and the knee as if they were going to run a three-legged race. "That oughta stop some of this silliness," he said. "When you get so sick of being tied together you don't want to fight, let me know."

Sarge put the two men in the front of the marching columns and hustled them forty-five minutes out. Jumping jacks were hard to do, but they managed squats and push-ups. They snarled at each other and, if no one was looking, tried to deck the other. The lectures in the morning turned to threats of breaking up the 442nd into labor battalions.

Finally, an invitation came from the Jerome and Rohwer internment camps for representatives of the 442nd to visit one weekend.

The camps were in Arkansas, about two hundred and fifty miles away. The men chosen were told they had been selected because they were such good soldiers. Abe was relieved to see Shug go as one of ten representatives of their company. He took his ukulele, a deck of cards, and some of the cash he'd won over the last few weeks. He smiled and waved at Abe as the truck pulled out. Abe relished the two glorious days without his taunts.

When the Buddhaheads returned, something was different. They didn't boast about their time in Rohwer or Jerome, although Abe learned there had been a dinner hosted by the camp followed by a dance.

In bed that night, Shug finally asked Abe the question all his islander buddies wanted to know. "You came from an internment camp, right?"

"Yeah, Minidoka."

"Were your people rounded up and taken from your home?"

"Off a fruit and vegetable farm. My brother really worked hard to save it, but when our mother's appendix burst, the family savings went toward her medical bills. My family is working as hired help on a farm in Eastern Oregon out of the military zone. George—that's my older brother—found a loophole to keep the family there instead of in an internment camp. Me? I couldn't leave the people I'd met at the assembly center. I had to see if I could help them."

"And so you went to live in a concentration camp?"

"Yep."

Shug rolled over in bed and looked intently at Abe. "Why'd you do it?"

"Do what?"

"Volunteer! Seems to me you'd resent these *Haoles*."

"*Haole*? What's that?"

"Our word for the blond, blue-eyed whites that ran the plantations."

"I have to show I'm a United States citizen, as loyal as any immigrant, and that I love the ideals this country stands for. You know. With liberty and justice for all."

"Sheesh. Liberty and justice? In Arkansas, folks live in a boggy, forested camp worse than any Army barracks. There are military guards in watchtowers. The military *we're* a part of."

"Sounds about right. But better to fight to put an end to this than stay inside those fences."

***

The next morning, Shug said to Abe, "Let's go tell Sarge we're ready to take off these ropes."

"You sure?" Abe didn't know if he could trust Shug.

Shug hesitated and then met Abe's eyes. "Yeah. But will you tell me one more thing?"

"Sure."

"How come you mainlanders don't shoot craps or play poker? You too pure?"

"I supposed it looks that way," Abe said. "I send the extra pay for my brother's medical schooling and a new stake for my family. Pretty hard to gamble it away when it's needed at home."

"Ouch. Sure had the wrong idea about you guys." Shug put his arm around Abe's shoulder as they managed the awkward gait to the company headquarters. "Think we could win the three-legged race?"

"I'll bet we could."

Chapter Thirty-Seven

George

If George had known how wonderful it was to be married, he'd have done it sooner. Molly brought joy and laughter into the family. Chiharu gained a genial woman who spoke Japanese better than George or his siblings. Pamela delighted in Molly when she talked about books, authors, and music. Thomas stilled under her hand when she absent-mindedly rested it on the back of his head. The magic George felt from his relationship with Molly bewitched the whole family.

It was obvious from the beginning that Molly had been a city girl. George didn't like Molly working in the fields, but she refused to be coddled. She learned how to handle a hoe, and gradually, her stamina improved. Chiharu taught her how to take care of their family's garden, and she was quite proud of the strawberries they harvested. He could tell she was homesick as she wrote to Mary and Kameko and her parents nearly every day, so he promised she could go to Minidoka to visit after the harvest.

He appreciated their surroundings through Molly's closer, more intimate eye. He'd noticed the quail, but Molly doted on the birds with their curious topknots. She laughed as she watched the row of youngsters following their mother in frantic, tiny steps, hurrying as if afraid of being left behind. She confused the names of the many black ones—blackbirds, crows, starlings, magpies, ravens. At least the magpies had white on their wingtips.

"What a terrible name for those pretty birds!" she exclaimed.

Molly noted the repetitious coo of the doves but thought the meadowlarks' song the most beautiful. George surprised her one day, whistling the many-noted melody of its call. She beamed at him when the bird answered.

"Don't flowers grow in the wild here?" Molly asked. She had George slow down when they drove by the Hertzog's place so she could look at the flowers planted in the corners of the yard.

"Sometimes, you'll see Indian paintbrush growing in the spring. But flowers need water, and the Allens haven't encouraged their growth," George said. "Perhaps you could get to know Mrs. Hertzog better and ask for lilac starts or iris rhizomes."

"Maybe," Molly said.

Mae Hertzog's stiff responses to Molly's first attempts at friendship had probably precluded that. No, George thought, she wouldn't be asking any favors of Mae.

One day, he surprised Molly with a seed packet of wildflowers. She read the names aloud, "Black-eyed Susan, yarrow, cornflower, daisies, cosmos, and poppies. Are all husbands as wonderful as you?" The kiss he received as thanks reinforced the worth of such efforts.

"If you plant them near the fence line, they'll get water from the irrigation rows. And you can sprinkle some seeds near the vegetable garden. Just scratch up the soil some with a rake."

She read the directions on the seed packet and set out to sow some color near the bunkhouses.

Every Friday night or Sunday afternoon, the family would visit the other Japanese in their community at Cow Hollow. George wanted Molly to meet other women and perhaps find a friend. Thomas and Pamela liked to see their high school friends, and George was pleased to introduce Molly to Doc and his former labor crew. Inevitably, a baseball game would begin, and Thomas and George took positions on one team or another. Molly sat with the other wives, girlfriends, and sisters who cheered them on.

Sometimes, George would be drawn into issues at the camp. The men were determined to put in running water, a sewer system, and remodel buildings into apartments. Once that project got started, George helped out over six weekends to dig all the ditches and connect the pipes.

Slowly, Chiharu replenished the money in the colorful tin. With no loans or mortgage, the wages the family earned from the Allens paid for their few needs. If George could find additional work with the

Hertzogs or another family, he squirreled the money away. Abe sent a dollar each week in his letters, specially earmarked for Thomas. The money represented the family's future, but George puzzled what that would look like. He realized he liked the Eastern Oregon community and began to look into ways he could resettle here. At first, it didn't look very positive.

The farmers' grange in Vale urged its members not to sell or lease land to the Japanese. "When the war is over, let the itinerant workers return to the coastal communities. We don't want Japs here!" one editorial urged. It went on to encourage farmers to house the temporary labor help, but "don't make them too homey!" George saw ads of farmers selling out, leaving for the shipping yards or manufacturing plants elsewhere in the country. He wished he could take advantage of the homesteads gone bust or the sagebrush-covered land where the government ditches made the desert bloom.

It wasn't just the attitude in the community that stopped him. He needed enough of a stake to buy a pickup and a tractor, plus all the implements like a plow and a harrow. He understood now why his father had been so proud of his 1934 black coupe and John Deere tractor.

One day, Ed, Rex, and George were discussing that week's newspaper articles.

"I understand some wealthy men in Ontario are buying up the land," Ed remarked. "They're installing Japanese families on acreage to rid the land of sagebrush and dig the ditches. They stand to profit after the war when the men come home. Lots of folks will want to buy land that has been cultivated and worked on for a couple of years."

"Will they sell to us?" George asked.

"The Japanese have a reputation for honesty, industry, and hard work," Rex said. "There's always a place for folks who enrich the land and community."

George thought about the conversation for several days. He hadn't really thought about where his family would go after the war. Molly was worried about her family too. Her aging father wouldn't have the physical ability to farm. Gradually, a plan took shape in George's mind. He'd lost everything in Toppenish, but that didn't mean he couldn't make a go of it again. He remembered his lesson learned last winter, though. He needed his family's approval.

The family settled outside one evening after all the chores were done. Chiharu sat on the step of the porch, dish towel in hand. Thomas and George sat on the crabgrass patches that grew out of the packed, smooth dirt. Molly and Pamela poured tea for each. Pamela brought out the first cups for her mother and Thomas, while Molly finished the last three. The two young women sat on a blanket, back to back, and stretched their legs out in front of them.

"Look," Thomas said. "The first star is out."

"Star light, star bright, first star I see tonight. Wish I may, wish I might, have this wish I wish tonight," Pamela recited. She closed her eyes for a moment.

Molly did the same, and George wondered what his wife was wishing for.

"I have a couple of wishes myself," he said once she opened her eyes. "But we'd have to work for them to come true."

"You know, it's bad luck to tell someone else what you wish for," Molly teased.

"I know." George paused. "I was thinking about us staying here in the Treasure Valley after the war is over. What do you think?" He looked around, including Molly and the family in the question.

"The Allens are good men. We've not been this comfortable since before we were forced out of our farm in Toppenish," Thomas said.

"Mother?" George asked his question in Japanese for her.

"Many aunties here for me to talk with," Chiharu told him.

"I am glad there are girls my age who share similar stories," Pamela added.

"I'm hoping to start over," George said. "Find some land we could buy, or at least lease."

"Thomas and I aren't much help," Pamela said. "We still have to finish high school. Maybe we could start small, like raise chickens and sell the eggs." She repeated her idea in Japanese for her mother, and Chiharu nodded her head.

Thomas thought some more. "I know my dream of being a doctor will take quite a bit of our family's savings. Maybe I could start studying some of Doc's medical texts and go on calls to understand basic first aid. I've thought of joining the military as a medic. After the war is over, I'd have a jump-start on my training."

"I know this might add to our burden," Molly interjected, "but I would like to bring my family here from Minidoka."

"We can do that. We'll add them to our plan." He reached over and kissed the side of her face.

"We're going to need a whole lot of chickens," Pamela joked.

"And a whole lot more stars to wish on," Molly added.

The weight on George's shoulders eased just a bit. He was so grateful the family was willing to take small steps to a new future. Even if the future meant more responsibility for him.

CHAPTER THIRTY-EIGHT

MOLLY

Molly had never experienced homesickness before. Although George made her very happy, she just wasn't used to living without her sisters, father, and mother. Molly received letters from her family almost every day. Mary occasionally mentioned Abe, enough to let Molly know they were still communicating long distance. Mary made sure she sent the camp newspaper as well.

Kameko wrote of her classes and classmates, dances, baseball games, and of sewing her own clothes. Her father wrote of the internment camp's issues, the food, hospitalizations, and lectures he was attending. He'd started a garden, both for aesthetic purposes and for additional vegetables. Her mother couldn't write in English, Molly couldn't read Japanese well, and so Molly missed her mother the most. She was surprised at that, as she and her mother disagreed about so many things. She searched out clues of what her mother was doing in the other letters.

Molly thought of the homesickness her mother must have felt. She'd left Japan as a young bride of only seventeen and never returned. Molly and her sisters didn't know her grandparents, uncles, aunts, or cousins who remained behind. At least her children would have grandparents and an extended family.

Before Molly left Minidoka, her mother warned her of the mother-in-law. "In Japan, a woman married and left her home for her husband's. The man works outside the home while the mother-in-law rules the household. She can make life miserable for her daughter-in-law."

Molly was surprised at her mother's warning but heeded it. She made an extra effort to please Chiharu. Every morning, Molly rose earliest. She lit the fire in the stove and prepared tea. Chiharu could then wake to a warm kitchen. By beginning each morning with an act of love and esteem, Molly hoped to endear herself to her mother-in-law.

George inadvertently caused a rift between Chiharu and Molly by encouraging Molly to work with his mother on English. He asked that instead of speaking Japanese in the home, they speak English, translating into Japanese only when it was necessary for Chiharu. "We want to assimilate into the American culture, not stick out," he explained. "It's important that Mother learn English too. If we coddle her by allowing her to function in Japanese, she'll never learn."

Molly tried to name all the furnishings, the pots and pans, and the dinnerware. She asked Chiharu to repeat the names of the birds and the plants in the garden. Molly had attended Japanese school in Portland but didn't understand how to teach verbs, tenses, and sentence structure in English. It wasn't much fun, and Chiharu couldn't seem to remember one day to the next. The more George insisted on English, the more English Chiharu forgot. Molly felt trapped in the middle.

"I'm not suited for this," Molly said to George. "I've never had to think about how a person learns another language. You and I just grew up with both at our disposal."

"Perhaps Pamela can help you," George suggested. "She might have an idea. You mustn't stop your lessons."

Molly despaired. When she talked it over with Pamela, they decided to work on some simple spoken sentences in a dialogue form that Chiharu might use ordinarily. Writing, using a whole new alphabet, was out of the question. Together, Molly and Pamela conversed in the simple phrases. Chiharu nodded, but added in Japanese, "The English sounds hurt my ears. I understand the meaning when I hear you practice, but the words fly out of my brain when I have the rare opportunity to speak it." Whenever Molly would ask a question in English, Chiharu acted deaf. Nothing was working.

One day, Ed brought down some socks for Chiharu to darn. He brought a large-eyed needle, wool thread, and a wooden block to put inside the sock. He said loudly to Chiharu, "I have some socks here I'd like you to darn. You know how to darn socks?"

Chiharu tilted her head to one side and looked up into Ed's face. She shrugged and put out her hands, palms up.

At least she didn't pretend to be deaf, Molly thought. She watched, curious as to how the two would communicate.

"Here. Let me show you," Ed said. He put the tools on the table, sat down, and threaded the needle. He tied a knot at the end and showed her how to weave the thread in and out. "See? That is darning a sock." Then he let her try. They were so involved in the task, their two heads together, both graying, a huge man looming over a tiny woman, that Molly could observe without being intrusive. When Chiharu completed the first heel, Ed beamed at her, and both laughed together. He left another six or seven socks that needed darned. When he came to collect them, he gave her a nickel. Chiharu bowed to him, and Ed shook her hand.

The next time George came in from the field, Chiharu proudly said to George in English, "I darn sock." She showed the coin to him, deposited it into the tin, and patted the lid. "Good for plan."

***

The next day, Molly was outside hanging up the washing on the line to dry when Ed walked by. His overalls were worn out at the knees, and one strap was loose without a metal button.

"How are the socks Mrs. Yano darned?" Molly asked.

"Holding up," Ed said.

"You know she could probably fix those overalls too."

"Think so?" Ed inspected the wear and tear of his work clothes. "Might make it through another season that way. I'll ask and see what she says."

Soon Chiharu not only cooked for the Allens' noon dinner, but she sewed as well. She patched the men's overalls, sewed on buttons, and turned the collars of their shirts. She made short-sleeved shirts out of the long-sleeved ones when the elbows wore out the cloth. Her economy in making the clothes last longer and look better made Ed and Rex delighted.

"We don't look like old hayseeds anymore," Ed said. He didn't seem to mind the nickels and dimes he paid for this new look.

When Chiharu also began doing the two men's laundry and ironing, Molly helped but made sure her mother-in-law collected the money. They hung more shirts, underwear, undershirts, and denim overalls on the clothesline than before. Chiharu asked Molly the names for sheets and towels. Soon, she was changing and remaking the beds too. The men left her to it and paid her fifty cents a week. She modestly showed George her earnings but rattled the coins as she added them to the tin. Molly hid her smile at her mother-in-law's small vanity.

Chiharu didn't respond to the overt language instruction, but once she wanted to know a word in context, she didn't forget it. George seemed pleased with her progress, raised his eyebrows at Chiharu's pride in helping the family progress, and minded less when Molly, Pamela, and Chiharu spoke Japanese in the cookhouse.

Molly heaved a sigh of relief. She'd passed the first test as a daughter-in-law and wife.

CHAPTER THIRTY-NINE

ELLIS

Ellis stood up from the beet field to wave at the passing mailman. He stopped his truck and rolled down the window. "If I'd known you were so close to the house, I would have given you the telegram instead of your ma. I don't know what's in it, mind, but news is always best when it's shared." The man ground the truck's gears into first and lurched away.

Ellis squinted down the road and saw his mother spreading a white sheet over the farmhouse's fence. It was the family's signal that a telegram had arrived. With Sam, Donald, and Luke in the service, any one of them could be coming home on leave. Ellis yelled at his father a couple rows over. They were nearly finished with the Allens' first round of thinning and weeding the beets. His father would be reluctant to leave the field when the job was so close to being done.

His mother was sitting at the round table when Lee and Ellis clattered down the stairs. She didn't answer Lee when he called to her. Both Lee and Ellis slowed as they approached her. She leaned on her elbow, her left hand supporting her chin. The other held the opened telegram. She sat unnaturally still, her eyes vacant.

Lee knelt beside her and asked gently, "What is it, Mae? What does it say?"

She turned to look at him but didn't speak. Then she slowly lifted the telegram. Lee took it from her and read it aloud to Ellis.

LUKE   HERTZOG   KILLED   IN   MEMORIAL   DAY CELEBRATION **STOP** AIRPLANE COLLISION **STOP** OUR CONDOLENCES **STOP** II CORPS COMMAND

"What does it mean, an airplane collision? I don't get it! Luke is dead? Our Luke?" Ellis's voice rose with each question. "Let me see that thing." He read it through twice more as if he could squeeze more information from the few words.

His father pulled up a chair next to his mother and gathered her into his arms. She looked stiff, frozen, unyielding. As he ran his hand up and down her back, rocking her, she slowly crumbled into him. "Our boy, Lee. Our boy is gone."

"Shh. Hush. I know, I know," Lee said as Mae's tears fell down her weathered cheeks and dripped onto his work shirt.

There was nothing Ellis could do to ease his parents' grief. Nothing he could do to change those terrible words in the telegram. His father closed his eyes and rocked his mother, shedding tears of his own. Ellis had never seen his father cry. Throwing the telegram down on the table, he ran out of the kitchen, up the stairs and out the door, slamming it behind him.

Luke, his spunky, rebellious brother, was dead.

***

Three weeks passed. His mother was barely functioning, and Ellis, Emily, and Lee found themselves taking over her responsibilities. She lay on her bed, sometimes with the pillow pulled over her head. When she roused herself enough to eat something, Ellis felt more hopeful that the family would be able to survive their grief.

The last time Mae had dressed was for the memorial service, where she had woodenly accepted people's condolences. Afterwards, she had taken off her shoes and laid down on her bed. Both Ellis's grandmother and aunt had gone in to hold her hands and offer words of sympathy, but that was the last company they'd had. Now, Mae padded around in her cotton nightgown, seldom combing her matted hair or washing her face. His father tried to reassure Emily and him that their mother would be fine, but the comforting words evaporated in the home's stillness. It would take time, his father said. Ellis's own grief seemed swallowed by his mother's.

Emily was doing her best. She fixed all the meals, baked the bread, and washed up. Neither man would say anything if the meat was burned or the bread doughy in the middle. Ellis milked all the cows and gathered the eggs morning and evening. He'd turn on the water for the garden in the late afternoon while his father worked in the fields later and later, trying to make up for the loss of their labor. The house was slowly deteriorating, dust accumulating on the piano and chair legs.

The Allens and the Yanos were quietly supportive of Ellis's family. One evening, Chiharu appeared in the Hertzog garden, weeding and watering in his mother's place. She'd pick what produce was ripe and leave it in the bucket by the door. Ellis tried to thank her by giving her some of the vegetables, but Chiharu would have none of it.

All he could understand was her daily inquiry, "Mother good?"

"No. Mother not good," and he'd imitate her sleeping with his cheek resting on his hands.

"Sad. Too sad." She would nod, turn around, and walk back down the road to her home.

After three weeks, this too became part of their daily life. Ellis didn't know what it would take to get his mother back on her feet.

One evening, after Ellis had finished the milking, he spied movement through the backyard. As he rounded the corner, he saw his mother. Her hair was wet, limp and tied at the base of her neck. She was wearing one of her faded cotton dresses with an apron over it. At first, Ellis was pleased to see her. But when she bent down and picked up a stick, he realized she was angry. She tested the stick's strength by hitting it against her thigh, then rushed through the gate. What was she doing?

"Noooo!" Ellis heard his mother yell. She ran through the garden, slipping and sliding in the water-filled rows. Crushing whatever plants were underfoot, she raised the stick and brought it down hard. As Ellis ran, he realized his mother was beating Mrs. Yano.

"Get out! Get out!" Mae shrieked. "Stealing our food out of our mouths? Get out!"

Chiharu raised her arm to protect herself and backed away from the fury descending upon her. "No! No! Mae. I help. I help!"

Ellis threw an arm around his mother, pinning the stick to her side. She struggled to get away, but Ellis pulled her back. With one arm around her, he twisted the stick from her hand and threw it down. She panted and tried to break his hold, ready to attack again.

"Stop! Stop it!" Ellis shouted. "What do you think you're doing?" Using both arms now, Ellis dragged her back out of the garden.

"I go. No more help. I go." Chiharu's hat had been knocked askew, and one shoulder of her blouse was torn. She backed away from them until she reached the road. Then Chiharu limped away, occasionally looking back.

"Mom, you beat her! You may have hurt her. What were you thinking?" Ellis had never physically restrained his mother before. He slowly released her, and she spun around to face him.

"That Jap was stealing from our garden. You bet I beat her. I'll do it again if she dares show her face here." Her face was twisted into a snarl. In the struggle, her hair had come undone. It was tousled, damp, and hung in her face. "Is that what's happened since I've been sick? You let them have anything they want?"

Ellis spoke through his clenched teeth. "She's been helping in the garden while you've been in your bed. She refuses to take anything for her labor. She's being neighborly." Ellis paused, catching his breath. "She comes up here every day and spends two or three hours keeping your garden for you. Before she leaves, she asks about your welfare as best she can." He looked hard at his mother. "You've made a terrible mistake."

Bewildered, she looked around the garden. Crushed, broken plants were smashed into the mud. She'd overturned the bucket of produce, spilling green beans hither and yon. The rows were flattened, and water flooded the area. Ellis walked over to the hydrant, pulled the handle down, and shut it off. He turned back to his mother. "I've never been ashamed of you before, Ma. But I am now." He paused. "How are you going to fix this? And not just the garden. Mrs. Yano is the most gentle and giving woman I know. I used to think that of you, too."

Ellis turned around. He found the stick his mother had used and broke it over his knee. He broke the halves into half again and dropped the pieces onto the ground. He left his mother standing forlorn in the garden.

***

For three days, his mother's fury took a different direction. She got up every morning, dressed and slammed pans around while she fixed breakfast. Then she cleaned. She barked orders at Emily as they dusted, swept, and mopped every nook and cranny.

One day at the midday meal, Emily finally broke down in tears. "What is wrong with you, Ma? You're angry every day, and everything I do is wrong. Luke was my brother, you know. He belonged to me too."

Emily ran out of the house, and Lee abruptly rose from the table and went back to the fields. Ellis sat there and stared at his mother. After a few moments, she began to speak.

"I remember when Luke was born. First child and born on my birthday. He was like a gift to me from God. Your father and I hadn't been married for a full year yet. I'd bundle Luke up and follow your pa into the fields, walking beside him, talking." She paused and smiled a little. "My mother was horrified, of course. Taking a newborn into the open air. And those times couldn't last. I got pregnant with Donald, and it became too much. But I'll never forget those times as a new bride with my new husband and my precious first born." She turned to face Ellis.

"I am angry, but if I'm angry at anyone, it would have to be God. The Lord giveth, and the Lord taketh away. Dust to dust and ashes to ashes. Such platitudes for grief." She bowed her head and began to cry again. "I'm so sorry, Ellis. Sorry for the way I've acted and the people I've hurt. I have to accept that my dearest Luke is dead."

Ellis pulled his mother to him, and she cried on his shoulder. Her tears washed away the image of that furious stranger he had seen.

Chapter Forty

Abe

Abe hated Mississippi. The summer heat and humidity increased to the point that he couldn't sleep at night. Even though the windows were open all night, it didn't stop Abe from sweating. The cold showers of April turned to lukewarm showers in June. And he'd never seen so many snakes in his life. He'd killed rattlesnakes in Minidoka and in Eastern Oregon, but here there were also copperheads, cottonmouths, corals, and more. One man in his company swore they made great eating and captured a snake whenever he could. Abe avoided them, careful not to disturb them on the hikes his company took.

The men also encountered chiggers, ticks, and poison oak. Shug told Abe the plant didn't exist in Hawaii.

"Really?" Abe said, surprised. "I memorized a saying in order to recognize it—'Beware of shiny leaves of three.' It's the oil on the plant leaf that will get you itching."

"And it's really hard if you get it on your hands," someone else said, elbowing Shug. "Makes peeing a challenge."

Abe laughed. Since he and Shug had become friends, humor made the tough training bearable. Abe's knowledge of ticks also came in handy. He'd spotted one burrowed in Shug's calf. The Hawaiian tried pulling it out with his fingers.

"That won't work. You'll leave half of him in there," Abe said. "Give me a match, or I can use a lit cigarette."

Wordlessly, Shug handed him the one he had in the corner of his mouth. As Abe held the cigarette at the end of the tick, it began backing out of Shug's leg.

"I'll be damned," Shug said.

"You might check out your more private parts. Ticks love to travel up the body from the boots." Abe laughed at Shug's quick step into the shower area.

Both Abe and Shug lost weight in basic training. No matter how big they were, each man received the same packed lunch: one baloney sandwich, one peanut butter and jelly sandwich, and an orange. The men were hungry all the time. At least they were as tall as the white sarge. The smaller men took three steps to his long stride and sometimes ran to catch up. Even the smallest in the group—five feet and one hundred five pounds—struggled to maintain his weight. Abe's company used their pay to buy candy bars and sweets at the PX to keep the weight up.

The first time the Buddhaheads went to the PX in Hattiesburg, Mississippi, the white GIs there refused to let them buy anything and called them 'Japs.' They came back and told their story to the rest of their buddies. Abe knew what was coming. The next opportunity to go to the PX, about thirty Hawaiians headed out. When the GIs again refused to sell them anything, the Hawaiians began a brawl. The fight wasn't over until every GI there was beaten. When Colonel Pence learned of the free-for-all, he lectured his men again about fighting but made sure a PX was established for the 442nd.

After the men returned from their visit to the Rohwer and Jerome internment camps, they also wanted their own USO club where the women from the internment camps could come for dances. Once a building was set aside, the women traveled round trips of five hundred miles for a single Saturday night. Abe and Shug decided to check it out, but both found it disappointing for different reasons. The women couldn't understand the Hawaiian pidgin, so there was little conversation. And the ratio of men to women at least seventy-five to one. Abe watched the dancing but missed Mary and left early.

Shug stayed for the beer if nothing else. "Some of them women were looking for specific volunteers from their hometowns or from their camps. I got to dance a couple of times, but one beauty claimed I was too rough," Shug complained. "Maybe next time will be better."

***

Abe was in his thirteenth week of basic training, with just another one to go, when the 100th Battalion returned to Camp Shelby in mid-July 1943. The troops had been on maneuvers in Mississippi and Louisiana, and they looked beat. The 100th joined the 442nd on Saturday morning for inspection and then got leave for the rest of Saturday and Sunday. Abe didn't even try to go to the USO, instead opting for the movies. The theatre seated two thousand men and had two showings a night. After that, he joined other soldiers in the lounge where men were playing card games. Abe went to the library side for some peace and quiet so he could write to Mary and his family. On Sunday, he and Shug gathered around various members of the 100th, listening to their stories and becoming acquainted.

On Monday, after a morning of physical training, men from the 100th Battalion shared the stories of their training and encouraged the men of the 442nd to learn as much as they could. "If you can make it through Camp Shelby, you can survive anywhere." The 100th Battalion received its colors the next day, July 20, and began to ready itself for combat. Their motto was, "Remember Pearl Harbor."

Abe and Shug became more thoughtful about their role in the Army. Their duty as soldiers weighed more heavily.

"How long do you think this war will last?" Shug asked Abe.

"It's been a year and a half," Abe said. "Allied forces just invaded Sicily last week. It's not some walk in the park."

"You think it'll last long enough for us to get there? We still have forty-some weeks of training to go."

"We'll get there," Abe said. "I just hope it's over before my little brother enlists next year. He wants to be a medic."

"We'll always need those," Shug said.

***

Before the 100th Battalion left for overseas, officers from the Military Intelligence Service came to interview the men from the 442nd Regimental Combat Team. They were looking for men who could speak, read, and write Japanese. Many could speak a home vocabulary but weren't literate at all.

Abe kept his head down, unwilling to go to Camp Savage in Minnesota. No way did he want to teach Japanese to others, translate documents, or interpret for the Intelligence Service. He ducked and dodged the officers, the interviews, and the large group lectures. He'd rather do latrine or KP duty than get removed from the 442nd.

When he skipped the lecture, he didn't realize Sarge was taking roll. "Where were you, soldier?" Sarge asked when he found Abe afterward.

"I had stomach issues, sir. I stayed close to the latrine," Abe lied. He stood at attention, looking straight ahead.

"You should know better than to try that excuse on me. After chow tonight, you're to report to HQ for latrine duty."

"Yes, sir." Abe didn't realize the MIS officers were quartered there.

It was nearly 2300 hours when Abe finished cleaning the showers, toilets, sinks, and counters. An officer he didn't recognize came in to wash his face and hands prior to retiring. Casually, he spoke to Abe in Japanese. Abe answered him in English but didn't get by with it.

"Speak Japanese, soldier, when I speak to you in that language," the officer commanded. "You're Abe Yano, correct?"

Abe stood up and realized all his efforts to avoid this interview had failed miserably. He'd only succeeded in shining up the officers' latrine.

"Yes, sir."

"We've been looking for you, you know. Your paperwork was flagged back in Minidoka as being a *kibei.*" The officer pulled out a couple sheets of paper from his back pocket. On it was Japanese script. He handed the first one to Abe.

"Start reading, private."

Abe took the papers. He read a simple story similar to the elementary school texts. It probably covered three hundred *kanji.* The officer grunted and took it from him. The second sheet was about Mount Fuji's eruption in 1707. There were a couple of *kanji* symbols unfamiliar to him, but the geological language was still within Abe's ability. He'd finished eighth grade in Japan before he'd come home and probably retained knowledge of eight hundred *kanji.* The officer held out his hand, and Abe returned the second sheet.

The third sheet was in cursive script. In spite of himself, Abe began showing off, reading the personal letter from a soldier to his wife. The letter ended abruptly in the middle of a sentence. Abe turned the page over, looking for the rest of the story and wondering what happened to the soldier.

"I always guessed at what that letter said," the officer commented. "I'm still trying to understand *sasho*. How'd you learn it?"

"It's the style my mother's letters were in from her family in Japan."

"Any chance with this?"

Abe studied the characters. "*Heiga*?" he asked.

The officer nodded.

"No, I'm not familiar with military or technical terms."

The officer handed him a final document. It was his transfer order to Camp Savage in Minnesota.

Abe's heart sank. The reporting date was August 23, 1943. Basic training would be over by then. He wondered how many others from the 442nd RTC would be transferring with him.

CHAPTER FORTY-ONE

GEORGE

The Yano family was finishing their supper when they heard a knock at the door. George thought it was probably Rex, ready to go out irrigating. He opened the door to find Mae Hertzog standing there with a basket of green beans and peas.

"I came to apologize to your mother. Will you let me speak to her?" Mae asked.

George couldn't find his voice. Mae Hertzog was the last woman he'd expected to see at their front door. He felt his mother's hand on his arm, moving him out of the way. He backed up but stood there protectively.

Chiharu bowed to Mae, and Mae awkwardly bowed back. At first glance, they couldn't have looked more different. Mae towered above Chiharu, taller by at least six inches. Mae was bigger too, with long fingers, square shoulders, and long, narrow feet. Chiharu was a diminutive woman. Her black eyes contrasted with Mae's gray ones. Yet both women had weathered faces, covered their faded dresses with aprons, and were used to hard work. Both had silver-streaked hair. Both worked on the farm. The two women looked at each other, puzzling out the similarities rather than the differences.

"Mae good?" Chiharu asked.

"No, Mae not good. I . . . I am so sorry, Mrs. Yano. I was angry, out of my head with grief. I lost my first son. I can't explain myself. I've never been so full of rage. And I took it out on you . . ."

George translated for his mother.

"Chiharu okay."

"My mother forgives too easily," George spoke over Chiharu's head. He was bewildered at his mother's kindness. This woman had beaten her, ignored her in the fields, and radiated disapproval at Chiharu's mere presence.

"I'll make it up to her. I'll do whatever I need to. I was horrible." Mae took off her hat and put it on Chiharu's head. "Here. I ruined yours."

Once again, George translated. "You know you tore her blouse too, but she's already mended that."

"I can't apologize enough," Mae said. "I have something for her. Would you translate for me?"

"I guess." George gave the family a look that released them from the room. Thomas picked up one of Doc's medical textbooks and went to his bunk in the next room. Pamela and Molly gathered the dishes from the table and began heating the water to wash them. "Why don't you come in and sit with Mother at the table."

Mae sat the basket of vegetables at her feet, reached into the pocket of her apron, and brought out a satin flag with three stars on it. Two were blue and one was gold. She smoothed it out on the table, her hands trembling, and bit her bottom lip. "Mrs. Yano, this is a flag that mothers of servicemen put in their windows to show the neighbors how many sons they have fighting for America."

George knew of these flags and had seen this one in the Hertzog's kitchen window. He translated for his mother and then waited for Mae to continue.

"This first blue star is for my second son, Donald, who was the first to sign up. He was only eighteen but had no plans to go to college, so after asking us, we agreed he could go. He's still training in the United States." Mae smiled a little as George caught up.

"The second blue one represents Sam," Mae continued. "George met him in the fields last year. Sam wants to fly warplanes, but I asked him if he couldn't sign up for transporting men and cargo. I don't want him to kill anyone." Mae paused as a tear trickled down her cheek. She whispered, "I don't know if my boys heed my wishes."

Chiharu nodded and said something in reply. "Our sons leave their mothers and follow their own paths."

George thought of Abe receiving his mother's blessing as he left the CCC camp and joining the other internees at Minidoka. Now he'd volunteered for the Army. Abe was certainly following his own destiny.

"The gold star symbolizes the ultimate sacrifice of a son killed in service to his country. This is my Luke, the oldest son, and the cause of my tremendous grief." Mae stroked the gold-colored star with her fingers.

"Poor Mae," Chiharu said and put her hands over her heart and bent her head.

After a shuddering breath, Mae picked up the flag and, folding it gently, returned it to the apron pocket. From the second pocket, Mae took out another white, satin flag with one blue star in the center. "This flag is for you, Mrs. Yano. You also have a son—Abe, I believe his name is—serving in the armed forces. I hope you never have to replace this blue star for a gold one."

Chiharu spread out the flag and stroked the blue star. George couldn't believe what he heard and sat mutely at the kitchen table. Molly came over, put her hands on George's shoulders, and quietly explained.

Chiharu caressed the satin material and whispered, "Abe." She nodded and looked into Mae's eyes. "Friends? Mae and Chiharu, friends?"

"Yes, that's right." Mae offered a wobbly smile. She reached across the table and squeezed Chiharu's hand.

Mae handed Chiharu the basket of vegetables and waited until Chiharu emptied it onto a clean dish towel. They walked outside to the garden, and the women talked as much as they could, pointing to this plant and then another. George stood at the window and watched.

"I can't believe what just happened," George said. "If it had been me, I wouldn't have let that woman into the house."

Pamela walked past him with the tin bowl full of dishwater to empty outside on the growing wildflowers. Molly joined him at the window. "And there wouldn't be a war if the women were in charge."

CHAPTER FORTY-TWO

MOLLY

Molly felt horrible. She was nauseous, and smells made her sick.

When Chiharu found her bent over at the end of the garden row, her hoe on the ground, vomiting in the weeds, she asked, "What is wrong, Molly? Are you ill?"

She described her symptoms as best she could in Japanese.

"Do you think you are pregnant?"

Molly was horrified. "Of course not, Mother-in-law. George and I have decided to wait to start our family."

"Ah. Babies come in their own time, you know."

"But George is adamant. He insists we wait."

Chiharu nodded her head and smiled a little. "Men do not control the universe, my daughter-in-law. You will discover this soon, I think."

That night, Molly told George about her vomiting, smells, and the days since she had her last bleeding. He didn't understand her cycle or what to expect.

"Are you sure?" he asked. His bewilderment endeared him to her.

"Not yet. I'll wait a bit more. I've never been pregnant before, you know." Molly kissed George and smiled at the worry lines on his forehead.

After two more weeks, she asked George to take her to see Doc at the CCC camp. While he examined Molly in a back room, George waited outside in the reception area. When Doc finished, he joined George while she dressed. She listened at the partially open door to hear how George would take the news.

"Congratulations, son. You will be a father next spring."

"What? You're sure? How can this happen?"

Doc chuckled. "I assume you know."

Molly smiled at George's naivete.

"What do I need to do? How can I help her?" George was embarrassed to admit to the doctor that he only understood the basics about pregnancy.

"Have you ever seen anything born before?"

"I saw a cat give birth to kittens. Calves from cows."

"It's not exactly the same." And so Doc gave him an overview of what he could expect during pregnancy, birth, and motherhood.

Molly listened carefully. Her own mother had told her little. Eventually, she opened the door and stepped out. George beamed at her, and she smiled tentatively. "I'm sorry. I know you wanted to wait."

George hooted with joy, lifted her off the floor and spun her around. When he put her down, Molly leaned her head onto his chest.

"A baby, George. We're going to have a baby."

***

Molly knew impending fatherhood gave George more to worry about. He wanted a bright future for his son—or daughter—but he was convinced their first child would be a boy. One evening, he spoke to his mother about the child's future.

"I've given this a lot of thought, Mother. If we are to be accepted as American citizens, we must speak English. Our child must speak English only. We have a future in this country if we fit in and adjust to the culture. We cannot be both Japanese and American. Do you understand? I don't want you teaching our child any Japanese. It's for the best."

George was firm in his beliefs. *Too firm*, Molly thought.

"*Hai*." Chiharu hung her head and stared at her hands folded in her lap.

Molly thought of the pain it would cause Chiharu not to be able to understand one's own grandchild, especially her first.

"*Yes*, Mother. Not *hai*." George got up from his chair, impatient with her. "Yes," he repeated.

"Yes," Chiharu whispered.

Life could be so cruel, Molly thought. She renewed her vow to teach her mother-in-law English. Perhaps the baby's arrival would provide as much incentive as the coins Chiharu added to the tin. She studied her husband's set expression. He was so determined to control life. He needed to learn to bend, like the trees in the wind. She thought he had learned that lesson, but perhaps it was one George would need to realize over and over. Molly examined the tiny stitches she was sewing in a baby's gown. Perhaps this would be her role in their marriage. She determined to bring up the subject again when George would be more amenable to considering both sides.

CHAPTER FORTY-THREE

ELLIS

It had been one year since Jeannie and Jimmy had drowned. Although Ellis's grief had faded, the anniversary brought back nightmares. Butch left him alone, but an occasional shoulder nudge or smirk let Ellis know all was not forgotten. And now his dad was drilling the Adrian Home Guard, and it included Butch. Ellis would see him every Saturday evening all summer long.

One night after the drills were over, Ellis saw Butch seated on the bleachers overlooking the ball fields. He was absorbed in his thoughts when Ellis approached him. "Know what day this is?"

"Yeah." Butch scowled at him and scooted over, putting more space between them.

Ellis sat down. He wanted to patch things up. "I was just thinking about Jimmy and Jeannie. Sure do miss them."

"Me too. Jeannie had so much spunk." Butch leaned back and put his elbows on the wooden row behind him. "I haven't found anyone else close to her."

"You know Jimmy had a crush on her?"

Butch rubbed his hand over his face. "Who wouldn't? She was a firecracker." He looked at Ellis and nodded his head. "You're the only one who misses them as much as I do. That don't mean I forgive you for their deaths. I can't imagine standing there, watching them drown, unable to prevent it."

"It haunts me," Ellis admitted. "I dream about it all the time and still I can never change what happened."

"I know that. And I can't stop blaming you for it. Guess it'll always be that way." Butch punched Ellis lightly on the shoulder. "See you next week." He joined his father at their pickup.

Ellis sighed with relief. That was as close to a ceasefire as he was going to get. He'd take it.

***

A week later, the guard was warming up with their calisthenics when Ellis saw the Butler pickup pull in. It was a dirty, black 1937 Ford. Junior was driving, and he parked cock-eyed instead of pulling in straight. Ellis was signing the men in and frowned as the father and son walked over to the field with their shotguns. Something was wrong, but he didn't yet know what.

Lee showed two men how to thrust and parry their guns as if they were using bayonets. Butch joined right in with the others, but Junior stood aside, watching.

"Ya gotta lunge harder!" Junior yelled belligerently at his son, swaying on his feet. "Ya can't stick a bayonet into a Jap with that easy poke. He's gonna kill ya first."

Lee headed to Ellis to take over the sign-in. He stood beside Junior, talking quietly. Even so, Ellis couldn't help but overhear.

"You're a bit late tonight. You stop at the Bright Spot before you came to drill?" Lee didn't have to ask; Ellis could smell the liquor on him.

"Only had a nip. We was early, and I just couldn't get the truck to drive by." Junior smiled and clapped Lee on the back. "I know ya tole me I had to be sober. It's the firsh time."

"I can't let you drill with your gun if you've had anything to drink. Why don't you give it to me."

"Sure thing. I'll start lunging with a pretend gun." Junior laughed at his own humor but handed Lee his weapon. Lee checked the gun. It was unloaded.

"And now I need you to go home. I'm recording a demerit next to your name. This is your only warning. Next time you have something to drink before drilling, don't bother coming."

Ellis held his breath. Junior was known for being physical.

Junior was slow in understanding, but his eyes turned from brown to black. "Gimme back my gun, then."

"I'll bring it out to your place tomorrow. Butch should probably drive you home."

Junior didn't move his eyes off Lee's face. "Butch! We're leavin'. Come on over here."

Butch jogged over. He stopped beside Ellis, keeping a safe distance from his father.

"I'd like you to leave your gun with me." Lee reached out to Butch and grabbed it. "I'll bring them out to your place tomorrow."

Butch's shame slowly burned a fiery red up his throat to his face.

"Mr. Hertzog here don't want any Butlers in his precious guard. We're going home." Butch started to protest, but Junior cuffed him on the back of his head.

Lee and Ellis watched the pair walk over to their pickup. From a distance, Ellis heard Junior growl, "Get over there. I'm drivin'." The pickup bucked a couple times before he peeled out, spewing gravel behind him.

"Sorry you had to witness that, son," Lee said. "Let's join the rest of the men."

Ellis knew Butch was going to hold it against him that Junior had been drunk and Lee had kicked him out of the practice. The shaky truce they'd managed to forge was undoubtedly broken.

***

Ellis clattered down the stairs on his way in to dinner after irrigating the lower fields. He'd heard some disturbing news from George just a while ago and he needed to talk to Pa about it. He washed his hands in the bathroom, dried them, and then let himself into the main rooms. Ma and Emily were just setting the serving bowls on the table. The family bowed their heads as Pa blessed the food, and then Ellis came out with it.

"Doc was hit by a dark truck last night when he was walking back to the CCC camp. George stopped to tell me the news on his way back from the Ontario hospital."

"Oh, no! Is he going to be all right?" asked Lee.

"Too soon to tell. The truck knocked him in the ditch and kept on going. Doc managed to make it to the next farmhouse, and the farmer there took him to the hospital. George said he ruptured a kidney and has cuts and bruises all over his face and body," Ellis related. "Thing is, the pickup had to cross to the other side of the road to hit him."

"Does the sheriff know who was driving?"

Ellis shook his head. "Only that the truck was dark. The headlight on the driver's side could be bent. They figure that's what hit Doc in the kidney. They're guessing the owner lives close to the CCC camp."

His father frowned. "It could be Junior. He lives over that way. Drives a dark pickup. I don't know if I'm right, but there's one way to find out. Let's return the Butlers' guns, pay a neighborly call."

***

When Lee pulled in, he stopped his truck beside Junior's. Ellis could see the headlight was knocked askew, and the bracket that held it was cracked. Butch opened the door and stood there in his jeans and t-shirt. Ellis sank down into the seat. After a couple of moments, Butch closed the door behind him and walked up to the Hertzogs. He had a black eye, and his lip was swollen and cut.

"What are you doing here? I thought you didn't want nothin' to do with us Butlers."

"I brought your shotguns," Lee said. "Is your pa around?"

"Pa's passed out. You won't be able to talk to him until at least this evening."

"Your ma?"

Butch looked at the ground and dug a hole with his boot into the soft, powdery dirt. "She's too ashamed to come out." He looked up and bawled, "It's your fault, ya know. He beat us both when we got home."

"Your pa the one who hit the Japanese on his way home last night?" Lee nodded toward the crooked headlight. Ellis couldn't believe he'd asked straight out.

Butch looked like he'd been pulled up short. "What Japanese?" he asked.

"It was Doc. Remember the one who wrapped Jimmy's ribs after the run-in with the train?" Ellis said.

Butch nodded sharply. "He's not dead, is he?"

"No. He has a ruptured kidney," Lee said. "He can live on one if they can't save it."

Butch studied the ground. He slowly covered up the hole his boot had made and tamped the dirt down.

"What makes you think Pa done it?" Butch kept his eyes on his boots.

"The headlight on your pa's pickup is knocked askew. I don't remember it being that way last night at the drill for the home guard."

Butch nodded and looked Lee in the eyes. "So now what? You gonna get the sheriff?"

Lee studied the boy. "Yes. You're going to have to tell the story. You were with your pa."

"Maybe I fell asleep on the way home and didn't see nothin'."

"The sheriff will arrest him."

"Maybe. But it won't stick."

"A hit-and-run is a serious crime."

Butch reacted angrily. "My pa's mean. If he wakes up, he'd let you know it too."

"He probably would try." Lee paused as he watched Butch. He reached over to Ellis and got the two shotguns. "Here," he said to Butch. "You might want to keep them out of sight for the next couple of days." Lee thought for a moment. "The sheriff will be out here soon. Are you willing to tell him the truth?"

"I'll get beat again. No way I'm talkin' to the sheriff!" Butch cried.

"Guess we'll have to leave it in the sheriff's hands, then." Lee put the pickup in gear and backed out of the drive.

"I didn't tell you nothin'!" Butch yelled. He threw a handful of dirt at Ellis's window.

Ellis recoiled and then looked at Butch through the back window. Butch shook his fist at them as Lee drove off. Ellis wondered what Butch would do now that Ellis had seen him humiliated twice. Butch was like a boil ready to burst.

CHAPTER FORTY-FOUR

ABE

Camp Savage had a familiar feel to it. It was built by the Civilian Conservation Corps, and the buildings and layout were similar to Cow Hollow. The state highway and railroad ran parallel to the camp, and the Minnesota River was just a half mile away. The barracks looked the same, smelled the same, and drew the same scorn from the new recruits. One difference was immediately apparent, though. Prejudice against the Americans of Japanese ancestry, or AJAs, didn't exist. No one called them "Japs," and there were no signs over the restrooms or drinking fountains delineating who could enter or drink the water. The tension in Abe's shoulders relaxed a bit.

The soldiers met the commander of the Military Intelligence Service Language School on their first official day, August 23, 1943. Colonel Kai E. Rasmussen spoke to them in Japanese. Abe sat up, straining to hear, surprised by the colonel's fluency. Colonel Rasmussen explained he had been a language attaché in Japan until 1940. In his welcoming speech, he emphasized that the school was an arm of the intelligence service, and the men needed to keep the school and its purpose a secret. He warned that letters home would be censored. Then he introduced the head instructor of the MISLS as John Aiso, a civilian and an attorney prior to accepting the role at MISLS in October 1941.

Mr. Aiso stood in front of the soldiers, hands clasped behind his back and feet shoulder-width apart. He studied the men for a long moment before he began speaking in Japanese. "You have been brought here to study hard and to learn much in a short time. You represent your communities, your parents, your brothers and sisters.

Make them proud of you! I expect patriotism in the face of prejudice, as well as self-discipline and the fulfillment of your duty to the country you were born in." His voice boomed across the room as he explained the language exams and what they would learn.

"Prove your loyalty! Hold your head up and serve honorably the United States of America." Aiso bowed to the students and returned to his seat.

Abe wiped his sweaty palms on his trousers. Maybe this wouldn't be as easy as he thought.

The men were divided up according to their last names and given a place to report for the language tests. Abe located the classroom and then found his name at a desk. Two sharpened pencils waited for him. The man at the front of the class was dressed in a suit and tie, obviously a civilian. Would the soldiers give him the respect they would give an Army instructor? Guess he'd find out. Abe sat down and watched the other soldiers enter and find their seats. The men exchanged small talk while they waited.

When every seat was taken, the man in front stood up and rapped his pen on a glass for their attention. The room fell silent. "This language proficiency test is very simple," said the man. "You have a thousand *jouyou kanji* characters to translate into English. The character is listed, then used in a sentence to give it context. The test begins with the most common vocabulary and increases in difficulty. When you reach the point you can't translate any more characters, you may turn your test in to me and return to your barracks. Any questions?" No one raised a hand. "Good. When you receive a test, you may begin."

The test reminded Abe of memorizing his multiplication tables in elementary math. This time, however, no one wanted to be the first one finished. After an hour, Abe had translated four pages. No one had given up yet. In the second hour, the trickle of soldiers turning in their tests turned into a deluge. In the third hour, only four men remained. Abe still had three pages to go. He began skipping the unrecognizable characters to see if there were any others he understood. Scowling at the pages, he guessed at a couple—they sort of looked familiar—but finally gave up. As he turned in his test, two more soldiers stood up and brought their tests forward. Only one man was still at it.

Outside, the bright summer sunshine felt good on Abe's face. He turned to the short soldier next to him and asked, "How do you think you did?"

"Good enough to be in the top group," said the soldier.

"Me too," chimed in the third. "Are you both *kibei*?"

"Yep," Abe said.

"I'm more literate in Japanese than English," admitted the second soldier.

Abe reached out his hand. "Abe Yano." He shook hands with both soldiers. "I have a feeling we're going to see a lot of each other."

"Ken Ogata," said the smaller soldier. "I nearly washed out of Basic. What a relief to receive orders for the language school." Ken was probably five foot two and barely a hundred pounds. He was peppy, though, and cracked a smile.

The third soldier introduced himself as Masayuki Higa. "Aren't you the guy who was always getting into fights with Shug?"

Abe admitted he was. "I wanted to stay with the four-four-two fighting beside Shug. I'll miss that big lug."

"I tried to stay away from those melees," admitted Masayuki. "Didn't look like too much fun." Masayuki stood about five-foot-six, wore glasses, and was mild-mannered.

"You guys have family in the internment camps?" Abe asked.

"Poston, Arizona," Masayuki said. "Parents and two younger brothers."

"How about you?" Abe turned to Ken.

"Manzanar, in California," Ken said. "I'm an only child. You?"

Abe nodded. "My mom, two brothers, and a sister are working as itinerant laborers for two farmers in a little town in Eastern Oregon outside the military zone. My older brother just got married. I spent the winter in Minidoka in Idaho."

Just exchanging the minimum information about each other gave them a common bond. The three men hurried to the mess hall. They were hungry and knew they'd be the last ones in line.

***

Abe, Ken, and Masayuki all qualified for the upper division classes. So did the soldier who was still working on the test when they left the classroom. They weren't alone. Of the two hundred fifty soldiers from the 442nd, about seventy men were assembled in the long and skinny classroom for the upper division.

Ken led the way to the front of the classroom. "I can't see over the other men's heads."

Abe chose a seat in the second row behind Ken, and Masayuki sat next to Abe. The soldier who had finished last on the test arrived late and found the only desk vacant next to Ken. Nodding briefly to Ken, he sat down.

At their desks were *Naganuma* readers, volumes one through three, developed in 1931 by Naoe Naganuma, who worked in Tokyo for the United States. The oral method of teaching Japanese was part of the Naganuma method, using the vocabulary in many contexts. The MISLS instructors wrote both the military language text plus a *Heigo Tokuhon* reader of military vocabulary. Those volumes were plopped down next to the readers.

Abe opened the Naganuma reader, curious as to where he'd place himself. He recognized many of the characters in volumes one and two, but most were new in volume three. Here come the flash cards, Abe thought. Then he opened the *heigo* text and shuddered. It looked like he was going to learn all about armaments, tactics, field service regulations, and how to interrogate prisoners of war. Abe lacked technical military vocabulary. More flashcards. He sighed at the hard work ahead.

An AJA man in uniform entered the classroom and went to the front. Abe listened as the man spoke rapid-fire Japanese, his pronunciation flawless. Abe was able to follow most of what the soldier said, although his mind felt rusty and slow. The more specific vocabulary about the Japanese military went right over his head. The class was absolutely still, straining forward, concentrating on understanding.

The instructor explained that each man would be in class seven hours a day, with two hours of supervised study each night. Exams were held every Saturday morning. On Wednesday afternoons, the soldiers would participate in conditioning marches. Ken turned around to Abe and scowled at that news. Every Monday morning, the soldiers would either move up into a more advanced section, stay in the same class, or move down. Some re-sorting was to be expected; however, the instructor warned, about ten percent of the group would fail to graduate, which could be for academic or non-academic reasons. "All students will undergo the scrutiny of a background check to make sure of their loyalty and patriotism to the United States. These are conducted by the Counter Intelligence Corps, or CIC. If you hear any discussion or see any action by a fellow soldier that would be considered disloyal, it is your responsibility to report that information to your sergeant."

Abe didn't like the thought of informants. A snitch. A betrayer. But whoever they might be, they wouldn't find anything on him. His face hardened. He'd do more listening, more studying than talking. He'd be an exemplary student. For the first time, he was glad Shug hadn't come along. Abe decided he couldn't let another person get close to him. He'd rather be aloof than compromised.

CHAPTER FORTY-FIVE

GEORGE

Two days after Doc had been injured in a hit-and-run incident, George found out Sheriff Hamilton had arrested Junior Butler. Ellis and Lee had reported Butler's pickup damage and that Junior had been drunk the night before at the Home Guard's training. That night, the sheriff had woken him from a drunken slumber and jailed him while the case was being investigated.

George knew the sheriff from his early days at the labor camp, back when they were trying to establish the rules and curfew for the Japanese workers. He also remembered the worker who had been beaten up by a farmer. Abe had been incensed at the charge against the farmer for disturbing the peace, feeling it had been much too lenient. George decided to go talk to the sheriff about the investigation and the charge against Junior Butler.

Sheriff Hamilton was in his office when George arrived. "You here about Doc?" he asked.

It'd been a year and a half since George had spoken to the sheriff. His golden-brown eyes were alert and curious. George knew he didn't miss much.

"Yes, sir." George removed his hat. "I have a few questions I'd like to ask."

"Come on back," the sheriff replied.

George followed him into a conference room. Apparently, the sheriff's own desk was too public. George appreciated the privacy. The long table was dotted with coffee stains, and the room was cooled by an overhead fan. The sheriff gestured to an empty chair and sat in one across from it.

"How's Doc doing today?" the sheriff asked. "I haven't had an update yet."

"His blood pressure stabilized, and there's no more blood in the urine," George reported. "He still has multiple bruises and a couple of sore ribs, but none broken."

"So, the kidney doesn't have to be removed?"

"The surgeon said we have to wait and see. Doc still has low back pain."

The sheriff picked up a pencil abandoned on the table and ran his fingers down its length. He tapped it on the table a couple of times. "You said you had questions?"

George cleared his throat. "You've arrested Junior Butler. Have you charged him with anything yet?"

"He's in the drunk tank. Unusual to hold someone there for two days, but I thought I'd give his wife and son time for their bruises to heal."

George felt a pang of anger. "He beat his family and ran down Doc?"

The sheriff narrowed his eyes as he studied George. "Now, we haven't proven that he was the one that knocked Doctor Yamaguchi into the ditch. Doc couldn't identify the truck except to say it was a dark color. That could mean most every truck in the county. He didn't see who was driving."

"What about the Hertzog's report that Junior was drunk, and the headlamp was knocked down?"

"You heard about that, huh?"

"They're neighbors of ours," George admitted.

"You know how many times Junior has been drunk?" The sheriff leaned toward George and looked him in his eyes. "And the truck damage? Who knows when or how that headlamp was knocked askew? For all I know, Junior coulda punched his wife into the car, and that's how it was done. Or Junior ran off the road into a ditch. Or Butch ran it into a ditch. We're not even sure who was driving. A defense attorney would have a field day coming up with reasonable doubt in this case."

"But you and I know he did it." George clenched his hands into fists.

"Maybe. But that's a problem," the sheriff said, tipping the chair back on its legs. "Butch wouldn't say anything to me. He hid behind his father the whole time I was there."

George mulled that over. "So, Junior gets away with it?"

"Let's say Butch changes his mind and is willing to testify against his own father. The jury is convinced and finds Butler guilty. Then what?" the sheriff asked. The chair clunked as the sheriff put it back down on the floor.

"Butler goes to jail, and Doc gets justice? Sounds like a fair outcome to me," George said. He squinted his eyes at the sheriff.

"Fair. Now *that's* an interesting word." The sheriff banged the tabletop with his flat hand, scraped the chair back, and began pacing back and forth. "The War Relocation Authority would be all over this case. If the prosecutor proves Butler hit Doc *because he's Japanese*, then all of you Japs head to an internment camp so you'll be safe. The farmers lose all the labor they need. Some go bust. You all lose the ability to earn a decent wage, attend public school, or live outside barbed wire fences. Think that's fair?" The sheriff turned on his heel and glared.

George sat still, his mind turning over the sheriff's words. He chose his next words carefully. "That's a compelling argument, Sheriff," George said. "How hard is it to build a case against Junior?"

The sheriff stood behind the chair, rocking back and forth on his heels. "Butch is the lynchpin in this case. If he refuses to testify—or tell the *alleged* truth about what happened—his father goes free. I can't try a man for driving a dark pickup and having a loose side mirror."

"But Doc's in the hospital!"

"Now there's a fact. That's the only one I can find in this whole investigation." The sheriff cocked his head. "Any more questions?"

George realized it was futile to continue. "So, Junior Butler will be released?"

"Probably in the morning. I'm stretching out the length of his stay as it is."

George scooted his chair back and stood to leave. The two men shook hands, and George put his hat back on.

"Relay my concern to Doc about his injuries. I hope he continues to heal."

"I'll do that," George muttered.

"The law is all shades of gray, not just black and white. Sorry this case isn't more cut and dried," the sheriff said as he escorted George to the front door.

George laughed bitterly. "Sheriff, you don't need to tell me that. Tell it to Doc."

CHAPTER FORTY-SIX

MOLLY

Once the harvest was over and her morning sickness had abated, Molly left to visit her family in Minidoka. It had been eight months, the longest she'd been separated from them. She hadn't revealed the pregnancy to her family, as Doc had told her to wait until after the first trimester. She hugged the navy-blue wool coat around her, hiding an instinctual caress of her belly. The small roundness could only be seen with close scrutiny.

In the letter to Mr. Stafford to ask permission to visit, she'd signed her name *Molly Mita Yano*. She wanted to make sure he drew the correct conclusion. Mr. Stafford responded affirmatively and said he'd have a car waiting at the Eden siding to meet the train.

Molly peered out the train window as the engine pulled up at Eden and spied Mary standing by a black Ford, a soldier in the driver's seat.

"You have a good visit, now," the porter said as he put down a step and held her hand as she descended. Molly picked up her pace as she and Mary hurried to greet each other. "I've missed you so much," Molly said as she hugged her sister.

It took longer than Molly thought it would to check in at the administration building. Afterwards, she and Mary hurried through the pathway to the family's barracks. Stopping outside the door, Molly slipped off her shoes and then glimpsed her family over Mary's shoulder.

Kameko squealed and ran over to hug her oldest sister. "I'm so happy to see you!" She held Molly by both arms. "Doesn't look like you've done anything to your hair since you left. It's longer than I've ever seen you wear it."

"I like your new hairdo," Molly said. Kameko had cut her hair to curl just under her chin, long enough to tuck the sides behind her ears.

"I'll give you a new 'do before you leave," Kameko promised. She moved aside as their father came forward.

"*Konnichiwa*, Daughter," greeted Kentaro. "It is kind of your husband to allow you to visit your parents."

Molly kissed him on the cheek. "It is wonderful to be here, Father. You are looking well. No recurrence of pneumonia?"

"None. Nothing to worry about," he said and smiled reassuringly.

She turned to her mother, Tak`e. Her hair was a bit grayer, but otherwise she hadn't changed much since Molly had seen her last. "Mother. I've missed you."

"Let me take your coat, Daughter." Molly shrugged it off and handed it to her mother who hung it up on a nail by the others. "You are with child?" Tak`e asked shrewdly.

Molly's face lit up. "*Hai*. The baby should be with us in early spring."

Her mother held her out at arms-length. "It's going well?"

"Just a little sickness at first. I am very healthy now."

"This is good, Molly," her father beamed.

Tak`e patted Molly's hand, a small smile lighting up her face.

"I knew it," Mary declared. "I just didn't want to spoil the surprise by asking first."

Kameko clapped her hands. "I'm going to be an auntie. How wonderful!"

Tak`e pulled out a wooden chair. "Eat." She uncovered a plate of chicken, rice, and green beans. "Are you tired from your journey?"

Molly shook her head briefly but couldn't say anything with her mouth full. She sighed as she ate another mouthful of chicken and rice. It felt wonderful to be in the bosom of the family again.

***

The next day, Molly noticed that a second family shared housing space with the Ashida family next door. "Weren't there also some extra cots in the recreation area?" she asked her father.

"Do you remember the loyalty questionnaire?" Kentaro asked.

"Of course," Molly said. "But that was last winter."

"We worried at that time that there would be consequences, that *Issei* would be sent back to Japan or families separated."

"Has something happened?" Molly asked. She knew being far away meant she missed the nuances of camp news and how it impacted the Japanese.

"The loyalty questionnaire divided many camps into two sides: those who said yes/yes and those who said no/no on questions twenty-seven and twenty-eight. Do you remember?"

"Yes. These were the ones that Stafford rewrote for us here at Minidoka."

"And we were the most loyal of the camps. But we still had about three hundred and thirty people who answered no/no. Many others were angry with the American government, and the split between those considered loyal or disloyal created much more trouble at the Tule Lake Internment Camp than here. Men loyal to the Japanese Empire, the *Hoshi-dan*, started a physical regimen in the morning, all wearing scarves around their heads and chanting Samurai slogans. All camp members had to speak Japanese, and the *Hoshi-dan* threatened the yes/yes families. Even high school children were getting beaten for their beliefs."

Kentaro told the story in a low, dispassionate voice, sitting on his cot. Molly moved closer, both to give him comfort and to hear better.

"Officials relocated all of the region's so-called 'no/no boys' to Tule Lake, including the three hundred and thirty people from here, and now call it a segregation camp. They've redistributed other families across the northwest. For us in Minidoka, it has caused a housing shortage. Some families are doubling up, and others are having to sleep in the recreation centers. The crowding will ease once farmers need help in the fields in spring."

"What about the people in the segregation camp? Do we know what's happening to them?" Molly asked.

"The *Tulean Dispatch* was shut down in October. Other than personal letters, it is difficult to know," Kentaro said.

"What about here in Minidoka?" Molly was troubled.

"There is more grumbling. We still sent over three hundred volunteers for the Army, more than any other camp. I hope we'll get through this troubled period."

Molly nodded. She wanted to remember the details to share with George when she returned.

***

Molly had a list of things she wanted to do while in Minidoka. One was to visit Miss Shepherd in the fifth-grade classroom where she had worked. The third day, she walked over to Stafford Elementary, timing her arrival for the end of the day when Miss Shepherd could spend a few minutes chatting.

The children were just being released, and Molly waited for a few minutes. She was pleased when some of the children remembered her and called out their greetings. Molly stepped into the classroom and called, "Miss Shepherd? It's Molly Mita."

Miss Shepherd looked up from the stack of papers she was grading at her desk in the back of the classroom. "Molly! But it's Molly Yano now, isn't that right? It's so good to see you."

"I wanted to be sure to visit you. I'm staying with my parents for a week and I brought you a present," Molly said. She brought out a bag of apples she'd been saving and a rectangular tin filled with sharpened pencils and red pens, erasers, and several rulers.

Miss Shepherd laughed. "What else could a teacher want? You've doubled my teaching supplies. And red apples! They look delicious. We don't see many of those in this desert."

"We have farmers from Hood River bring them to Eastern Oregon. No teacher ever gets enough thanks these days, and you were so good to me." Molly sat in a student desk near Miss Shepherd.

"Do you think you'll be a teacher someday?" Miss Shepherd asked.

"Not this year," Molly said. "I'm going to have a baby in the spring."

"Oh, how wonderful! You'll make a great mother."

"I wanted to ask you if I have a girl, would it be all right to name her Alice after you?"

Tears welled in Miss Shepherd's eyes. "It would be an honor, Molly. I couldn't be more delighted."

Molly stayed and talked to her mentor for an hour, sharing details about her new home, George, and her in-laws.

"I have a surprise too," Miss Shepherd said. "I'm getting married in the spring after school is out. This may be my last year teaching."

"Oh! Who is the lucky man? Do I know him?" Molly asked.

"I met him at church in Jerome. He's a widower with three children, all in elementary school there. I'll have a ready-made family."

"The children will miss you," Molly said.

"Yes, I suppose so." Miss Shepherd looked around the classroom. "I've taught them what all fifth graders need to know, but they have given me an education too." She looked wistful and bit her bottom lip. "I'll never forget my experience here in Minidoka. I feel as though I've lived through history. I've learned so much about the Japanese, their culture, their values." She wiped tears from her eyes.

Molly gave Miss Shepherd a moment to collect herself. She noticed the children's work on display on the classroom walls and wove her way to the nearest examples. A poem illustrated by a student caught her attention. Miss Shepherd joined her. "That's one of my star pupils this year," she said. "There are always a couple from each class who seem destined to make a mark on the world. I'm humbled to be their teacher."

"They are lucky to have you." Molly read a couple more poems and then said, "I must be going and let you get on with your work. I hope your future family appreciates you half as much as we have. Goodbye, Miss Shepherd." Molly squeezed her hands.

"Goodbye, Molly. I hope you'll write to me. I'd like to know what becomes of you once this wretched war is over."

"I will. I'll let you know if a little Alice arrives."

Miss Shepherd laughed and walked arm in arm with Molly to the door. They hugged each other goodbye, and Molly left. After a dozen steps, she turned to find Miss Shepherd still at the door. They waved to each other again, their final farewell.

***

One evening, while Kameko was cutting Molly's hair, Mary sat near them, working on an embroidery project. She was working on a traditional picture of a geisha in a red kimono looking into a mirror. The girl's back was to the observer, but her face was visible in the mirror. The white makeup, red lips, and black eyebrows almost hid the beauty of her face. Molly was always amazed at the artistic talent Mary showed with a needle and thread.

"How often do you hear from Abe?" Molly asked.

"At least once a week and sometimes two," Mary said. "Doesn't he write home also?"

"Yes. The last letter we received, he told us that new instructors had arrived from the battlefields of the Aleutian Islands. They told Abe and the other students more of what they could expect to do in the field once they graduate."

"He tries to be light-hearted with his news to me," Mary continued. "I guess the language school also accepted men of Chinese ancestry, thinking they would find it easier to learn the Japanese *kanji* characters, but they can't keep up with the AJAs. Abe thrives on competition. I can just imagine him studying an hour more each night just to show them up!" Mary shook her head at Abe's folly. The three sisters laughed together.

"Did he tell you the story of the invasion of Kiska Island?"

Molly shook her head.

"The Japanese Imperial Army had abandoned the island two weeks before the Americans got there but left behind rice, bamboo shoots, and kegs of soy sauce. Kegs! The linguists were so happy to find a way to spice up their rations." Mary laughed at Abe's rendition.

"Whenever we receive a letter from Abe, he sends a dollar or two to add to Thomas's college savings," Molly said.

The girls sobered at Molly's reminder of what all the interned Japanese had lost.

"I wonder what Father's plan is for after the war," Kameko said. "We've been at Minidoka for over a year. It seems forever." She trimmed a couple inches off Molly's hair, so the shimmering black curls rested on her shoulders. She combed the hair all the way around, checking to make sure it was the same length.

Molly thought of her request to George, to allow the Mitas to live in Eastern Oregon with them. He'd agreed, but would her father want that as well? She only had one more day before she was to return to the Yano family. She didn't want to share her thoughts with her sisters until she'd talked it over with their father.

***

In the late afternoon, Molly and her father walked through the camp. They admired the gardens created while she'd been gone. Many Minidokans used greasewood carvings and rocks to intersperse plantings, creating beauty in defiance of the bleak desert of Idaho.

"*Otoosan*, have you given any thought to where you'll settle the family after the war? Will you try to move back to Portland?"

"I don't know if we'll be allowed back in western Oregon, Momoe. I have thought about it, but I have no control over much of our lives," Kentaro said.

"What about living near us in Eastern Oregon?"

"And farm? I have no experience in farming, no money for equipment." Kentaro shook his head. "I would not want to add to the burdens of your husband."

"What if we found a small store? You still have money from selling merchandise, don't you?" Molly wanted to give her father some hope for the future.

"And who would be my customers? It's more than having merchandise to sell."

"There are many *Issei* and *Nisei* living in the area now, many more than before. We are finding our way in the new community. Think of them and what needs they might have." Molly glanced at her father's face. To her relief, he seemed to be thinking about what she was saying.

"And George? Have you spoken to him about this?" His question was full of nuances—his pride, his squelched hopes, his shame. Molly answered very carefully.

"The Yanos have a plan for the future and, yes, it includes our combined families. You know that Mary and Abe are writing to each other and thinking of their future also. I would have two sets of grandparents for my children, aunties too. At least think about it, Father. You don't have to give an answer yet."

"I haven't been able to think of a future for so long," Kentaro mused. "Or to contemplate anything after the war."

"I know. Abe and Mary are waiting too."

"We'll see, Daughter. This idea of yours has merit. I must confer with your mother and determine whether a Japanese-owned business might succeed. What is the name of the largest city near the farm where you're living?"

"Ontario."

"Ah, yes. I remember the name now. Ontario." Kentaro clasped his hands behind his back and walked on, their conversation over for now.

***

Molly kissed her family goodbye the next morning. "I'll write to you and let you know how the pregnancy is going," she said to her mother.

When she kissed Kameko, Molly thanked her for the new hairdo. Her father gave her an awkward hug.

Mary walked to the camp's gate where a soldier was waiting to take Molly to the train. "It was a wonderful visit," Mary said.

The two sisters held each other in a prolonged embrace.

"I don't know when I'll be able to come again," Molly confided. "Perhaps next year after the harvest, when the baby is six months old."

"Or when the war is over," Mary said, "whenever that is. It can't go on forever."

"Take care of our folks." Molly knew she had to leave or she'd miss the train. She wiped the tears from her face and stepped out of the camp. Through the wire fence, she said one last goodbye, "*Sayonara.*"

"*Sayonara.*"

Molly watched her sister from the window until the car rounded a curve and she was out of sight.

CHAPTER FORTY-SEVEN

ELLIS

By the end of the harvest of '43, Ellis, Emily, Thomas, and Pamela had spent countless hours in the fields working together. The last load of beets lumbered to the Overstreet Beet Dump at the end of October, and school finally began. Ellis was relieved to finish the physical labor and start classes.

Thomas and Pamela attended high school in Adrian, just like the Hertzog children. The Yanos rode the first route to school, catching it at their corner. Ellis and Emily rode a different bus, walking down the road to its stop. Ellis wondered later if it would have been easier on Thomas and Pamela if it had been clear from the beginning they were friends. As it was, neither Ellis nor Emily had a chance to smooth the way for them.

When Ellis and Emily entered the high school, the hallway was abuzz about a fight in the gym between Butch, his friends, and the new Japanese boy. The principal had just broken it up, and the offenders were waiting in the office.

Ellis was surprised to find Pamela there as well. He hustled into the office and slid into the seat beside Thomas. "What happened? How'd you get into a fight so soon?"

"A kid named Butch had a couple of his friends try to beat me up."

Pamela sat there, arms folded in front of her, leaning back in the chair. Her eyes were closed, but tears still tracked down her face.

"Why's Pamela here?"

"The group surrounded us. Guess the principal figured she was somehow involved."

"Butch and his friends? I heard you threw two of them over your back. Kids are saying they didn't have a chance."

"What do you mean, they didn't have a chance? We were the ones outnumbered five to two! It was more than us being the new kids. We're the new *Japanese* kids. Are they forgetting who started the whole thing?"

"Ellis!" The principal came out of his office with Butch. "What are you doing here, talking to those two? They're in trouble."

"They're our neighbors, sir. They've been helping out the Allens and us all summer. Surely, Pamela didn't do anything wrong."

"Nevertheless, I want you to leave them alone. Go on to class."

"Yes, sir." Ellis headed out the door. "Good luck," he whispered to the Yanos.

"Butch, you go on too. I'll call you back if I need to clarify anything."

By fifth period, Thomas and Pamela were in class. Apparently, a visit from Ed and Rex Allen and George Yano convinced Mr. Patterson that the Farm Security Agency wouldn't be pleased if Adrian High School couldn't provide a safe place for the two students. No punches were thrown, although Pamela had been terrified. Mr. Patterson brought in Butch and his friends and talked to them sternly about the needs of their farming community and that they would be suspended if there was any more fighting or egging on others to fight. Patterson might have hoped the conflict was over, but the struggle just continued below the surface.

Ellis wasn't prepared when Butch and his friends started calling him Jap lover. He found folded up notebook paper in his locker with the two words on it. The boys called him the slur throughout the day. He tried to shrug it off, but the words bothered him. Finally, on his way home from school, he brought up the subject with Emily.

"Butch ever call you a Jap lover?" he asked.

"Yeah," she admitted. "Once."

"Didn't it bother you?"

"Not much," Emily said. "Besides, it's true, you know? I love Pamela and Thomas, as friends. They're certainly smarter and nicer than Butch. That's how I got him to stop."

"How?"

"I told him I'd rather be a Jap lover than a Butler lover any day!"

Emily laughed. "You should have seen his face." Emily glanced over at Ellis. "Name-calling bother you?"

"More than it should," Ellis said. He walked the last steps into the yard. "I wish I could have seen Butch's reaction. That was a smart retort."

***

A couple of weeks later, right before lunch, Ellis received a note from Mr. Russell, his music instructor, asking him to visit the practice room after he finished eating. He needed fifteen minutes of Ellis's time. The request wasn't unusual, as Ellis was the accompanist for the choir during concerts, and the Christmas one was coming up fast. As he headed toward the room, Pamela was in front of him.

"You going to see Russell too?" Ellis asked.

"Yes," Pamela said. "He wants to hear me sing as I'm new to the school. He walked in front of the choir yesterday and stopped to ask me to come in today. I'm so nervous."

"Don't be. Russell often works with individual singers during lunchtime."

"Ah. Here you are." Mr. Russell greeted Ellis and Pamela.

Ellis sat down at the piano.

"The first thing I want to do is test your vocal range," Mr. Russell said to Pamela. "But let's have you warm up first. Ellis, would you play a C scale?"

Ellis ran his right hand up the keyboard and back down one octave.

"Now Pamela, please sing that scale on an 'ah.'"

Thus, the trio began twice weekly vocal lessons. Mr. Russell's coaching enhanced Pamela's technique and helped her with breath support and clearer vowels. Ellis learned the various scales and drills that Pamela needed to practice. She had a wide range and a pure tone and developed from a second soprano to a first. Ellis and Pamela practiced at the Hertzog home twice a week also, and Emily occasionally joined them.

By Christmas, Pamela was ready to sing a solo of Schubert's *Ave Maria,* one of Ellis's favorite hymns. At first, he was too rigid in the timing, forcing Pamela to follow him rather than the other way around.

"I'd rather sing that more legato," Pamela requested. "You know, like a prayer."

As they worked together, Ellis's fingers began to breathe at the same time Pamela's voice did, and his tempo slowed or quickened depending on her phrasing. The music finally sounded like the blessing it was.

"I've never sung in front of people before," Pamela confided to Ellis one day after practice. "What if I get stage fright and forget the words?"

"I find that if I concentrate on the music instead, getting the message of the piece to the audience, I do better," Ellis said. "It's not about you as a singer, but you as a channel for the beautiful melody. Don't worry. You'll do great."

On the afternoon of the concert, Ellis took a deep breath as Pamela and the rest of the choir filed onto the stage. He certainly didn't want to be responsible for ruining the Christmas program, a highlight of the music department. Adrian High School's student body was seated on chairs across the gym floor, the seniors in front, as was their due, and teachers scattered throughout the audience. Pamela would perform her solo between the choir numbers and the band's selections.

When it was finally their turn, Pamela stepped forward in her green robe with a gold stole, the Adrian Antelope's school colors. She smiled timidly at Ellis as the choir exited behind her. Ellis began the introduction, and Pamela started to sing. At first, her voice trembled, but with added volume, the thin soprano became richer, fuller, and more robust. Ellis's steady rhythm lent strength and then a surge to the lyrics. At one point, Pamela held a note extra-long and looked to Ellis, subtly nodding at him when she was ready to continue. At the conclusion of the piece, she ended it in full voice, gradually softening, until Ellis played the last prayerful notes.

The audience clapped and rose to their feet, their faces filled with the beauty Pamela's solo had given them. She bowed, and Ellis stood to acknowledge the applause. As he looked out into the audience, he caught Butch's smirk and paused. Butch was looking from Pamela to Ellis and back. He caught his breath, unable to look away from the malice in Butch's face.

Chapter Forty-Eight

Abe

"You feelin' okay?" Masayuki asked one day.

"Sure," Abe said as they walked across a skiff of snow to the classroom, leaving their grassy footprints behind them.

"Thing is," Masayuki continued, "I was awake when you left for the latrine, and you didn't come back for a couple of hours. You sure you don't need to see the doc?"

Abe chuckled.

"And I noticed the same thing a couple of nights ago," said Ken.

Abe laughed a bit harder. "I'm okay, guys, really. Happy to know you're so concerned."

"I don't think stomach problems are a humorous issue," Masayuki said. "I've seen a doctor a couple of times now."

Abe laughed again. "Promise you won't tell on me?"

"Sure."

"Of course."

"That's where I go for more study time," Abe explained. "Haven't you ever needed a couple more hours to read?"

"You head there for the *lights*," Masayuki said, "not the actual head."

The three men laughed together at Masayuki's play on words.

"No wonder you do so well in class," Ken said.

The laughter relieved some of the stress they were under. No matter how much they learned, more lessons stretched out ahead of them.

Abe opened the classroom door. Today's subject was how to interrogate captured soldiers. Afterward, Abe was glad they'd laughed while they could. Much of the lecture covered the propensity of Japanese soldiers to commit suicide rather than lose face by surrendering. The instructor had been on the island of Attu in May of '43. When the U.S. troops surrounded the last Japanese soldiers, they had blown themselves up with grenades. Abe, Masayuki, and Ken all wore grim faces by the time the presentation was over. Lunch was a quiet affair.

***

John Aiso, the senior civilian instructor at Camp Savage, kept the students aware of former students' or instructors' achievements on the battlefield during monthly gatherings. The first Silver Star was awarded to Kazuo Kozaki, a former instructor, after he was wounded in action. General Willoughby, an Australian, did the honors. In November '43, in the South Pacific battlefield, Dye Ogata was buried alive in his bunker after a bomb hit nearby. He managed to dig himself out and was awarded a Purple Heart. Unfortunately, the AJAs' success on the battlefield changed the minds of the politicians in Washington, D.C. On November 18, after the many successes of the 100th Battalion in Europe, and the praise interpreters received in the Pacific, the Selective Service reinstated the draft for AJAs, including those in the internment camps. The IV-C draft classification was eliminated.

Abe knew many of the no/no boys wouldn't react too kindly to the new status. As the winter proceeded, news came of the arrests and convictions for two hundred and sixty AJAs who resisted the draft. The headlines bothered Masayuki and Ken as well.

One night, the three men talked about Tule Lake Segregation Camp and of the burgeoning requests of internees to expatriate or repatriate to Japan after the war. Their discussion didn't go unreported. Before Abe knew it, they were called into the administration building for questioning by the Counter Intelligence Corps. A snitch had turned them in for "unpatriotic conversations." The trio argued their rights to talk about Tule Lake—freedom of speech—and swore their loyalty to the United States.

"We volunteered," Abe reminded them.

They were warned that further talk could earn them dishonorable discharges and placement into Tule Lake themselves.

Abe clenched his jaw until his teeth hurt, held his head high, and concentrated on his studies. He was due to graduate on January 15, 1944. He was anxious to take leave so he could see his family and stop by Minidoka to visit Mary. He was ready to do his part in the war, whether the CIC believed it or not. Time seemed to drag.

***

In December, MISLS received several bundles of captured documents from the Pacific front. These weren't the pristine materials from the school, but a glimpse at what the translations, interpretations, and analyses would really be like. Abe found a military doctor's leather, blood-soaked diary in among the stacks and decided to read it in his spare time. It was written in *sasho*, the Japanese cursive writing. He checked out the small journal from the instructor and was given three days to return it.

Abe discovered the doctor had joined the Imperial Japanese Army in 1940 after he had practiced medicine for a couple of years. The diary began with a wedding and contained a picture of his bride in a traditional white kimono with a white hood. He talked of his duty to the land of his birth and the obligation to serve in the Army. After consuming so much military jargon, the diary was a welcome window into the life of an ordinary man. In a way, Abe felt like he was intruding on the man's inner thoughts. It made him feel only slightly better to know the man was dead or had escaped, leaving the diary behind, and would never know of Abe's secret curiosity.

On the second night with the diary, Abe read about the doctor's experience in the Aleutian Islands, on Kiska and Attu. He described setting up the field hospital and treating the wounded. Abe was near the end of the diary at lights out, so he set it aside to finish the third night. He wondered if he would find out how and under what circumstances the doctor escaped or died.

On the final night with the diary, Abe read about how the doctor knew the Japanese were losing the battle of Attu. He wrote of sacrificing his life for the emperor. The men who could still fight got up from their hospital beds, took their rifles, and joined the last frantic *Banzai* charge. Those men who were too injured knew that the

Americans would capture them shortly. The doctor went from bed to bed, helping each wounded man kill himself through *seppuku* rather than becoming a prisoner of war.

"And now it is my turn," the doctor wrote on the last page.

Abe closed the diary and held it next to his heart. He thought of Okimoto and his death. In a way, Okimoto's sense of honor was reflected in the doctor's diary entry. Abe understood why the Japanese did this—it came from the Samurai's code of honor—but could not imagine choosing suicide. Or, more horrifically, helping someone else. Abe closed his eyes, and in the darkness of the night, he contemplated the fate of the doctor, his patients, and his cousins.

CHAPTER FORTY-NINE

GEORGE

The fields and the farmers rested during the winter of '43 into '44. There was no need to rise at dawn and labor until dark. What work there was could be done in the outbuildings. Rex, Ed, and George would build a fire in an old oil drum stove to warm up the tool shed and work together. George helped repair the equipment and sharpen the tools, but there were days of leisure where nothing seemed urgent and he spent time with his wife and family in the kitchen, drinking hot tea or coffee, reading the newspapers, and listening to the news.

When Molly returned to Adrian after her week in the Minidoka camp, she shared the news of Tule Lake Segregation Camp and the ultimate unrest caused by the loyalty questionnaire and the Selective Service reinstating the draft for AJAs. George registered for the draft, but as a farmer, he was unlikely to be required to serve in the military. With Molly pregnant with their first child, George didn't want to leave his family. He didn't know how they would survive without his income. The threat of being drafted added to his steady diet of worry.

Sitting across the table from George, Molly said, "My father chewed on the idea of a small store, perhaps in Ontario, catering to the needs of an AJA community, but I don't know if he's financially able to open one on his own. Do you think we'd be able to help?"

Chiharu rocked back and forth in the chair that the Allens had given her, listening and hand stitching a baby blanket.

"We'll do what we can," George assured her. It was just like Molly to think of others first. Here they were, living in a bunkhouse, and Molly wanted him to help her father. George sighed. It was tougher to account for a growing family than he ever realized.

With their harvest money, the family agreed to buy a car. George found a '37 Plymouth sedan and had been washing it ever since. No wonder his father had been so proud of the family car in Toppenish. However, the family still had a long way to go to recover all they'd lost. How many years would it be before they'd be able to buy a tractor and implements? A house and at least forty acres? And Molly's family needed a step up too.

George followed the news of the war over the winter. President Roosevelt had traveled to Cairo to meet with Chaing Kai-Shek and Churchill and then to meet with Stalin and Churchill in Tehran at the end of November. The Italian front consumed most of the Allied efforts, as well as bombing Berlin. In the Pacific, the Japanese and Allies fought over Guadalcanal, and then Japan bombed Calcutta, India. It was truly a world war.

One afternoon shortly before Christmas, George stepped out to the mailbox and found a letter from Abe. He brought it into the bunkhouse to share with the family. Abe's letter to his mother was written in *sasho*, the cursive characters George had no idea how to read. Even Molly found it difficult, and she was more literate in Japanese than he was.

"My son, I cannot translate into English what Abe has written. May I read it in Japanese?" Chiharu asked. Although she had been very diligent in her study of English, she was nowhere near fluent.

"Of course, Mother. I appreciate you sharing the news," said George. He sat back in his chair and put a hand over each knee, waiting for his mother to begin. He was uncomfortably aware that Abe had never sent a letter to him since their falling out in Cow Hollow.

"Dear Mother," Chiharu read, *"I have only one month left of language school, and I can hardly wait to graduate on January 15. I will be able to take a three-week leave of absence to visit you, although I will also stop at Minidoka to see friends there."* Chiharu frowned. "Who could be so important that he would not come home for his entire leave?"

George caught Molly's eye but said nothing. The extra stop was Abe's story to tell. He hoped he and his brother would have a chance to make up after their differences. It had been nearly a year and a half since they'd seen each other. With the Toppenish farm lost, George wondered if he had made a mistake trying to save it, sending money for the bank to gobble up. He didn't know if he owed Abe an apology for taking Thomas's college savings, or if Abe owed him one for pushing him into the woodpile. Guess they'd hash it out when Abe came home. He missed his brother. He listened as his mother relayed more of Abe's military life:

It is snowing in Minnesota, but that doesn't stop us soldiers from our weekly march in full gear. The biting cold makes my mind sharper and helps me concentrate when it is time for more study. I wish I could have heard Pamela's solo for the Christmas Concert, but hope she'll sing for an audience of one when I arrive.

Pamela lowered her eyes demurely when Chiharu glanced up at her. She must have written to Abe about her solo. George was proud of Pamela. His little sister was growing into a lovely young woman.

Thomas sat in front of the potbelly stove, his arms wrapped around his knees, absorbed in the news. Abe always asked about Thomas's studies with Doc and the advanced biology class he was taking on his own. He would be graduating in the spring and intended to enlist as a medic. George remembered when Thomas announced this decision and looked at him to see if he would object. Molly had reached for George's hand, probably worried at what he would say in reaction. George had squeezed Molly's hand and then focused on her soft, swelling belly and the promise of a new generation.

"You need to do what your conscience tells you to do," George said quietly, reluctantly. He knew Thomas needed to choose his own path to adulthood. "Be true to yourself, little brother."

George found he couldn't control Thomas's destiny any more than he could Abe's. He knew he needed to quit trying.

When Chiharu finished reading the letter, she carefully returned it to its envelope. She took out the two dollars Abe had contributed and put it in the colorful tin sitting on the window ledge. The letter itself joined the others Abe had been writing in a cache stored in Chiharu's suitcase.

Just before Christmas, Thomas came into the bunkhouse with a large sagebrush to use as a holiday tree. "What do you think? We could trim it up a bit."

George was so proud of the idea, he got into the spirit too. "I can make the stand."

"What about origami birds, popcorn strings, and red bows?" Molly suggested.

They wrapped gifts in newspaper, tied them with red and green yarn, and put them under the "tree."

Pamela and Thomas eyed the finished product. "It is a good tree," Chiharu declared.

"Well, at least it's unforgettable," Pamela said, and everyone laughed.

On Christmas Day, Rex and Ed came to the bunkhouse for dinner. They contributed two pheasants they had shot while George and Thomas fished for steelhead. Chiharu, Molly, and Pamela worked all morning making sticky rice balls and added baked carrots and mashed potatoes from the garden. After dishing up, they took turns expressing what they were grateful for and enjoyed the camaraderie around their small table.

After they shared the feast, the family and friends opened their gifts. Chiharu gave the finished baby blanket for George and Molly's baby who was due in three months. She also cut down a dress for Pamela. George bought everyone oranges and nuts as a treat. Pamela baked Ed and Rex an apple pie she'd learned to make in home economics and gave each of her brothers a wool scarf.

Toward the end of the evening, Ed and Rex went outside to get their gift. It was a rocking cradle for Molly and George made of dark, solid wood. Chiharu then brought out a small, padded mattress she'd covered in the soft cotton of flour sacks.

Molly petted the cradle and wept in her joy. "Thank you. This is so wonderful. Our child will grow up surrounded by kindness." She spoke to Chiharu in Japanese, thanking her mother-in-law too.

A package had come for Molly and George from the Mitas. It was filled with homemade gifts for their first grandchild. Molly oohed and aahed, holding up each item for George to admire. There were several nightgowns made of soft cotton, with embroidery on the front and at the bottom.

Molly examined the exquisite needlework. "Mary must have made these." A deep blue silk bonnet came from Molly's mother. A baby's rattle and a mobile of origami figures completed the package. Nothing was more special than celebrating the coming of the first grandchild.

Ed and Rex told of other Christmases they'd experienced during the cold winters in Alberta. They loved to laugh and sometimes crowded anyone else's stories out of the conversation. The Yanos, however, laughed right along with them, happy for their company. George sighed in contentment and reached for Molly's hand.

CHAPTER FIFTY

MOLLY

Molly burrowed deeper under the blankets. George's gentle breathing and warmth made more sleep a tempting choice. Yet the baby inside her tumbled around, sticking a foot up here and a shoulder there. She lay on her back, touching her belly, tracing the movements.

George put his hand over hers. "Let me feel." Molly put his hand where the baby was most active. George propped himself up on an elbow and grinned. "Hope we can keep up with this fella when he's born."

Molly smiled sleepily. "You're so sure it's going to be a boy."

"Yep. Going to name him James," George said. "Do you want to give our child a middle name? I know it wasn't customary for us, but for our children, why not?"

"We could give the child an English first name and a Japanese middle name. I'd like to name a girl 'Alice' after the teacher in Minidoka."

George leaned over and kissed her stomach. "Hello, Alice or James, whichever you are."

"I need to get the fire started in the stove to warm up the kitchen," Molly said.

"Let me do it today. You take the extra rest." George slipped out of the covers and tucked the blankets under Molly.

As he slipped out, Molly drew the second pillow near her to retain some of the heat. What a lucky woman she was. As the baby did another somersault, it kicked her full bladder. Nope. No more sleep for her. Molly threw back the covers and quickly dressed. At least George would have the fire going after her trip to the outhouse.

During the dark winter months, the family often gathered in the kitchen to be near the stove. If it was just Molly and Chiharu, the space felt cozy. Once Pamela and Thomas returned from school and George from work, it became more crowded. Molly opened the door to the bedroom Pamela, Chiharu, and Thomas shared so it would warm. Thomas frequently studied lying on his single bed while Pamela used the kitchen table. They all listened to the radio for an hour between five and six o'clock when the news came on, especially if President Roosevelt was giving one of his fireside chats.

One afternoon, just a week after school resumed after winter break, Molly was cutting out a pair of yellow rompers when Pamela and Thomas came home. Chiharu was mending one of the Allen men's coveralls where the knees and elbows had worn through. Pamela made hot tea for everyone, and Thomas took out a mug for George. Pamela sat next to Molly and blew on the tea.

"How do you know if a boy likes you?" Pamela asked.

Molly looked up at her young sister-in-law who was biting her bottom lip. "Sometimes, it's hard to tell. Sometimes it's easy, like a boy asking you to dance several times in one night. Is someone sweet on you?" Molly tried to keep her tone light. They were speaking in English, so she didn't think Chiharu was listening.

"This boy has been staring at me, just kind of following me around with his eyes."

"A Caucasian boy?"

"Of course." Pamela sounded a bit exasperated. "There's only one other Japanese boy in the school besides Thomas and me."

Molly bent over the pattern as she continued cutting out the baby outfit. Her own father wouldn't allow her or her sisters to consider someone outside of their race. She didn't know how George would feel about this new wrinkle in the family.

"Do you like him as well?" Molly tried to sound nonchalant.

"He's just kind of creepy. He hasn't done anything to complain about—he just makes me feel uneasy. He was part of the circle of boys who wanted to fight Thomas that first day of school, but he's left us alone since then."

Molly's ears pricked up. At least Pamela didn't like him. It didn't sound as though she had anything to tell George after all. "Is he in any of your classes?"

"No, he's a senior. But just this week, I've seen him in the hallway outside the music room—twice." Pamela shuddered.

"If he makes you uncomfortable, it's probably best just to avoid him."

"That's what I've been doing," Pamela replied. "His name is Butch."

***

Molly watched Pamela carefully for another week. Each time she thought she might bring up the subject of Butch, Thomas set up his study area at the kitchen table. Finally, she decided to accompany Pamela down to the Hertzog place for her singing practice.

"Mind if I join you?" she asked Pamela. "I've been cooped up in here all day, and Doc tells me I need the exercise."

"Not at all." Pamela and Molly put on their coats and hats. Since neither of them had gloves, they put their hands in their coat pockets and set out.

The air was crisp and clean. Snow on the ground crunched under their feet, the cold turning their faces numb. The Hertzog farmhouse was about a half mile down the road, which gave Molly a decent walk without tiring her.

"How are things going with the boy who was ogling you?" Molly asked.

Pamela frowned. "I think he's listening to my lessons with Russell. Whenever Ellis and I leave the music room, he's there leaning against the wall."

"Has he said anything to you yet?"

"Sometimes he'll say hi to Ellis."

"Do you feel safe with Ellis beside you?"

"So far. Don't worry, Molly. I'll let you know if the situation gets any weirder."

"We could always involve Thomas, have him look after you."

"I've thought of that. But I don't want Thomas to get in a fight. He promised the principal he'd stay out of trouble. He told George the same thing. I'm okay for now."

Molly nodded. "Think I'll head back. Just keep me aware of what's going on."

CHAPTER FIFTY-ONE

ELLIS

Basketball season started after the holidays. To Ellis's surprise, Thomas tried out for the team.

"Heck," Thomas said, "it's my senior year. If I'm ever going to play for the school, it has to be now."

He and Thomas played one-on-one using the basketball hoop Lee had put up for his sons. The hoop had an unforgiving metal backboard. Any near miss sent the basketball flying. Thomas's shooting steadily improved over the fall and winter. He knew how to guard a player on defense, and his ball handling was faster. Even so, Ellis was surprised when Thomas made the cut for varsity.

Racial tensions simmered under the surface at the high school, and Ellis knew he wasn't the only one bothered by it. At basketball practice and sometimes in games, Andrew Brecht stewed visibly when the coach played Thomas as guard instead of him. Ellis's ball handling saw him starting as the first guard position, but he never knew who would be playing as the other one. And if Adrian found themselves ahead by a comfortable margin, the coach would pull him off the court, leaving Andrew and Thomas to play together. That's when the race issue was at its worst. Andrew refused to pass the ball to Thomas, and the team played an uneven game until the coach subbed in Ellis for one of them. One night in the locker room, the team's frustrations came to a head.

"What's with you, Brecht?" Stan, the center, yelled at Andrew. "You know the plays as well as I do, but you botch them every time. We almost lost the game when you came in for Hertzog."

"Yeah," Alfred, a forward, chimed in. "You got something against passing the ball?"

"Ain't passin' to no Jap," Andrew muttered. It was loud enough for Thomas to hear.

"You're selfish!" Thomas countered. "You'd rather us lose than pass to me."

Ellis had never seen Thomas lose his temper before.

"There's a difference, you know, between a Jap and me," Thomas continued. "I'm an American citizen, born and raised. And don't tell me I'm the enemy! Your name is German. That mean you'll go fight for Hitler?"

Andrew and Thomas were standing nose to nose now, and the noise caught Coach Hamm's attention. He stormed out of his office.

"What's going on?" The coach seemed as upset as the team. "Oh, it's you two. Can't get along on the court and can't get along in the locker room. Well, I've had it up to here!" He drew a line across his throat with his hand. "Tomorrow, I'm sending you through some drills. The one who does better will stay on the team. The other one moves down to junior varsity." The coach stomped back into his office and slammed the door, punctuating his frustration.

The team turned their backs on the two near combatants and quietly got dressed.

Ellis walked out of the locker room with Thomas. "Good luck tomorrow," he said.

"Thanks," said Thomas. "I'll need it."

***

The next afternoon, Coach Hamm incorporated the JV and the varsity in the contest between Thomas and Andrew. Word spread throughout the high school, and Butch showed up to watch. Ellis had no idea how Butch managed to skip out on the class where he was supposed to be, but he wasn't surprised to see him. Andrew was one of his buddies. What did surprise him was when Pamela and Emily sat down in the bleachers to observe the contest. Soon other students dribbled in until nearly twenty kids were in the stands. When the principal joined them—and didn't send them out—everyone relaxed. Now it was okay to make some noise.

Coach Hamm ignored the spectators and, working from a series of pre-planned exercises, made the boys race from one end of the gym to the other. Andrew won that competition, though Thomas bested him at the foul line by making seven of ten. During head-to-head layups, Andrew made more, but later, Thomas hit more mid-range jump shots. The contest was as close as could be.

Next, Hamm set up a line of wooden blocks and had the boys dribble around them, changing hands as they went. The next time through, the coach timed them. Then he sent out defenders and tried some three-on-three plays, then three-on-two. He paired the two boys as if they were on the same team, and Andrew refused to participate in the drill.

"What is it about 'team' you don't understand?" the coach yelled.

"Pair me up with someone else, and I'll show you what I can do," Andrew said. "I can out-maneuver Thomas any day."

Thomas put his hands on his hips and glared at Andrew. Here it was, the issue out in the open for all to hear.

The gym quieted. Coach Hamm tilted his head, bounced a ball from one hand to the other, and inspected Andrew up and down. "Can't do that, son. You've made my choice easy. You'll play JV from now on."

Andrew slammed his basketball down so hard, it bounced over his head.

"And now you owe me twenty-five laps—unless you want to be cut from JV too."

Ellis could tell Andrew had to fight to bring his rage under control. He took off jogging around the gym.

"Show's over, folks. Why don't you head back to class?" the principal said, standing up from the bleachers.

Ellis watched his sister and Pamela follow the other students out the double doors before the coach started practice again. Butch stopped Andrew for a few words until Hamm saw them.

"Brecht!" he shouted. "Now you owe me fifty!"

Andrew shook his head and started running again. Butch shot the coach a dirty look and walked out.

***

A couple weeks later, Mr. Russell again asked Ellis and Pamela to come to the music room to prepare for the spring concert in March.

"Any idea what Mr. Russell is planning?" Pamela asked Ellis as he began playing the chords for her warm-up scales.

"After your solo of 'Ave Maria,' my guess would be another showstopper," Ellis said.

Mr. Russell came out of his office, carrying some sheet music. "I have something special for you to try. You ever heard of opera?" He raised his eyes to take in the two students.

Pamela shrugged. "I've listened to it on the radio, but my brother always changes the station."

"Sopranos get their own arias. I have one here made famous by Puccini called 'O Mio Babbino Caro.' It's in Italian, but I think you can handle it. It'll be a stretch for you too, Ellis." Mr. Russell went over to his prized record player, cranked up the spring drive before turning it on, and set the needle down carefully on the black disk. "Listen."

An orchestra played the opening bars, and then a rich, beautiful voice began singing. The aria was only about three minutes long, but haunting and lovely.

When it was over, Pamela said, "She sounds so sad."

"She is," Mr. Russell replied. "She wants her father to give her permission to marry a young man, and the father is against it. 'Pieta' means 'have mercy.'"

"Do you have the rest of the translation?"

"It's on the back of the score. We don't have an orchestra, of course. Ellis here will have to imagine harps and violins. I've never had a student I thought could handle the vocals. Let's go through the pronunciation and then give it a whirl. Play it through a couple of times, Ellis, while Pamela gets the Italian down."

When Russell was satisfied, Pamela and Ellis immersed themselves in the aria.

"That's it!" he cried. "This song was made for your voice. We'll work on phrasing and dynamics tomorrow. Take the music home with you, Ellis. Pamela, why don't you copy the words down and practice the Italian? You'll absolutely entrance the audience."

Ellis and Pamela walked out together. Butch was standing in the hall in PE clothes, arms folded over his chest. He'd obviously been listening to them practice. He bent over the drinking fountain and took a noisy slurp. Wiping his mouth with his arm, he said, "You hornin' in on my girl, Hertzog?"

Pamela's face colored up, and she shot back, "I'm not your girl! Quit saying that!"

Ellis stepped in front of her. He reached behind and grabbed her hand. "Come on. I'll walk you to class." He drew Pamela to the opposite side of Butch, and they hurried down the hall.

They had walked a few feet when Butch ran up behind them. He rammed his shoulder into Ellis, knocking him into Pamela. He nearly fell, but Pamela grabbed and steadied him. Butch continued down the hallway, laughing.

When he'd disappeared around a corner, Ellis asked, "Is Butch bothering you? I thought he only picked on me."

"He's got this crazy notion I'm his girl. He won't leave me alone." Pamela lowered her voice. "I'm afraid of him."

"That makes two of us," Ellis admitted. "But he's a senior. He'll be gone soon. Try to stay out of his way."

"I'm trying to, believe me."

After that incident, Ellis kept a careful watch on Butch and his interactions with Pamela. Butch stopped a couple of times at her locker and talked to her, but Ellis had no idea what he said. Most of the time, Pamela walked with other girls or her brother. Butch would leave her alone then. Only one time did Ellis see her wiping tears from her face as she hurried down the hall. Butch followed her, sauntering, a smile at one corner of his mouth. Ellis didn't know how to ask Pamela if she needed help. Surely, she would tell Thomas if there were any danger.

Chapter Fifty-Two

Abe

When Abe arrived in Minidoka to visit the Mitas, Director Stafford welcomed him warmly. The irony of Abe returning in his uniform to see the Mitas who were interned by his country, the one he was defending, was particularly painful to him. Stafford, however, wanted him to be sure to see the Honor Roll sign that had over four hundred names of Minidokans who were currently serving in the U.S. Army. More names were being added as the draft was reinstated.

Abe walked to the Honor Roll sign. At the top, a huge, fierce bald eagle towered over the volunteer's names. Centered in the middle, words read: "Minidoka Relocation Center, Hunt, Idaho, Serving in U.S. Army." To the left was a quote from Secretary of War Henry Stimson: "It is the inherent right of every faithful citizen, regardless of ancestry, to bear arms in the Nation's battle." On the right were President Roosevelt's words from a year ago, when he activated the 442nd Regimental Combat Team: "Americanism is a matter of the mind and heart. Americanism is not, and never was, a matter of race or ancestry."

Huh, Abe thought. Too bad the president hadn't applied the same logic to internment. He started around the sign but then saw the ornamental garden behind it. The landscaper had used basalt rock, trails, flowers, and trees to create a place of peace and meditation. He doubted he'd return to the site, so he dropped his suitcase at the beginning of the trail outlined by pebbles and wandered through. It was a cold day, the nipping wind urging him on. Abe thought he'd spend more time here in warmer weather, but that wasn't his lot. It was now or after the war.

After he'd traced the trail, he stopped in front of the sign again. Many men with the same last name had volunteered; he counted nine Satos. He wondered how many would not return. The 100th Battalion had just reported 580 casualties, with 142 killed or missing in action. The men Abe served with in the 442nd had not been deployed yet—they still had three months of advanced training to go. Abe would be reporting for duty the second week of February. At least he'd managed to get through Basic Training before the MIS recruited him.

Mary was waiting for him. It wouldn't do to show her his dark thoughts. He picked up the suitcase and walked on to the barracks for single men. He'd stow his gear and then find his girl.

***

When Abe knocked on the Mita's door, Tak`e answered. Tak`e was the only one home—Kameko was in school, Kentaro was shoveling coal, and Mary was at work in the school's administration office. They bowed to each other, and Mrs. Mita invited him inside for a cup of tea.

"Is your family well?" Abe inquired. He saw his picture by Mary's bed and the wooden statue Okimoto had carved him.

This simple question released a torrent of information about Kentaro's improved health, Molly's pregnancy, and her own arthritis. Abe listened politely, nodding at appropriate times. Tak`e wound down slowly and then giggled behind her hand.

"I am like the magpie, loving the sound of my own voice," she said. "How is your life, Abe? You have been gone for nearly a year."

Abe summed up his basic training experience. When he told her of the story of cleaning the officer's latrine and the quick Japanese reading test the officer gave him, Tak`e's eyes shone with amusement. He talked about Shug and the difference between the Hawaiians and the mainlanders, and how long it took for the two groups to get along. Just as he was finishing, Kentaro opened the door and came in.

Abe stood up, and the two men bowed to each other.

"I wondered who it was that was making my wife laugh! I should have known it was you. We've been expecting you. Please, will you join us in our mess for the noon meal? I believe Mary will meet us there."

"I would be honored." Abe thought he might have to wait until

Mary completed the day's work but was pleased it would be sooner.

Kentaro ushered his wife and his guest in front of him. Bundled up against the cold, they discussed the news on their way to the mess hall. When Mary joined them, Abe smiled at her across the table. He knew there would be no opportunity to see her alone. And he was right. Mary returned to work, promising they'd have some time together soon.

***

Mr. and Mrs. Mita, Mary, and Abe ate dinner together too, with Kameko tagging along. Abe stood and bowed to many internees who came to greet him. After dinner, the parents, Mary, Kameko, and Abe retired to the recreation hall where Kameko practiced for an upcoming ping-pong tournament. Abe and Mary watched, Abe noting that Kameko needed to practice her backhand. He discussed the technique and then sent several balls to Kameko's left side, where she worked on her backhand stroke.

"That's it," Abe said. "Watch your opponents and see if they can hit with the backhand. Might be an easy way to get some points."

Abe returned to the Mitas just when Kentaro and Tak`e were getting ready to brave the weather back to their compartment.

Mary put down the letter she was writing and looked up at Abe. "You looked pretty confident in ping pong," she said. "Perhaps you should register for the tournament too."

"I didn't want to tell Kameko, but I'll be one of the officials. One of the recreation officers asked me today as we were leaving the mess hall."

"She'll be nervous, but that girl has a level of concentration when she wants something," Mary said.

"Who ya writing to? Should I be jealous?" Abe's heart was doing its own flips now that he was alone with Mary for the first time.

"I kept my word. You're my only soldier boy," Mary said softly. "No, I'm writing to Molly. The closer she gets to the baby's due date, the more nervous she feels. I try to reassure her, but I've never had a baby either, so I don't know how to help."

"How's George doing with his pending fatherhood?" asked Abe.

"You don't know?" Mary asked. "You still haven't made up with him?"

For the first time since he'd arrived, Abe's face clouded over. "When I get home, George and I will have some time together. I have every intention of getting our disagreements out into the open. We've both had time to grow up and see things from a different perspective. I just can't find the words to say it in a letter."

"Do you have something to say to me that you can't say in a letter?" Everything about Mary went still. Her intent gaze made Abe feel as though she could see right through him.

Abe took her hands in his. "You're my girl, Mary. I don't want anyone else." He hesitated. He hadn't anticipated saying anything so serious so soon. "I looked at all those names on the Honor Roll when I came into camp, and I wondered how many of those men won't come home." Abe looked down at their intertwined hands. "I hope to marry you, Mary, if you'll have me, but after the war. Would you wait for me?"

"I don't know if I can just wait around," Mary said frankly. "What if I join the service too?"

Abe looked into Mary's eyes. "I don't know of a *Nisei* women's group yet, but it may be coming. Is that something you want?" Abe's hands were suddenly clammy. It was one thing for him to risk his life serving his country. He wasn't sure he wanted Mary to do the same.

"It's something I've been thinking of. I could even teach Japanese reading and writing. I'm quite literate too, you know." Mary smiled her small, reassuring smile.

"But after the war, when everything has settled down . . ."

"Yes, Abe. I will marry you then."

CHAPTER FIFTY-THREE

GEORGE

George squeezed the family into the car to meet Abe at the Nyssa train station. When he caught sight of his brother, Abe looked spiffy in his Army uniform, appearing like the professional soldier he was. Before their mother could ask him pointed questions, Abe picked her up and swung her around, flustering and delighting her.

George shook Abe's hand, both brothers eyeing each other. Then Abe turned playful as he yanked his sister's ponytail, patted Molly on the stomach, and asked Thomas, "Play any basketball lately?"

***

Abe breathed life into the family. In the short time he was home, everyone laughed and told jokes. They reminisced, reliving stories of their father. His mother made his favorite foods, and for a bit, the ugliness of war, internment, and prejudice receded. George sat in the background and let Abe enjoy the limelight. At the end of the week, he and Abe made time to talk alone.

"How's your training going? Glad you joined up?" George asked as the two brothers walked in the winter's brisk air.

"So far, so good," said Abe. "I learned and relearned a lot of Japanese. We had great instructors. It's a top-notch language school."

"You'll be heading for the Japanese front?"

"Looks that way. Not sure Hitler is real fluent in Japanese."

George smiled at his younger brother's quip and then asked a more serious question. "Will you be fighting or staying on the back lines?"

"Both, I imagine. I learned all about weapons and fighting too. There's an urgency to get us out there. I could be interrogating the men who surrender, reading captured documents, intercepting communications. It's up to the MIS where I go and what I do." Abe stopped and shook his head. "I've already told you more than I should. I'll write what I can."

"You have a special reason to come home? Mother is doing her own interrogating about your stop at Minidoka."

"I do." Abe didn't dance around the question at all. "I hope to marry a Mita girl myself."

"Mary?"

Abe nodded. "You seem surprised."

"She's quiet, is all. I'm amazed you noticed her with all the other girls flocking to you."

"That's why I'm attracted to her. With Mary, I don't have to entertain or pretend. She accepts me as I really am, deep down."

"You're not marrying before you ship out?"

"No. If something were to happen to me . . . It just doesn't seem fair." Abe looked at George. "You and Molly will help her if something happens?"

"Of course, we will. She's family."

Abe paused. George was expecting the next question. "So, we lost the farm?"

"Yep. It was like pouring money down a rat hole. I need to apologize for raiding Thomas's college fund from Mother's tin. It wasn't the only time, I'm afraid. I also had to take all of the savings to pay the hospital bill following Mother's appendicitis."

George expected Abe to blow up at him again. Instead, Abe nodded. "I've learned we can't always anticipate calamities. One of the Minidokans died on my watch. I should have seen it coming."

"Was that the old man who carved so beautifully?"

"Yes. How did you know?"

"I saw the carving he made you when I went to Minidoka to marry Molly. I read the engraving underneath. It sounded as if you were close."

"We were. He was like a grandfather to me." Abe was quiet for a moment. It felt good to George to be with his brother again. Abe cleared his throat. "I'm way past blaming you for whatever decisions you felt you needed to make about the farm, the family. Sorry I pushed you down. I've regretted that day and our estrangement for a long time."

"It sure got my attention," George said. "That winter was a cold one. We weren't speaking, and Molly and I weren't writing. I was sorry you'd enlisted and that I missed your send-off. We could have patched things up then."

"How are you managing with the family and Molly's pregnancy all on your shoulders?" Abe asked.

"I'm starting from scratch, seeing as I worked myself out of a job." George smiled wanly. "There are over eight hundred Japanese settled in Malheur County now. A lot of folks don't want to sell their land to us, but a few are willing to lease it. We're making inroads. We're lucky we found the Allen brothers. Not sure we'd have survived without their help."

"I want to help out the family too," said Abe. "I've saved most of my pay since I joined up. I want you to take it and start a new venture. When I come back, I'll join you." Abe took money out of his pocket and offered it to George. "I've arranged to have my pay sent to you directly, minus a couple of bucks each month. I'll need some walkin' around change."

George stood there, hands on his hips, and looked down at the cash in his brother's hand. For a moment, he wasn't sure he could take it.

"I lost our whole stake," George managed. "What makes you think I'll do any better the second time around?"

"I trust you. It's not like you lost the farm because of poor management. You had a bit of help from the war hysteria."

Reluctantly, George took the money. "What do I do with it?"

"Lease some land? Start small, but keep at it. You'll figure it out."

"And grow what?"

"Potatoes."

"Potatoes?"

"Sure. Soldiers eat them every day. What's that saying? Napoleon said it—in French, of course. 'An Army marches on its stomach.' By the time you need to plant next spring, you should have enough to buy some equipment."

"Thanks. You know I appreciate it. To give me a second chance . . ."

Abe put his hand on George's shoulder. They had walked down the full length of the road as two men, but when they turned and headed back, they were brothers again.

Chapter Fifty-Four

Molly

Molly had one hand on her back as she felt the temperature of the dishwater with the other. Her pregnant belly was so large she had to stand sideways to be close enough to the sink. The baby could come any time now. And yet she was smiling to herself. Pamela was at the table, supposedly studying, but she had a faraway look on her face. Molly wondered if Pamela still had an issue with that boy she'd talked about. Molly tried to be available for girl chats, but Pamela hadn't shared anything else troubling.

"Oh!" Molly felt underneath her stomach.

"What is it? What's wrong?" Pamela asked.

"I don't know. I felt a clunk. The baby shifted, and now I'm wetting myself." She looked down at the puddle forming under her.

Pamela saw it too. "I'll go get Mother."

Molly stood there horrified. The fluid ran down her legs and into her socks and shoes. She'd had no contractions to warn her the birth might begin soon.

Chiharu rushed in. She got a pan and placed it between Molly's legs to catch the liquid. "We need to get you in bed. It would be better to be near the stove where we can boil water. Will you be all right if I ready my bed for you? You do not feel faint, do you?"

Molly tried to assess how she felt when she heard the bell ring outside. It rang several times, stopped, and then began ringing again. George would be home soon. That was the family's signal to come to the house. Did she need to protect George from the sight of giving birth? It wasn't normal for the husband to be in the room when the wife gave birth, but then she wouldn't be in the hospital. They had arranged for Doc Yamaguchi to tend to her.

Chiharu returned to the kitchen and led Molly to the next room. She had closed the curtains and stripped the bed of all but a clean bottom sheet. Molly let out a groan as the first contraction began.

Chiharu bent down to take off Molly's anklets and shoes. "Can you take off your dress? I will get your nightgown." She hurried out once again.

Molly struggled with the wet dress. She pulled it over her head and dropped it in a sopping heap on the floor. She shivered as another contraction began. The baby would be a week early, not so much to endanger its life. She tried to think beyond the contractions to holding the baby in her arms.

She heard George on the porch speaking with Pamela. He came into the bunkhouse and approached the closed bedroom door. "Molly?" he called out. "I'm going to get Doc. I'll be back as soon as I can."

"I'll be fine with your mother and Pamela watching over me." She tried to reassure George as if she gave birth every day. Another contraction began. They were still several minutes apart. She gritted her teeth against the pain.

Chiharu reentered the bunkroom. She had a pan of warm water and a washcloth with her. Gently, she cleansed Molly's body and put her warm nightie over her. Molly lay down on the bed, a pillow under her head. Chiharu draped a clean sheet over her.

Pamela came into the room hesitantly. "Can I help? Anything I can do?"

Chiharu gave Pamela instructions about timing the contractions. She put the wet dress and socks into the pan and took them out to wash. Pamela sat there with George's watch. When the next contraction began, she wrote down the time it began and when it ended.

Molly looked at her young sister-in-law. "You know this could take more than a day, don't you?"

Pamela nodded.

"Do you have a story you could read to me to take my mind off of all this?"

Pamela nodded again and grinned a bit. "Ever read *Jane Eyre*? That's one of my favorites." Pamela opened the family's trunk and got it out. With an interruption every now and then, the two sisters-in-law escaped for a bit into England.

***

Six hours later, Molly was roused from sleep by a knock on the bedroom door.

"Molly? It's me. Can I come in?" George said.

Molly could hear the hesitancy in his voice. "Yes, George. I'm decent."

George opened the door and poked his head around it. He held his hat in his hands. "You mad at me?"

"Mad? Of course not," Molly said. "Come in and meet your son."

George shut the door quietly and padded across the room. Molly closed her eyes in response to the kiss on her forehead. She watched George bend over the crib as he met their son for the first time. He ran the back of his hand down the baby's sleeping face and drew it back quickly when the baby stretched out one arm, grimaced, and sighed.

"Hello, little fella. I'm your dad," George whispered.

Molly had never seen him so gentle. She patted the bed beside her, and George eased himself down.

"How'd you manage without Doc?" he asked.

"Ed Allen delivered him," Molly said. "I guess he'd been a help to the women on the bald prairie back in Alberta. Said our son made an even dozen."

"Ed?" George sounded amazed. "I did bring Doc. He had an emergency to attend to when I arrived at Cow Hollow. He told me the first baby could take hours, so we had plenty of time."

"Guess I fooled him." Molly pushed up and started to fuss with the pillow.

"What are you doing?"

"Trying to sit up," Molly said. "Now, hand me the baby."

George gave her a panicked look. "I've never held a baby this small. What if I break him?"

"Just put one hand under his head and neck, and one hand under his back. His head is too heavy for his neck to support just yet. That's the only caution Ed and your mother gave me."

George carefully scooted his hands under his son and lifted him gently. "Not much to him." He slowly brought the baby to Molly.

Molly put the baby on the bed between her covered legs and untied the bottom of the small nightgown. She pulled it up to reveal the baby's tiny toes, feet, and legs. "See how tiny he is? Ten tiny, tiny toes." She glanced up into George's eyes. "I counted them."

"What are we going to call him? I'm afraid Alice will have to wait for us to have a daughter." George grinned.

"I thought we'd settled on James," Molly said.

"James, it is." George soothed the black hair on the baby's head. "You ready to see Doc? He's late, but he said he probably should examine you and James and ask you some questions."

"I'll bet Ed has filled him in on a lot, but of course, he can come in," Molly said. "By the way, Ed said with how easily this first one came, I could safely have a dozen."

"Let me get used to one first," George pleaded. "Then we'll see."

Molly smiled to herself. She knew how to bargain with her husband. Her mind was set on four. A dozen was out of the question.

CHAPTER FIFTY-FIVE

ELLIS

With the March spring concert rapidly approaching, Mr. Russell needed an accompanist frequently. Ellis had permission from Coach Hamm to be late for PE, and Mr. Russell tried not to detain Ellis too long. The afternoon PE classes were held outside as the students rotated between track and field and baseball or softball. Pamela sang the Italian aria first and then left the music room for home economics. Mr. Russell asked Ellis to stay and play for a second soloist.

When Ellis left, he went through the double gym doors, crossing the floor to the locker room. The light filtered into the gym from the windows in the doors and the exit signs but still filled the area with shadows. He heard a cry and a thump. What was that? Ellis looked around. There! In the back corner. Ellis tried to make out what was happening when he realized it was Butch and Pamela. He had Pamela pinned down underneath him with one hand over her mouth. Pamela's skirt was pushed above her hips as she fought to break free.

"What are you doing?" Ellis yelled. He rushed forward and bowled over Butch, but he righted himself and jumped quickly to his feet.

Pamela scooted away, holding her blouse together and straightening her skirt. A knot on her forehead was swelling, and her hair was mussed.

"You!" Butch pointed his finger in Ellis's face. "You keep interferin' where you're not wanted. First you drown Jeannie, and now this. Pam was givin' me a little sugar, weren't ya, Pam?"

"You liar! You attacked me!" Pamela ran to Ellis and got behind him.

Butch began circling around them, his fists clenched. His eyes squinted in concentration, and his blond hair hung across half his face. He licked his lips.

Ellis bobbed and weaved to stay between Butch and Pamela. His left fist was clenched, his right arm keeping her close behind him. "I always knew you were filth," he spat.

"I'm gonna enjoy beatin' the crap outta you. And then I'm gonna finish what I started." Butch smirked.

"Go!" Ellis yelled to Pamela.

She backed up to the gym door but hesitated.

Butch tossed his hair out of his eyes. His fists were clenched in front of him. Ellis was limber, ready, his deep blue eyes open wide.

"Go! Get some help!" Ellis called again.

As she fled, she heard the unmistakable sound of flesh hitting flesh.

***

By the time Coach Hamm and Pamela returned to the gym, boys from the PE class had separated the two. Butch had a bruise on the side of his face, and Ellis had a bloody nose.

"You boys had enough?" Hamm roared.

"No, sir," Ellis said. "I want to finish this thing once and for all."

Coach turned to Butch. "You?"

"Bring it on."

Hamm turned to the other boys. "Thomas, see if you can get that bloody nose stopped. Alfred, you go get the gloves. Stan, pull out the floor mats. We'll do this right."

Other boys from the PE class entered the gym and started to help with the setup. Even though gloves were often used to settle scores at school, the buzz of speculation about what caused this dust-up hummed as the ring took shape.

Ellis tried to calm down. He was so angry, he shook all over. He couldn't believe Butch had assaulted Pamela. He'd been wrong trying to stay out of Butch's way. It had made him bolder, more certain no one would stand up to him. Now Ellis had to face him, make him back down.

"So Butch is finally gettin' his way, huh?" Thomas said. "He got you mad enough to fight him? What'd he do?"

"He attacked Pamela! He had her pinned underneath him when I heard her scream."

"Whoa! He went after my sister?" Thomas glared at Butch, doubled up his fists, and started over toward him. Ellis grabbed his arm.

"This is my fight. Not yours. You know he's been after me."

"But it's my sister!"

"You'll get expelled if you get in a fight. You know that! Let me handle this." Ellis was determined to fight Butch.

Thomas turned back and took a long look at Ellis. "Are you up to this?"

"He stepped over the line from bully to criminal. I'm going to teach him a lesson." Ellis was quieter now, more determined. "And I'll fight him again and again if I have to."

Thomas looked around to see if he could spot Pamela. She had disappeared from the gym. Then he studied Ellis. He held a rag to his nose to stop the bleeding. "Okay. I'll be in your corner. What's your strategy?"

"He has longer arms than I do and he's taller, but I'm quicker on my feet. I plan to get close to him and do a lot of damage in short spurts." Ellis took off his shirt, revealing the sleeveless t-shirt underneath.

"He'll be watching you, waiting for you to make a mistake. He's tough. He might try something sneaky."

"Keep an eye on him for me," Ellis said. "You may be able to spot a weakness I won't."

Andrew glared at Thomas as he put Butch's gloves on. Ellis wondered where Pamela was and if she was all right. He hoped she'd found Emily. He mentally shook his head. He had to keep his wits about him to beat Butch. He couldn't let his concern for her distract him. He spotted Pamela and Emily hurry into the gym with the choir director.

Hamm inspected the makeshift ring. There were no ropes, but mats outlined the floor. The boys had stools and a bucket of water with rags ready at the corners. Alfred had the timer and the bell at a desk on the side. Most of the junior and senior boys were standing around the edges just off the mats.

"You boys understand the rules: no illegal punches, no holds. There will be three three-minute rounds. Put down your dukes and go to your corner when you hear the bell. If both boxers are still standing at the end of round three, the PE boys will call the winner. All right. Touch gloves and come out fighting."

Ellis heard Emily shout, "You can do this, brother! We're behind you all the way!" Her single voice released the tension, and other voices rose in encouragement.

Butch used his long arms to jab Ellis's shoulder and knocked him backwards. Ellis started dancing lightly on his toes, both gloves protecting his face. He wanted to give Butch the message this wasn't going to be an easy win. He waited until Butch threw another punch and then, instead of stepping back, used the temporary space to get closer to him. He delivered three sharp jabs to Butch's stomach and then a left to his chin. Butch's head snapped back, and Thomas yelled encouragement from Ellis's corner. Butch shook his head as if to clear it and then narrowed his eyes. It looked like he got the message.

The first three minutes flew by. Butch jabbed Ellis frequently, but that gave Ellis an opportunity to sidle in for his own quick punches. At the end of the first round, both boys were breathing hard and sweating.

"Way to go," Thomas said as he gave Ellis a ladle of water and a wet towel to wipe his face. "You've got an advantage in being a southpaw. It surprises him over and over."

Thomas moved to massage Ellis's shoulders. "You both have a lot of stamina. I'll bet you can go the full three rounds, so long as you stay away from his right. He doesn't have your footwork. He's not as fast. Hang in there!" Ellis stood up at the sound of the bell, and Thomas pulled the stool from the mat.

The second round had barely started when Ellis got in one of his quick combinations. He was in close enough that when Butch stepped back, he tripped over Ellis's lead leg and fell backwards onto the mat. Some of the boys laughed, and Butch's face darkened.

Ellis stood breathing hard in his corner while Hamm counted to eight. He noticed Butch could not defend well against both his straight left and his overhand left. The difference in Ellis's stance, leading with his right foot rather than his left, opened up angles.

Butch's face flushed with anger and humiliation as he slowly stood up. He would fight harder than ever now.

Hamm brought the two boys back to the center of the ring again and dropped his hand to restart the bout. Butch came at Ellis hard, and his right cross landed solidly. Ellis grunted at the pain. He ducked the next swing and danced backward into the center. When Butch faced him again, Butch changed his stance to a square one. He was trying not to get tripped up again.

The students were loud now, no one voice piercing the din. Bam, bam, bam. The blows hit one after the other, both fighters serious, intent, dripping sweat, and tiring. Ellis mixed up his punches with some right hooks and jabs along with his straight lefts. No matter where Butch defended, Ellis found a way in. He couldn't hit as hard as Butch, but his punches were as steady as spring rain. When the bell rang to end round two, Hamm had to step in to stop them. The students chattered and hooted as the fighters took their last break.

As Thomas wiped Ellis down, he talked to him until the time was nearly up. "Remember your gunslinger shot you use in basketball? Put all your strength behind it. It might leave you open, so hit hard and make it count."

Ellis nodded. He was breathing hard, and the spring in his step was nearly gone.

The first time Ellis tried to drop his left for an uppercut, Butch nailed him with his right fist. Ellis dropped to the mat. He ran his tongue over his teeth and found that his mouth was bleeding.

"Stay down, Hertzog," Butch growled. "I've won this fight, and you know it."

Ellis groaned and rolled over to his knees as he listened to the count. When Hamm got to eight, Ellis put his left foot on the mat and pushed himself up. He flicked his sweaty black hair out of his eyes and spat the blood out of his mouth. "I'm not quittin'. Not now, not ever."

Before they could resume the round, Hamm called a timeout. "Thomas! His mouth is bleeding. If you can't get it stopped in two minutes, fight's over." He turned to Alfred. "Two minutes. Then ring the bell."

Butch swaggered over to his corner and sat down. Andrew rubbed him down and talked in his ear.

In his corner, Ellis took a couple mouthfuls of water, swished it around, and spat it out, red. He was so tired. His body ached. He didn't drop his eyes, though, and tried to gauge Butch's energy. He had to be tired too. Ellis pictured Pamela in his head. He couldn't quit. Not after what Butch had tried.

"You dropped your left shoulder," Thomas said. "That was the tell. He'll be watching for it again. Try an overhand left first. You have a couple of minutes to decide this match. Watch him. If he can't win legit, he'll find another way."

The bell rang. Ellis stood up. He was steadier on his feet. Butch was cockier, sure now he was going to win. Ellis began to weave and dodge, not as fast as he was in the first round, but fast enough to penetrate Butch's defense. He landed a one-two combination close in. Butch tried to back away so his long reach would be more effective. Instead, Ellis followed him, landing an overhand left to Butch's face. Now Butch was struggling to get away. Ellis punched him in the stomach, trying to find an opportunity to land an uppercut. Then he danced backwards, giving Butch a chance to come at him again. He didn't want to win by a decision. If he could, he wanted to knock out Butch.

Butch approached Ellis cautiously. Both fighters were barely standing, their stamina almost gone. Ellis watched him, waiting for an opening. There it was! Ellis hid his left hand with his body until it exploded under Butch's chin. A left-handed uppercut, like his gunslinger basketball shot: odd-looking but effective. Butch's head jerked back, and his feet flew out from under him. He was down!

The boys cheered wildly. Mr. Russell clapped and whistled through his teeth. As Hamm counted to ten, Ellis swayed on his feet. He wiped the sweat from his brow with the glove and turned to look for Pamela. He spied her at last, hiding between the taller boys, tears running down her bruised face.

Butch got up and staggered to his stool as Hamm raised Ellis's arm above his head, officially declaring him the winner.

Ellis turned around and trudged back to his corner. He'd done it. He'd knocked down the bully both of them were afraid of. He'd won.

Someone yelled, "Ellis, look out!"

He glanced back in time to see a bucket coming toward his head. It hit him once and then again before Ellis fell to his knees and blacked out.

CHAPTER FIFTY-SIX

ABE

Abe gazed out on the atoll of Eniwetok from the bow of a destroyer. His MIS language team was going ashore soon, along with the 110th CB, the Seabees. Their job was to restore the airfield there in the Marshall Islands. Abe was charged with interrogating Japanese prisoners.

Eniwetok Atoll arose from volcanic eruptions and consisted of forty islands forming a circular coral reef. The islanders called the atoll "a gift of gods," and the Spanish explorer Alvaro de Saavedra called the island "The Gardens." It didn't look like that now. After continuous bombardments from the USS Colorado, Tennessee, and Pennsylvania, and the cruiser USS Louisville, and then air attacks, the islands were a battered, cratered, bloody mess. Any palm trees still standing looked like skinny, charred hat racks.

As the Seabees unloaded their equipment, Abe and his team waded ashore. This was the first battle aftermath Abe had witnessed. In all, over eight hundred Japanese soldiers had been killed or committed suicide. Body parts lay helter-skelter, an arm here, a leg there, a torso without a head. Craters from the bombardment made the land look like egg cartons. He couldn't comprehend the absolute destruction before him.

A *Samurai* war song, grieving the dead, wove through the sounds of the equipment, the shouted orders, and the men talking all around them. Abe couldn't tell where the song was coming from. The lieutenant leading them didn't stop to gawk. He directed the interrogation team to the temporary headquarters where they were to get their orders. The forlorn keening was louder the closer the men got to the POWs, who numbered over a hundred.

Abe was taken to one site where three men had been stripped down to their skivvies.

"Why are these men nearly naked?" Abe asked the sergeant.

"We don't want to get blown up from a hidden hand grenade. In earlier battles, the Japanese soldiers pretended to surrender and then evaded capture by blowing everyone up."

Abe grunted and then began to speak to the first prisoner. The man's accented Japanese was the first clue.

"No wonder this man didn't commit suicide like so many of the others," Abe said. "He's Korean. The Japanese enslaved a bunch of them to build the airfield. I'll bet most of these prisoners are Korean."

Abe spoke to the other two captured men. Korean. "We're not going to get anything from these men other than the awful stories of their treatment. Take me to more POWs. We should be able to sort out the men fairly easily."

Abe and two other interrogators moved on from small group to small group. In the end, only twenty-three Japanese had surrendered. The mournful lament came from a man sitting on his shins, hands on his knees. His eyes were closed, his face grimy. Clearly, he was frightened, certain of torture by the Marines.

"Can you get the songbird to quit squawking?" A sergeant gestured to the man. "He's driving our men nuts."

Abe crouched down on one knee and, using a conversational tone, first assured one man and then the next that the Geneva Convention would be followed as to the treatment of prisoners. The soldiers would not be killed or tortured. Abe's low-key manner paid off. The singing broke off abruptly, an eerie stillness replacing the dirge.

"Thanks, Yano. You've earned yourself a cigarette." The sarge handed him one out of his breast pocket.

Abe put it in his mouth, and the sarge lit it for him. He stepped back in among the prisoners and handed it to the forlorn man. The man looked at Abe in his American uniform and murmured his thanks.

The MIS team began a methodical interrogation of the Japanese prisoners, taking one at a time and then sequestering those who had been questioned from the others. The Japanese hadn't been trained on what to do if they were captured. U.S. soldiers knew to offer their name, rank, and serial numbers. The Japanese had been told to kill themselves and never surrender. Perhaps because of Abe's initial humane treatment of them, they slowly opened up about what they thought had gone wrong at Eniwetok, where other bases were being reinforced, and any future attacks the Imperial Japanese Forces planned.

"One of the prisoners said he was aware of a plan for a counterattack in early March," Abe told his lieutenant. "We should look for some corroborative documents, and if we can find additional proof, let our higher-ups know."

"They'll want to know more than the specific date. They'll want to know where and in what strength the Japs will attack. Your prisoner couldn't provide more than that?"

"No, sir."

"Go back through the prisoners you've already talked to and see if this is the real deal. I don't want to report a rumor. In the meantime, I'll tell the others what to ask about."

Abe began talking to the prisoners again. Three more men confirmed the counterattack, and then the translators found the outline of a battle plan. The MIS team proved its worth quickly.

***

When Abe had time, he wrote to Mary and his family. Occasionally, he'd write to Shug, still in training for the 442nd RCT. Ever mindful of the censors, he couldn't describe much of what he did. He managed to write a few funny stories, usually of him and the team goofing off. Anything that didn't scream of death and destruction. Mail call saved his sanity. A month after the event, Abe opened a letter from George and learned he was an uncle. Mary wrote of her love for him, and Thomas described Coach Hamm's decision to keep him on the varsity basketball team. The letters described a reality so far removed from his current one that Abe wondered if he'd ever be able to return to civilian life.

Abe tried to harden himself to the horrors of war so that his basic humanity might survive. But his compassion—what he had thought of as his Achilles' heel—made him an excellent interrogator. The prisoners opened up under his watchful eye, revealing far more than he and his superiors originally thought possible. He had to remind himself that just days before, these same soldiers would have gladly killed him.

One memory he couldn't get out of his head, especially in dreams, was the mourning song of death. The keening, high-pitched, plaintive melody continued to haunt him. Perhaps it would forever be a cost of war.

CHAPTER FIFTY-SEVEN

GEORGE

George heard the gong ring several times, stop, and then ring again. It was the family's signal to come in from the fields. He'd seen Emily run by. Whatever the emergency, it must involve the Hertzogs too. He hoped the boys hadn't been in a fight. As he ran across the corrugations, he could see Molly waiting for him.

"What is it? What's happened?" George panted. He searched Molly's face for a clue. "Is it Mother? It's not James . . ."

"It's Pamela."

"Pamela?" George was startled. He couldn't believe she was in trouble.

"She was assaulted at school."

George took a deep breath. "Assaulted? By a boy?"

Molly nodded.

"What happened?"

"She's all right—just a knot on her forehead, a torn sleeve, and a button missing on her blouse." Molly quietly said, "I think someone tried to rape her."

"Rape?" George's face darkened. He started to walk around her, but Molly grabbed him by his arm. "Be gentle with her. She's still in shock."

George nodded. Molly followed him back toward the house, but first he stopped by the outside faucet to wash off the dirt from the field. He dried his face with his handkerchief and wiped his hands too. He stood still for a moment, trying to calm down and think. His sweet little sister had been assaulted. Almost raped? He opened the door of the kitchen. "Why don't you give us some privacy?" he asked Thomas.

"Sure." Thomas slipped out the door.

George sat down at the kitchen table and faced his sister. Pamela's usually smooth pigtails were out, and her shiny black hair fell around her face, hiding the knot on her forehead. He reached over and gently pulled Pamela's hand, holding a cold cloth away from her forehead. "That's some bump you've got."

His kindness and concern brought Pamela to tears. As Molly ran the cloth through cold water again, George asked, "Can you tell me what happened? I want to know everything, even if it seems embarrassing. I'll simply listen."

George held her hand as she began to tell him about Butch, and how Ellis had come to her rescue, and how frightened she'd been. Her story was disjointed as she described Butch's unwanted attentions and how he wanted her to be his girl.

"Pamela," George said softly. "Do you think he would have raped you if Ellis hadn't interrupted him?"

Pamela looked at George. Her eyes brimmed over with her tears, and she nodded.

"But he didn't rape you? He was stopped in time?"

"Yes." Her whispered answer was some small comfort. "But after the fight, Butch gave Ellis a concussion, hitting him over the head with a bucket. The last time I saw Ellis, he was sprawled out unconscious on the gym floor."

George took a deep breath. "Let me see what I can do. I'll be back soon."

George stopped in front of the Malheur County Sheriff's Office. The sheriff hadn't been much help after Doc suffered from the hit-and-run, but maybe this time he could be. George took off his hat and left it on the front seat. He hoped he looked presentable. If only his hands would stop shaking.

"Afternoon, ma'am," George greeted the secretary. "Is the sheriff in? I'd like a word."

"Just a minute," she said. She walked back to the conference room, spoke a few words, and then beckoned George. "Come on back. The sheriff will see you now."

George nodded his head as he passed. He peered around the door and saw the sheriff shuffling papers onto one of three piles.

"George! You caught me doing the job I like least in the world. What can I do for you?" The sheriff reached across the table to shake his hand.

George didn't know where to begin, so he started off with the facts. "My sister and our neighbor boy were assaulted at Adrian High School this afternoon. You'll remember the boy that did it: Butch Butler."

"Butch, huh? What makes you think an incident at the high school should land on my desk?"

"Butch was trying to rape my sister when Ellis Hertzog stopped him. Coach Hamm didn't know why Ellis and Butch got into a fight, but he let them duke it out with boxing gloves."

"How'd Ellis get assaulted if they were wearing boxing gloves? Sounds pretty organized to me." The sheriff frowned.

"After Ellis had been declared the winner, Butch hit him over the head with a metal water bucket—twice. My sister said he was knocked out. Probably has a concussion."

"Okay. Let's take this back to the beginning. Tell me the whole story."

The sheriff reached for a pad of paper and a pen. He began taking notes as George relayed the story. After he finished, the sheriff scratched his head with the end of the pen.

"I know you want me to run right out there and arrest Butch, but I'm going to have to do some investigating first. See if this rises to the level of a crime." Sheriff Hamilton looked up from his notes. "I want you to do some thinking too. Do you want your sister to testify in a court of law? I've seen it be pretty painful for the victim. She'd have to prove it was sexual assault, not mutually agreed to."

"The lump on her forehead should help with that. Ellis can testify too."

"Ellis is also a witness for Butch—he didn't complete intercourse."

George gripped the chairback so hard, his fingers turned white. Anger swirled in his brain, interfering with the cool logic he needed to convince the sheriff.

Into the pained silence, the sheriff spoke once more. "Let me talk to the Butlers, Ellis, and Principal Patterson. See what I can do." He cautioned George. "Let me handle this."

George nodded curtly.

When George got back to the farm, he stopped first at the Hertzogs. Emily responded to George's knock and led him downstairs into their living quarters. Ellis was lying on the couch, his head wrapped in a gauze bandage showing faint tinges of pink.

George walked over to Ellis and shook his hand. "Thanks for standing up for my sister."

"Sure," Ellis said. "I'll do it again if I have to."

George turned to Mae and Lee. "I went to the sheriff. He said he'd investigate, but I don't know if he'll actually do anything. He may try to pawn this off onto Principal Patterson as a school issue. He said he'd come out tomorrow after he talked to the Butlers and Ellis here." George's frustration made his voice flat. "I don't know if there's anything else we can do."

"Patterson told us he'd expelled Butch for the rest of the year. He's a senior. He'll get his diploma but won't be allowed back at school or at the graduation ceremonies. At least that's something," Lee said.

"Huh." George looked down at the floor. Some justice. Not enough, but some. George shook Lee's hand, nodded to Mae and Emily, and squeezed Ellis's shoulder in farewell. "Thanks again, Ellis."

He thought he would feel better than he did at the news of Butch's punishment. Instead, he felt numb.

***

The next day, the sheriff arrived at the Allens' farm. Molly directed him out to the field where George was working. When George saw him coming across the field, he stopped and leaned against the long hoe.

"What'd you find out?" George asked.

"I convinced Butler to take his son to Boise to enlist. Put him on the train to Fort Lewis last night. He won't be around to bother your sister for a while."

George pursed his lips and nodded. Nothing more he could do. He hated not being in charge when his family was hurt. Without another word, Sheriff Hamilton turned around and walked back to his car. George thought it all over while he finished the row he was on and then headed in for an early lunch. He had no idea what his sister would say.

"*Shikata ga nai*," Pamela whispered.

To George, the words felt like a gut punch. There it was again. Hopelessness and stoicism all in one tidy phrase. It wasn't enough to take away the store, his father's car and tractor, the farm. Now his little sister had been damaged too.

As he walked woodenly back to the fields, he felt bereaved. Just when he thought all was right in his small family, he was slapped down again. Perhaps his mother was correct. The gods grew jealous at man's good fortune.

Chapter Fifty-Eight

Molly

Molly, George, Pamela, and Thomas sat outside on the porch. James was asleep, but at two months old, it was never a sure thing. The sun set over the high hill across the road on this first warm night in May. Pamela's bruises had faded, but the trauma wasn't behind her. Molly worried about the injuries Pamela hid. George was introspective, quieter than Molly had ever seen him. If that wasn't enough, Thomas had just enlisted. He had two weeks before reporting for duty.

Molly still questioned his decision to join the war. "Why do you want to fight at all? Many young men in other relocation camps refuse to enlist until their civil rights are restored."

"Other relocation camps? You mean at Tule Lake Segregation Camp. No thanks." Thomas glanced at the darkening sky. "If I'm designated as a medic, I won't carry a weapon, except perhaps a personal one for my own protection. My job will be to save lives, not end them. I know all the first aid Doc could teach me. I can give injections, apply tourniquets, and fix bandages. I'll learn from other medical personnel and be on my way to being a doctor when I get home."

"Isn't it more dangerous to be a medic?" Pamela asked.

"It's not supposed to be. The Geneva Convention specifically says that knowingly killing medics is a war crime." Thomas reached over and squeezed Pamela's hand. "I'll be okay, Sis."

"How about you?" Molly asked Pamela. "Are you going to be okay?"

"I don't know. I'm on the graduation program to sing the aria

Mr. Russell wanted me to perform at the spring concert. With Ellis's concussion and my—well, it just didn't happen. Ellis and I have practiced, but I just can't get through it.

"There's just something missing between Ellis and me," Pamela said quietly. "The music doesn't bring us together anymore. We used to breathe at the same time, move to the cadences in the same way, express the poetry of the lyrics through the pacing and dynamics. Now, it's broken, shattered. I just don't know how to fix it."

Molly despaired. She didn't know how to put the pieces back together again either.

CHAPTER FIFTY-NINE

ELLIS

With his high school graduation in sight, Ellis knew it was his turn to enlist. If he was drafted, he lost the ability to choose which service he wanted to join. With his two brothers destined to fight in Europe, he decided to go to the Pacific war front. He'd join the Navy and see where it took him. His folks gave him permission to go to Boise with Stan and Alfred. He'd have a two-week leave afterwards, just enough time to graduate and pack his bags.

He hoped to tell Pamela his news and see if he could break through her quiet grief. He'd been to see her before but only managed to talk with Thomas instead. It was okay to be Thomas's friend, but after the attack in the gym, Pamela was quickly cocooned by the whole family.

When he reached the bunkhouse, he knocked hesitantly on the door. Chiharu answered.

"Is Pamela home? Wondered if it would be okay to talk with her." Ellis didn't know how much Chiharu understood. Her English was sketchy at best.

Chiharu nodded and pointed to one of the chairs on the porch. Ellis sat down to wait. When Pamela came out, it was obvious she'd been sleeping.

"Did I come at a bad time?" Ellis asked. "I didn't mean to disturb your nap."

"It's fine. Mother thinks I've been sleeping too much anyway," Pamela said flatly. She sat on the chair next to him.

"I came to tell you that I've enlisted in the Navy. I'll be leaving right after graduation."

"Thomas is going too. Boys must be born with itchy feet—can't wait to get away from home." She spoke into her lap.

Ellis felt dismissed and couldn't think of anything else to say. He regarded Pamela carefully. Her dark hair was loose, hiding most of her face. He didn't know what she was thinking, what she was feeling. He just couldn't reach her.

"Pamela, I'm sorry I didn't protect you from Butch. I should have been with you and walked you to class like we always did. I'm so sorry you got hurt—that he hurt you—that I didn't stand up to him sooner." Ellis turned in his chair as he pleaded with her. "Please forgive me. I hate that our closeness, our companionship is fractured."

Pamela raised her head and peered at him. Then she whispered, "I should be apologizing to you. I didn't want *you* to get hurt." Her voice became stronger, impassioned. "I can't get the sight of you lying on the gym floor—unconscious—out of my head. I thought Butch had *killed* you."

She sat back in the chair, looked up at the slanted roof, and blinked her eyes several times. Ellis thought she was trying not to cry.

"I'm not worth the sacrifice you made to defend me." A minute ticked by. "And it feels like Butch got away with it."

Pamela, her shoulders rounded, slunk down in the chair, her feet straight out, hands clasped in her lap.

"So that's what you've been doing? Blaming yourself for that creep's bucket bashing?" Ellis knelt beside her so he could look into her eyes. "He didn't win, Pamela. He lost in front of all the boys. His buddies saw him for the coward he is. I can't tell you how many students have thanked me for standing up to him. I'm just sorry I didn't do it sooner."

Ellis reached out and lifted Pamela's chin. He looked into her eyes for a long moment. "And I'd do it again in a heartbeat."

"Oh, Ellis." Pamela's tears finally fell.

Ellis dropped his hand onto hers. He squeezed them and bit his lip as he watched her cry. "I can't stay very long. I told Ma I'd do the milking."

Pamela wiped the tears off her face.

"Walk me back?" Ellis asked.

Pamela nodded. She stood up and stepped off the porch with him. She waved at her mother through the window, indicating what her intentions were. Chiharu nodded.

As the two friends walked onto the road, Ellis glanced back and saw Chiharu come out to the porch to watch them go.

***

If Butch had enlisted to escape the consequences of his actions, he was simply the first of the seniors to go off to war. Ellis, Stan, and Alfred all left on June 1, 1944. Stan and Alfred joined the Army and headed to Fort Lewis near Tacoma, Washington. Ellis teased them that the Navy's song, "Anchors Away" was a better anthem than the Army's. That evening at the train station, the three boys gathered with their families. Even Thomas and Pamela showed up to say goodbye.

Ellis was glad to see the spring back in Pamela's step. He shook hands with Thomas. "You leavin' soon?"

"Yeah," Thomas answered. "Apparently, the Army can wait until we finish thinning the beets."

The conductor yelled over the heads in the crowd, "Two minutes! All aboard!"

Ellis turned to his father and, instead of hugging him, shook his hand.

"Goodbye, Dad."

"Good luck, son. Hope the Navy is good to you."

He turned to his mother. Mae's hands cupped his face, and she looked long and lovingly into his eyes. "Come back to me." She hugged her son close to her.

"I will." Ellis choked out the words. "Take care."

Pamela and Emily stood together, arm in arm. Ellis yanked Pamela's pigtail and then kissed his sister on her cheek. "Be good, you two."

"All aboard! Final call!"

Ellis ran up the steps, then turned to wave one last time as the train pulled out. He was relieved the goodbyes were over. He joined Stan and Alfred, anxious to have one last bull session before he lost sight of them too. He'd be back home soon. The war couldn't last forever.

EPILOGUE

George pulled the truck into the driveway of his Toppenish farm. His used-to-be farm. In the three-and-a-half years since he'd been gone, the new owners had painted the house white with red trim. The orchard in the back had suffered a bit but had been recently weeded. The acreage was under someone's capable care. A car was parked in the shed, one that had been manufactured before the war. Looked like the folks here were doing all right.

He cut the motor, opened the door, and stepped out into the fall sunshine. The sanctions for the West Coast Japanese had been lifted late in 1944, right before the Supreme Court ruled that interning people who had committed no crime was illegal. By the end of 1944, a third of the folks in the various internment camps had resettled. George kept his promise to Molly and brought her parents and Kameko to Ontario soon after. He used some of Abe's money as a down payment to buy a small building where Mr. Mita set up a store catering to the needs of the local Japanese Americans. The family lived on the second floor.

The war ended after the atomic bombs dropped on Hiroshima and Nagasaki, forcing Japan to surrender. Japanese Americans could now travel in the former military zone of the western states. The only active camp was the Tule Lake Segregation Camp. The U.S. government was still trying to decide the fate of the people there who had wanted to give up their citizenship and be sent back to Japan. An attorney, Wayne Collins, with the American Civil Liberties Union, went to bat for them and obtained a court order to stop mass deportation of both willing and unwilling *Issei* and *Nisei* by ship. It was a mess George knew would take a long time to sort out.

This was George's first opportunity to come home to Toppenish. The door opened when he started toward the house.

"You need somethin'?" A pregnant white woman about George's

329

age stepped out, a young child hanging onto her leg. She was barefoot, with blond, shaggy hair, wearing a red checked apron over a nondescript dress.

George shaded his eyes with his hand. "I'm George Yano, ma'am. I used to farm this place before the war. I was hoping some family things we had stored are still here."

"The house was looted before we came. Wasn't much left. I did find a box with some books in it, but I'm not much of a reader. We repaired what we could, but there weren't any treasures."

"I'll take that box of books. They were my sister's." George glanced about. "Your husband around? I'd like to talk to him, see what he knows. You the owners now?"

"Just tenants." The woman paused, obviously assessing George's intentions. "My husband is picking apples out yonder. You're welcome to ask him any questions you might have. But I don't think he'll know much."

"Thank you, ma'am."

"No trouble. His name is Jack. You might just holler. He'll answer."

"Thank you."

George walked behind the house, following the path he and his own family had used for so many years. This was the orchard where his father had died. He hoped to visit the grave one last time.

He searched for Jack as he surveyed the red apple crop and noted the health of the trees. Empty wooden crates and fruit baskets lay scattered here and there. Farther on, he saw full boxes waiting to be picked up. When he thought he was close enough, he called, "Jack? Can you hear me? Jack?"

"Over here."

George saw the legs of a man on a ladder, propped against a tree. "Hello. My name's George Yano. I used to pick apples in this orchard."

"Yano, huh? You here about the farm?"

"No. I lost it during the war when I couldn't pay the mortgage and taxes."

"You in the 442nd?"

"I wasn't, but my brother was. You know about the combat team?"

"I fought alongside them in Italy and France. They were the most decorated bunch of guys in the Army. 'Go for Broke!' That was their motto. Sure lived up to it. Your brother come home?"

"He did. He's in school, training to be a doctor. Lots of his buddies didn't make it, though." George thought of the reckless charge to save the Texans' lost battalion in the Vosges Mountains in France at the end of October 1944 after Thomas joined the unit. Under enemy fire, he'd tended to wounded soldiers and, despite a bullet wound in his thigh, dragged many to safety. He'd been awarded the Purple Heart and Bronze Star.

"Lots of men didn't come back. I was one of the lucky ones." Jack climbed down from the ladder. He was barechested and wore a bib overall. Holding out his hand for George to shake, he asked, "What can I do for you?"

"I met your wife when I pulled up. She said the house had been looted before you moved in. You know any more than that?"

"Not much. I mended the table and a couple of the chairs that were broken up, but everything else was gone or ruined. A couple of trunks had been opened, and the contents strewn about. If I'd known you were coming back, maybe I'd have tried to save some of it, but it looked pretty useless to me."

"*Shikata ga nai.*" George muttered the phrase under his breath.

"Say again?"

George sighed. He couldn't believe he'd said that. "Nothing we can do." He should have realized the empty house was ripe for looters. "Then maybe you'd be so kind as to move your car out of the shed?"

"Maybe." The man looked puzzled. "Mind if I ask what for?"

"Buried treasure," George replied.

***

An hour later, George was heading back to his new home. His family had been treated well there, Ed and Rex were much like family, and the Yanos had decided to stay. He found forty acres close by to lease and planned to plant potatoes in the coming spring. James had a little sister now, named Alice. His mother had slowed down but took care of the young ones if Molly needed. Pamela joined Thomas at the University of Oregon, majoring in voice.

Abe re-upped to serve in Occupied Japan for the U.S. Armed Forces. Mary must have tired of waiting for him to come home.

She entered the Women's Army Corps in January 1945—also as an interpreter—and joined him there, helping the war-torn country get back on its feet. They had submitted their paperwork and were waiting for permission to marry.

He'd heard through his mother's friendship with Mae that the three Hertzog boys had survived the war. The two older sons had taken advantage of the GI Bill and were in college. Ellis had six months more to serve. He was on a minesweeper now, clearing out the mines on the Yangtze River and in the harbors of China. George would never be able to repay Ellis for saving Pamela from Butch. But she wouldn't have to worry about him ever again. He'd been killed in the Battle of the Bulge in Germany just after Christmas in 1944.

George looked down at the Samurai sword, his father's watch, and the elaborate Geisha doll—remnants of their lives before the war. Pamela's books lay on the floor. He smiled, thinking about bringing something home to his mother, something to remind her of the past as they worked to rebuild their future. It would be an emotional homecoming.

ACKNOWLEDGMENTS

This story is rooted in Eastern Oregon, where my grandparents raised their family and I was born. In helping Grandma Edith Kurtz write her life story, I found out they had hired Japanese Americans to work their fields in 1942. Growing up, I had Japanese-American friends in school, but didn't know they had settled in the Treasure Valley as part of the internment of thousands of West Coast Americans of Japanese ancestry. As I worked to uncover the story, I spoke with Paul Hirai, an uncle of a Nyssa classmate, Brian Hirai. The kernel of this story began then and resulted in *A Shrug of the Shoulders*.

I am grateful to the many friends and instructors who guided this story. First on the list is Alan Rose—writer, teacher, and organizer of the local *Wordfest*—who helped me find my voice as a writer. Others include Mary Stone, Steve Anderson, Dave Rorden, Ned Piper, Jaimee Walls, Robert Griffith, Michael Kruger, Debbie Cardiff, Peggy Ryan, and our seminar group: Carrie, Suzanne, Debz, Linda, and Lori. My father, Dudley Kurtz, answered many questions about the farming sections, and my husband, Bud Cockrell, questioned the same details and sent me back to the research. I'd also like to thank Mike Iseri for checking the last names of the Japanese Americans who still live in the Ontario area, and for reading the manuscript to check for cultural flaws in the story. Morgen Young was also in Ontario working on a story of Russell Lee, the Farm Security Administration photographer, and verifying the Nyssa Japanese American labor camp. We shared research and a drive through the farm fields.

ABOUT THE AUTHOR

Elaine Cockrell grew up amid sugar beet and wheat fields on the family farm near Adrian, Oregon. She lived in a multicultural world with Basque sheepherders, Mexican itinerant fieldhands, and Japanese-American families, most of whom settled there in World War II. She left the area for four years but returned to Eastern Oregon University, where she became an English teacher. She spent her years in middle school and high school, teaching literature and writing, and producing yearbooks and newspapers. She finished her career as a middle school principal.

Now writing in retirement in Longview, Washington, she set her novel in the farmlands of her youth.